SAVAGE ALLIANCE

SAVAGE LAW: BOOK 6

SAVAGE ALLIANCE

SAVAGE LAW: BOOK 6

KIRBY JONAS

Cover design by Pat Heath

Howling Wolf Publishing
Pocatello, Idaho

Howling Wolf Publishing
1611 City Creek Road
Pocatello ID 83204

For more information about Kirby's books, check out:

www.kirbyjonas.com
Facebook, at KirbyJonasauthor

Or email Kirby at: **kirby@kirbyjonas.com**

Manufactured in the United States of America—*One nation, under God*

Publication date: September 2020
Jonas, Kirby, 1965—
Savage Law 6: Savage Alliance / by Kirby Jonas.

ISBN: 978-1-891423-05-5
Library of Congress Control Number: 2020915601

To learn more about this book or any other Kirby Jonas book, email Kirby at kirby@kirbyjonas.com

To Alex, Sam, Megan, Caleb, and Kathryn

And to the memory of the real Mike Fica,
who will live forever in our hearts

CHAPTER ONE

♦ 1973 ♦

Las Vegas, Nevada
Private office on the top floor of the Flamingo Hotel
Friday, February 2, 9:45 A.M.

"I want them dead. Both of them. *All* of them."

Paolo Oronzo Rustichelli de Castiglione was as large and as difficult as his name. The nickname Porc, which emerged conveniently out of his initials and fit his size triumphantly, was rumored to be of his own invention. It made addressing him easier on the tongue, but gathering the nerve to speak to Paolo de Castiglione—and refer to him as "Porc"—was always a ticklish prospect, and an occasion saved up for only the most special circumstances.

Around boisterous and impolite card tables, it was often a topic of conversation what was bigger in girth—de Castiglione's eyebrows, his fingers, or his cigars—but it was universally decided that it was easy to tell his fingers apart from the other two. They weren't as smoky as his cigars, and slightly less hairy and a little more jointed than his eyebrows, every one of them was overloaded with rings of enormous value, and they were generally jabbing you in the eye—if only in a figurative sense.

His eyeballs and his mustache seemed to have been drawn on with one dot each and a couple of slashes of a fat black Sharpie marker, respectively, and the same marker had put the lines of hair on the backs of his fingers and made the hundred or so slash marks from far back on the crown of his head to the base of his bony skull.

The one thing on Porc de Castiglione besides his eyeballs that seemed small, but only in proportion to everything else, was his ears, which were dwarfed by his cheeks and jowls, and his evil reputation might have been the only reason someone hadn't skinned out the bags under his eyes to use for shot glasses.

Scabs Ravioli, who was not near as delectable as his name, and Menny Marcello stood in their black business suits and conservative ties with their hands folded in front of them across the desk from de Castiglione and listened to their marching orders: *Head to a little town called Salmon, Idaho, forthwith. We have people in trouble, and you have two men to kill, or more—the sooner, and the deader, the better.*

Porc de Castiglione leaned back in his chair, probably only to put his back momentarily in a different position rather than because he wanted to appear relaxed in front of Ravioli and Marcello. "The word is coming back to us very late, so I hope we still have time. Angel Medina and his stupid ex-cop of a brother got themselves in it up to their eyebrows. We don't have time to find out what they've said or even if they are still on our side. They made mistakes, and it's up to you two to troubleshoot.

"The local law enforcement is another question. Sheriff Coal Savage. You might ignore his comic book-sounding heroic name and try to consider him just another country bumpkin. Don't make that mistake. He is a heavily decorated ex-Marine and soldier of both of our most recent wars and lately an agent with the FBI in Washington. He is seasoned, and he will have friends just like him. Take nothing in this place at face value.

"The prosecutor is another story. A fat man. I mean *big.*" He drilled his underlings with a challenging look, but of course neither was fool enough to bring up the obvious comparison with Porc. "His name is Mike Fica, and he is one ambitious s.o.b. on his way to the top of the food chain. You will not know by looking at him or talking to him. He is like a sleeping rattlesnake.

"Two men to kill. Understand? The Medinas cannot stay where they are with these two men working this case. And this must never—and I am saying *ever*—reach back to us. Or even to this state. Capiche?"

Scabs Ravioli cleared his throat. He hated it when de Castiglione tried sounding more Italian by using corny Italian words. They only made him look like a sap. But of course he would never say it. "Sir, this isn't an item where we should go off half-cocked, so I would like to clarify. You want them dead. No questions asked. No nothin'."

"Exactly. Hang out. Do your magic. Be your sly, charming selves." These words came as comical to Scabs, because where his young, very handsome partner might be charming, he himself was anything but. "I'm asking for the heads of two men. But if you don't like what you learn while you're there, burn them all. Every last candle. Think of this Salmon, Idaho, place as your great big mess of a birthday cake. Do this right and you'll both come back here reaching for some pretty high places—not to mention the biggest bonus you ever saw. Capiche?"

Again, Scabs cringed inwardly at that word, but both men nodded, knowing just as well what it would mean if they *didn't* do it right. They waited. You didn't just walk out on Porc de Castiglione without an invitation, any more than you would walk in without one.

"Go and do it. Keep in touch. And you know how."

They both knew how. *Keep in touch* meant often, and only through payphones. Generally, Castiglione's hitmen didn't even get in the habit of using the same payphone twice in a row. Luckily, there seemed to be a phone booth around every corner and in the lobby of every hotel.

Scabs Ravioli and Menny Marcello boarded a Learjet 23 on a private runway west of Vegas and left the ground half an hour later, Scabs already snacking from a jar of homemade pickled garlic and a box of Ritz crackers as he gazed down at the vast face of the desert below, and Menny kicked back in his seat with his hands folded over his midsection and his eyes hidden by jet-black Ray Bans with gold frames.

The Idaho Falls airport where their assigned car awaited was only an hour's flight away.

Lincoln, Nebraska
Friday, February 2

Former FBI agent Sam Browning sat in his cushy blue La-Z-Boy in front of a brand-new Zenith colored TV watching Charlotte and Mike Bauer act stupid on *The Guiding Light*. He wasn't watching because he was interested in the plot line whatsoever but because it was a good nine months before football games would begin to air again. It was then that his beloved Huskers would once more start knocking heads into the turf, but those were college games, and he wouldn't see most of those on the tube. Which was why when he left his gainful—although extremely frustrating, even aggravating—employment in Washington, D. C., and moved away it was straight back to his hometown of Lincoln, Nebraska, home of the University of Nebraska, the Memorial Stadium—and the Cornhuskers.

The heavy, but gracefully sculpted muscle of a gym fiend prodded a T-shirt bearing the red and white of the Huskers in every right direction and to every ideal proportion, and a ball cap of what had once been the same colors, but looking now as if he had run it several times through a greasy bicycle chain, sat brim-low over his eyes, covering a crewcut crop of white-blond hair.

On an end table to his left sat a "Thermo-Serv" plastic stein half full of cold coffee the color of the midnight sky—a mug that any good guesser would have known had a picture of smiling blond, red cowboy-hat wearing Herbie Husker on the front of it, with the great big blue N on the front of his overalls that stood for— Well, anyone who knew Sam Browning knew what the N stood for: NEBRASKA! His big right hand cradled a stein that was the twin of the one to his left, but that one was half full—for the fifth or sixth time since eleven that morning—of peach and lemon juice and Smirnoff vodka. Just because.

Browning's wife, Megan, thought he was at work. She had no reason not to. She didn't know he rented this tiny one-bedroom apartment on the back of a farmhouse on the edge of the little dot on the map northwest of Lincoln called Prairie Home, which literally wasn't far removed in ambience from *Little House on the Prairie.* As she sat at home doing wifely or motherly things, she thought her husband was off making big business deals, selling corn harvesting machinery all over the Midwest for John Deere. For if he wasn't, then how was he providing their nice Swiss-style five-bedroom home on D Street and 20th, with their wonderful view of the huge red brick First Plymouth Congregational Church, right across the street? And how did he afford their royal blue 1971 Monte Carlo parked in the long, marble-smooth driveway, with its 454 beneath the hood and its immaculate black vinyl top?

Contrary to what his wife believed, Sam Browning was not, in fact, making money. He was waiting to make it. It was just that when it did come, it came in hefty spurts, so hefty he had to have them split into increments and fake checks written out to him from a checking account of his own making, under the name of Robert N. Trader (who was supposedly his boss at John Deere but who really didn't exist, because "Trader" was Browning). Most evenings, unless he was on a job, Browning came home to his wife and children for the night. And the next day he went to "work", or, more accurately to sit in his apartment, waiting for phone calls—big phone calls. Every other week, on Fridays, he returned from "work" after a generally very boring stretch of watching soap operas and reading Western, espionage, and bad detective novels all day long, and handed Megan the receipt from his latest bi-weekly deposit into his *real* bank account, that of Samuel R. Browning.

And then one day he would take a call that would send him off to some strange, unknown place in his own country or some exotic (or semi-exotic) place around the world—selling corn harvesting machinery, of course.

The phone sat next to his right hand, near the bottle of Smirnoff. When it rang, he jerked. Then he swore. It was a ritual as old as time, always performed, like a classic opera, in the same rhythmical succession: Startling ring, heart-stopping convulsion, and a good pair of cuss words—sometimes three or four, if he had been particularly engrossed in the spell-binding doings of the good-as-real-life characters on *As the World Turns, General Hospital,* or, like today, *The Guiding Light.*

Browning picked up the phone after it had disconnected immediately, then rang again after fifteen seconds. Secret spy code stuff. "Yeah?"

Yeah. The voice was scratchy.

"Hey, Q," said Browning. On the other end of the line was his best friend, who was actually more of a brother, Alex Martinez, better known as Q. The Q stood for Quezada, his middle name that he never used but which he had signed up under in the service: Alex Quezada-Martinez. "You mad?"

Mad? Why?

"You sound mad."

I always sound mad. You don't remember telling me that?

Browning laughed, flashing bright white teeth, the quintessential model for Crest commercials, if he had ever wanted to get into another line of work. "Well, you do. What's happening?"

Not a thing. Selling real estate in this city stinks.

"Sorry. You could always go back to the FBI."

Right. And then who's gonna be here to babysit you?

Browning gave another laugh, then chased it with a quick swallow of Smirnoff. "Wanna come out? Shoot, there's gotta be a half-dozen houses you could sell in Prairie . . . What's the name of this place again?"

Judas Priest. Really? Prairie Home. You been drinking all day?

"Oh yeah! Shoot. Prairie Home. Well, I'm watching *The Guiding Light,* Q. What else am I gonna be doing but drinking?"

Good point. So really, what's goin' down? I'm getting restless over here. Want me to go check in on Megan?

"Like I'd trust you with her!" said Browning in a good-natured growl. "Go get some rib eyes and come over. I'll grill 'em up."

After a moment, long enough for Alex Martinez to look at his watch, he replied, *It's almost quittin' time. You really wanna go hit the gym on a gut full of meat?*

"That's like asking a lion if he wants to roar!" Browning said, giggling. "Is it red and bloody? Then yes!"

I'll see you down at the gym, Martinez said. *And if you're wondering, no, I didn't sell any homes today. And there probably isn't one stinking house anyone would want to buy in Prairie Home, either.*

The phone line went dead. Alex Martinez wasn't big on goodbyes. Browning set the phone down and stared at the TV screen. On *The Guiding Light,* Charlotte Bauer had been pretending she was pregnant, which she really wasn't, and the court had finally granted a divorce to her hubby, Mike, so he was going to get shut of her forever now. And Browning wanted to pull his .38 from the holster that was fixed to the side of his La-Z-Boy and shoot one or the other of them through the knee. He would have if he thought they would feel it and if it wouldn't necessitate having to buy a new TV set so he could see what they were going to do on the show tomorrow.

Sam Browning sipped Smirnoff, peach, and lemon and wished he was watching the Huskers tear up the grid iron. He thought about work. His *real* work. His work almost nobody except Q knew about, and for which he was glad. If some people knew, he would have to kill them, and he didn't always enjoy killing dumb people—only ones that were bad. Although it didn't hurt his feelings if the bad people he killed were also dumb. That was sort of double satisfaction.

Sam Browning had a good, warm feeling deep inside, and he hoped it wasn't merely the Smirnoff. There was a great big job heading his way, and a pay-off the size of the infamous *Sea of Red*—that is, the Memorial Stadium, home of Huskers football.

Sam smiled and closed his eyes. He drifted off and began to dream, and he wasn't dreaming of *The Guiding Light*.

Salmon, Idaho
Friday, February 2

Coal Savage pulled up to the stop sign coming off Highway 93's north stretch onto Salmon's Main Street. A gust of breath escaped him. It felt somehow as if he had been holding it, at least figuratively, since driving away from Oglala, South Dakota, and the odyssey of hell he and Maura PlentyWounds had just gone through.

He looked up Courthouse Drive, toward work, and he felt absolutely no compunction for not having been back sooner. For one thing, his vacation from Salmon had turned out not to be any kind of vacation at all, but rather going from one big house afire into another.

He found himself feeling suddenly impatient as he waited for several cars from each direction to pass. His feelings must have shown, for he felt Maura's hand on his leg, and she gave it a little squeeze and a shake. Somehow, that touch both thrilled and calmed him. He turned his head to smile at her, then pulled onto Main and headed east, on the final stretch for home.

Coal and Maura hadn't stopped to eat anything since breakfast. They hadn't discussed not doing so, but there seemed to be a shared feeling inside the Thunderbird that all they wanted to do was make it back home as fast as Thunderbird-ly possible, back to people who loved them, and to a place where they could feel safe once more. It had been a long time since either had felt safe.

For many miles Coal had pondered on the remainder of the journey home after passing through Rapid City. The nights had been idyllic. Not in any sensual way, because the two of them had done nothing physical whatsoever but share one casual kiss, that very Friday morning before checking out of what would be their last hotel of the trip. Of course they had snuggled close each night, but for some reason they both had been content simply to lie there in each other's arms, feeling warm and safe and knowing they had survived hell together and come out stronger on the other side.

The town looked peaceful. People hustled about, all bundled up in heavy coats even though a bright sun flooded the world, glaring off new snow that had fallen since their departure a week earlier and was heaped along the edges of the sidewalk. A few Christmas wreaths and some garland still remained from the holiday season some folks couldn't quite bid farewell to. They hadn't turned on the radio, so there hadn't been a chance to catch a weather report, but from the rosy-cheeked looks of people on the sidewalks it didn't appear to be any warmer here than back in Oglala.

Something about being back home made Coal hate the lidded box between the seats even more, for he had a feeling Maura would have been snuggled up against him right now if she could. The most she could do was turn toward him and reach across with her right hand, taking his biceps. That would have to be enough unless Coal could manage to find himself a bench seat and have it installed in the car, and for the few times he and Maura were together maybe it wasn't worth the effort.

He slowed down when they neared Maura's. When he looked over at her she was already watching him. "Am I dropping you off?"

"I don't know. My choice?"

"Yes. Your choice."

"Then please don't. I'm not ready."

"Okay." That didn't surprise him, and he couldn't say it upset him either. He wasn't ready to be away from her yet either, not when so recently he had believed her gone forever.

With still a mile to go, a beautiful teal Lincoln Continental passed them heading toward town.

Coal whistled and looked over at Maura, who had also seen it. "That's going to be my next car," he said. "I noticed *they* didn't have to sit a mile away from each other in the front seat."

With a thoughtful nod, Maura threw a glance after the Lincoln. "A mile. Hmm. That car was bigger than it looked."

Coal laughed, and it felt good. Right now, his whole world had become a dream—not a nightmare like it had been for what seemed like weeks on end. "Fine, have it your way. A mile, ten feet. Who's taking actual measurements? When I can hardly even smell your hair anymore I know it's too far."

On they drove, laughing, and at last Coal turned the incredibly smooth wheel of the Thunderbird, and its tires met frozen Savage Lane. In less than a minute more, putting the car in park in the yard outside the front of the house, they saw the front door explode outward, and two streaks, one black and one tan, rocketed off the porch just ahead of an army of bodies with joy-filled faces.

Now they were truly home.

CHAPTER TWO

Friday, February 2

The teal Lincoln Continental was as silent and streamlined spearing along the highway toward Salmon, Idaho, as a blue shark cruising a clear-water Tahitian lagoon. With its white convertible top and suicide doors, the Lincoln spun heads and broke necks everywhere, and its owners treated the car, in spite of its habit of guzzling gasoline like a fat man at a pop-drinking competition, like a member of the family.

Blond Becky Fairbourne sat beside her husband Grant, with their two girls, Nella and Jill, and their five-year-old Michael asleep in the back seat, and little Jonathan fighting to keep his eyes open on the seat between them.

Life was an adventure, and the massive 462 V-8 under the hood and its three hundred forty powerful horses, like a Roman chariot, were carrying them home.

Becky was beautiful. She knew it because Grant told her—every day. Almost unfailingly as they woke up in the morning, and without exception when they lay down at night—or at least when he wasn't working the graveyard shift. And even then he tried to tell her as often as he could from the office phone down at the Caldwell, Idaho, PD, where he was a decorated patrol officer.

Or more accurately, Grant *had been* a decorated officer in Caldwell. He was employed now as a county deputy, at least until he heard otherwise, of Lemhi County.

Becky's hair was long and straight, and this sunny Sunday afternoon it flooded down over a teal blouse with white piping and a huge collar, a blouse she wouldn't realize for at least a decade was about the ugliest thing she had ever put on. Even in spite of her glasses, with their thick black frames, Grant swore she was gorgeous—maybe even more so while wearing those glasses—and Grant was the wonderful kind of husband who could make her believe it.

Without trying to draw his attention, Becky leaned back against the seat and turned her head to look at her husband. Grant was thirty-two years old, an eight-year veteran of the Caldwell Police, and, if anything, living with a wife and four children had made him even more handsome than the day her first view of him nearly knocked her backward off her seat in the Challis High School cafeteria. At the time, she had recently become a student there after her family relocated from Sandpoint, in the far northern netherreaches of the state.

Grant had short hair of a deep chocolate color, and eyes of the same, a strong chin and jaw, straight nose, and full, honest mouth. He was tall and muscular, much of his build being due to genetics but thanks also to a high polish brought on by his big pastime of lifting weights. He was a dream of a man, a great provider, and she had sworn when they moved out of Challis that she would love him to Caldwell and back. That had been a joke between them ever since.

Grant had been aching for so long to get back to what he referred to as "God's country," which to him was the Salmon-Challis area, that the day he came running in from work to tell her he had seen a notice of emergency hiring at the Lemhi County Sheriff's Department, Becky knew the writing was on the wall: Yes, they would be going home, for who in their right mind would turn away a golden employee like Grant Fairbourne?

Saturday, February 3

Grant Fairbourne woke up Saturday morning when his wind-up alarm clock rang at seven o'clock. He rolled over, grinned with his eyes half shut, and told his golden-haired Becky how beautiful she was. With her eyes puffy and red, without a fleck of makeup, her hair in disarray, and her nightgown skewed around on her body, she told him what a great liar he was, and he laughed.

After a fierce kissing session while the kids were still sound asleep, ignoring Becky's terrible morning breath because he knew he had it too, he told her she was the most wonderful kisser he had ever seen, for a dragon, then jumped backward out of bed in time to dodge the back of her hand.

"Get out of here!" she said. "You don't smell like any lilac yourself."

Giggling with delight, he went over to start the long and arduous task of forcing the kids out of bed. "Get up, guys. We're all going to a restaurant to eat breakfast."

The very notion of going out for food was novel enough to force five-year-old Michael (who looked so much like his father had at his age that Grant teased Becky about how she could never deny he was his son) up out of bed in a heartbeat. With his hair sticking every direction except where his mother had combed it the day before, he was getting dressed before it registered on Nella, who was nine, and Jill, who had just turned seven, that their father had said the word "breakfast."

While Grant was rousting the older kids, Becky plucked three-year-old Jonathan out of the bed where the four children had all slept together, the wrong direction, and cradled him in her arms for a few minutes, gazing down at his curly yellow hair and his soft, perfect lips. She looked over at her husband, who was preparing to get in the shower. "You know what, Grant? You could never deny this little guy is mine." She grinned when she said it and then stuck out her tongue playfully.

Grant laughed, grabbing his underwear, socks, and pants from his nightstand. "Okay, dopey—he *did* come out of you, after all. It's a little harder to deny a child under those conditions. I'm just not sure he's mine!"

She gave him a shocked face. "Oh, come on! I guess he does look like you too—a little."

After breakfast later, Grant took the family back to their motel room. He had badly wanted to see the local sheriff, Coal Savage, again the day before, prior to the start of the weekend. It would have been nice to visit with him under more normal circumstances than the first time, where a manhunt he had volunteered to take part in after a knifing at a local store had gone bad. It had turned out that the suspect was a good friend of the sheriff's, and the man had ended up jumping off a cliff right in front of him and a woman who was apparently the sheriff's girlfriend. Both the sheriff and the woman were taking a trip out of town the next morning when he met them, so the hiring interview Grant had talked himself into basically by the skin of his eyeballs was brief and bizarre. However, at least it had gotten him the job.

But when Grant went to the jail to test his chances of a casual visit with the sheriff, Jordan Peterson, Savage's deputy whom Grant had gotten to know a little bit the week before, told him the sheriff wasn't back from his trip yet.

So Grant had returned to the motel and spent the remainder of the evening snacking on apples, potato chips, and Hostess Twinkies with the kids and Becky and playing board games on the bed with all the covers thrown off.

Grant came out of the bathroom after they returned from breakfast, went over and kissed his wife and reminded her how beautiful he believed her to be. She smiled up at him from where she sat on the bed. “Even with my dragon breath?”

“Now it’s pancake breath, and you’re even *more* beautiful.”

She giggled again. Grant made her want to. “You gonna try the courthouse again?”

“Yeah. I doubt I’ll be too long. But since Jordan said Sheriff Savage had called a couple days ago to say they were on their way back, I’m hoping he might stop in today. At least I would if I just got back from a trip that long. I guess if he’s not there we’ll drive around and enjoy the valley—maybe even go to Challis and visit Mom and Dad for the weekend—and then we’ll come back Monday to see the sheriff. And maybe we’ll start looking for a house if we have enough time.”

“Okay. Exciting! Come here.” She made him bend down to kiss her again. “Good luck, baby. Knock ’em dead.”

“Ha! That might not be the best phrase to use around here after the other day!”

Grant stopped one last time on his way out the door to turn and smile at Becky, blowing her a kiss. “Did I ever tell you how beautiful you are?”

She was saying something back to him as he shut the door and started down the hall, whistling the theme from *The Andy Griffith Show*.

Saturday, February 3, 10:00 A.M.

Scabs Ravioli rubbed his knuckles. They still hurt where he had plowed squirrely Bobby Vigliaturo right on the knife-sharp cheekbone in his most recent bare-knuckle fight, a week earlier. Scars of a hundred different ages made a sort of macabre work of art out of his knuckles and his fingers, where the black hair that remained peppering the backs of his hands was more or less non-existent since it had no interest in trying to grow through all the scar tissue from fifteen years of what some people referred to as "stupid bare-knuckle boxing".

Scabs didn't understand that way of thinking. After all, what more useful pastime could there be, especially for a man who might be called on at any time to utilize his fists? He had always grinned to think how awkward it would be stopping someone who wanted to fight him because he wasn't wearing the proper hand protection.

Scabs's real given name was Saverio, but it was a name mostly lost to him because it was seldom used. The name Scabs had come to him honestly, from all the healing wounds he often wore so proudly on his hands and face after his bare-knuckle bouts.

Scabs rubbed a little more with his other hand on his battle-tattooed knuckles, then gave them a final dusting with a couple of swats. Looking over at Menny Marcello and holding up his right fist, he said, "Hey. Look at that, would you? The scars are almost healed. I think my body's adapting an' healin' itself faster than it even used to when I was young."

Menny scoffed. "I bet. I think your brain's just mush and you can't even remember how fast you used t' heal up."

Scabs laughed. He didn't care what Menny said. They were pals. They said a lot of mean-sounding things to and about each other, like any good pals do.

"I still can't believe this car," said Menny, slapping the steering wheel. He ran his hand back over his smooth, perfectly oiled black hair, which framed a face with modest sideburns and perfectly trimmed eyebrows. He glanced in the rearview mirror and couldn't help a little smile. He should have been a model.

"What about it?" said Scabs. "You still gripin'? You'd crab around about somebody givin' you a Ferrari."

"Ah, you're an idiot, Scabby. We're supposed t' be on a job, right? Be inconspicuous. Why do they think it's okay t' reserve a Jaguar for us? An' where'd some piss ant place like Idaho get a Jag for rent anyhow?"

Scabs laughed, and he let his eyes scan the car again. The midnight blue vehicle with its tan interior was immaculate and just as gorgeous as the moment he laid eyes on it. Which was exactly why Menny didn't like it, oddly enough—because it was too beautiful and too conspicuous. Ironically, Menny's personal vehicle back in Vegas was also a Jag.

"Come on, man! Guy like you, so into his looks—you'd think you'd shout for joy gettin' a Jag reserved for you. Relax. It's all part o' the show."

Menny looked over at him, trying to be angry. Finally, he fought back a smile. "You got any gum?"

"I got some Skoal. An' pickled garlic."

"No *thanks!* The car stinks bad enough already. Why can't you chew bubblegum an' eat candy, like any regular jerk?"

"'Cause maybe I ain't no regular jerk. I'm Scabs Ravioli."

"Yeah! See? You could be eatin' a jar o' ravioli, just like your name. Actually sounds good, now that I think of it. I'm starved."

Scabs scowled at his partner. "When aren't you starved? Man, my mama'd roll over in her grave she heard you say that. Canned ravioli! That's it. I swear you're turnin' into a damn American."

Menny Marcello laughed and watched a pronghorn dart across the road a ways in front of them. "Next one o' them comes across in front of us I'm gonna stop an' shoot it."

"Settle down! I think they're kinda perty myself. You'll have your chance to kill somethin' soon enough." Scabs leaned back in his seat and slipped his sunglasses on once more. "Wake me up when it's over, would ya?"

CHAPTER THREE

Salmon, Idaho
Saturday, February 3

Coal tried to sleep in the next morning, but he hadn't been smart enough to put earplugs in at the end of the late-night party his mom had held in his and Maura's honor, and now the kids, who had managed somehow to get in bed earlier than the adults, were up watching Saturday morning cartoons—*The Flintstones,* specifically.

That's what Coal learned when he stumbled from the bottom of the stairs toward the kitchen with coffee on his mind and heard "Yabba dabba doo!" accompanied by some strange comical instrument on the TV in the front room. Through the cloud of his exhaustion, the kids looked like wax figures molded in place on every sitting space in sight.

The dogs didn't, however. The moment they caught him up and awake, they came padding in to be his faithful companions wherever he went in the kitchen. He remembered Laura trying to train Shadow to stay out of the kitchen so she wouldn't be in the way. Maybe he should do the same. But then she would look at him with those big, soft eyes, and he would cave.

It dawned on him once he reached for a porcelain mug that he could already smell coffee, and his favorite mug sat right in front of the coffee pot. Connie had been doing everything she could, it seemed, to make Coal and Maura's transition back into real life as seamless as possible after they had somehow managed to give her the brief outline of what had happened to them over the last week. They still hadn't been able to share all the details, and perhaps they never would. As with Korea and Vietnam, there were some things simply better left untold.

Coal filled his mug and took a sip that burned his lips and the tip of his tongue. So he took another sip to make sure he wasn't imagining how hot it was. No, it was indeed too hot. But it tasted odd, at the same time, so he took another sip. Still too hot. But not so hot that he couldn't tell it was not any coffee he would have made.

Frowning, he took his burned tongue and his cup and walked in his stocking feet down the hall. Katie's door was partway open, so he glanced in, surprised she would neglect that detail. It was a mess, with clothes and books on the floor, and a bra hanging on the back of a chair. A feeling of nostalgia washed over him—not brought on by a teenage girl's bra, of course! It was the fact that she had one at all. When had Katie Leigh ceased to be his little kindergarten girl? He forced away his all-too-frequent regrets about all the time he had missed with his children and continued down the hall.

Connie's door was shut tight. He put an ear close to it. Connie had been up as late as he and Maura. So she might have gotten up to make the coffee, then gone back to bed. After all, it was only fifteen or twenty minutes after eight. But no, this was Connie Savage. She would have to be dying of some disease as yet unknown to man to be found in bed after eight o'clock.

Reaching down with his left hand, he feathered the knob, easing the door open and peeking in. The bed was half empty, and Connie's boots were missing. Just as he had guessed.

Maura was nothing but a big lump of rumpled blankets. Part of Coal wanted to creep in and snuggle under the covers with her. It had gotten to where it seemed natural. However, trying to justify it to his mom, with all the children in the house, that was an elephant he had no interest in trying to tackle to the ground. But still . . .

Walking soft on the shag carpet, he went to Maura's side of the bed. He sipped Connie's hot black water, frowned once more at the lack of taste and the overabundance of heat, and looked down at the woman's face, peaceful in sleep. She had earned this sleep. This and a thousand other quiet mornings like it.

An almost painful urge swept over him to kneel down and kiss her pouty lips. But then she would wake up, and he would have taken away one of those thousand quiet mornings he knew she deserved, so he turned to go.

A rustling behind him as he touched the doorknob again preceded the soft voice. "Hey."

He looked back and smiled. Maura blinked her eyes several times, trying to get them to open wider.

"You turning into a hit and run driver?"

"What's that?"

Maura giggled, the sleep in her eyes and in her voice. "You drive in here, ogle me while I'm sleeping, then race off?"

He couldn't help but mimic the woman, although he preferred to think of the sound he made as more of a chuckle than a giggle. "You looked so peaceful I didn't want to wake you."

She struggled up, the covers falling down off her nightshirt—which since they hadn't gone back to her house yet was actually one of Coal's own shirts, a blue and gray plaid one that in the right light made her smoky blue eyes come to life and covered just enough of her thighs to be good and immodest.

"So you're just gonna make me miss all the cartoons?" she said.

"Oh, shoot! Right. You wouldn't want to do that. You might miss *H.R. Pufnstuf.*"

She grinned, making her eyes almost disappear. It wasn't a normal look for her, because her eyes weren't exactly narrow. "Nope. I'm afraid we don't get that station here in the big city. So . . . want to come to bed for a while?"

He made a rueful face. "I wish I could. But with the kids all here . . ."

"Yeah." She sighed. "I already thought of that, so I was sort of kidding. But I almost wish we were still traveling."

"Me too. You want some breakfast?"

"Sure."

"In town?"

She hesitated. Too long.

"Not ready, huh?"

She made a tall shrug with one shoulder. "Not sure. You?"

"Well, even if we don't get *H.R. Pufnstuf,* we *are* back in civilization, you know."

"Hey now." She lowered her eyebrows. "The Rez wasn't *that* bad, was it?"

He stared down at her. For a moment he wasn't even sure how to reply. "Uhh . . . Yeah. It was that bad."

She gave him a little smile, and this time a shrug that deserved both shoulders, holding them up by her ears for a couple of extra seconds and looking at him. As she got out of bed, he pretended to try and ignore the smooth, slightly dusky skin of her legs blazing out from under his shirt, tan not from the sun but from her Indian heritage. He chased out of his mind the thought of how that skin and much more could have been his for the taking if he had been a different man, and if they had been that kind of friends.

Reaching out with both hands, she pried the coffee mug out of his hands and turned to set it on the nightstand. Then she swiveled back to him and eased her arms around his middle, stepping in to hold him gently, as he did her.

Coal didn't care about Maura's breath. In truth, he didn't even notice it when she raised her face to him and he gently kissed her. It was her warm, wavy hair enveloping his face as he snuggled into the side of her neck that lured him the most. As he drew the scent in through his nostrils, he thought of the counselor in Idaho Falls, Nancy Pearson, and his promise to get the girls back there. That promise, if he was a good friend, should include Maura as well. And then he thought what an odd and uncharacteristically male thing that was to think about at a time like this, and how he must be getting older than he had believed.

"Kiss me again." Maura's voice was soft. Almost fragile. He took her words not as an off-hand suggestion but as a plea.

Even as their lips met, as soft as newly washed silks melding together of their own weight, Coal jerked at the sudden sound of the phone ringing. He swore. Into Maura's mouth.

By the second ring Maura had pulled away from him and was laughing. "Did you just swear in my mouth?"

He was pretty sure he blushed. "I think I might have."

"Well. That tasted weird." The phone rang for a third time, proving that Connie was still outside and the children were all still glued to the Flintstones.

It was Coal's turn to laugh, even though the phone was not so far out of reach behind Maura. "Oh yeah! Like you've never tasted swear words in your mouth before, Miss Prissy Prude."

"Miss Prissy Prude?" She looked at him as if he had two noses. "Where'd you pull that out of? Never mind. Aren't you going to get the phone?"

It was on the sixth ring. Any normal, polite person would have hung up by now. With a sigh, wondering what disrespectful lout was on the other end of the phone line, he stepped around her and picked it up. "Hello."

Coal? Is that you?

He heard the strained, faintly familiar voice of a man on the other end of the line. Strained, and maybe scared.

"Yes, this is Coal. Who's this?"

Coal, it's me, man! Mikey. Parravano!

"Oh! Hey, Mikey! You all right?" The last time he had spoken with his old high school buddy, the man who as a boy used to idolize him for what he considered to have been saving his life, was when he was gleaning information about Ray and Angel Medina from him.

No!

Mikey's answer took Coal aback.

"What's wrong? Are you in trouble?" Even as Coal asked, he had no idea what he could have done to help his old friend, clear down in Vegas as he was, but after Mikey had saved his bacon so recently he would sure do anything within his power if he needed his help. He had the jolting thought that perhaps the Mob had somehow learned of Mikey's tipping Coal to the operation they had attempted to pull off behind the Hargis place. If they had, Mikey was dead!

Coal, listen man. Listen. It ain't me that's in trouble.

"What's that again?" Coal was trying to shift gears, and it was still too early after only five hours or so of sleep.

It ain't me that's in trouble. It's you!

CHAPTER FOUR

Maura looked sharply from the phone to Coal. From that look he guessed she could hear at least part of what Mikey Parravano was saying.

"Why? What are you talking about?"

Coal. I need you to get out of there for a while, man. Like maybe for a week or two. Can you do that?

"Slow down a little," Coal said. "I'm having a hard time keeping up."

Sorry, buddy. But there ain't a lotta time. I gotta get off the line, and you gotta get outta there. Presto. Fast!

"Mikey, I just got back from a trip. I've already been gone a week."

It doesn't matter. You gotta go. Just get out— Aw, crap. Hey. Bro, I gotta go. Just get outta there! The last sentence was spoken in a hiss.

"Mikey, wait! What's going on?"

Mikey's voice dropped almost to a whisper. *Sorry, I gotta go. I'll try t' call you back.*

"No! Hang on!" But Coal's voice was almost shouting over a line that had already gone dead.

He looked at Maura, as he continued holding the phone to his ear without thinking about it.

"What is it? Did he say you're in trouble?" If Maura had been having a hard time opening her eyes all the way only minutes ago, she didn't any longer. They were open wide.

"Yeah." Slowly, he let the phone fall to the side of his leg. "Yeah. But that's all."

She searched his eyes. "Who was he?"

Coal explained how he knew Mikey Parravano, from way back when he had stood up for him against bullies at school, to his role in the Mob, and how Mikey had been instrumental in Coal's getting information about Angel and Ray Medina and the Mob's hideout operation behind dairyman Bern Hargis's place.

"So . . . Coal, is this about . . ."

Maura PlentyWounds had never been a cop. She had never been in any kind of position where getting intelligence was a requirement. But she was no fool. She jumped to the same conclusion Coal had, and he saw the realization when it leaped into her eyes.

"Yeah. It's something to do with the Medinas."

Maura's face paled, even in the dimness of the room. "What are you going to do?"

Coal's mind raced. Still hanging on to the phone, he brought up both hands to Maura's shoulders, holding the left one and resting his fist full of phone on top of the other. He blinked rapidly. "I've got to think. I need to get on the phone."

"With who?"

Blankly, he stared at her. Who? He wasn't sure. The FBI? The judge? Prosecutor Mike Fica and his deputy, Bryan Wheat? His own deputies? The police? The correct test answer would probably be all of the above. And maybe the PD in Idaho Falls as well. Just how far-reaching was the Las Vegas Mob's intelligence network? Did they know the prisoners had been moved?

Coal swore. Mike Fica had been right to fear something like this. Somehow through all the events that had taken over Coal's and Maura's lives of late he had forgotten all about Fica's premonitions, but now they stared him boldly in the face.

He had to do something. To be proactive. But he had no idea how. Why had Mikey hung up on him? He feared for the life of his old friend.

Coal went upstairs to get dressed, and the .44 in its hunter holster slipped onto his pants belt as naturally as his wallet went into his pocket or his watch strapped around his wrist. But he feared which of the three might be called upon more in the near future, and that fear brought him swooping backward to the war he and Maura had just come through. With acid flooding his stomach, any interest he had had in eating had flown.

Coming down to the kitchen, Coal found Maura sitting on one of the stools, while Connie was mixing up biscuits, and bacon grease was melting in a saucepan for gravy. Maura jumped up and met Coal partway. “You okay?”

He looked at her, searching inside for an answer. A shrug was the best he could do. When he looked over, Connie was watching him. By the look in her eyes, it was plain Maura had already told her about the phone call, and he wished she had kept it between them until he could decide what to do.

He stared back at Connie, who looked concerned but also a little demanding. “What?”

“What? What are you going to do, Son?”

“Ha! I wish I knew. Mikey couldn’t even give me any real information. But I have to guess from what he said that somebody’s coming up here to do some killing.”

Connie stared, and blinked. She looked down and started stirring her biscuits furiously. Coal stepped closer and closed his fingers over her spoon hand. “Hey. Don’t start getting yourself in a lather, Mom. Okay? Don’t make the kids’ breakfast into pieces of wood.”

Her face flashed up, and her eyes came into his. They were wet. With her jaw clamped, she stared at him, then finally managed a little smile. He knew she was recalling the times she had given him the same advice: If you stir your pancake or muffin batter, biscuit dough or pie crust too long, they'll turn as stiff as boards.

He brought a hand up and cradled her cheek. "Mom, it's going to be okay. The Medinas aren't here, and I'd bet if anything that's who they'll be after. Whoever's coming will see they're gone and probably just leave. They can't stay up here forever."

Connie pursed her lips, fighting emotion. Finally, she drew in a deep breath as he dropped his hand from her cheek, and she looked down and resumed stirring the biscuit ingredients together more slowly.

"Sometimes I almost wish you hadn't come home, Coal," she said as if speaking to her biscuits.

"I know, Mom. Me too."

It was almost like she hadn't heard him as she kept talking, now sounding almost matter-of-fact. "It seems like everything in this valley has fallen apart since just before you came home. Life isn't supposed to be this way." After a long pause in speaking, she said, "Where is that salt, anyway? Did I put the salt in?" She ducked her chin deeper. She was hiding her tears.

Coal stepped closer and took the wooden spoon out of her hand, giving it to Maura. He folded his mother into his arms, and then he prayed, which he realized sadly how seldom he thought to do.

Coal Savage, a man alone, had come up against the Mob.

Hell might not have followed him and Maura home from South Dakota, but it had certainly found him here. Again.

Thinking he should make his mother think of something else, he said, "Thanks for the coffee."

She didn't look up at him. "I hope you liked it. It was Sanka decaffeinated and Pero."

Coal smiled to himself. Why was he not surprised? "Well, it was delicious," he said, then prayed she would never make it for him again.

Maura got her coat on when Coal did and followed him outside. He didn't tell her not to, because he didn't mind having her come out and give him a more private goodbye, but he had no intention of letting her go into town with him.

On the porch, he turned to her. "What are you doing?"

"Huh?"

"I'm going to the jail. By myself."

She searched his eyes. Then she tried to harden her expression. "Well, I came out to see Chewy and Dart and the horses."

In the bright morning sun, as clouds of frosty-looking steam erupted from their mouths and hung for moments on the crystalline air, Coal gazed at Maura. How did the blue of her eyes keep startling him so, when they had known each other for so long and had stood so close together, or lain in each other's arms, so many times? In the fresh morning light, they looked bluer than ever right now. And clearer.

"I'll go with you," he said, wanting to hold her, wanting to kiss her, afraid because the kids might look out the window at any moment, and he wanted nothing they saw to give them false hopes. Thanks to Laura, when it came to relationships Coal was a coward, and there wasn't any getting around it. He wondered if he ever again would be able to stop being afraid of relationships.

They walked out to the barn and opened the door, and Chewy and Dart bolted out and ran around them in circles for a while before letting Maura crouch down and pet them. They followed them to the horse corral, where the horses were finishing up the last of their hay.

Maura's big black, Homer, stood segregated in a separate pen because he was a bully and because he and Connie's big old gray, Cody, would have otherwise tested each other in battle, and Coal didn't like to see horses with the ends of their ears bitten off, or something worse, like a broken leg. Looking at Homer, the horse Maura had said would be his if they ever went riding together, Coal found himself wondering if that day would ever come. It seemed like life on the Lemhi, at least for Coal Savage, went from one bad scrape to another faster than a fat man moving down a dessert bar.

Coal didn't want to leave Maura, so the horse-watching, and the dog-petting, took up twenty minutes or more, all while no one spoke, because neither had the nerve or even knew what could be said.

Finally, Coal cleared his throat. "I guess I'd better get into town."

"Can I go?"

"I already answered that, didn't I?"

"Why? It's not your town."

That almost made him laugh, and he had to fight it back. "That's true. But it is my truck."

"I have a truck too." She folded her arms across her chest. "Coal, please let me be with you. It'll be fine."

He stepped into her and grabbed both her arms, making her react instinctively by trying to jerk back. Her eyes, filled with sudden shock, were raised to his face.

"Don't you understand? I almost lost you in Oglala. I can't do that again."

"You won't."

"Maura. Stop. Anyone comes to this town to kill me, it isn't going to be some schmuck looking for a drug fix, wanting some quick money. It won't even be like the Iron Ropes and the rest of those would-be gangsters on the Rez. The Mob doesn't hire bumbling turds to assassinate people. Do you understand? They hire pros. And pros are ruthless. They'll go after their target by any means, and nothing is off-limits. They'll use anything they can find against you. They'll kidnap wives, kids . . . girlfriends. They could use bombs, sniping, poison. All of it. And more. You can't be seen with me anymore. At all. And that's the end of it."

Maura was too shocked to speak. She stared at him, making no further attempt to pull away from his grip on her arms.

"Don't follow me, Maura. If I see you anywhere outside this yard, you're nobody to me. I don't even know who you are. Is that clear enough?"

Dropping her arms, he whirled and started away. He didn't make it ten feet before spinning back. Maura stood there waiting for him.

Coal practically plowed the woman over in his rush to get back to her. He crushed her in his arms, kissing her passionately, almost ruthlessly. He wanted to tell her he loved her, yet he didn't dare. She hugged him like she would never let go, but at last, when he relinquished his hold, she dropped her arms away, burrowing her hands in her pockets like she was digging deep for change. Her eyes were wet as she stared at him, and her face was flushed, only partly from the cold.

"Coal, you have a whole bunch of people who'll be waiting for you. You've got to come back. Safe."

A thought struck him, and he sent it through his blender of a decision process—fast and furious. "Can I use your house?"

"What?"

"I need to use your house."

"I'm not sure what you mean."

"I can't be seen back here until whatever this is is over. That's what I mean. It has to look like I'm living alone. You can stay here with Mom. You can even sleep in my bed. Please. Don't make me beg."

"Of course you can stay at my house. You don't even have to ask." As she pulled the house key out of her pants pocket, she asked, "How long?"

"I don't know. I won't know until it's over."

"How is it ever going to be over? And how would you know if it was? It's not like the Mob's going to run out of people—or post a notice saying they give up."

He knew one certain answer to those questions, a tragic one. So did she. Neither of them could speak it. He turned again and didn't look back at her for several feet. He stopped and turned. "Could you tell Mom and the kids I'll call them soon?" He couldn't bear to go inside and ruin their Saturday. Maura gave him a brisk nod in reply. He guessed she was unable to speak.

At the truck, he carefully walked the circumference of it, looking for tracks in the snow. He did the same with all the other vehicles, including Maura's Travelette—Ebenezer. He didn't seek Maura out again until the truck engine was warmed up and he was backing out of the yard. She was standing in the same place, her hands remaining buried in her pockets.

She yanked one of them loose and waved. She had started to bring it back down, but stopped and instead blew him a kiss.

He gave her a wink and his best put-on smile—and wondered if they would ever see each other again.

CHAPTER FIVE

On a whim, before driving into town Coal pulled off at Maura's. He sat and scanned the yard and outbuildings with his revolver drawn, resting on his leg. He didn't know why. Since they had driven right on past the house the day before, it didn't seem like anyone could know about Maura . . . yet. But he had seen strange things while he was in Asia, and more of them while he was with the Bureau. Besides, this was a habit he was going to have to get in, because apparently life away from Washington, D.C., for him, was nothing but another war zone.

Stepping out of the pickup, he visually scoured the yard. Other than some deer tracks and a set of fox prints, the snow was undisturbed, either by tires or by human footwear. He went up on the rickety porch, swearing once again as he creaked across it that he was going to come over and build her a nice new one the first chance he got.

Inside the house, it was cold. Listening carefully, he could hear the water running in the kitchen sink, and when he walked closer he saw the pencil-lead of water streaming down into the basin. *Good girl,* he thought. Maura had left the water on to keep her pipes from freezing. He opened the fridge, then the cupboards, wanting to know what he would need to buy when he was in town. He was going to buy plenty extra for her, to make up for what she was doing for him, and for all she had meant to him.

Checking around one last time, he didn't even know what for, he went back out and drove slowly into town. A couple of vehicles passed him on the way. He looked at them closely. Both had Lemhi plates.

It took a while to get up to the courthouse because he stopped at every motel and hotel along the route, and even went out to the Stagecoach. He was looking for strange vehicles. Remarkable vehicles. Nevada plates would have been the most notable sign of all, but improbable to find. The Mob was unlikely to be so obvious.

Of course he didn't find any local plates at the hotels or motels, but most of what he did find were vehicles from nearby counties—mostly Bannock, Bonneville, or Bingham, known to locals as "the Killer Bees", because they were generally there to help reduce the area's wildlife population—and some out of Montana.

He drove up to the courthouse and was about to turn in, but at the last second he drove on by, watching the building closely as he passed. He went up to Todd Mitchell's place and checked on Jan and the boys, trying to act as natural as possible. The woman's embrace left his clothes feeling a little dirty, and smelling oddly like fried bologna, but even so it warmed him up inside. He wished there were some way without being offensive to teach these folks something about hygiene.

"Todd called me and said he took two steps," said Jan after a few minutes' small talk, and after thanking him again, profusely, for all the food he had brought up to her and the boys before his trip.

His heart jumped at the welcome news. "That's great! I'm so happy to hear that." And he truly was. Just for that moment he was able to put aside whatever danger he was in. His deputy was improving. Maybe in time he would be back. He had almost stopped daring to hope.

"Yeah." Jan nodded, making a loose strand of unwashed hair slump into her face, which she hurriedly fixed back behind an ear. It was a habit that seemed to have bent both of her ears permanently forward, not so much as to look bad, but noticeable.

"I sure hope he gets back here soon. I miss that boy."

"Thank you, Sheriff. He told me he misses you too. I . . ." She stopped.

"What is it, Jan?" He didn't know how her first name had slipped in. He didn't remember ever calling her anything but Mrs. Mitchell or ma'am before. But it seemed right to use it now.

"I don't know how much I ever told you thanks for everything you've done for me and the boys, and what you did for Todd. For not givin' up on 'im."

He stepped close and cupped one of her shoulders. "That's my pleasure. It really is. I couldn't find a better deputy."

Jan's eyes got misty and, looking awkward, she stepped in and gave him another hug. She held on so long that he finally brought up a hand and pressed her head closer to him. Maybe Jan could have used a few lessons on cleanliness, but she was a lonely woman in need of a soft touch and a kind heart. If he couldn't do anything else, at least he could offer that.

Before he got back to the courthouse, he saw a car coming from the other direction slow down and then turn in, driving toward the parking lot. He felt himself stiffen. It was the same teal Lincoln Continental he and Maura had passed on the way home . . .

He stopped in front of the driveway, looking toward the back. He couldn't see the Lincoln, but there was no other way out of this parking lot. It was back there. Somewhere.

He drew the .44 again and set it on the seat beside him. Easing down on the clutch, he put the pickup in first and crept up the drive.

The Lincoln sat sleek and beautiful in the middle of the lot—empty. This being Saturday, there was only one valid reason that car would be here—sheriff's office business. He pulled the pickup all the way around the lot so it faced back out, then parked.

With his pistol in hand, he got out, carefully studying the lot, and every part of the courthouse he could see. There was nobody in sight.

He stepped closer to the jail, crouching down to look through the window. He could see the torsos of two men, one of them good-sized. The other appeared to be his night jailer, Vic Yancey, who had been stepping up and working more hours lately. The men seemed to be involved in a casual conversation.

Holstering the Smith and Wesson, Coal stepped down the stairs and pushed the door open. He was gratified to see the big smiles that came to the faces of both men—young Vic, and his recently hired deputy, Grant Fairbourne.

"Hello, Sheriff!" Grant was first to recover from the surprise of his entrance, and he leaped forward and extended his hand.

Coal shook, smiling back. It was a smile of relief as much as one of happiness. "Don't tell me that beautiful Lincoln out there belongs to you! How did I miss that when you were here before?"

Grant laughed. "I'm not sure. But it was here."

"Man, you might want to have second thoughts about coming to work in Lemhi County. You'd never have been able to buy that with anything you made here."

"That's all right. I've already paid it off."

After making sure to greet Vic, a man of nineteen, with big brown eyes, curly brown hair, and the pretense of a mustache, but no stylish sideburns anywhere on his horizon, Coal turned his attention once more to Grant. "What brings you back again so soon?"

"I'm ready for work," said Grant, beaming.

Calculations flashed through Coal's brain. "It hasn't been two weeks."

"No sir. The chief in Caldwell told me he appreciated my two weeks' notice and would have given me a good recommendation anyway, but it sounded like your call for help was urgent enough that he thought I should get over here as soon as I could."

"That's pretty nice of him. I'll have to give him a call and thank him."

"I'm sure he'd love to hear from you. So what's the plan?"

"Well, for starters if you want to go down to McPherson's and pick yourself up a cowboy hat, feel free. It's sort of the casual uniform standard around here."

"Except for Jordan," Grant pointed out, a little shyly.

"Oh, right. Well, you know, I've never said anything to Jordan about it, and he never asked. I don't think he has the right shape of head for a hat."

"Yeah, you're probably right. Anyway, I have hats already. I am from Challis, remember."

"I do. And it sure is good to have you. So how are you fixed for living quarters?"

Grant told him about their motel.

"Then first thing Monday morning let's get you down to a realtor. I'm going to guess you're wanting to rent?"

Grant stared at him for a moment. A look of disappointment came over his face. "Oh. Yeah, we were thinking about buying something, but I guess now that you mention it renting would be safer for a while."

Coal thought back on what Jan Mitchell had just told him about Todd, but he didn't want to disappoint Grant with the news. "Yeah. Sorry about that. I'd hate to see you get into a new house just to have to turn around and sell it if things don't work out long-term. Why don't you show up here before nine on Monday? You brought your own iron, right?"

"Yes sir. Just a thirty-eight."

"If you think about it and have the inclination, I'd like to see you carrying at least a .357, but the .38 will work for now."

After Grant headed back to his hotel, Coal spoke for a while with Vic Yancey. He realized he had never taken the time to get to know this young man, who seemed pretty sharp. He certainly knew his job well and kept the jail in perfect shape.

Coal found himself starting to feel distracted after a while, his mind wandering back to the morning phone call from Mikey Parravano. Vic seemed in the mood to talk, in spite of having been up most of the night, but Coal knew he couldn't give him his full attention at the moment.

"Hey, Vic, I have some stuff I have to take care of this morning, but do me a favor, would you?"

Vic stared back at him. "Sure, Sheriff. Anything."

"Okay, first off, you have to start calling me Coal. Second, let's take a Saturday sometime soon and grab a bite to eat or something after you've had some rest. I think we ought to get to know each other a little better."

Grinning, and his eyes lighting up, Vic replied, "That would be great! Later today would be good for me, if you have any time. I usually try to be back up by one or two, so I can sleep that night."

"Then let's shoot for that—say maybe two o'clock?"

Coal put out his hand, and Vic Yancey shook it eagerly. Even as distracted as he felt, it made Coal happy to see the light that had come over Vic's face.

"See you at two."

"See you—Coal. And thanks!"

After Vic left, Coal sat at his desk and shuffled through his Rolodex. He made a call to police chief Dan George, and another one as a friend to Bob Wilson. He also called Lyle Gentry, the temporary state bull. He would have called Jordan Peterson, but he wasn't sure of his sleeping schedule.

His last call was to prosecutor Mike Fica.

The cheery voice of the lawyer came over the other end of the line.

"Hey, Mike. Coal Savage."

Hello, Coal! How are you? How did your trip go? Small town Salmon.

Coal gave a dry laugh. "Well, we survived. I'll tell you all about it sometime."

Okay, said Fica with a little chuckle. *Sounds portentous.*

Coal had to laugh. "Yeah. Portentous. That's exactly the word I was going to use."

Fica's giggle was infectious. *So what can I do for ya, Coal?*

"Well, Mike . . . You know, I wouldn't mind seeing you for a bit. Is that possible?"

You mean now?

"Sure, if you have time."

Well, uh . . . Damn! Now this does *sound portentous! Sure, Coal. Sure thing. Where are you?*

"Up at the office, but I can come to wherever you are."

No, no, that's fine! The family's all here, and it's pretty noisy. I'll just swing up there. It won't take me five minutes to get there. I just live down on Gwartney.

Three minutes later a big blue van pulled into the lot. Coal watched it from the side of one window, wishing he had asked Fica what he would be driving. When the door opened and the shape of a man squeezed out the opening, there was no doubt who it was, even from behind. Fica was one large man, but somehow he got around fine. Someone had even told him Fica was a referee for high school football games and a Boy Scout leader as well, so his weight didn't seem to hinder him whatsoever in life. It just made him memorable.

The prosecutor came down the stairs, and Coal had the door open for him when he reached the bottom. Fica's happy greeting, big smile, and firm handshake warmed Coal's heart. He had never felt more immediate friendship with anyone than he did with Fica, and he didn't normally feel that way about attorneys.

"Come on in," Coal invited. "Can I make you some coffee?"

"Nope, don't drink the stuff. I don't suppose you have any Coke, do you?"

Coal laughed. "You don't drink coffee, but you drink Coke? Sorry. I'm about as likely to have cocaine on hand as Coca-Cola."

Fica giggled gleefully. "Oh! Well, I'll take some of that then."

Coal couldn't help another laugh. Mike Fica always had a way of making people do that, and even more importantly of making them feel like old friends.

With a long sigh, Fica said, "Yeah, the Coke's a bad habit, I know. Wouldn't have had my nice figure without it, though."

After answering questions once more about his own welfare and that of his family—whom Fica didn't even know—Coal turned serious. "Mike, you remember having me move the Medinas to the Falls?"

"Sure."

"Well, you were right. I think it could be worse than you were thinking, though."

Fica's stare was almost blank. The only emotion Coal might have read into it, and that could only have been because he was looking for it, was worried anticipation. After several seconds he said, "Why, what's up?"

"I got a call from an old friend of mine I used to go to school with here. Somehow he got mixed up in the Mob down in Vegas. He's the one I got hold of to crack the Medina case. Anyway, he called me up in a panic this morning to tell me I had big trouble coming my way because of this mess."

Fica listened intently. When Coal stopped talking, both of them sat still, but Coal had a feeling Fica's mind was running a hundred miles an hour behind those narrowed eyes, which were made narrower by the pressing upward of his rotund cheeks.

"Did he say anything specific?"

"He practically begged me to leave town for a week or two."

Fica swore. "Oh crap. Then somebody's coming up here. I was afraid of that, but I was sure hoping we could avoid it if we sent the Medinas somewhere else fast enough. You think maybe they just don't know we moved them yet?"

"Aw, I don't know, Mike." Coal swore as he stood up. "I know you're the one who came up with the idea to move them. I was an idiot not to think of it. But I don't know if you've thought any farther ahead."

"Ahead? What do you mean?"

"About you. And me. And our families. Friends. The courthouse. Mike, this is the Mob we're talking about. If it was important enough for them to send somebody up here, they're not just going to skip on down the road because the Medinas aren't here, or because I leave—which I can't do anyway. If they can't get the Medinas right now, or me, I'm afraid where they might go next."

Once again, perhaps Coal saw it only because he was looking for it, but Mike's already rather pale face seemed to go a shade more ashen.

"You mean me, huh?"

Coal nodded, his mouth twitching involuntarily. "I don't want to scare you for no reason, Mike, but . . . They're smart enough to know if they can stop you they stop the trial. At least until we can regroup. They might even go after Bryan Wheat."

Again Mike swore. "Man, Coal. You sure know how to rain crap on a family get-together."

* * *

When Coal met with Vic Yancey at Wally's later, he broke down under the beautiful, warm smile of Karen Richardson and ordered hot chocolate for the two of them, and two of Wally's prize cinnamon rolls. He would have to try and make sure it was the only big treat he had all week, but how did a mere human resist the charm of such a cute, lovable waitress, and a warm, buttery cinnamon roll fresh out of Wally's microwave oven? He caught a certain look in the eyes of young Vic when Karen brought their sinful order back out to them, told them to enjoy, then moved on to other customers.

"Cute girl, huh?"

Vic jerked his eyes away from Karen and looked at Coal. His face reddened. "Uh, yeah. She's pretty cute."

Coal laughed. "Downright beautiful, buddy. I don't blame you a bit. If I were your age I'd be looking too."

Laughing, Vic said, "I don't think her mom and dad would let me get within ten feet of her."

"You never know what a good recommendation might do. But then again, maybe you should wait till she at least turns eighteen."

Vic laughed again and sipped at his chocolate.

"So I was thinking, we've never had a lot of time to talk. What do you do for fun, anyway, Vic?"

"Oh, lots of stuff. I love to shoot."

If Coal hadn't been so distracted, those would of course have been words to win his heart. He forced himself to forget about the Mob and Mikey Parravano for a while, and he and Vic talked about guns, hunting, riding horses, fishing. Vic turned out to have much in common with Coal, even in the way of his taste in entertainment. He was a huge fan of Marty Robbins and The Sons of the Pioneers, and he thought Jim Reeves sang like a meadowlark—which was true.

Vic told him about his family, way out south of town, his twin sisters who were about the same age as Wyatt and Morgan, and about a fun, loving family life he had grown up in. When they got ready to part ways, Coal found himself regretting it. He was amazed how good it had felt simply to sit and talk, like two normal people, to forget all his worries, to see how much an old forty-two year-old man could have in common with one who was only nineteen. He had enjoyed every minute with this young jailer, and he started to think Vic Yancey might have a promising future in law enforcement, especially if he could get over a little touch of shyness. He might even have a greater future if the smile Karen Richardson flashed him on their way out meant anything.

CHAPTER SIX

Lincoln, Nebraska

Alex Martinez drove a 1968 Mustang coupe. Born in a deep blue color known as presidential blue, the car had been rear-ended by a drunk driver when it was two years old and he was still living in D. C. and working at the Bureau. On a whim, he had chosen to have it repainted not in its original color, a color he had seen his car's double of on the streets of D. C. far too many times, but in a color the owner of the auto body shop called flake orange. The "flake" in this case had been added on top of a rusty orange color after the fact, and it sparkled like diamond flecks in the sun. Although the Mustang only bragged a 289 under the hood, the carburetor had been bumped up to a four-barrel, along with other special modifications, and it would blow the doors off most anything around if someone wanted a race, at least for the first block. Not that Martinez was a show-off—but if someone was fool enough to challenge him, he was not about to let his pride and joy be insulted.

Martinez had been told his features were classic, with a heavy dose of Indian blood giving him the sharp nose of a hawk, shiny, deep black hair, and black eyes it was said could bore right through a person—especially one with whom he was displeased.

With a third-degree black belt in judo, a decent command of several other martial arts and boxing, along with a credo of Mexican machismo that he would let himself die before he let himself be beaten, Martinez was no man to trifle with.

Like his best friend Sam Browning, Martinez had won the stripes of a sergeant, with his chosen branch being the Marines. And while Browning had completely left the service, Martinez remained in the reserves. Once a Marine, always a Marine.

Martinez had never married, but not by his own choice. He simply had yet to find the right woman. In that way Browning was lucky: He had found probably the one woman who would put up with his work and travel schedule—although heaven forbid Browning's wife ever learned what his real "work" was.

Martinez pulled the sleek, shiny Mustang into the parking lot at the Lincoln Children's Zoo. The place was fairly new—only about seven years old, he'd been told. But they had done a fantastic job of making it into a destination for the entire family.

Feeling stupid for being here alone, he drove the Mustang slowly around the lot, looking for the Brownings' Mulsanne blue seventy-one Monte Carlo. By the time he had made it twice around the lot, he had to start wondering if the Brownings had forgotten him.

And then there they were.

The immaculate deep blue Monte Carlo glided off the road, and almost immediately an arm shot up out of the passenger side and started waving maniacally. Martinez allowed himself a smile. He wasn't known for his award-winning, toothy grins, but seeing Sam, Megan, and their two children always made him happy. And Megan's big wave reflected how relieved she must be to know she would get to spend time around someone who wasn't as cracked in the head as her husband. That thought gave Martinez another subdued smile as he pulled the Mustang—with a lot of arm power, because it didn't have power steering—into a parking space. He knew Megan really didn't think that about her husband. Somehow, Browning had tricked her into thinking he walked on water.

As Browning's luck would have it (he led a charmed life), a pickup pulled out of a parking space toward the front of the lot just as he was coming in, and within a minute of leaving the road he was shutting off the Monte Carlo.

Martinez, wearing a black ball cap with a big gold USMC on the front, a black T-shirt stretched over his vee-shaped torso, and blue slacks, came up out of the Mustang just as a brown-haired boy of six years old came bounding over with his arms outstretched and gave him a hug around the waist. This was Caleb, Browning's oldest. There was nothing in the universe that could bring a tear to Martinez's tougher-than-basalt Marine eyes, but if there had been it would have been the affection of Browning's family. Martinez for years had longed for a son of his own. But Caleb Browning might be as close as he was ever going to get.

"Hey, buddy!" he said, crouching down to pick Caleb up and walking toward Megan and Sam, who was carrying their four-year-old, Kathryn.

As they stopped a few feet from each other, Megan said, "I hope you know now you've picked that little stinker up you're going to have to hold him the whole day."

Martinez laughed. "That's okay with me."

But it wasn't with Megan. "Okay, Caleb. Let the rest of us have a turn."

Martinez set the boy down, and Megan gave him a bearhug, followed by another when Martinez knelt down to Kathryn's level. The blood coursing through his killer of a Marine heart turned ten degrees warmer. He loved this family.

When Martinez stood up, Browning's hand shot out, and Martinez shook it. "Hey, Vike. Good to see you didn't forget me."

Browning's call sign in the Army had been Viking, because apparently his size, muscle, and blond hair put his buddies in mind of a Norseman. Martinez had long since taken to shortening it, because anything that *could* be shorter should be.

"Heck no! Never," replied Browning. "You ready to go see some animals?"

Martinez couldn't hold back a chuckle. They had been here only a little over a month ago, for the festivities of Christmas, so it wasn't as if this was going to be something new and exciting. But hey, the dating scene for Alex Martinez, in spite of his astounding good looks and gorgeous car, wasn't exactly flourishing. In fact, it was barely alive and kicking. There was nothing he would rather be doing than spending the afternoon with his adopted brother and his family.

It wasn't long into the fun zoo experience when Martinez remembered the one thing he didn't like about spending time with his adopted brother . . .

They were standing in front of the sun bear cage, watching the bear stroll casually along just inside the bars, when someone nearby dropped a cup of soda. It didn't make a loud noise, but it was loud enough to draw Martinez's attention. As he looked over, a heavy-set man in a white T-shirt and jeans raised a hand to the much-smaller woman who was apparently at fault for knocking the pop on the ground. He managed to hold himself back from striking her, but instead he verbally crushed her, in spite of twenty or thirty other people standing about, including Browning's little kids.

"Jean, judas priest! I'm sick of your fumble fingers. Idiot."

Martinez felt his blood pressure go up, but there was no physical violence, and this wasn't his business. This jerk didn't deserve a wife at all, much less one as sweet-looking as little Jean, but life wasn't always fair. Unfortunately, Sam Browning was what one would call an infamous sheepdog, and he always had to ramp things up beyond the casual. Sam's red neck—which at the moment was literal, not just figurative—was a bad sign Martinez always watched for, and all too often found.

Before Martinez could step over to grab his friend's arm, and his attention, the pressure in the boiler blew a valve.

"Listen, you ass—that was your fault, not hers."

Martinez's heart leaped, then fell. Here it went again: the beginning of the end for a nice family outing. He heard the plea in Jean's voice as his own words were drowning it out.

"Come on, Vike, let's head over to the elephants. It's not worth it, bro."

Browning didn't hear him. The listening part of Sam Browning had shut down. Browning the sheepdog hated bullies—the wolves of Browning's world. And Browning never walked away from a wolf in need of a lesson.

Apparently, the bull-necked wife-bully could hear only one thing as well: Browning's cutting remarks. He didn't care that Martinez, and his own wife, were trying to avoid a scene.

"Mind your own business, Blondie, or you're gonna find your butt on the ground."

Browning took a step closer. Even with both his hands still down at his sides, he was in fight mode, and this idiot was clueless. He had no idea in the universe what a Green Beret could do to sever him from his happy day of wife-belittling.

"By who?" demanded Browning, his face appearing calm except for the red that was fast creeping up it from his neck.

Martinez didn't want to say anything, but in the hope of saving this potentially wonderful day for the family, he had to.

"You might want to back off, mister. Sam's a Green Beret."

The bully's eyes flickered. No one in his right mind would buck a Green Beret, except for perhaps another Green Beret. In today's atmosphere, there couldn't be anyone left who didn't know the Green Beret reputation. Everyone at least knew about the John Wayne movie, even as inaccurate as it might be.

The bully forced a grunt and spat hard on the pavement. "Like I give a crap! Green Beret!"

Poor Jean took one last chance and jumped in again, looking up—*way* up—at Browning. "Please, sir, it's all right, I—"

Whatever the woman was saying vanished for Browning and Martinez when her husband, thinking Browning sufficiently distracted, took a swing at his chin.

Within the beat of a heart, every shocked ear around heard the back of the man's skull snap against the asphalt. He was dazed, as anyone would be, and his eyes took on a glazed appearance. But Browning had no way to know if he was down for good. Neither did Martinez, and now that the ball was rolling downhill he was done stepping in. He wasn't going to stop Browning's train only to have the man come up with a gun or knife and hurt his friend while Martinez was pulling his attention elsewhere.

Martinez reached down and grabbed Caleb, stepping back as Megan pulled Kathryn out of the way.

Browning leaned forward and grabbed the front of the fallen man's shirt while he was trying to get his bearings, and then, while everyone looked on with open mouths, he raised him up slightly and powered two blows to his chin, both of them slamming the back of his skull to the asphalt anew. This time the affect was that the man's eyes slowly rolled back in his head as Browning continued watching him, and then as they went shut he let go his hold on the now-rumpled shirt, and the man's head thunked back to the asphalt and lolled to one side.

His wife screamed, and a nearby little kid cried in horror. Apparently, that was his father on the ground.

Martinez grabbed Browning's arm, making sure to speak his nickname to him, very firmly, before he did so. Browning came around, his right fist cocked. He blinked and stared at his friend.

"All right, bro, it's just me. We'd better get out of here. Fun's over."

Browning blinked once more. Then he did so again, a mad flurry of blinks, and looked over at Megan. An apology was in his eyes, but she didn't need it. She took his arm, her mouth set, her eyes disappointed. "Come on, honey. The animals don't seem all that active anyway."

Reaching down, she picked up Kathryn, then turned her eyes to Martinez. "Hey, can you get Caleb's hand?"

Martinez went her one better and picked the boy up. Both kids seemed pretty shaken. He looked at Browning. "You comin'?"

His friend stood staring down at the unconscious bully. Almost reluctant, he turned and followed them away, looking back only once. At the zoo gate a man in uniform was on the phone. He looked up sharply as Martinez and the family filed through the turnstile.

"He did what again?" the man yelled into the receiver.

Martinez heard him and swore. "Hustle up, guys. I'll hold off the cavalry."

With strides any military branch would be proud of, Martinez and Browning headed for their cars. Megan almost had to jog to keep up.

As they neared the Monte Carlo, Martinez looked back to see two determined-looking men in uniform headed after them. He set Caleb down. "Hey, bud, run along with your mom and dad, okay?" Then he turned and started walking back.

He knew Browning didn't like having to run, but the way things were with him and his livelihood he could hardly afford to sit in jail—something he never thought much about until it was past too late.

Martinez heard the Monte Carlo fire up behind him as the two guards picked up their pace. He walked to meet them.

"Hey, guys. What's up?"

One guard, a stocky blond with a big mustache, looked at him. "You with that guy?"

"What guy?" The other guard had already started past them. Martinez turned and yelled sharply at him, making him spin around. "I'm with the FBI. Can you tell me what's happening?"

Something about those three initials seemed to hold great sway with people, probably because they watched too much TV. The man turned back. "You're FBI?"

"Yeah." With great satisfaction, in his peripheral vision he saw the Monte Carlo speed out of the parking lot.

The second guard whirled back and saw the same thing. It was too far away to see the plate. "Hey! Who was that?"

"I'm not sure," Martinez said with a shrug. "The woman just asked me to carry her son for her, so I did. Is there a problem?"

The heavyset guard swore. The guards looked at each other, then at Martinez. "Uh, no sir," said the heavyset one. "I guess not anymore."

Fifteen minutes later, Martinez sat with the Brownings, chilling out in a McDonald's two miles away. Browning fidgeted, continually looking out the window. It was sad that problems with Browning were frequent enough they actually had to have a nearby meeting place decided on before they started any activity, in case something went south. Martinez had learned this lesson long ago.

He stared at Browning, his mouth firm. He had made eye contact with Megan numerous times, but no one spoke, not even the children. At last, Martinez said, "Hey, sorry, Megan. We'll be right back." He stood out of the booth and looked down at Browning. "All right, Vike. Come on. We need to talk."

Browning looked up. The normally whitish pink of his skin was long since back to its normal color, but he had a strange shine to his eyes. "Huh?"

"Come on, get up."

Browning turned his eyes to his wife. Without saying anything, he struggled out of the booth, then followed Martinez into the restroom. Once the door swung shut, Martinez looked at him. "That was sure smooth back there."

"What?"

"Oh, for hell's sake." Martinez's eyes were hard, but he didn't bother raising his voice. "You act like you're still in junior high. I've told you a hundred times I can't keep bailin' you out of crap."

It went unspoken, but was still somehow amusing, that even after a hundred times Browning didn't change.

"What'd you want me to do?" Browning asked with no conviction.

Martinez stared at him, letting the moment of silence sink in. "Is that even a real question?"

"Yeah."

"I wanted you to walk away. I wanted to stay at the zoo with Caleb and Kathryn and for once let them have a normal outing with their dad. I don't know how Megan puts up with you, man. What the hell goes through your head?"

Browning's jaw set. He probably thought he was totally in the right, and he was probably starting to get angry. Martinez could only push things so far, because no one knew what might happen if a real fight ever erupted between the two of them. And no one would have wanted to find out.

"I'm not standing around while some poor woman gets bullied. If you want to that's your business."

Martinez sighed. "Man, we've got to get a new job. You've got way too much steam building up. Just don't forget, you don't have a *real* job, buddy. If you keep doing stupid crap, eventually I won't be able to get you out of trouble. And if it's bad enough, neither will they."

Browning blinked. "They?"

Martinez stared back at him, waiting for him to catch up.

"Oh. 'They'. Well, they can't afford not to have my help."

"Don't get cocky. There's other people out there who are willing to off people and do other bad crap in exchange for money."

"Sure. But not people who do it all as good as I do—and with a conscience."

And Browning was right. Martinez couldn't even argue the point, although it seemed ironic to talk about a man who often had to kill other people for a living doing it with a conscience.

"Come on, man, let's go eat," Martinez said with a sigh. "But do me a favor: If the little girl back there making your Big Mac forgets and accidentally put pickles on it, please don't break her arms off, all right?"

CHAPTER SEVEN

Salmon, Idaho

The immaculate paint of the Jaguar XJ was a hue known as ocean blue, about the darkest a blue could be without being black. The plates, white with the upraised green lettering and the "Famous Potatoes" logo of Idaho, marked the car as nothing special to Salmon, only another misguided visitor, this one with the "1A" designation of Ada County. The plates had been put on shortly after driving away from the rental car company, whose Bonneville County plates had been on the car originally.

The Jaguar sliced along Main Street like a blued gun barrel, its tires humming a quiet tune as they crackled on loose bits of gravel and ice. Even with the Idaho plates, Menny Marcello felt as self-conscious inside the flashy Jag as a debutante at her first ball, with a broken high heel.

Scabs Ravioli looked over at him, sensing a tension in the car thick enough to spread on his Ritz crackers. "Jeez, brother, look around, will you? We've gone down almost the whole street, and I've only seen one person turn and look at us. You gotta relax!"

"Shut up!" Menny growled. "I *am* relaxed, all right? I'm relaxed! Any more relaxed I'd be asleep."

Scabs laughed. "Yeah, you seem like it. Just drive to the hotel. We can walk anywhere we want to in this two-dollar town if it makes you feel better. It's small enough—*Matthew.*" He said that last in a joking tone to remind both himself and Menny—who on his birth certificate was known by the given name Menneghetti—that while they were in Salmon, Menny was a dopey rich guy named Matthew Hardigan, and he was Bryn Renault, and both of them were looking for a nice inexpensive cabin they could purchase for weekend getaways from Boise—the "big city". Every piece of identification on them, including the fake registration and insurance on the car, reflected those names.

"Maybe walking *would* make me feel better," agreed Menny.

"Yeah. Because you look so much less conspicuous than the Jag."

Menny looked over at his partner and allowed himself to smile. He knew Scabs was having fun with him. Menny, who was ten hard years behind Scabs in age, and still young enough to care about such things, was widely recognized for his good looks and charm—and humble about it too. So yes, perhaps walking around wouldn't help them to be inconspicuous either. But the good thing, the thing that made him most relaxed, was knowing that nobody anywhere had photographs of either him or Scabs marking them as wanted men or even men of interest—legally speaking. That fact was confirmed on a regular basis by people who would know—

those being people in the FBI and different agencies who pretended to be "for the people, of the people" but whose biggest paychecks came not from their government day jobs, but from the Mob.

As they crossed the bridge over the rolling Salmon River and pulled onto Highway 93 heading north, Menny pointed at the Stagecoach Inn and exclaimed, "There it is!" Scabs laughed. Menny sounded like a kid who had just spotted the candy store.

"Yeah, there it is. Home sweet home."

They parked and went inside, where Scabs registered for a room visible from the parking lot while Menny ogled the good-looking woman in black-rimmed glasses behind the desk who had introduced herself as the manager, Julie. Scabs, even while he was engrossed in the paperwork and concentrating on making sure to put his correct incorrect name on the registration slip, saw Menny making his eyes and wanted to elbow him. Menny tried so hard to pretend a desire to be inconspicuous, yet he didn't mind making eyes at the women and certainly didn't mind them looking back. It happened every place they went.

Going back out to the Jag, Menny parked it exactly in front of their room, whose sliding glass door made it accessible from outside. He wanted to be able to look out at any time and see what kind of attention the car was drawing. If it started feeling too hot here, he was going to get out of this deal, Porc de Castiglione be damned.

After they took their suitcases in, leaving all the other important tools of their trade in the trunk, only to be brought into the room late in the night, Scabs flipped the TV on and threw himself on the bed, pushing pillows up against the headboard behind him. "That was a nice little display out there at the desk." He was trying to sound casual.

Menny turned and stared at Scabs like an old cow chewing its cud. "Huh?"

"The girl?" Scabs said, throwing his eyebrows up as he slapped his accusing stare into the younger man's face.

"What are you talkin' about?"

"Oh, jeez, Menny! I think Julie's expecting you to ask her on a date. If you'd kept it up, she'd've been askin' for a cigarette."

"What'd I do?"

Scabs grunted. "Cut the stupid act, man. Mr. Inconspicuous!" he scoffed good-naturedly.

Menny only grunted in return as Scabs lay there looking at the television screen, wishing he had some nice little kid to change the channels for him, having already forgotten that last exchange.

"So what do we do next?" Menny asked finally.

Scabs turned his hand over, directing a casual finger toward the Zenith as if Menny was on drugs. "TV?"

"Huh." Menny grunted once more and gave a big shrug, glancing around the room. "Well, I'm gonna take a nap. We might be here a while."

Scabs already knew that. This wasn't his first time out of the chute. One time he and a former partner had been forced to spend an entire three months getting to know their hit before they even dared to make a move. That one ended up being worth sixty thousand dollars, which was pretty phenomenal considering the average yearly wage in America was a little over nine thousand that year and a good physician might make fifty. But then physicians had insurance to cover their mistakes. If guys like Menny and Scabs made a mistake, there was nothing that could cover it. Death would be merciful, and prison the alternative.

Menny got on the second queen-sized bed and lay on his back with his eyes shut. The pillow felt like a pile of cotton. The room, in spite of what had turned out to be ice-cold air outside, was warm—even toasty. For a while, he could hear Scabs chuckling at *Hee Haw*. Menny had always found the show inane, but he enjoyed the sound of Scabs's laughter. Any other day it would be contagious. Now it just lulled him. Between his partner's soft chuckling, the warmth in the room, the comfort of the pillow, mattress, and covers, in minutes Menny was gone.

And he didn't even dream of shooting anyone, or of making them into a towering fifty-foot ball of flame. Instead, he dreamed of silly laughter, pickled garlic, and Ritz crackers.

* * *

Coal Savage wasn't exactly sure what to do. This appeared to be a waiting game, at least unless and until something bad happened or he heard something more from Mikey Parravano. If Mikey was even still alive.

It was two o'clock, Saturday afternoon, and he had been hanging out at the office most of the day simply because he had no other plan. Even as distracted as he was by the thought of mortal danger, he had been able to do quite a bit of work on the budget, including fitting in a certain amount for emergency wages—which meant Grant Fairbourne. He had also done an awful lot of going over a seedling of a plan he had in his head to go to the county commission with a plea for two more permanent deputy spots. It was a big request, and he figured he wouldn't get it, but he was hoping by doubling the number he wanted it would create somewhat of a smoke screen, and then a single deputy wouldn't seem so hard to swallow. Lemhi County was simply too vast to be handled by a sheriff and two deputies. A bare minimum, for a place like this, would be himself plus three, and in reality even that was a joke. But if he could push the idea for another man through, Grant would be assured a permanent spot—and the more he was around that young man, the more he hoped he would be able to stay.

He decided to take a chance that Jordan Peterson might already be up getting ready for work, and he drove over to his house. The deputy wasn't up yet, but before Coal got back to the pickup he heard the door open behind him and Jordan yelling, "Hey, Coal!"

Turning, he went back. Jordan extended his hand, more of a habit than anything, and Coal shook it. "Good to see you back, man! How was your vacation?" Coal guessed the biggest thing on Jordan's mind was Maura, but to his credit he didn't mention her.

Coal's eyebrows went up, and he sighed, glad to know the whole story of Pine Ridge so far had remained within his own family and with Maura. "Well, buddy, that's a long story I'll save for another time. The best thing I can say is we survived." He knew that was starting to be a canned answer, but in this case nothing else fit so well.

Jordan blinked rapidly, trying to clear sleep from his eyes. "That doesn't sound good."

"Well, we're in one piece. But hey, there's a reason I had to wake you up, and I really apologize. Looks like I caught you right in the middle of some good sleep."

Jordan grinned, his eyes almost disappearing. "Don't worry about it. I'm still young."

"I hope what I'm about to tell you doesn't keep you up until your shift. The short of it is we've got some real trouble."

Jordan looked startled. "Somethin' I did?"

"No, no! Not you. Sorry to scare you. No, I got a call from my informant friend in the Vegas Mob. He tried to get me to leave town for a week or two, but he had to hang up before he could give me much detail."

Jordan kept staring, his face blank, but concern building in his eyes.

"Meaning, if my guess is correct, that the Mob has sent some trouble shooter up here because of the Medina brothers."

"Trouble shooter?"

"Yeah. Headhunter. Hitman. Assassin. My guess is they came up here most likely to take Ray and Angel out."

"Really? Kill their own men?"

Coal nodded briskly. “Sure. They’re a liability now. It’s just a guess, mind you.”

“But they’re not here. So …”

Coal studied his deputy, waiting to see if he caught on without further prodding. He didn’t, and that didn’t surprise Coal. Any normal person would come to the conclusion that by moving the brothers away they had avoided an issue.

“Things should be good then, right?” Jordan finished his thought.

“I’d hope so, but I’m guessing not. They’ll eventually figure out where those two are, I have no doubt of that. I’m sure they’ve got informants everywhere. But I think it would be hard to get into a facility as big as the Idaho Falls jail without a lot of work. So what move’s going to be Plan B if they can’t silence the Medinas? They have to silence the witnesses and prosecutors on the case.”

Mouth ajar, Jordan stared for a couple more seconds, then clamped his mouth shut, swallowed, and swore. “Coal, that’s bad.”

Coal only nodded in response. “I don’t have a clue what we’re looking for, Jordan. Not the foggiest. I just wanted to warn you to keep an extra vigilant eye out. Be watching for anything out of the ordinary. Any new cars around, any people you’ve never seen—especially if they don’t seem to fit in around here. Especially this time of year, now that most of the tourists are gone, there’s a look to the locals—the ranchers, cowboys, miners. The lumber men. You know what I’m talking about, right?”

“Sure, I think so. I’m looking for somebody that looks like a big city thug.”

Coal chuckled. “I wish it were that easy. But it won’t be. If the Mob has sent someone up here, it’s going to be someone with a really good story about why their appearance is different, or someone who has gone to extra lengths to fit in. Either way, these men are going to be pros. Top notch people. If you see them in the bars, they may be pretending to drink, but it’s a good bet they won’t actually be swallowing much. That doesn't mean they won't act drunk. I guess what I'm trying to do is scare the hell out of you, Jordan. And I'm sorry. But unless I miss my guess, they're here, or they soon will be, and we can't afford to miss a trick. You being a deputy could make you a target too."

What might have passed for fear came into Jordan's eyes, but he clenched his jaw and remained silent.

"I don't think that will be the case, all right? I think they'll be after me, and maybe the prosecutor. Because if they start out killing deputies, they know things are going to get real hot around here, real fast. The faster they can get to their main targets and put them out of the picture, then get out of town, the safer they'll be. And these guys don't make a living by taking unnecessary chances. They'll be as safe as anyone you know."

"At least for themselves," said Jordan.

"Yeah. *Only* for themselves. The opposite of safe for me."

When he left Jordan's, he decided to make another stop he wanted to even less. That was at the hotel where Grant and his family were staying. Coal hadn't been thinking very clearly when he came in that morning to find Grant with Vic Yancey. He should have let everyone know what their situation was from the very first.

After knocking on the door, Coal waited only a few seconds for it to be answered by a pretty blond woman in glasses. Her eyes dropped immediately to his gold badge. "Oh! Hello. I was expecting my husband. Are you Sheriff Savage?"

Coal nodded. "I am. Mrs. Fairbourne?"

"Yes, that's me. It's so good to meet you."

"You too. Call me Coal, would you?"

"I'd love to. And it's Becky." The woman's hand was soft, but her grip was pleasantly firm.

Coal could see a couple of kids past Becky, but by Becky's first reaction to his appearance at the door, Grant evidently wasn't here. He was about to ask for his whereabouts when he heard someone coming up the stairs and turned to see his new deputy top out on the landing.

"Hello, Coal! I'm surprised to see you twice in one day."

"Yeah, me too. I forgot to tell you something earlier, and it's pretty important for you to know." He instinctively thought to go down the hall with Grant to break the news, but then he thought how much he would hate to be left out of something this big, as a lawman's spouse.

"Ma'am, can the kids stay alone for a minute? What I need to tell Grant you should probably hear too."

Looking bewildered and a little worried, Becky turned back into the room to tell the kids she would be down the hall, and then she followed Coal and Grant, leaving the room door unlatched.

Coal turned at the end of the hall. "Grant, there's something up that you've got to know about. I think I've already told you about our recent case with the Mob, and how we had to take our two prisoners to Idaho Falls for safe keeping. Well, I got a call from a friend of mine in Vegas who has Mob connections, and he didn't tell me any detail, but from what he could say I think the Mob has sent some more of their people up here."

Grant and Becky exchanged glances. Grant wasn't big city, but he was savvy enough and had been a cop long enough to put the puzzle pieces together quickly. Becky still looked confused as he reached down and took her hand.

"They're going to come and try to kill your prisoners, right? To keep them quiet?"

Coal nodded. His eyes flitted over to Becky, but then back to Grant.

"And when they're not here … They'll be after you. And maybe the prosecutor."

To say he was "proud" of his new deputy for his insightful deductions was probably too much, but in a way he was. "That's what I'm afraid of," he said. "You caught on quick."

Grant took a deep breath. "So what now?"

"I just needed to tell you so you'll know what you're walking into and so you can be on the lookout for anything strange."

"I sure will, Coal."

"And another thing: This is the Las Vegas Mob we're dealing with. The Mafia. Grant, I won't blame you one bit if you have second thoughts about taking this job. At this point you really don't have any dog in this fight." He looked over at Becky. "And you have every right to be concerned too, ma'am."

Becky looked at Grant and squeezed his arm. "Grant knows what I'll say. And I think I know what he'll say too."

Grant nodded and met Coal's eyes dead-on. "You've heard the old term in Western novels about riding for the brand, right?"

"Of course."

"All right then. I signed on for this Salmon 'brand', Coal. What kind of man would I be if I turned tail and ran at the first sign of danger?"

Coal drew in a deep breath and stuck out his hand. "Thanks, Grant. I really can't thank you enough. And thank you, ma'am," he told Becky. "You just keep an eye out, Grant, and keep your family safe."

* * *

Becky Fairbourne pressed her backside up against the inside of the hotel room door, shutting it firmly behind her and her husband. Grant, taking two steps into the room, turned to meet her gaze.

"Are you okay, honey?" she asked.

Grant almost laughed. *"Okay?* Are you?"

"I'm fine, but … You never expected to walk into something like this, did you?"

"Of course not. It's a small town. This kind of stuff doesn't happen." He stepped closer and took her arms. "You want me to change my mind, Beck?"

"Uh-uh. I knew you would make the right decision. But I'm scared. I really am."

"Me too," he said in a whisper. "But let's not let the kids know."

He went to the bathroom, and when he came back out later Becky was on the bed reading a book to towheaded three-year-old Jonathan. Grant came and sat down on the other side of her, stretching his long, muscular legs down the length of the bed as he leaned his back against the headboard.

"Hey, Jonny. Can I talk to Mom for a second? Hold on just a bit, okay, bud?"

Jonathan gave his dad and mom the "serious" look, then gave his father a big nod. "Good boy. Beck, I did some praying."

"What? You mean just now?"

"Yeah. And I already know the answer."

"Okay?" She studied his eyes. "What do you know?"

"I think I was inspired to take this job. I think Coal Savage is really going to need me right now, and maybe God even put me here to save his life."

She stared at him until tears filled her eyes to match the goose bumps on her arms. Slowly, she began to nod. "Okay, honey. If that's the answer you got to praying, that's good enough for me. You will be careful, right?"

"Of course. I wouldn't leave my family alone."

* * *

Coal found himself at a loss. After leaving the Fairbournes' hotel, he drove the GMC up the Salmon River valley, past the snowy reaches of Carmen and the picturesque ranches strung like worn-out Monopoly pieces along the river. He hung a left after

North Fork onto the gravel road that would have taken him all the way to the end of the road at Corn Creek, had he wished to go.

As he drove, his actions mechanical, he mulled over his situation. Just yesterday if someone had asked him what he knew about surveillance, and phone-tapping, and many other things that had engulfed his mind today, he would offhandedly have told them he was quite familiar with all that. But now, with this deadly dilemma staring him square in the face, he realized he didn't really know all that much. He could answer basic questions, and it would be easy to figure out how much the Bureau was able to do about things as simple as tracing phone calls and finding people who didn't want to be found. But what he didn't know was how much the Mob knew—or how much they could easily learn through sources of their own.

And then, in time, reality set in. He could not allow himself to be so naïve as to think the people who were after him didn't know everything there was to know. They knew enough to kill him, in a big, loud bang, or silent as a whiff of wind. He could die in a hit and run accident, by a long-range rifle shot, a close-up round to the back of the head or the chest from a .22 with a silencer. They could even use drugs to make it look as if he had died from a stroke or heart attack. And considering all he had been through recently, why would anyone question it, especially in a backward little town like this? Or if they did, so what? They couldn't afford autopsies here, and even if they could prove he died by nefarious means the assassins would be gone, and there would be no witness left to tell the story. It would forever remain a case unsolved.

It was then he thought of his friend Andy Holmes. Andy would be on the witness list too. And Andy had no idea his life could be in danger.

Coal had come up to a place where the elements had caused a ton or so of rock to roll down off a hill onto the road, completely blocking it. He needed to call it in, but he couldn't raise dispatch on the radio, and he didn't even feel like taking the time to stop in North Fork and use their phone.

Jockeying the pickup around on the road, he finally got it turned around and gunned it, flying around the curves of the muddy gravel road as fast as he dared with the mighty, icy Salmon plunging along close by.

When he reached North Fork, he saw someone getting out of a pickup, and he recognized his old friend Travis Woolsey, from Pocatello, who was a big fan of fishing the river for steelhead. His wife, Tamberli, was getting out the other side with a big smile on her face. Whipping over, Coal stepped out of the truck long enough to greet Travis and Tamberli with a hug and tell them about the rocks on the river road, then ask them to notify the County. Then he got back in and continued speeding toward Salmon.

At last, he flew past the Shady Nook, then the little box building that was the home of KSRA Radio, who at that moment had Elvis Presley telling the world to "clean up your own backyard".

Left on Main. Over the river bridge. Screeching to a stop in front of Ken's Automotive, he jumped out of the truck and went inside. Ken Parks was just sliding under a blue Studebaker when he heard his bells chime, and he slid back out and looked up.

"Oh, hey, Coal."

"Hey. Is Andy in?" Coal didn't realize it until that moment, but he was almost out of breath.

"Sure, I think so. At least I've been hearing somebody over there."

Relief washed through Coal. "All right, get up and come with me."

Ken must have known by the tone of Coal's voice something was wrong, because he got up without one single smart aleck comment.

"What's goin' on?"

"I'll tell you and Andy at the same time."

As they stepped into Andy Holmes's body shop, a man popped up from the far side of a fifties Oldsmobile he was sanding on. It wasn't Andy.

The man, wearing greasy blue overalls and cowboy boots, with a mostly bald head, a horseshoe mustache, and glasses, set down a sander and came around the car. "Can I help you?"

"Looking for Andy," Coal said.

The man shook his head. "He never came in today."

Coal's heart leaped. "Why?"

"He called and told me he was sick."

"Coal," Ken cut in, "this is Brian Howell, new in town. He just started working for Andy a week or so ago."

Howell came around the car, looking as if he was trying to tear off his right hand with a rag before he shoved it out to Coal. "Hi there, Sheriff." When he stopped in front of Coal he noticed the man was pretty short, yet he carried himself well, had a good build, and seemed taller than he was.

"Hi." Coal didn't feel his normal affable self. But knowing Andy had at least called in made him feel better. "Good to meet you, Brian."

"Same here. Anything I can help you with?"

"No, thanks. I really need to talk to Andy. I'll try to raise him at his house. But if you hear from him first, can you have him give dispatch a call?"

"You betcha, I sure will."

Coal and Ken left, and they stopped in Ken's shop before Coal went out the front so Coal could tell his friend what he had intended to tell both him and Andy: to be looking for any odd strangers who might stop in.

Driving back to the jail, for lack of anything better to do, Coal said hello to Vic Yancey, who had just come in. "You trying to get a raise, Vic? You're not supposed to be here for several more hours."

The young man laughed. “Naw, I just figured I’d stop by and say hi on my way to go eat.”

“Great. Hi,” said Coal with a forced chuckle. “Say, do we have anyone in back? I totally forgot to check when I was in here earlier.”

“Yes, sir. Some guy Jordan brought in for fighting at the Owl Club. Jerome Fishman?”

Coal chuckled and repeated in a derogatory voice, “Sounds like a fishy name to me. The Owl Club, huh? Should be re-named the Fight Club.” To the sound of Yancey’s laughter, Coal went into the cell block to see a man with red hair and a thick mustache that was turning gray around the edges sitting on the only occupied cot. He didn’t say anything, just made eye contact with the man, raised a hand by way of greeting, and stepped back out.

After leaving the jail, with no intention of going back that day, Coal drove to Andy Holmes’s house and knocked. He could never bring anyone to the door, but it was no surprise since there was no car parked anywhere nearby. When he left, he drove to Saveway Foodtown, keeping a close eye in his rearview mirror, and parked in front. For a long while he sat studying cars that passed, as well as any that were parked along Main.

Finally, he got out and went to the phone booth in front of Saveway. Dropping a dime in the slot, he dialed home. Only one lousy day, and it hadn’t seemed so long being away from his loved ones since Vietnam.

CHAPTER EIGHT

Scabs Ravioli's stomach was growling, but Menny Marcello's quiet snoring sounded so peaceful he didn't have the heart to wake him. Besides, he was in the middle of *Hee Haw* and didn't want his partner awake right now anyway. Menny had no respect for anything on television and would talk right over it like it meant nothing in the world.

Then Menny stirred, and the peaceful feeling was gone. "Hey! Man, what time is it?"

Scabs dragged his eyes away from the country girls in the plaid shirts and cut-off blue jeans to look at his watch. "Just past six-thirty. Why? You got a big date with Julie?" He looked back at the TV screen.

"Yeah, I got a big date, dumbo," Menny said with pretend scorn. "Come on, man, we need to get up and do somethin' to get the blood movin'. I'm goin' to the jail."

Those words jerked Scabs's attention away from his show. "The jail! What for?"

"For starters. That's what. We get in there, make sure the Medinas are in there, and bam! Half our job's over. If we can figure out a way to burn those two bozos right away we can get out of this hillbilly town and go home."

Scowling, Scabs looked back at his show. Well, one *Hee Haw* was almost like the next anyway. "All right, well we better get goin' now then. I got a World War Two show comin' on at nine, and I ain't gonna be too happy if you make me miss it."

"Oh, Judas! You and your boob tube. Come on. We can get somethin' to eat too, before all the stores close."

Now Menny was singing Scabs's tune. He had touched on something much closer to his heart than simply going to the jail to check in on Angel and little Rey. He wasn't in any hurry to off them anyway. Fact was, he kind of liked little Rey, even if Angel was mostly an ass. But food? Yes, that was worth leaving the show in the middle for.

Both men popped open their suitcases and changed into clothing much more suited to this area: Levi's, plaid shirts, and hiking boots, all strategically aged to look like "Matthew Hardigan" and "Bryn Renault" wore them around as a matter of course.

Scabs shrugged into a slick blue down coat, which felt warm from hanging near the radiator. He pushed the drapes aside a couple of inches and looked out into the darkness at the Jaguar. First thing he was going to do when they got back to Vegas was to head down to the Jaguar dealer. After riding in that thing, he had to get one for himself.

The racking of a pistol slide across the room drew Scabs's attention, and he saw Menny take his gun off cock and lean down to blow into it, clearing it of any dust it might have picked up. Menny was always prepared. No one could take that away from him.

Scabs went to the dresser and shucked his Ruger Standard from its holster. This little .22 auto looked a lot like the World War II-era Lugers, and for that he admired it greatly. It had a four and three-quarter inch barrel and could hide snugly behind his belt without much discomfort, but more importantly, when up close and personal, and fitted with a silencer, that pistol could put two quick rounds into a man's heart or the back of his head, leaving very little blood, no exit wound, and the opportunity for a nice, smooth exit from the scene without anyone being the wiser.

That little Ruger had snuffed out thirteen and a half lives, and Scabs remembered every tiniest detail of every hit. The "half" was because Turdo Gagliardi had been such an ugly, monstrous, downright hate-able "turd" of a human being that Menny couldn't agree to let Scabs take him alone, and he had insisted on donating one of his own hollow points to the cause. The funniest part was that it was Menny's first hit, and when the deed was done, before they could even get out of the apartment, Menny had to run to the bathroom and puke his guts out in the toilet. It was different for Scabs, who had taken to offing a target like a falcon to flight.

Scabs eased back the slide partway, glimpsed the brassy glitter of a round in the chamber, then slammed it back into its holster, which he clipped down behind his belt. He watched Menny screwing a silencer on his pistol, which was about to make it twice as long as normal.

"What are you gonna do with that?" asked Scabs.

"What?"

"That silencer. How'll you hide it? It's gonna look like you got a banana down your pant leg. Or somethin'."

Menny busted up laughing. "Okay, well, great. We just go in there shootin' around drawin' attention then?" he asked after getting control of himself.

"I don't think you gotta worry, Menny. Nobody's gonna be around this time of night. These twenty-two's aren't gonna make any noise outside the jail—at least not enough to bring anyone runnin'."

"Okay. No silencer." Menny screwed it back off his pistol and tossed it on the bed, then pushed the door open a couple of feet and peeked out into the quiet lot.

"Come on, it's clear."

They slipped to the Jaguar and got in. It fired up as if it had been running only ten minutes ago. Menny fondled the steering wheel like a girlfriend.

"Gettin' used to it, aren't you?" said Scabs with a grin.

"I was always used to it," said Menny. "But I still say it draws too much attention."

Scabs wouldn't admit it for anything, but he agreed with Menny. He wished the big boys had seen fit to rent them something a little less conspicuous. Which was why his birthday present to Menny was going to be stopping in one of the lots around town when they got a chance and picking up something that wasn't quite so noticeable—that is unless they got really lucky, finished both hits tonight, and could head out of this town posthaste.

Menny followed the carefully written-out directions up to the courthouse, where they made one pass, turned around a few blocks up, and cruised slowly back. The air was bitingly cold tonight, and no one was out.

The Jag made its smooth turn into the parking lot, and Menny shut down the headlights and put it in first gear, so he wouldn't have to be on the brakes so much. They puttered through the lot, which was mostly empty except for one old junker and two cars with government plates.

Stopping in the deeper shadows, Menny put it in park and drew a deep breath. Scabs looked at him blandly. "You okay?"

"Sure. Just gettin' psyched up."

"Well, let's do this thing, shall we?" Scabs threw open his door. They had disabled the overhead light switch by shoving a short piece of dowel into the hole with it and taping it in place to hold it in even with the door open, so no light ever came on.

Buttoning up their coats, they made their way casually toward the jail. There was supposed to be one guy who was normally here at nights, a kid named Victor Yancey, with no street smarts or experience beyond the walls of the jail. Easy to fool, and easier to kill.

Making no noise but without looking like they were trying to be quiet, they stepped to the jail, and Scabs went down the stairs first, while Menny waited on top, keeping his eyes open.

Scabs slipped a glove on one hand and tried the knob. It was locked. Taking the glove back off as he looked up at his partner with a cautionary glance, he slid it into his coat pocket with its mate and knocked three times on the door. He could see the kid inside, sitting at a desk with his feet up.

The kid jerked and jumped to his feet, sending a startled look about the room as if he had been dozing off. It took him a few seconds to get his bearings, it seemed, and then he looked toward the door. Scabs smiled and waved at him.

The jailer smiled back, dumb kid. Then he came to the door and opened it as if he had seen his grandmother outside, not some complete stranger with a fighter's face.

Scabs stepped inside, and he could hear Menny following him down the concrete steps.

"Hi. Can I help you?" asked the jailer.

Scabs gave him an amiable wolf-in-sheep's-clothing smile. "Sure, I'm hopin' so. My name's Bryn Renault, and this is my brother-in-law Matthew Hardigan. We were kind of hoping you might have my cousin in here. We've looked everywhere else, and somebody said he might have been in a fight and got arrested."

The young jailer chuckled, nodding knowingly. "Oh yeah. We've got a fighter back there, all right." He didn't even ask for a name. "It's not supposed to be visiting hours, though."

Scabs felt lucky to have guessed correctly that someone might be in here for fighting. It didn't hurt that Salmon had a big reputation for men who liked to fight, apparently for lack of anything more entertaining to do around these parts than drink and knock each other around.

"Sure, I was afraid o' that. But we're from out of town, and we might be driving out early in the morning. I wouldn't take more than a minute. Fact, I can just peek in and make sure it's him."

"Is his name Fishman? Jerome?" asked Yancey.

"Uh …" Caught off-guard, Scabs stared at the jailer.

Behind him, Menny gave out with a laugh. "Oh, that's rich. Fishman? No, his real name is Dave Roberts. That guy's an incurable liar. He's constantly givin' the cops a fake name."

A disgusted look came over Yancey's face. "Great. Well, I'm glad you two came in. We have him booked as Fishman."

With that, Yancey walked to the wall and picked up the ring of keys. Going to the cellblock door, he pulled it open, stepping in as Scabs pushed aside his coat to grab the butt of his Ruger. Oh, this was going to be far too easy. They would be home by tomorrow night!

Scabs's trained eyes scanned the cells in less than a second. All were empty except one, and a red-haired man with a graying mustache was sitting up on his metal cot, blinking his eyes as if he had been fast asleep.

It wasn't Angel Medina. And it wasn't his brother Rey.

Hastily, Scabs dropped his hand from his gun butt and smoothed his coat down over it. He watched the prisoner carefully to make sure he hadn't seen anything. It was plain the man's eyes were full of sleep. It took him several moments even to focus on young Yancey.

"So your name isn't really Fishman, is it?" Yancey's voice was testy. Fishman stared at him, looking bewildered.

Scabs came up beside the jailer. "Hey, deputy, my mistake. That isn't George." Menny jabbed him in the back. His mind flashed back, and inwardly he groaned. "Oh, brother, I must be tired. I mean Dave. Sorry, I have another cousin named George."

Yancey stared at him, and Scabs had the feeling the young man hadn't even caught the slip. "So this isn't the guy?"

"No, no. Not him. So … He's the only one in here? Quiet place."

Yancey nodded. "Yep. It's been pretty quiet for a couple weeks." He turned and looked back at the prisoner. "Sorry, man, I guess they're looking for somebody else. Go back to sleep."

Scabs and Menny turned and went out in front of Yancey. Scabs's heart was racing. So was his mind. As Yancey shut the door and hung the keys back up, he turned around, and Menny said, "A couple weeks of quiet, huh?"

"Yep. Thank heavens."

The partners feigned laughter. Menny said, "Yeah, thank heavens. Except I'd sure like to know where Dave is since he's not here. I always heard this was a pretty wild town for fighting. I'm surprised you only have one guy in there."

Yancey nodded, sniffing. He was starting to take on the appearance of someone who thought he was important. Shades of Barney Fife on *The Andy Griffith Show*. "Ha! You heard right. Especially the last couple months, this valley's been crazy."

"Oh yeah?" cut in Scabs. It had taken him a moment, but now he was catching on to what Menny was trying to do. Might as well play along now and pretend he had had the same idea all along. He glanced over at the clock on the wall, checking to see how close it was to the start of his war show, then returned his eyes to the jailer. "Say, I don't suppose you're plannin' on drinkin' all that coffee, are you?" he asked, pointing toward the half-full pot. Setting the stage to get a real conversation going with this kid.

"Oh, heck no! I don't even drink it. If you seriously want some, it's yours, but I bet it's been here eight hours or so."

"That's all right with me," said Scabs, going over and picking up a mug, which he raised to his nose to sniff. "Are these clean?"

"Yeah, I think so."

Scabs smiled wryly to himself as he poured the mug full. Whose lips had already touched this, he wondered. He couldn't imagine even for a second a bunch of hick lawmen washing their cups out before setting them down.

Sipping at the coffee and trying to give Yancy a smile as if it actually tasted palatable, he said, "So what's been goin' on around here? What's so crazy?"

"A lot of stuff. We had a string of murders—assassination-style. Then some kids got kidnapped, more or less, and they were kids our sheriff had living with him. One of them was the daughter of the old sheriff, and he was one of them that got assassinated."

"You're kidding!" said Scabs. "In a town like this?"

"Shoot, that's just the beginning. One of our deputies went over to check on the kids, and the couple who stole them bashed him in the head and took off down the river. The sheriff chased them, and they ended up going off the road and into the river. Both of 'em died."

"That's insane! Sounds like some crazy movie of the week!" said Menny, shaking his head, his eyes big.

"Then we had another murder, and this one was bizarre. A couple of guys from the Mob, down in Vegas, were up here trying to set up some kind of operation where they were gonna hide important criminals out. But they got found out, and the sheriff chased 'em down the road—same road the other guy and his wife ran off of, actually. Their car broke down—the sheriff had sabotaged it—and they ended up stealing some other guy's car and shooting him in the head, right in front of the sheriff."

"No!" Scabs said, acting as if this were all the biggest news story he had ever heard. "What happened?"

"Well, he caught 'em and brought 'em back—after shooting the one in the arm that did the killing. Oh—and then another guy was up here from down south. This colored guy. Friend of the sheriff's. He ended up stabbing some guy, and when the sheriff went to get him he jumped off a cliff right in front of him and killed himself."

This Victor Yancey was really on a roll. Scabs had to hold back his amusement at his little tell-all monologue.

"That's flat-out unbelievable. I would have never dreamed so many far-out things could happen in a little place like this. But … What about those two Mob guys?" he asked, trying to bring his voice back to sounding casual. "They sound like some pretty bigtime bad guys. How come they're not still in here?"

"Oh, the sheriff didn't want to keep them here, on account of the Mob connection. He hauled 'em over to the jail in Idaho Falls—until the trial."

Inside, Scabs swore, and it was all he could do to keep a straight face. *Until the trial!* That could literally be months. And who knew what kind of damage those two morons might do before then, if they sat in jail long enough and had the right pressure applied to them?

Scabs felt sick. He glanced over at Menny, and his partner closed his eyes and gave a little shake of his head. The writing was on the wall. Until they could figure out a way to infiltrate the Idaho Falls jail, there was only one thing left to do: kill anyone who might be a witness in this trial, and whoever the prosecutor was who was handling the case.

Scabs took another long drink of the worst coffee he could remember and looked at Yancey, trying to seem as innocent as a two-year-old.

"So I remember when we were here before we got to be pretty good friends with your prosecutor, Brad Niems. Is he still around?"

"Niems?" repeated Yancy. "I never heard that name before. Our prosecutor's name now is Mike Fica."

"Fica … Fica! Oh yeah. I think I met him too. Drives a light yellow Chrysler? Lives on Church?" He was thinking fast, making up details, and naming the first street he remembered passing on their way into town.

Yancy looked thoughtful for a moment. "No, you got the wrong guy. Fica's never lived on Church that I know of. He lives on Gwartney and drives a dark blue van."

* * *

Coal was sitting on Maura's couch reading a battered copy of *To Kill a Mockingbird.* Like some weird creep, he had gone into her closet earlier and pulled out one of her shirts, and it was now draped over one shoulder. He missed the heck out of Maura, and the closest he could get to having her with him was the smell of this shirt he had seen her wear shortly before their trip out of town.

The ringing phone made him jerk and swear. Apparently that was a ritual that could be played out anywhere, not just at home. He debated whether to pick it up. After the seventh ring he did. It was Nadine, working night dispatch.

Hi, Sheriff. I was starting to wonder if you were actually there.

"Sorry, Nadine. I wasn't expecting any calls here. What's new?"

Yeah, your mom gave me this number. Well, I just got a call from Deputy Price, over in Challis. He says they picked up a guy over there on one of our warrants. They wanted to see if somebody can come get him first thing Monday morning.

Coal sighed. He thought about calling the Custer County sheriff's office and offering to get whoever this guy was tomorrow, but it was Sunday, after all. It could sure wait one more day.

"All right. Did they leave a number?"

Nadine said yes and gave it to him. After she hung up, Coal contemplated making the call right then while he was thinking about it, but he was in the middle of his book, and on top of that he was enjoying the smell of Maura's shirt and didn't feel like disrupting the ambience. So he didn't.

Monday, February 5

Coal spent Sunday sitting alone and reading, longing to be with his family and Maura. The next morning he was up early, but because he was in a hurry he had to settle for a couple hundred pushups and some squats for his workout. He showered, trying to ignore the fact that this was Maura's shower, and how many times she must have stood in here looking so darn … Shaking his head to clear it, he turned the water all the way over on cold, felt the shock of it hit him like a bucket of ice, rinsed off, and got out.

He dried off and dressed, and after putting seven eggs on to fry and a piece of wheat bread in the toaster, he called Andy Holmes's number and then Mike Fica's. He warned them both that he would be coming by to visit with them as soon as he got back from picking up his prisoner in Challis.

After breakfast, he raced the pickup way too fast out along Highway 93, with the river rolling by on his right, big and slow and icy. He picked up his prisoner, a poacher by the name of Walt Ledley, whom they'd been looking for now for seven or eight months, and the two of them tore a path back toward Salmon in a silent pickup cab, Ledley with one hand cuffed up to the gunrack on the back window. It looked pretty uncomfortable, so Coal thought of all the game Ledley had taken out of season and was comforted.

Only because Coal paid no attention to speed limits, took some dangerous curves nearly on two wheels, and passed some other cars he should not have passed, when he got Ledley back to Salmon it was only 8:30, still early enough that Andy Holmes and Mike Fica might still be at home, and both of them lived conveniently near each other on the same street, so if Coal could get rid of his poacher fast enough he could drive down and see them before they went to work.

He managed to get rid of Ledley fairly fast, only because Jordan Peterson was still at the jail when he got there, and since Grant Fairbourne was there as well, after calling Andy and Mike to tell them he was on his way, he took Fairbourne with him with the idea of getting to know him better.

They had just come off Courthouse Drive onto Main and made the turn onto Water Street, which would take them to Gwartney, where both Andy and Mike lived, when a huge bloom of flame and smoke burst into the sky to their left, appearing over the rooftops like a giant orange cauliflower. The concussion followed a second later, rocking the pickup and almost making Coal swerve off the road as he heard Grant Fairbourne utter a word he would never have expected to come out of him.

With his mouth open wide, Coal came to a stop in the middle of the road, leaning over to look at the black smoke rolling skyward from where the explosion had been. It was exactly in the direction of Gwartney, where Andy Holmes and Mike Fica called home.

CHAPTER NINE

Coal gunned the pickup and flew around the corner down Gwartney. He slammed on the brakes just shy of South Terrace. There on the other side of the intersection was a large white house with a red brick wainscot and people running around outside in hysteria. Coal had never been to Mike Fica's house, but the vehicle engulfed in flame in the driveway was a van the same size as Fica's, and, as far as he could tell through the flames and smoke, the same color.

"My hell," Grant Fairbourne said beside Coal, his voice almost a whisper. He had no sooner spoken than the hinge of his jaw loosened again, making his mouth fall back open, and he stared at the wreckage and the hysterical people all around.

As two police cars swerved off the next street and skidded to a stop on the far side of the house with the burning van, Coal jerked out his .44 and got out of the truck. With the door still open, he scanned both ways up and down the street. Every person he could see either stood in apparent shock staring at the destroyed vehicle and the shattered windows of the house or ran around crying. One of them, a young man, kept trying to get into the vehicle, but the heat drove him back each time.

“Come on!” Coal yelled at Grant, and he reached back into the cab and yanked a shotgun off the rack in the window. When Grant caught up to him at the grill of the truck, he thrust the shotgun into his hands. “Rack it and keep your eyes open!”

With that command, Coal advanced, the revolver in both hands and up to chest level, but with his finger out of the trigger guard. “Clear the street!” he yelled. “Clear the street!” A few people numbly obeyed. Most of them didn’t even hear. On the other side of the fire, Bob Wilson and the second police officer were trying to do the same—remove anyone who didn’t need to be out in the open.

Swiveling to the left and right, Coal scanned each house as he passed, each garage, shed, or vehicle. He was literally back in the war, and the enemy could be hiding anywhere. As he passed Andy’s house, he was vaguely aware of his friend standing there in his Levi’s and an untucked long-sleeve shirt, his feet bare.

“Coal! What the hell’s going on?”

“Andy, get in your house!” Coal barked. “Don’t touch your car until I come check to make sure it’s okay! Go!” He had no time to sound civil or make any further explanations.

Grant Fairbourne moved along a little behind Coal and to the right. Like any good pheasant hunter, he had the shotgun halfway to his shoulder and ready, watching, waiting, expecting his game to erupt from anywhere, at any time.

Several dogs were barking in the neighborhood from different locations, and one of them howled mournfully. Coal made sure to locate every one of the dogs he could, watching its mannerisms, trying to make sure what it was looking at, if anything.

Coal’s heart could not have been much lower in his chest, but the closer he got to the burning van the blacker it seemed to feel. There was a woman and three children all holding each other and crying not far from the van, and here he hesitated. Finally, he had to move on. This wasn't the time for introductions.

Once he and Grant had gone down the street half a block, clearing it as much as they could, and checking in every vehicle for any suspect who might be hidden there, they returned to the scene of destruction. Soon, they heard the wail of a fire engine and an ambulance. At that point Coal moved toward the mourning people still huddled some thirty feet from the van.

"I'm sorry, folks. I need you to go back in your house or else to a neighbor's, all right? I'm real sorry, but whoever did this might still be around. Please."

In shock, the woman and her loved ones slowly moved away, none of them speaking, now and then looking back toward the burning wreckage. Half a minute later Coal turned in time to see the last of them disappearing into a neighbor's house, and the door shut behind them.

The fire engine had pulled up, and a handful of firemen stood outside now with dirty gray hoses, from the nozzles of which shot great streams of water while the engineer stayed at the truck making sure they had a constant supply of water although they had yet to hook up to a hydrant. Police chief Dan George had also pulled up, somewhere behind Coal, and he came alongside him, staring at the burning van. He didn't speak.

Forgetting that it wasn't really his jurisdiction, Coal went to the only man among the hose-tending firemen wearing a yellow helmet instead of black. "Hey there."

The man turned. When he saw Coal's badge, and the police chief behind him, he shut the nozzle down. "Hey. What's up?"

"You the captain?"

"Yes, sir."

"Hey, this is going to be a crime scene, so as soon as you think it's safe, can you and your man shut down the hoses so we can look around for evidence?"

"You bet. I think most of the damage is already done anyway."

"Go ahead and knock it down as much as you can, though. No point burning up anything else that might be used as evidence."

The man continued spraying, now concentrating on letting his stream of water go up in the air and lob down on the fire, forming a graceful rainbow.

Coal stood beside the man, still keeping an eye around for anyone who looked suspicious. Grant Fairbourne was just behind him.

At last, when there was nothing left but little puffs of smoke now and then, the fire captain shut off his water and gave the throat-cutting sign to his engineer. In moments the whine of the engine slowed, and gradually the flow of water stopped altogether. The fireman on the far side of the van let his hose fall slack. He looked toward the captain as if for a new order.

The captain, a tall, rangy man with a handsome face and honest-looking eyes, set his hose down and walked over to Coal, working the glove off his right hand and holding it out to shake. "Gary Hirschi," he introduced himself. "I'm not sure we've met before."

Coal shook. "No, I'm pretty sure we haven't. Coal Savage."

"Sure," said Hirschi. "Everybody knows you."

"Probably not such a good thing right now," said Coal. He didn't offer any explanation.

Hirschi then looked beyond Coal and greeted Chief Dan George, who said his name back to him, quietly. When Coal returned his eyes to George, he looked sick.

The other fireman set down his hose and walked over, pulling the helmet off and looking a question at Hirschi. Coal suddenly recognized him. It was Brian Howell, the man he had met working at Andy Holmes's auto body shop.

"Howdy, Sheriff," said Howell. "I didn't expect to see you again so soon."

"And I wish you hadn't. Not like this."

"That's no joke," said Howell, looking back at the charred van.

The medics were standing not far away. It was Jay Castillo and Ronnie Davis—one of Coal's favorite people paired with one of his least.

Coal started to say something, then let out a long sigh and walked closer to the van. He sensed George, Hirschi, and Howell following him.

At the van, which was recognizable as Mike Fica's even though it had little paint left on it and all the windows had shattered, leaving square bits of glittery glass strewn all over the ground, Coal looked in. It was a grisly sight, something he had seen enough in Korea and Vietnam to last a hundred men's lifetimes.

Brian Howell swore and backed away. Hirschi stared, kneading his forehead. The police chief simply turned and stared at Coal. Coal had a feeling he had never seen a burned body before—or the remains of one.

"You know him?" Coal asked Hirschi.

"I think it's Mike Fica, the prosecutor. His van, anyway. And his house."

"I thought so," agreed Coal. He looked toward the neighbors' house into which he had seen the distraught family disappear. "I'm guessing that was his wife I saw earlier, and two or three kids. Does he have a teenage boy?"

"Yeah." Hirschi's face, besides the shock, was sad. His eyes indicated he wanted to say more, but he didn't.

Coal turned to Grant. "Hey, will you go back to the truck and get on the radio? Ask Flo to send the coroner."

By this time, Ronnie Davis and Jay Castillo had wandered close as well. Davis must have had a crystal-clear memory of his past associations with Coal, judging by his tight lips. It was Jay who did the speaking.

"It doesn't look like you need us, huh?" Jay's face was pale even under the olive-brown tone of his skin.

"No, I'm afraid not."

"Is that Mike Fica, do you know?"

Coal nodded, and Jay bunched his lips and shook his head sadly. "Man. How did this happen?"

"I'm not sure yet." Coal was lying, of course, but not completely. He knew it was a bomb. He knew the Mob had set it. He just didn't know the details.

When Grant came back he was no longer carrying the shotgun. Coal wished he hadn't made that decision, but it was something they could talk about later, away from listening ears. He took a moment to introduce Grant and the police chief to each other. Chief George was slowly regaining his composure.

Coal asked Grant, "You ever see anyone that died in a bomb or a fire?"

"No sir. I've been lucky."

"Well, your luck just ran out. Might as well put it behind you."

Grant's face paled, and because of his Caucasian skin it had the ability to turn much paler than Jay's had. He didn't want to go look, but when he read the look in Coal's eyes he did anyway. Chief George walked over with them. When they stepped away, Grant looked even more sober than the teetotaler he was. Both he and the chief looked like they needed to leave.

"Sorry, Deputy. I figure in this career you need to get used to everything."

Grant nodded but didn't speak.

The coroner, Kerry Updyke, pulled up, and Chief George gathered himself together enough to speak with him briefly. Coal was guessing there really wasn't any reason for Updyke to be here other than in his capacity as an undertaker. Anyone with eyes, even a four-year-old kid, could have proclaimed Mike Fica gone.

Turning his head, Coal looked again toward the neighbors' house where the Fica family had gone for refuge. "I was first on the scene," he told Chief George. "I can talk to the family if you want."

George nodded slowly. “I guess I should probably at least go with you. I’ve known Fica a long time. And I know the family.”

“All right. You can do it alone if you’d rather.”

“No, I’d like you to come. Moral support.”

“Sure.” Coal looked over at Grant, feeling sicker about the task of talking to the Fica family than he had about seeing the charred remains of a man he knew he could have grown close to. “This will be a hundred times worse than looking at burned bodies.”

Grant turned his eyes in the direction of the neighbors’ house. “You mean … You want me to go?”

Coal chuckled without humor. “I’d like you to *do* it. But yeah, I think you should go with us.”

And so the three of them walked toward the house. Coal could hear his boots crunching in the snow, but he couldn’t feel them hit the ground.

CHAPTER TEN

After Chief George, the fire crew, and the ambulance left, then Kerry Updyke with his grisly burden and the second policeman, Coal, Grant, and Bob Wilson remained to cordon off the crime scene. The whole time Coal was stringing the tape, he could not stop thinking about Rainey Fica and her children, grief-stricken and in shock, unable to stop crying while the neighbors tried to stay clear of the room they had granted them refuge in. He thought about that family, and he couldn't escape the fact that it could just as easily have been him, and someone else going to talk to his family.

Chief George had gone to contact Lyle Gentry, the state bull, who would be in charge of setting up a crime scene investigation. Coal would have liked to be involved in that, and he needed to. This wasn't the type of scene he would come across often and get chances to snoop around in. But he doubted he would be here much. He had other things he needed to do, and he needed to do them fast.

Sitting in his chair at the jail, Coal watched Grant Fairbourne, standing across the room from him, try to fumble his way through making a good pot of coffee with shaking hands.

Coal flipped through the Rolodex until he found one of the numbers he had long ago made certain he would have access to. This man was going to get sick to death of hearing from him, especially since he never called to check on him or just exchange pleasantries. Whenever Coal called, it meant something bad had happened—or was about to.

Six rings. Seven. Eight. The man on the other end of the line had been trained in the same impolite school as Coal. The phone finally rattled, and a distant-sounding voice said, *Yeah, Nwanzée.*

"Pick up the damn phone, Tony," Coal chided.

Hey-hey, brother! What's happenin'? Oh no, don't tell me. It's somethin' bad, or you wouldn't be callin'.

Coal cringed. The truth hurt. "I'm sorry, Tony. You're right."

Oh no, man! I was just havin' fun with ya. What's up?

"Tony, you remember that deal with the Mob we had a while back?"

Sure, of course. I ain't that old yet.

It was a stupid question. Coal should have worded it differently, but right then he didn't care. He wanted to laugh at Tony's remark, but there was no sense of humor left in him.

"Well, we've got trouble. I mean *real* trouble. I got a call from my informant friend in Vegas, and he practically begged me to leave town for a week or two. Then he had to go, so I never got any details from him. I'm still waiting to hear back from him, but I have a feeling I might have heard the last of him—literally."

Sorry, bud. So you got anything else to go on?

"I do. Unfortunately. We had a car bomb go off an hour and a half or so ago. It killed our head prosecutor." He saw Grant cringe as he said it, and he was pretty sure he cringed a little as well. It was still hard to believe Fica was gone, and especially the *way* he had gone.

Tony swore. *No! Oh, man, Coal—I'm sorry! What about the prisoners?*

"We moved them to Idaho Falls a while back."

Tony swore again, softly. *That's too bad.*

"Too bad why?"

Too bad 'cause maybe if you hadn't moved them then the hit might have been on those two and they woulda left the rest of you alone and gone back home. Can't have trouble back home if there ain't any birds left to sing, right?

Coal sat silent for a moment. His mind roiled. A sick feeling began to creep through him. Tony might be right. Maybe if they had kept the Medinas here Mike Fica would still be alive. Maybe with his own suggestion to move the brothers, Fica had unintentionally committed suicide.

When Coal hadn't responded for a while, Tony's voice came back on. *Hey, brother—you all right? Can I do anything?*

Coal took a deep breath. He knew what he wanted to ask his old partner, but he didn't know how to word it. As always, he was going to have to bull right in and pray Tony would understand.

"Tony, I told you: I'm in big trouble. You know the Mob. You know the kind of lengths they'll go to."

After a drawn-out silence, Tony finally said, *Sure, man. I do.*

Come on, Tony! Don't make me come out and ask you this, Coal begged silently. He looked over at Grant, who was trying for all he was worth to pretend he wasn't listening yet hung on every word. He wished he had found some job for the young deputy to do, somewhere any place but here.

"So … Ah, hell, Tony. I'm in a corner. These guys could do anything. They could go after my family. Set bombs. Poison. Maybe—"

Tony's merciful voice finally stopped him from repeating himself anymore. *Coal. I get you, brother. I get you. Hey, where you at? Give me a number and maybe a half hour to an hour I'll ring you back. You know, I'm at the office now.* He made certain to enunciate that last very carefully, and Coal understood. Certain things, highly sensitive things, should never go over the phones right there at the Bureau, in the highly self-important Department of Justice building.

"I understand, buddy. I'm at my office now too, but I'm going to give you a different number, all right? Then make sure you give me at least forty minutes to get there before you call it. Got a pen?"

Yeah, shoot. Not a figure of speech Tony should be using right then.

"Two-O-eight, seven-five-six, ten-ten. Got it?"

Tony repeated the number back to him. *That it?*

Coal confirmed it was Maura's number, and they hung up. With his heart pounding, he stood out of his chair, the fingers of both hands pressed down on the desk top as if he needed the support. Grant looked over at him. "The coffee's hot. I think I got it right."

After all that trouble Coal couldn't tell him no thanks. He walked over and picked his favorite mug off the shelf, a drip glaze stoneware mug that looked like it had been soaked in different levels of creamed coffee for extended periods of time. It was a gift his mother had sent him two years ago for his birthday, a gift he cherished. Pouring the black brew up to the mug's rim, he raised it and took a sip. Grant was watching him.

"It's perfect, Grant."

The deputy only nodded. He tried to smile, but it came to his face looking like someone had kicked him in the groin and he was trying to tough his way through it.

"Hey, you all right?" Coal sipped the coffee again. It was near boiling, but he had to get it down and get on the road.

Grant nodded again. Coal studied him closely. "You're not, are you? I don't have much time right now, but …" He suddenly wished he had given Tony a longer amount of time before calling him. "Listen, you need to talk?"

The deputy's face had turned pale once more. The memories were too vivid. "I just never saw anything like that." His voice was quiet. He couldn't meet Coal's eyes.

"I know. Believe me, I know." He thought back to Korea, and to Nam, both of them worse than what he had seen today, and many times over. He thought about men who had been bombed with napalm, some of whom had survived the attacks only to die later, after excruciating days in the hospital. "Listen, Grant, I'm going to give you the rest of the day off. Go see your wife if you want to. Or if you'd rather wait, I'll try to get back here as fast as I can, and we can sit and talk. But I've—" He stopped himself abruptly. "On second thought, hang on."

"No, boss, wait." Coal turned to see an almost panicked look on Grant's face. "I think I should stay on duty."

"Grant, I'm serious. I don't want you to."

"But …" Grant stared at him. Coal could see he had something else on his mind, but the younger man held it in.

"Hold on, buddy."

In a rush, Coal went back to his desk and dialed Tony Nwanzée's number again. This time it took only three rings to pick up, but it was a secretary, not Tony. When he asked, he was surprised to hear they were able to catch his old partner on his way out. After asking Tony to give him another couple of hours and telling him he would call back to let him know exactly when he could be reached, he said goodbye and turned back to Grant. Too many times in Coal's life he had rushed off to something he thought meant the world only to ignore another human being in distress.

He was not going to let Grant Fairbourne start out his first real day of work like that, hung out to dry by the one man who was supposed to have his back.

"Now we can talk, Grant. We'll take all the time you need."

It took quite a while for Coal to get Grant to open up and talk. Talking out emotions wasn't a cop thing, any more than it was a Marine thing, but Coal knew a lot of men who could have been helped if they had only opened up. He was a psychologist by no means, but at least he knew how to listen.

What Coal didn't intend was for Grant Fairbourne to break down at one point in tears. It didn't last long, and he brushed them brusquely away, but the effect was the same: Grant had let another man—his boss, no less—see him cry. Coal assured him it wasn't the end of the world. "Bud, I'm tired of people acting like men aren't supposed to cry. It's not like you're blubbering on the floor. You just saw something pretty traumatic. It isn't good to hold it in."

Finally, when it seemed like there couldn't be much left to say, Coal could still see Grant acting fidgety. He studied him, but Grant wouldn't meet his eyes.

"All right, Grant. I have a feeling you have something else you need to say."

Grant looked at him then. For the first time since they started talking, Coal saw him give a little smile. "You're kind of a mind-reader, Coal."

"Why do you think they pay me so much money?"

This time, Grant laughed. "Yeah, there is something else. I just don't know how to say it."

"Just spit it out. I've heard some pretty crazy things."

"It's just … Well, taking the rest of the day off. I don't feel good about it."

"Why?"

"Because something told me …" He paused, then finally let out a sigh. "This is going to sound stupid, but I prayed this morning after you left my room. Man, something told me I was going to have to be around to save your life."

The conversation had ended up way longer than Coal had expected, but out of the whole exchange that last part was of course the thing he couldn't shake.

Regardless of Grant's plea, Coal insisted that he head home, and sent him off with one last bit of fatherly advice: take a circuitous route through town before going to his hotel and watch for cars that appeared to be sticking unnaturally close to him.

It was twelve-fifteen by the time Coal placed the phone call to Tony Nwanzée letting him know when it would be safe to call him at Maura's, then went to the parking lot. He checked around for anything that looked suspicious under and around his pickup, made the drive out to Maura's, and pulled into her yard. It felt disconcerting not seeing the horses come to stick their heads over the top fence wire. He was so used to their greeting. And no Chewy and Dart, either.

With a sigh, he got out, walked up the creaky steps onto the rickety porch, and christened it once more with a few obligatory curses as he swore once again he would come back soon and build a nice new one. He went inside, picked up the phone and its base, and sank into the worn-out sofa to wait for Tony's call.

When the phone rang, he was dozing off. He jerked and cursed it, cursed himself for jerking, then cursed one more time for cursing, and picked it up on the second ring.

Coal, it's Tony.

"Thank heavens. All right, buddy. I'm completely alone now. Did you get out of the office?"

I sure did. Wanna know where?

"Sure." Coal was lying. He didn't really care where Tony had gone, as long as it was someplace safe from listening ears. But obviously Tony wanted to tell him.

I'm calling from a phone booth about as close to work as I dared stay—clear over in Arlington. I'm at B & E's, remember? Bob and Edith's?

The name made Coal smile. It was a little mom and pop restaurant where he and Tony had spent many an enjoyable lunch hour away from the Department of Justice Building where the FBI headquarters was located. A place he had once dreamed of taking Laura on a date, before things with her went down the Potomac River. "I guess your goal's to make me salivate, huh, Tone?"

Ha! Yeah, sorry, man. I'll have a sandwich in your honor. With a quick and fun-loving laugh, Tony cleared his throat. *All right, brother, we gotta talk turkey now. For obvious reasons, I couldn't say what I wanted to before, but nobody's around to listen now, so let's lay this on the line before it's too late. If you don't mind me still being a little cryptic, I get why you called me, and I think maybe what we're talking about is not quite ... well, should I say 'sanctioned' by the powers that be? Is my understanding correct?*

"It is. I'm sorry, Tony. I know this is putting you in a bad spot morally, but I don't know what else to do, and I didn't know who else to turn to. It's my family we're talking about."

Not to mention you, Tony threw in. *I told you I get you, brother. I totally get you. Listen, man, this is ole Anthony you're talkin' to! We gotta do what we gotta do when it comes down to life or death, an' especially when family gets involved. I'm with you. But man, you gotta promise me: I never talked to you. At all. Right?*

"You know me better than to ask that. They couldn't torture your name out of me if things go south."

I know. I trust you right up with Jesus, brother. I do. So I did some checking around, made some calls over to some folks I know at the C.I.—well, never mind about who. Anyways, I got some stuff I'm not supposed to have, and for sure not to be using this way. I've got some strange-sounding code talk you'll have to jot down, and I've got a phone number. It's from out in Nebraska.

Coal let out a laugh. He couldn't help it, for he knew who Tony was talking about. "Oh, man! Are you serious? He just couldn't stay away from the home of the Corn Huskers, could he?"

Tony didn't share the laugh. *I guess not. So you're a smart man, Coal. You're already ahead of me. I know the guy's a little crazy, but you know he's the best, right? Best at what he does, any-*

way. And he's got ... Well, let's say our 'other friend' moved out there to babysit him and keep him on a straight line—as much as anybody can, at least. They're the only way I know to keep this quiet, man. And in the hands of a guy who knows everything the Mob does about trying to kill people—if not more.

Neither of them put a name with "he" or "they". They both knew who they were talking about, and there was something about voicing the names out loud over the phone lines that seemed dangerous.

"So you're sure Mart— You're sure the other half is still with him?" Coal asked.

As far as my informant told me. You joshin'? I think one of them would have to be dead to separate them. And poor Q, if he dies first I swear his head's gonna be mounted on ... his *wall.*

Again Coal couldn't hold back a laugh. "Good to have friends, huh?"

Maybe. I guess. Coal, you're gonna be going off the charts with trouble if things go wrong. There ain't gonna be no savin' you. You know that, right?

"What choice do I have?"

None. You got no choice whatsoever. That's what scares me.

Tony made sure Coal had a notepad and pen, and then he started reading off some funny code words, both clues and replies to those clues, the kind of silly stuff one might hear in a spy movie, or read in a Matt Helm novel—only now it was real.

When he finished, and Coal read everything back to him, Tony went silent for a moment. "You still there?"

Yeah, I'm here, man. Listen, I don't know where he is right now. I pray he isn't on some job already. You know—selling tractors or something, Tony said in a wry voice. *But you got all I got now. Use it wisely. And Coal? Good luck, brother. I'm only asking you one thing.*

"What's that?"

You gotta call me when this is all over, all right? I gotta know my brother's safe.

For a long time after they hung up Coal sat in silence, holding the phone in his lap, staring down at it. He thought about Washington, D.C., how hard his job there was, but how rewarding in so many ways, and how … safe. Of course it wasn't literally safe, but his family had lived so far out of town, and things with the Bureau were so secretive, that he never had to worry that anyone could find Laura or the children and use them against him. He and his loved ones no longer had that net of safety, not in the little mountain community of Salmon.

At last, he took a deep breath, and he dialed the first number. An answering machine picked up, and a half-familiar voice said, *Mick Spillane. Leave the message.* Coal scanned his notepad, then enunciated carefully, "Big green tractor. Black Redman. Four-Two-Zero, nine-seven-eight, three-two-three-two."

Scanning carefully over the paper again, making sure he had said everything the initial message was supposed to say, he reached out an almost trembling finger and pressed down on one of the two white buttons to disconnect the line.

Letting out a gust of breath he hadn't known he was holding, he let the handset settle softly onto the base and dropped his chin on his chest. Now he would wait. And waiting could be forever.

Before he could even think about getting up to feed a nervous hunger, the phone rang, vibrating on his lap, making him with a large amount of exuberance say a word he didn't often use. This had to be someone else, calling for Maura! What terrible timing! But he couldn't take the chance of ignoring them.

He plucked the phone off the base. "Hello."

There was a pregnant pause on the line. His heart started thudding faster.

"Hello twice, and once for the moon landing," he said, feeling foolish.

Hello is just hell with a donut for a caboose, a voice replied from what felt like a world away.

"And I have the donut here," Coal quipped, hoping he had really written this idiocy down exactly as Tony had told it to him. He waited for two seconds, half-expecting the line to go dead.

Is this really Black Redman? the voice said.

The silly code words were over. Now they were speaking in words Coal understood. "Black Redman" was the code name he had gone by back at the Bureau—"Black" for Coal, "Redman" for Savage. And Sam Browning was known as "Big Green Tractor" because that was his cover—a salesman for John Deere. Maura's number had been changed, to Tony's specifications, so that each digit was two digits higher than the actual ones, which had made the eight in the Idaho area code fall back to a zero.

"Vike!" Coal would continue being careful not to slip up and use Browning's real name. "Vike, is that really you? And yes, it's me, Black."

Red! Holy hell, man, I never dreamed I'd hear that cowboy twang again. How'd you get this number? This is only supposed to be used for ... Oh, son of a— Co— I mean, Red, you all right?

"First let me set your mind at ease—sort of. Nobody's going to get this number from me, and the source I got it from is safe. You don't have to worry about that."

I'm gonna take your word for it, brother. But you didn't answer my question. If you were calling just to be friendly you wouldn't have been talking in code. Something's wrong, man. What is it?

"I got in a bad spot, Vike. I mean *real* bad. The Vegas Mob's after me."

He went on to tell Sam Browning a condensed version of the story. He was telling the right man, because not only was Sam "Viking" Browning one of the guys Big Brother sought out when he needed some nasty, dirty, top-secret job done, but Sam hated the Mob with a passion. Not being able to handle the Mob as he saw fit, in fact, was the reason behind his untimely departure from the Bureau in the first place. And it was the reason he was now sought out for a high-dollar fee by another agency that he would wish could remain nameless, and in circles like theirs, it did.

When Coal finished the details of what he was up against, there were only a couple of things left that could not go unanswered.

"I'm out of my league, Vike. I don't know where else to turn."

You really want me in this, man? Which means Q, too, because you know we never work alone.

"I do."

You know what it means.

"I know that too. Vike, you're my only chance of surviving this. And my family's only chance, I'm guessing. But I need to know upfront how much it's going to cost me."

There was a long moment of silence, and then Sam's voice came back. *I should hang up on you, Red. What the hell kind of question is that between friends?*

"No offense. I just have to know I'll be able to pay it."

Pay it! It's the same price as everything else I ever did for you, ya prick. Two pounds of mixed chocolates. And it's Russell Stover's, or the deal's off. Oh—and since you questioned me, I want a handful of Milky Ways, too. In advance.

CHAPTER ELEVEN

Stagecoach Inn, same day

Menny Marcello lay back on his bed, snoring off and on. Scabs Ravioli sat in the only chair in the room, which he had pulled over halfway in front of the TV, but where he could see himself in the mirror. He was watching the television screen, but whenever a round of commercials came on, he studied himself in the mirror, after making sure his partner's eyes were still shut.

How had Saverio "Scabs" Ravioli gotten to be so old? So old and beat-up? In all fairness, he guessed the "beat-up" part was a given. All the years of bareknuckle boxing, in spite of the fact that he won most of his bouts, could not be claimed to have been his friend. Maybe he deserved to look this way. His eyebrows, far too sparse of hair among the thatch of scar tissue, looked swollen all the time, like his ears and his flattened nose. His eyes, always deep-set even as a child, were astoundingly so now after all the times he had taken hard fists to his eye sockets. The hair on his head was thin and graying, and his low-riding pencil mustache had maybe a total of ten black hairs left, with the rest all gone over to the snowy side.

And here he was—how old now? Fifty-eight, he was pretty sure. Or fifty-seven. In his line of work, who really cared? He had plenty of money—more, in fact, than any of his associates. Because Scabs knew how to save.

And he had a family, too. His wife was Nicola, who was round and fat like a good Italian wife should be, loved to cook linguini and, ironically, ravioli, and who made the best marinara on the face of the earth—or at least in Las Vegas. His oldest son, Giorgio, was a mechanic in Vegas—not the kind of fictional mechanic they made the Charles Bronson movie about the year before, a hitman like Scabs, but a real one, and one of the best in the city. All the Mob took their prized automobiles to him, and he was honest and fast—just like his father.

The other boy, thirty-three-year-old Nicoló, named of course after his mother, played the violin in the New York Philharmonic orchestra. Seeing him hold that instrument like a sacred lover, and coax magic from his fingers and his bow, made Scabs Ravioli the proudest father of all.

And then there was Viola—*Violet,* in English. She was married to a doctor, a cur who had taken her away from the family to live in London. Of all places! But beautiful Viola seemed happy, and she was raising five children of her own—hopefully not with English accents, heaven forbid! That was all Scabs wanted for his family: happiness.

Scabs and Nicola lived alone now, in an apartment off the Strip. Well, alone except for their schnauzer, Pieta, who mostly did nothing but eat, slurp wine, and pass gas, and two goldfish Nicola cherished, Baldini and Bud. Where the woman came up with names like that, Scabs had never dared ask. And how she could find anything to cherish in a fish was another question with no answer. But perhaps he should have been glad. Perhaps it was Nicola's ability to love even fish that had made her love him as well.

Thinking of his family made Scabs's mind turn to the man they had killed that morning. From listening to the radio, he and Menny had ascertained that the hit had indeed been a success. One dark blue van, blown to *paradiso*—or *inferno.* Heaven, hell, what was the difference, after all? Dead was dead. The once-blue van was black now, Menny had another notch carved in his bomb-making hands, and one prosecutor, Mike Fica, was off the case of Lemhi County v. the Las Vegas *Familia*, as the Mob liked to call themselves.

The only downside, and it was one that ate more and more at Scabs's heart as he grew older, was the thought of the prosecutor's family. The deejay on the radio had said he had a wife—had even called her by name—and … how many children? He couldn't remember anymore. But it was a handful.

Scabs didn't much care that the prosecutor was gone. But thinking about the man's family, now missing their father and husband, still mourning, of course, but probably also beginning to wonder how they would survive without their bread winner, that was the hard thing. That was the thing that ate at Scabs in his older age, the thing only strong drink or drugs could erase from his mind.

Was he getting soft? Was he going to turn into an old grandmother and have to go into retirement to preserve his sanity? It was ridiculous. He had killed twenty-four men, and he had never regretted even one. Or at least that was what the inner Saverio Ravioli told the outer Saverio Ravioli. But the families … The families … At night, the voices of the wives, and of the children, they had started to cry out to him, and in spite of everything he had learned, all the steel he had put around his heart since the beginning of this remorseless career, his heart had started listening.

Damn hearts. He looked over at Menny Marcello, who now slept soundly. Why did a good, strong man like Scabs Ravioli need a heart anyway? Apparently, in time all they did was cause a man trouble he didn't need.

Scabs's stomach growled, reminding him that he and Menny had last eaten early that morning in the far back of a place called the Salmon River Coffee Shop. Good food, but not enough to carry them through the whole day. But in spite of the growling of his stomach, Scabs found he had no appetite. He swallowed the acid taste in his mouth and reached for his can of Skoal, glancing over at the table, where the tools of Menny's trade were lined out and ready to go in case he and Menny chose to go with another bomb for their next hit. He packed his lower lip with Skoal and looked again at Menny Marcello. He remembered when he used to sleep that way, as if he had no care in the world.

That was before the ghosts began to haunt him.

Fifteen minutes later, Menny slept on, and the chew in Scabs's lip had done nothing to take the prosecutor's family off his mind. He could think of only one other thing to do about it, and that was to eat, and only one thing right now in all the world, including Nicola's pasta, would satisfy his hunger.

Getting up, he went to the door, looking closely at Menny, who didn't budge. He stepped out and walked down to Courthouse Drive, where he crossed over and went into the IGA grocery store. When he came out, he was carrying a paper bag that contained two cans of Skoal, a bag of Clover Club potato chips, a container of Knudsen sour cream, and a packet of Lipton dry onion soup mix. There was about to be a party at the Stagecoach Inn, even if it proved to be a party of one.

* * *

Maura PlentyWounds went back to work at McPherson's that day, and a part of her felt great. After being away so long, her senses had had a chance to clear out, and once again on stepping into the store, the door chimes seemed clearer, more musical, the colors of the clothing on the racks brighter, and best of all the leather goods smelled like leather. She had missed that, although she knew it wouldn't take long before the scent was lost to her once more—too much of a good thing.

McPherson's owner, Florin Beller, and the two other employees seemed tickled to death to see Maura back, and young, dark-haired Nellie Ferguson even ran over to give her a huge hug. Maura put on her best face, hoping she could pretend her vacation had been nothing but idyllic and that in time the lie would become her new truth.

After initial conversation finally died down, and Maura had told the others everything she hoped ever to have to tell them about Montana, Wyoming, Nebraska, and South Dakota, and she got her day's assignment from Florin Beller, she settled right into work, almost as if she had never left. It felt good to be doing a mundane task, taking clothing out of shipping boxes, ironing it, and putting it on hangers, and saying hello to passing customers or answering their questions while the scents of leather and cigarette smoke swirled around her in a pungent mixture that tickled her nose.

She found herself looking over at the hats, and that made her think about Coal. She had been quietly threatening to herself that she was going to get him a new hat and form it especially for the shape of his face, hoping to get him to wear something besides the silver belly Stetson he always wore, with the cattleman's crease in the crown and the brim that curved up on both sides to match his grin. She had to admit the hat was about perfect for him, and it certainly took nothing away from his handsome mug, but being a woman, she thought it would be nice once in a while to have a change—and it was going to be a drastic one. One day. Someday …

She put the thought out of her mind, knowing that with her week off she was going to have a tough enough time getting by as it was without spending frivolously on a hat Coal might not even appreciate. She would have to wait until she got her taxes back, maybe, or until she found a fifty-dollar bill lying in the gutter. A smile came to her face, and the voice of Florin Beller startled it away immediately.

"You must be thinking about your vacation," said Beller, who had stolen up in front of her in her reverie without her even noticing a movement. "That sure is a pretty smile, Maura. I'm glad to see you back."

Maura reached out on impulse and squeezed his hand. "Thank you, Florin. It sure is good to be back, too."

"Say!" Beller shook a finger at Maura and said, "I think I have something for you." He reached up to his right shirt pocket and unsnapped it, withdrawing what appeared to be a slip of paper folded in half. A note? "I thought you might be able to use this."

With questioning eyes, Maura reached out and took the paper from Beller, trying to read the cryptic look about his face. She unfolded it to see it was a check, made out in her name for the amount of one hundred dollars.

Her glance shot back up to his face, as he stood there with arms folded watching her. "What's this?"

"Oh, just a little something. To help you get by. I'm sure you didn't make much money while you were out gallivanting around the country."

A rush of tears filled Maura's eyes, and she stepped close and threw her arms around her employer, much to his obvious surprise.

"Thank you so much, Florin. You sure have great timing."

When she stepped away, he took her by both shoulders. "We love having you here, Maura. You're a great employee."

Florin went back to his office, and when Maura turned to her ironing again, her eyes were drawn once more to the hat rack. One hat of dark gunmetal gray sure was whispering Coal's name to her.

* * *

When Scabs returned to the room, Menny had been up and pacing the floor. He met Scabs at the door, startling him into taking a step back.

"Damn it, where'd you go?"

"Settle down, putz. I went to get somethin' to eat."

Menny leaned forward and peeled back one side of the paper bag, trying to see into its depths while Scabs worked on closing the door. Finally, in disgust, Scabs shoved his partner back. "Man, let me in, would you? You wanna go out in the hall and eat?"

Menny swore as the door shut and once again tried for a look down in the bag. This time Scabs shoved it up against his chest. "Here. Just take it."

Now with the bag in his hands and a good look in it, Menny looked back up at his partner. "You jokin'? That's what you chose? Out of a whole store?"

Scabs shrugged, feeling irritable because something like remorse still seemed to be scourging him deep inside. That damn prosecutor's family ... "Go back over if you want. There's nothin' stoppin' you." He yanked the bag back out of Menny's hands, tearing it halfway down.

"Jeez!" Menny raised his hands out to the sides, feigning a posture of surrender. "Don't have a cow, all right?"

Scabs, holding the torn bag of groceries, stared spears into Menny's face. "Have a cow? Did you actually just say that? You must be hangin' out at the junior highs again, huh? That where you picked up Lily?" Lily was Menny's girlfriend of over a year, a girl he loved dearly but looked to be fifteen years his junior.

"Funny. Hey, brother." Menny's face went serious, and he studied his partner for a moment. "Something eatin' you?"

Scabs shook his head. "Naw, come on. Let's eat this stuff—unless you wanna go find somethin' better." He started removing everything from the bag, tore open the onion soup mix and pulled out a metal spoon—he could have bought a bag of plastic ones, but only a moron would stir something with a plastic spoon—and then took off the sour cream lid and slowly stirred while pouring in the contents of the soup packet.

Menny, who had been so scornful of Scabs's choice of delectables only minutes before, ripped into the Clover Club bag and pulled out a handful of chips, taking one between thumb and forefinger and aiming for Scabs's half-finished mixture. Scabs jerked away defensively.

"Get back, ya worm! It's not finished. What kind of low-life would eat half-stirred chip dip?"

Menny laughed, then shoved the entire handful of chips into his mouth, crumbs scattering everywhere like a herd of escaping sheep. He said something that Scabs deciphered as "Better like this anyway."

Menny didn't seem to lack an appetite when it came to cleaning up chips and dip, but Scabs did. A fourth of the way through the bag, Menny leaned back, supported by the one hand, slapping his salty and greasy fingers on his pant leg. "All right, man. What's up? I can tell somethin's eatin' you."

Scabs avoided his eyes. "Sure. Would you cut it out? I was just thinkin' about that sheriff. Since we can't get to Angel and Rey, we've gotta get that sheriff, and fast. Wanna go case the courthouse and see if we can spot him headin' home?"

Menny shrugged and leaned over to study the remains of the potato chip bag. "Yeah, I guess we should. Another bomb, you think?"

"Yeah. These rubes won't even know what to look for." Even as he spoke, his mind tried to wonder if the sheriff had a family. He slapped the thought down hard and stood up. "Let's get going."

"Sure wish we had another car right now," Menny said.

"Oh my hell. Are you gonna get on that again?" Scabs growled.

"You think that sheriff isn't going to notice a fancy Jaguar sitting by the courthouse, and then it starts to follow him?"

Scabs frowned. He knew Menny was right, but he still couldn't admit it. He would just have to come up with some plan to nullify the danger of being detected. He had thought too much on his idea of renting a different car and decided he wouldn't bow to Menny's paranoia.

"Let's go, you worry wart. You want something else to eat?"

"Some Chee-tos and a package of Twinkies would be good. And a Pepsi."

"Twinkies," said Scabs in a scoffing tone. "The picture of health, that's what you're gonna be. Twinkies. I think I got a new name for you. Come on, Twinkie."

CHAPTER TWELVE

Judge Wiley Sinclair wanted a favor from Coal Savage. A favor that went almost above and beyond Coal's job. It was a favor to the judge, and against a criminal, or at least a potential criminal, he found particularly repugnant. Judge Sinclair took the time to call Coal personally to ask for the favor, and even in the tight spot Coal had found himself it seemed like a good idea to humor him. Besides, it might take Coal's mind off all that was going on, and right now his mind needed a breather.

Richard Parker carried the unfortunate shortened name of Dick, which especially considering his family name could lead into all manner of off-color jokes, none of which the generally proper, stern-mannered judge would indulge in, or at least he never had done so around Coal. Dick Parker, Coal learned, had drawn the good judge's ire when he and his lawyer managed to plead a charge of battery down to one of disorderly conduct, when the judge had observed the battery with his own eyes, and when it definitely did not match the definition of disorderly conduct. He had struck his wife, who had since left him, it was rumored, right on the sidewalk in front of Saveway Foodtown. Not only did the judge deplore violence, Coal had learned, but the mere thought of it being perpetrated against the fairer sex was something that drove Judge Sinclair to the edge.

To top it all off, and it was something Coal learned from Jordan Peterson, and not the judge himself, the judge in spite of the staunchly religious circles he seemed to associate in, had learned that Parker was purported, through evil rumors spread in bars and back alleys, to have some kind of unseemly relationship with the hogs he raised in a cluster of filthy pens behind his house. It was thought by the bolder, more ribald crowd, that the calling of animal husbandry might have taken on a whole new meaning out at the Dick Parker farm. It was also strongly rumored that this brand of animal husbandry had led to the fight on Main Street that had ended with Mrs. Parker being struck by the back of her husband's hand.

The short of it was, Judge Sinclair still wanted some of the justice of which he felt he had been deprived, and he was hoping Coal could get on the phone with people he knew and try to work up some kind of case against Parker that he could be brought back into court for. The judge simply wanted another shot at a degenerate and wife beater. It all seemed to come down to revenge, very unbecoming of a judge, Coal thought, but making him a lot more human than he had seemed when Coal first had to deal with him.

Jordan Peterson had a funny way of summing it all up that unfortunately came out in front of Grant Fairbourne when he said, "Yeah, that's what I've been hearing anyway. Between the pigs he raises and his wife, it sounds like Dick Parker forgot where he's supposed to park it."

"All right, Jord," Coal cut off his big deputy's laughter at its height. "I don't think Grant appreciates that kind of stuff."

Grant grinned. "Thanks, Coal, but I'm pretty sure I've heard a lot worse over in Caldwell." Jordan kept snickering as he walked over to fill a mug with coffee to get ready for the road, and Coal looked at Grant and just rolled his eyes. Grant laughed quietly. The look on his face said simply, *Boys will be ribald boys.*

With all that degenerate, yet in some dark sense humorous, clutter now polluting his mind, Coal left the office that evening with a folder of paperwork he needed to shuffle through and investigate, then fill out some forms and get them back to the judge first thing in the morning. He had intended on taking care of the unofficial investigation before he left the office and getting whatever he came up with back upstairs to Judge Sinclair's desk before he left town, so he wouldn't have what basically amounted to homework hanging over his head while he could otherwise be spending another highly entertaining evening sitting alone at Maura's twiddling his thumbs, working out, and eating jerky. At this point he didn't even like having a phone conversation with anyone in his house, for fear the Mob might have some way of tracing such calls. His biggest problem right at the moment was truly having no clue what capabilities the Mob actually had. Unfortunately, the judge had left the courthouse early, so out to the pickup to head home Coal went, with his assigned homework clamped in his left hand.

At the truck, he performed his now-normal routine of carefully scanning the parking lot, making note of each car, and whether it belonged to someone he knew, then got down to inspect the underside of the pickup and other vehicles close by. Everything seemed to be in order, and the two strips of duck tape he had carefully and strategically placed in the crack between the hood and front side panels were exactly as he had set them up as well. Feeling safe, he got in and fired the GMC up, letting it rattle and groan for a while as the engine and heater warmed up. Then he pulled out to Courthouse Drive.

As he sat at the street, he scanned it as carefully as he had the parking lot, then pulled out. Rather than go down the hill, he went up into the Bar neighborhood and drove a bizarre maze pattern down most of the tiny streets, watching in his rearview mirror. When he finally got back out on Courthouse and headed toward downtown, he was satisfied that no one could be following him.

Coal didn't see the dark blue Jaguar that pulled up to the stop sign at Main, coming in from Highway 93. He didn't see it wait for a few more cars to pass, then pull out onto Main, heading east—the same direction Coal was heading. And when he got out on the highway and opened it up, seeing a beat-up red Ford pickup right behind him, a pickup he had already recognized back in town, which belonged to an employee at Saveway, he took a deep breath and sighed it out, then leaned back against the seat, set his elbow on the arm rest, his chin on his hand, and drove. It was good to be alive. And he had to keep it that way, biding his time until Sam Browning and Alex Martinez—Vike and Q—rolled into Salmon like the Texas Rangers.

Coal pulled off at Maura's, watching the red pickup rattle past him on the highway. The driver raised a hand in high salute to him. The car after that, an aged Pontiac, was one he recognized from town as well. The one he didn't know was the next one, a dark blue Jaguar. But then he remembered another such car he had seen in the parking lot of the Stagecoach Inn. Tourists heading back out of town?

He turned his head and watched the car roll on east. Its brake lights never lit up, and its speed never seemed to slow. Then it was hidden from view as a logging truck lumbered by—hidden from view and forgotten. Thinking about logging trucks "lumbering" made Coal ponder with a bit of humor that maybe he should make up puns for a living—except he was so busy trying to keep from dying.

Sitting on Maura's couch, it was pretty straightforward work sorting through the documents the judge had given him on Richard Parker, and making some random, and sometimes slightly uncomfortable, phone calls to people he knew around the valley from the farming and ranching community. Coal finished in less than an hour and set the folder and his notes aside on top of the coffee table at the end of the couch, where he couldn't possibly forget to take it back to work with him in the morning.

He was watching the news when he realized his eyes couldn't manage to stay open, and they apparently didn't care that his stomach was digesting its own lining for lack of anything inside it. For the first time in a long time, he thought of alcohol—liquor, to be precise. He thought back on all the names he used to know fairly well, although never because he got drunk on any. In fact, he could probably count on one hand the number of times in his life that he could have been considered drunk. He simply liked the taste of liquor—not beer—and he liked the warm, relaxed feeling it gave him when he had a cup or so inside.

Seagram's 7, Jagermeister, Wild Turkey—which he knew Annie Price would have some of down the road a piece—Jameson Irish, Jim Beam bourbon, Crown Royal, and Fireball, which was flavored with cinnamon and was one of the most decadently delicious tastes in the known world. There were a lot more of them, and in his day he had lightly sampled several dozen, including some homemade brew that had probably singed hair off odd places around his body from the inside.

Coal let out a sigh. The thought of something warm in his gut was tempting, but he wasn't going to head back into town, for one thing, and for another, he didn't need to put himself in a state of being mentally impaired, not right now. The most tempting thing at the moment was to drive over and check on Annie Price, but he didn't dare take a chance on anyone with evil intentions seeing his truck parked at her place.

So he sat quietly with Walter Cronkite's manly, comforting voice droning on and on, telling lies on the CBS Evening News, and let the Sandman win the battle against his wakefulness. He could hear the fan of the furnace blowing, the house was warm and comfortable, set at sixty-eight degrees, and other than a whole bunch of professional, highly trained killers who didn't even know him wanting to scramble his brains with a .22 hollow-point or turn him into pink vapor with the blast of a bomb, the world seemed sparklingly friendly.

* * *

Maura PlentyWounds sat on a stool in front of the hat steamer after work was done. She had sat down the moment Florin Beller turned the OPEN sign around to show CLOSED through the glass in the door, and in her hands was a size seven and five-eighths dark gray Resistol hat.

"You'll lock it up tight when you're done, won't you, Maura?" Beller had come up behind her and softly laid a hand on her shoulder.

"Of course. You're sure it's okay for me to stay?"

"Oh, of course! You know, I've styled a lot of hats in my day, and there isn't anything I've found to do with my hands that's much more relaxing. It'll do you good. You've just got to promise me to make sure Coal comes in wearing it sometime. I want to see how it turns out."

"You can bet on it. Thanks, Florin."

"Sure, hon. See you tomorrow."

Beller picked up his coat, went to turn out the lights at the front of the store, and trailed out after the other girls.

Maura was alone. Alone with the now-fading smell of cigarettes and new leather and freshly ironed clothes, and ... In short, she was in her own kind of heaven.

The steamer had already heated up, and it let out an impatient and loud huff of steam as Maura turned to her work. She slowly turned the hat in her hands, looking it over, trying to decide what she would make of it.

As it was, the hat's crown, a six-incher, was shaped in the ubiquitous cattleman's crease, like what Coal normally wore, and the four-inch brim curled up on the sides in the typical western "grin". The edge was already bound, which would be a big plus to help it keep its shape, and it had a quarter-inch band the same color as the hat, a nice, conservative touch she knew Coal would prefer to something gaudy and shiny like leather and conchos.

But other than the bound brim edge and the band, Maura was having big visions for this new hat, and it wasn't going to look much like its original state when she handed it over to Coal.

She finished an hour later, not because she couldn't have done it quicker, but because she wanted it to have the extra loving touch and make sure not one single dent or bump remained in it. While the steamer continued to burp and hiss now and then, she sat back on the stool and turned the hat around and around in her hands. The cattleman's crease was gone, and in its place was a crown that looked flat from the horizontal position but from the top was dented in and softly telescoped. The brim was now almost completely flat, dipped down only a little on both the front and back.

Maura smiled with great pleasure. This hat said Coal Savage all over it. Maybe not the Coal of this modern day, but Coal had he been born in the last century, as she sometimes thought he should have been.

Her work here was done.

Sadly now, she had to go back to the Savage place and await the day she could present her gift to him. She had wanted to do that on her way home, but she had had too much time to think while reshaping the hat, and Coal's last words to her were all too clear and strong. She could never afford to go to him, to give anyone the chance to discover that they knew each other. That was Coal's wish, and she had to be true to it.

Supper at the Savages' was quiet. The twins, especially Morgan, tried questioning Connie several times about why their father couldn't be home with them at night anymore, but Connie's evasive replies, even to a five-year-old, eventually seemed to come across as the ultimate fence that could not be crossed, and then even the boys stopped asking.

Sissy, meanwhile, refused to kneel on her own chair, as she usually did to eat, and she stood close to Maura's right side, holding onto her arm whenever she could get away with it and causing Maura some practice in left-handed eating that she had never known she was in need of. Sissy would reach out almost gingerly, glancing quickly around to see if anyone was watching, and pluck bits of food off her plate to bring them to her mouth. It was a system that, unlike Maura's left-handed fork usage, appeared to be pretty well polished.

After supper was done and the dishes dried and put away, Connie sat down with the children and Maura to watch *Gunsmoke* on Channel 3, which didn't end until eight, right when the children knew they were expected to be making preparations to head to bed.

Immediately afterward, on NBC's *Monday Night at the Movies,* they were playing *Charro!,* and for a few minutes Maura thought Connie was actually going to let the kids stay up clear until ten to see it. As it turned out, Connie was just a huge Elvis Presley fan, along with being a fan of Westerns, and was too engrossed in the movie for the first twenty minutes or so even to realize the kids were all still sitting there.

But when the next commercial came on, she dutifully got out of her chair and rounded all the children up, herding them off to their various rooms for the night.

Maura loved Elvis too, because after all, who didn't, but the opening song had stirred her blood, and something Connie had confided in her earlier in the evening when they were out feeding the horses had got her creative juices flowing—which didn't happen very often. Connie had admitted she was getting worried about Cody, the aging gray quarter horse-Tennessee walker who still seemed to think he ruled the ranch. She could see the horse, now almost completely white, simply was not himself, and she had a growing fear that he would not be around much longer. Between listening to "Charro" and thinking about Cody getting on in age, the urge to write a song had spawned inside Maura, and it would not go away. It started out as only a title: "My Horse".

After Connie had made sure the kids all brushed their teeth and got in their pajamas, she came back to the living room, and Maura was there waiting on pins and needles.

Taking a chance, she interrupted the movie. "Hey, Connie?"

Connie managed to drag her eyes away from the rarely but majestically whiskered face of Elvis Presley at the first sound of her name. "Yes, dear?"

"Do you think Coal would care if I played with his guitar?"

Connie smiled. "Well, I can't imagine he would. No, not at all. But you don't want to watch the movie?"

"Well, I do, but I kind of have this song running around in my head that wants me to try and write it."

Turning more fully to Maura, Connie said, "I didn't know you write songs!"

Maura gave a little laugh. "I'm not exactly sure I do. I've done a few, but nothing I'd really ever want someone to hear."

With a friendly-looking frown, Connie said, "I sure hope you change your mind about that someday. I would really love to hear them."

"Really?"

"Well, of course! Listen, if you feel the need to create, why don't you run up and get Coal's guitar from his room. I know he won't mind. The quietest place to play it is probably down in the basement in Coal's weight room."

Somewhat regretfully, because she truly didn't want to leave Connie sitting all alone in the living room, Maura went upstairs. She felt a little strange going into Coal's room, but she didn't know why. They knew each other well enough by now! When she came back down with the guitar, in its case, she saw Connie's eyes glued to the television screen, and it took only a glance to see the woman wasn't going to miss her presence one bit. Smiling to herself, she went downstairs.

Maura had never been down in the Savages' basement, but she found the light switch easily enough and lit the place up. It was a jungle of weight equipment, jump ropes, a few full-length mirrors on the wall, and here and there a poster of someone Coal evidently looked up to, either movie stars like Clint Walker, William Smith, and Steve Reeves, or famous body builders like Larry Scott, the first Mr. Olympia, Dave Draper, or the huge black man, Sergio Oliva, known in bodybuilding circles as "The Myth". Maura smiled to think how impressed and surprised Coal would surely be by her knowledge of a world that was generally thought of to be strictly the realm of men. It wasn't that she was into lifting weights herself, but she enjoyed watching the success of those who put so much of their heart and soul into the whole daunting process.

Choosing a weight bench, Maura sat down and pulled out the guitar, doing her best to make sure it was tuned. She strummed a few chords, found a place she thought she would like to be musically, and started writing her song down in a notebook she had stolen from Coal's room when she got the guitar.

Singing the song, thinking of Coal, Cody, her own horses, and all the hell she had been through lately, brought back to Salmon alive only because Coal would not give up on her, at last the emotion overcame Maura, and she sat and sobbed quietly, the tears streaming down her face. She missed Coal right now. She missed him more than she had ever dreamed she could miss a man.

Because she thought she was alone, and being completely silent in her sorrow so as not to disturb anyone, the voice startled her so bad she almost threw Coal's guitar across the room.

"You really miss him, don't you?"

Connie, whose approach had been unfortunately about as quiet as a Navajo rug, was standing in the opening to the room, her hand resting on the wall.

CHAPTER THIRTEEN

Coal sat watching the movie *Charro!* Like his mom, he had always been an Elvis Presley fan, and in his opinion this movie, unfortunately one of only a handful of serious films the King of Rock and Roll had ever done, was among the hundred most watchable Westerns he had seen—and he had seen most that were worth watching.

He remembered a chilly, rainy evening in the middle part of March, 1969, when he and Laura had walked from the parking lot of the Pitts Theater, on Main Street in Warrenton, Virginia, into the warm, dim-lit theater lobby, to the smell of popcorn, heated film, and humanity itself. He recalled vividly that he was holding Laura's hand, and it felt good, for they had been apart for so long, while he served his last stint in Vietnam. He had only been home then for four months.

Unfortunately, once inside the auditorium, the musty smell of mold and the rot of old wood were added to the normal odors of the theater experience, for the old theater, opened in 1931, had gone dilapidated, and the roof leaked. On top of that, after stepping over the occasional water puddle to find a leather seat with minimal cracking and wear, once in a while in the dim light from the film, a roach could be seen scurrying over the top of a seat. The crowds in the once-magnificent, first-class theater had dwindled way down, and this Pitts Theater experience was bound soon only for the halls of the memories of those who had sat here in its glory days watching such heart-stopping films as *Gone With the Wind* and *The Wizard of Oz.*

On this rainy night, Coal and Laura had taken all the kids to a babysitter, which they did about zero times in never, and for once they were alone. They sat as far to the back of the crowded theater as they could get where there weren't any drips, and Laura began caressing his leg. The next thing he knew they were necking, and … Well, it was a great movie, a warm moment—in fact, one of their last of such moments—and a wonderful night to boot.

Right in the middle of *Charro!*, a strange and somewhat startling realization struck Coal. He had only ever had intimate relations with one woman, his wife, had only felt like he came close to it with one other, and that was Maura. Yet it was only at this strange moment during the middle of watching the whiskered Presley give the bad guys what for on Maura's little black and white television screen, that he realized his wife, and the woman he had come to care for so much, shared almost exactly the same first name—differing only in the first letter.

Coal pondered this for a few seconds, then laughed out loud. How had he, a man who prided himself on details, never tumbled to that before? He guessed it was only because an M and an L sounded so different, and because he had seldom had any reason to see Maura's name spelled out.

How quickly Coal's mind had slipped from Laura, with whom he had struggled and quarreled so much toward the end of their existence together, to Maura, with whom he had just spent an entire lifetime on the Pine Ridge Reservation in South Dakota, bringing her back, it seemed, from the brink of destruction.

He looked over at the phone, and he almost reached for it. There was a commercial on now, showcasing a long, red 1973 Lincoln Continental on the road. Beautiful car, but his mind hardly registered it. He was thinking of Maura. Of the kids, and Connie.

He missed home. He missed the noise and the ruckus, and a part of him even almost missed the occasional squabbles, or the rare-as-hens'-teeth irritated snarls old Shadow gave to Dobe when he got too pushy and playful. When would he ever be able to return to all that commotion ... and love?

* * *

Maura had absolutely no doubt that Connie had meant well when she came into the basement, sacrificing part of her movie, to make sure Maura was all right, and to let her empty out her soul, both in words, when she could manage them, and otherwise in tears. Connie had talked about the beautiful dark gray hat Maura had been so excited to show her. She had listened attentively as Maura, partially successfully, stumbled through the new song she had written, in between bouts of choking up with tears. They had talked about life, and of course they had talked about Coal, for in all reality, wasn't he the one thing that had brought them together, and the one person they both feared losing now?

Maura was sure Connie had the best of intentions, and yet all her efforts had served only to compound Maura's misery. She had just spent a few wonderful days, and then quite an ordeal, beside the man with whom she kept fiercely swearing to herself she was not in love. And now he was forced to be away from her, yet by such a short distance, and she wasn't even allowed to speak to him on the phone. Life to Maura had so often been excruciatingly cruel, but in its own way this seemed one of the cruelest blows of all.

Connie left, after a while, and when the movie ended she came back down one more time to check on Maura. Maura was able to successfully convince her that she would be all right, that she just needed some time alone with her thoughts. Connie told her she was going to go to bed, but would leave a lamp on, and she left her with some typical advice she often freely gave the kids, and sometimes even to Coal—to turn to God in prayer.

Maura followed that advice. Only this time the advice that should have been perfect ended up leading to trouble neither Maura nor Coal could have foreseen.

An hour after Connie had gone to bed, Maura had finished talking to God, and now she was quietly strumming her song again and trying to sing it, in a low enough voice that no one else could hear. The song was really coming together.

She couldn't stay away from Coal's guitar, or the song, and both of them made her think of him. She couldn't stop thinking about his hat, and the toil and care she had put into making it just right. She knew it would anger Coal if she pulled her very distinctive Ebenezer, the International Travelette, into her yard near his GMC, where passing motorists might see it—particularly if the passing motorists were also the men Coal believed were here to kill him and anyone else involved in the trials of Angel Medina and Ray Christian and who had already proved it, according to the news, by one explosion that morning.

But if she were at her house without her truck ... wasn't that something different altogether?

With her heart starting unreasonably to pound, and her breath feeling short, Maura closed the heavy wooden guitar case and went upstairs. She looked over by the front door, where she had set the cardboard box containing Coal's hat after showing it off to Connie and the kids. Her eyes went to her dark green polyester coat with the brown fur hood, hanging by Connie's Levi coat on the rack, also by the door.

She didn't know who had absconded with both of the dogs, but neither of them was here. She was completely alone. She looked again at her coat and drew a deep breath. What was it, maybe two miles from here to her house? Only two miles. That couldn't be so far to walk, even though she knew the temperature was supposed to hit down around ten below zero tonight, and the wind was actually blowing a little, a rarity of late.

She filled her lungs with another huge breath. Her eyes bumped from the guitar case leaning against the back of Connie's chair, to the hat box, to her coat. And last, they fell to the notebook she was clutching too tight in her hand, where the precious words of her new song were written down.

Stepping almost robotically, not even feeling her feet hit the floor, Maura went to the kitchen bar. With trembling hands she tore a sheet of lined paper out of the notebook and began writing a note to Connie, telling her not to worry. She would see her tomorrow. As a last-minute thought, she put some oatmeal chocolate chip cookies she and Connie had ganged up to make earlier in the evening into a towel, then a paper bag, and slipped them into the box carrying Coal's hat.

Then, putting on her coat and wrapping a heavy blue wool scarf around her face, she pulled on thick gloves, inhaled deeply once more, picked up the hatbox and the guitar, and stepped out into the frigid February night. She felt the instant bite of tiny gremlin teeth against her cheeks and nose, and her eyes began to water, as the full force of the wind and cold struck home.

* * *

After *Charro!* ended, Coal tried to watch the news. Too much detail about the explosion that took Mike Fica's life, destroyed his van and his family, made him shut off the TV and go back to the couch to sit there in silent contemplation. By now, all the ribald humor of the Dick Parker case, and the paperwork pertaining thereto, was forgotten. Coal could think only of Mike Fica and his family, and Maura PlentyWounds and his own family.

He went to bed missing the sound of the toenails of Dobe and Shadow on the wooden floor, then their paws thumping on the brown shag carpet, as they tailed him to his room.

It might have been an hour later, or it might have been two. He lay on Maura's bed, staring at the black ceiling, wishing he was looking up at summer stars somewhere in the mountains, snuggled up in a sleeping bag, his family surrounding him. His return to Salmon sure had turned out differently from his dreams. Then again, there had been no summer yet. There had been no opportunity to go camping with his family, no matter what had happened here otherwise. Maybe he wasn't giving the valley enough of a chance. After all, the turmoil and death that had been going on here since his return couldn't go on forever ... could it? Sometime in the near future, things would surely settle down, and he would—

A light tapping on the wall outside jarred him from his reverie, and in a moment he was on his knees on the floor, his shotgun clutched in his hands.

CHAPTER FOURTEEN

Coal heard the sound on the wall outside the house again, but this time much louder, more demanding. Certainly not a sound any hired killer was likely to make outside Maura's bedroom window at ... He looked over at the clock.

Midnight!

As Coal became aware of an insistent wind worrying at the eaves, and a light pattering on the roof, he heard the sound of a woman's voice from outside, and then again. The second time he thought he heard it calling his name! The whole scene felt like the middle of a horror film.

Coal stumbled across the room, fumbling along the wall for the light switch. The flat of his hand touched it, and he almost flipped it up, then thought better of it. He made his way blind back across the room and crouched way low, then hollered through the wall. “Who’s out there?”

“It’s me, Maura!” came the muffled voice.

Coal swore, and it was not in a good-natured voice. Maura! What in the name of— It was midnight! And he had told her she could not come here until this was all over. A feeling of controlled fury swept over him and flooded out every good feeling he had been having earlier in the evening, when thinking about Maura and his family.

He managed to get back across the room and this time flipped the light switch, exploding the room into bright light and blinding himself in the process. Throwing open the door, he went down the hall, turning on the light to the front room as he leaned the shotgun against the wall, with the TV stand for support.

Unlocking both the deadbolt and the chain lock on the door, he shoved it open only to have the wind tear it out of his hand, slamming it back against the outside wall before he could catch it. He looked out into the dim light to be bitten in the face by tiny particles of frozen snow, and it took less than three seconds to feel the deep, brutal bite of the cold. A glance over at the chattering thermometer precariously nailed to one of the roof supports declared the temperature to be eight degrees below zero!

As that shocking number registered on him, another thought hit Coal, and even as he focused in on what appeared to be Maura, coming around the end of the house, he let go of the door and lurched backward into the front room again. Flipping the light back off, he grabbed the shotgun and dropped to a knee.

He didn’t have time yet to be ashamed, only shocked, that he had allowed what sounded like Maura’s voice to draw him out of the house, un-armed. What if the Mob had gotten to Maura and been using her to get his guard down? He had been wrong before, and if this damn well wasn’t Maura, whoever it was would soon be picking buckshot out from among the shards of her head.

Kneeling there with the shotgun, he scanned the yard through the open doorway.

Maura came stumbling up the porch carrying something big. As Coal stared, she came in, a big box in one hand, and a guitar case in the other.

"Shut the door," Maura said as she went past Coal and over to the couch. It sounded like she dropped the guitar before Coal could reach out and get the door shut, lock it again, then whirl to switch the light back on.

He turned on Maura, feeling barely enough confusion to keep his mouth shut—a teaspoon of confusion infused with a trough full of anger.

Maura looked a spectacle. Even in her heavy coat, the exposed skin of her upper face was an ugly, mottled red, battered by the wind, snow, and cold. Her hands trembling, she was unwrapping a heavy scarf, her eyes on the floor as if she couldn't make herself look up at him yet.

Coal was able somehow to control his anger long enough to step forward and help Maura out of her gloves and coat. He accidentally touched the skin of her hand, and in spite of the thickness of her gloves, they were chilled. But what shocked him most was the horribly ruddy skin of her face, almost a look of chilblains. This was not the look of a woman who had driven over to see him, and yet even as he became certain of this, it wasn't the same thought that came out of his mouth.

"Maura, what the hell are you doing? Somebody's going to see your truck out there! I told you you couldn't come here!" His voice was anything but soft and welcoming. He recognized that, and couldn't stop it.

Maura's mouth dropped open, and she stared at him. For a moment, she was lost for words. Then the panther within her broke free.

"What am *I* doing? Listen, Coal, this is my damn house! I'll come over here if I feel like it! There's no law that I have to let you stay here, and you sure as hell don't own me!"

Coal swore. It sounded ugly and mean, even to his own ears. He was too angry to think about caring. "I don't give a— Listen here. I don't care if it *is* your house! We had a deal. You agreed in perfectly good English that you weren't going to let anyone know we were together. What the hell were you thinking? And besides, it's midnight. I don't believe this. You need to get out there and drive back to Mom's. Right now." He was speaking in tones he wouldn't have used on an errant Marine recruit.

After staring for another long moment, her eyes jumping back and forth between Coal's as steam built within her, Maura shook her head. She didn't scream back at him, as she very well could have. Instead, her voice lowered to a deadly tone. "Wow, Coal. You arrogant son of a bitch. You know what? It's going to be pretty hard to drive home, since I didn't bring my truck here in the first place. I walked."

Coal had started to open his mouth, but he forgot what he intended to say. His teeth clacked shut. He stared. The battered, half-frozen look of the woman kept slamming into the back of his mind, but the upset side of him wouldn't acknowledge it. He wasn't thinking any of the things he should have been thinking, the things like how much Maura meant to him, and how badly he wanted to protect her, especially after all they had been through. He could feel only sheer, overpowering anger, with no rational thoughts as to why.

God was surely merciful to Coal. To both of them. It took a drawn-out moment of silence, maybe a full twenty or thirty seconds of staring at each other, before things began to come into focus. Fortunately, God had closed Coal's mouth during all that time, forbidding him from making things worse than he already had.

Coal began to notice that on Maura's cheeks trails of tears now streaked down, disappearing under her jaw as she continued to challenge his stare. Her eyes were so full of moisture he wondered how she could even see him, but she kept staring, defiantly. Finally, in a much softer voice, the voice of someone who has been so upset, so angry, that he has lost all control of himself and can barely trust himself to speak, he said, "I don't understand. You ... You walked over here? All the way from Mom's? Maura ... why?"

The woman stared at him, her chest heaving. Her lip was trembling so bad he didn't know if she would be able to speak. "To see you. To be with you. Apparently because I'm an idiot." The words sounded bitter.

"But I told you ..." His voice, and his thoughts, trailed off, and he could only stare into her eyes.

"I know what you told me. You think I haven't thought about it all night? But I ..."

"What?"

"I thought if I walked and they couldn't see my truck ..."

Coal stared at her, feeling suddenly like a terrible fool. Emotion rushed through him, an emotion one hundred and eighty degrees different from the ones he had felt moments ago.

"Maura …"

He didn't know how it happened. A minute before, he would not have believed it, and even still it was like a dream. Without any awareness of his own movement, he was across the room now, and Maura was locked in his arms. Her lips, cold as ice chips, were on his. She was kissing him, almost frantically, feverishly, and the kisses he returned were the same.

It took him a moment to realize Maura was still crying, not softly this time, but in sobs. And still she kept kissing him. And kissing. Passionately, fervently. She pushed away from him just enough to find the top button of his shirt and began unbuttoning it.

For a moment, as her frozen, fumbling hands shook, it seemed she would get frustrated and tear the buttons all loose.

And then she had his shirt completely undone and was shoving it back off his shoulders, and when it had fallen her ice-cold hands were on the bare skin of his back, and he felt it, knew it, and yet no cold registered on his mind.

The kissing never seemed to cease. Everything else took place in spite of it, around it. When Maura started to unbutton her own shirt, and his own unsure hands took over the task, he knew deep down inside it was over. He and this woman had been through too much together. Too much togetherness. Too much emotion. Too much time to think about how close they had come to death so many times without ever having fully known each other. Like two broken ice statues in the fires of passion, tonight they were melting. Falling ...

Maura's shaking fingers pried his pants belt loose without his embarrassed realization that he had gone to bed dressed in everything but his boots. She let out a strange sound, half weeping, half giggle, into his mouth, and kept kissing him. He assumed the giggle was because of his wearing the belt to bed; he was too busy kissing her to ask.

And she drew him down with her onto the couch.

Tuesday, February 6

Coal blinked his eyes open in the yet deep black of the morning, feeling several sensations, having several recollections, all flooding over him at the same time. First, it was the feel of cold on his face, mixed with absolute warmth under the covers, utter opposites that melded together in a bizarre fashion to create an unlikely yet undeniable sensation of utopia.

The frigid air from outside, the sub-zero temperature augmented by the nearly ten-mile-an-hour wind that had been so rare in the valley of late, had infiltrated the walls of the house. The furnace struggled to keep up, and he hadn't heard the fan shut off in some time. The encroaching cold that seemed to be winning the contest had put a chill on his ears, nose, and cheeks. But the warmth coursing through his body from under the covers more than made up for any cold. It was the warmth of the flannel sheets and blankets themselves, coupled with the warmth of skin to bare skin, of Maura lying against him with one leg still across his, and her right arm drooped over his midsection.

The woman was snoring quietly, her face resting on his chest, her hair in disarray. He reached over with his left hand and laid it on her arm, stirring the covers enough to let a cool rush of air from the room down inside with them. But even that failed to stir Maura, and she snored on, a soft sound that, coupled with the hot breath against the skin of his chest, only added to the bliss of the moment.

Coal's other sensations and recollections were not so blissful, yet they were not unpleasant, simply confusing and perhaps provocative of strong, deep feelings. He thought back on his recent trip with Maura through parts of four states, through major bouts of emotion, and of how strong he had proved himself to be. He had intended to keep himself strong on that trip, and he had. And somehow Maura had gone along with it, even if she didn't know where his strength came from or even why he felt such strength was necessary. He had had a feeling during much of the trip that deep down she would rather he not be strong, but weak.

There had been plenty of time to think about that trip beforehand and to prepare himself for it. But there was *no* time to prepare for Maura's appearance here in the house during the night. And also perhaps way too much time before that contemplating what the two of them might have missed on their vacation, and, in the current state of affairs, what they might miss forever, if the Mob succeeded and Coal and his compatriots failed. He and Maura hadn't discussed any of that, of course. And he suspected it likely they never would. But he was betting she might have had a lot of similar deep thoughts since returning home, and on the last leg of their trip, after checking out of their last hotel room, knowing as he did they might forever have missed the chance to connect in the ultimate, intimate way for two people to demonstrate how they feel for each other. And all because he thought he had to be so strong.

Whatever forces had culminated in what happened last night, he recalled every moment of it vividly, and he couldn't pretend to regret a single one. He had forced himself to be too strong, too virtuous, for too long. He had asked too much of himself, of a man still in his prime who has lacked the sensations of physical and emotional love for too many years. The question remaining was one he couldn't be sure he would ever know: Would Maura, when she awoke, regret what happened in the night?

And there were bigger questions, questions Coal was not ready to tackle face to face: Where did last night leave them? Would either of them feel ready to go forward with the emotions they had unleashed? Would this prove to be the proverbial one-night stand, satisfying them both to where they could now move on with separate lives? And was either of them ready to brave the conflicting logistics of trying to stitch together two disconnected families? A man with the responsibility now of caring for six children, and a woman with two teenaged boys, one of whom Coal remembered as not being exactly into the idea of having a man around who was not his father? All were questions that, in this blissful, perfect moment, Coal had no interest even in thinking about, and he wished they would go away. So he settled his mouth and nose back down into Maura's tousled hair and closed his eyes.

Later, when he woke again, light was infiltrating the blinds. It was a diffused, dirty gray light he would have held back for several more hours had he the power.

He felt Maura's body, no longer only warm, but feeling hot against his. Yet even that heat could not stop him from thinking about the Mob. In spite of every intelligent thought he had tried to keep at the forefront of his mind, he had let his guard down, and somewhere, maybe just outside, they were waiting, closing in for the kill ...

CHAPTER FIFTEEN

Coal must have blinked his eyes louder than he imagined. He was positive he didn't make any other noise, yet Maura's soft voice came from the dimness, coming out as hot breath against the bare skin of his chest.

"Good morning, Mister."

"Good morning to you."

"You slept good?"

"Pretty much like a baby."

Maura laughed. "That proves you're a man."

He lay there for a few seconds trying to decipher her words before deciding to reply. By then, he realized it was just another cryptic female-ism she was waiting impatiently to clarify for him because in his male dumbness the answer would never come to him. "Why's that?"

"Because only a man would use that saying and think it fits. Babies wake up all night wanting something. I think after you went to sleep you slept more like an old man."

She tilted her face so she could see his reaction.

He laughed, just as quick with his rebuttal as she thought she was. "How do you know I didn't wake up all night wanting something?"

That made her giggle, and she laid her cheek back on his chest again. “Okay, you got me there. So ... what did you want?”

“You.”

After a moment of silence, she slid her hand down along the length of his thigh, then pushed herself up until her face was over his. She lowered her lips, and they kissed, and the fire came over them, the fire held back too long.

Later, they lay breathless, and the cold air in the room felt good on their partially uncovered, moist skin. Maura raised her hand and stroked the side of Coal’s face. She drew in a deep breath, and it made a throaty, satisfied, chattering sound as it came back out.

Her voice was soft as linen. “Hey.”

“Hey.”

“I don’t want to ruin this moment, Coal. In fact, I’d kind of like it to last forever. But ... I have to know something. You won’t hate me now, right?”

“Hate you? How could I hate you?”

She lay quiet for a while, formulating her thoughts. “Because you’ve tried to be such a gentleman. And I’ve made it so hard for you.”

They lay breathing deeply. Coal’s heart was pounding. This was the kind of morning after conversation where men often plunged through thin ice and never came back up.

“I don’t have any regrets, Maura. Is that enough of an answer?”

“Maybe. I just want you to know I didn’t come over here last night to seduce you.”

“I wouldn’t have thought you did.”

She lay and simply breathed for a while. “I really only came to give you a present. Maybe you could say two presents.”

“Yeah?” He tried to look down to meet her eyes, but she kept her face on his chest. And that was fine too.

“Yeah. I made you something. Well, kind of two somethings, really. You want to see?”

"Right now?"

"Uh-huh."

"It sure is cold, isn't it?"

She laughed. "Oh, yeah, I guess. But someone has invented these weird coverings called clothes that you can put on and they keep you warm."

He had to return her laugh. "Oh, right. I forgot about those."

"Yes, you did. Well, I'm going to get up, so don't look."

"Me? Never!"

Maura got out into the frigid air, and he watched her while she got dressed, the most interesting part being her act of trying to shoe-horn herself into ice-cold Levi's 501 jeans. He could tell by the way she kept her eyes averted the whole time that she knew he was watching. As she buttoned the second-from-top button of her navy-blue blouse with white piping, she looked down at him. "I hope you enjoyed the show. That wasn't very gentlemanly of you."

With another laugh, he said, "Oh, I'm sorry. I guess you got me mixed up with a gentleman."

"Uh-huh. I won't let *that* happen again. Do I get a show now too?"

"Nope. I'm not getting out in that cold."

She reached down and tried to whip the covers off him, but he knew her well enough to be prepared for that and had them in a death grip. She dropped her hand and stuck her tongue out at him. "Real fair."

He laughed again. She made laughing so easy when she was in a fun-loving mood. In the back of his head, however, in spite of the moment, he had started thinking once more of things that were not so much fun. He only prayed she wouldn't see those thoughts in his eyes. He was thinking of Sam Browning and Alex Martinez. And wondering if they would get to Salmon in time to save him, or if he would have to save himself. The Mob was coming, and no amount of love-making would hold them back.

Coal watched Maura walk out of the room, then jumped up and got his underwear and Wranglers on before she could return. He was pulling his second sock on by the time she made it back, and her eyes fell on him sitting on the edge of the bed. She frowned, but it was a good-natured frown, and it made him grin back at her. "Maybe next time."

She looked his bare torso up and down. "That's okay. I'm seeing plenty." As she spoke, she leaned his guitar case up against the bed.

"That case sure looks familiar."

"Well, it probably should."

"That's a heavy load. I still can't believe you walked all that way carrying all that stuff, and in that kind of cold." In truth, although he had ordered her not to, it warmed his heart deeply to think she had done that, merely for the chance to see him.

"Well, sometimes when you're desperate ..." Her voice trailed off, and he chuckled.

"So what do you have there?" He was looking at the hat box.

"Okay, so we might still have to do some work on it, but I did the best I could. Close your eyes."

"Can I get my shirt on first?"

She paused. "Nope. I kinda like you like this."

He studied her long enough to see she was serious, so he made up his mind to freeze a little longer. "All right." And with that he closed his eyes.

He could hear her open the box, which he had been around long enough to recognize as a hat box, but of course that meant little. She could have been keeping a rabid armadillo in it for all he knew.

He heard her pant legs swishing together as she walked around the bed, and then she was in front of him. "Don't open yet."

"Yes, ma'am. I wouldn't dream of it."

"I hope you're more trustworthy than you were a while ago."

"There was more at stake that time." He laughed as she smacked him in the forehead softly with the heel of her hand, and then he felt a hat sliding down over his hair. It was a little snug, but not terribly so. Probably only one decent soaking away from a perfect fit.

"Okay, almost ready. I'm just going to take your hands and walk you over here."

He felt her grasp both his hands, and he walked with her until she stopped. Then she took one of his shoulders and turned him a little. "Okay, open."

When he opened his eyes, he was looking into a mirror that hung on the wall over her dresser. He was instantly admiring a dark gray hat that made him look like a gunfighter out of some Old West photo. "Wow! Nice! Where in the world did you get a hat like this?"

"I made it."

"Made it? What do you mean made it?"

"Well, I should say I *re*-made it. It was like your other one when I bought it, other than the bound edge. I just thought you might look good in something different than a cattleman crease."

He recalled Maura making comments more than once since they had known each other about him trying a hat other than his silver belly cattleman. She must have gotten impatient with him.

Turning his head from side to side, and pushing a too-long strand of hair behind one ear, he said, "I like it. A lot. You really do know what you're doing at that hat steamer, don't you?"

"I hope so. You really like it?"

"I really do."

She smiled warmly, admiring him. "It looks perfect on you. Makes me want to throw you down on the bed again."

"Right, and take a chance on breaking a nice hat brim?"

With a giggle, she said, "Don't worry, this isn't one of those cheapie hats. It might bend, but it isn't going to break!"

He turned fully to her. “There’s only one problem I can figure out with this hat.”

“What?” Her eyes looked concerned.

“I’m not sure I can kiss you with it on.”

She stared at him, then jerked the hat off and threw it over the side of the bed. “In that case!” And she wrapped him in her arms and once more tried to start a fire with the friction from their lips.

When the kissing was over, they went in the kitchen, and Maura turned the furnace up. “Want some breakfast?”

“I’d love some. And then we’ve got to figure out how to get you out of this house without anyone seeing you.”

Her expression went a little sad. And perhaps a little frightened as well. But if that were true, she hid it behind her next words: “I still have one more thing, remember?”

“Oh! Yeah, right. The guitar.”

“Yeah. But let me get you some breakfast first.”

“Okay, if you’d like. In the meantime, I’m going outside to do a little reconnaissance.”

He put on his shirt and boots, then shrugged into his heavy blue and black buffalo plaid coat and wool gloves. He went to a window and pried a slat of the blinds downward, peering outside to study every inch of the yard. All was quiet and still. Picking up a pair of binoculars he had hung by the strap from one of the coat hooks at the front door, he stepped outside and almost instantly froze his nostrils together when he inhaled. Other than the wind not being as high as it had been in South Dakota, it felt even colder here than he remembered it being on their trip.

Stepping out to the barn, he climbed into the loft and threw open the front doors, which were opened to access the loft when hay was delivered. He sat a ways back in the shadows, on a bale of hay, and brought the binoculars to his eyes.

With painstaking care, he glassed the other side of the road. He studied the foothills, looking for anything that seemed out of place, any movement. He spied a herd of deer, browsing slowly along the far slope.

For fifteen minutes or more his eyes picked at everything he could see from this vantage point. Then he went back down and studied the layout from other places around the yard. He never saw anything that worried him or even interested him, other than a nice bay quarter horse a few hundred yards away across the road that he had never seen before, and a rangy white one, obviously a gray in its younger days, that put him in mind of old Cody. The thought of Cody made him nostalgic. He wondered how much longer that big boy was going to hold out, especially if there were going to be very many days this cold.

Finally, with the cold having made its way through his gloves, and the tip of his nose having almost no further feeling, he returned to the house. It felt excruciatingly warm, and the aroma of bacon and eggs almost made him swoon.

Maura looked up at him, watching his face for any sign. “Everything okay?”

He shrugged. “Yeah, as far as I can see. Maybe we got lucky for a change.”

She laughed. “Well, I thought that went without saying.”

“Ha ha. Wow, little miss, I think I’m starting to see a naughty side of you I didn’t know was there.”

“Want me to stop?”

“Did you hear me say that?”

“Okay then.”

He grinned. “Sure smells good. Is it ready?”

“It is, but I heated up the oven, and I’m putting it in there until I give you your other present.”

“Oh. Okay. Let’s see it.”

“You’re getting pretty demanding.”

“Yep.”

With a laugh, she went over to where she had laid his guitar on the couch with the spiral notebook. She picked it up. "Okay, you sit on the couch."

He obeyed. She looked so serious he didn't figure he had any other choice.

When he was seated comfortably, she pulled a stool over and sat in front of him. "Okay, now just remember, this isn't very polished. But I wrote something for you."

"You— Really? You wrote ... like a song?"

"Well, maybe *sort* of like a song."

They both laughed.

But Coal wasn't laughing when Maura sang her song to him. Although it wasn't polished, as she had warned him, and she was a little nervous playing and singing it, and even messed up the lyrics and the chords in a spot or two, the song brought out deep emotions in Coal as a lover of horses. She had titled it "My Horse," and it told the story of a man whose best companion was his horse, but that horse was now going lame, and was close, as she sang, to crossing over the "last Great Divide". It seemed as if she had been reading his mind.

In her slightly husky but very alluring singing voice, Maura picked the guitar and sang:

My horse, he knows me; he knows what I love;
He takes me to places that I'm dreaming of;
My horse understands me, he knows what I dream;
My horse is half-human, or that's how it seems.

He's been with me a lifetime, since his mother gave up
And I bottle-fed him, like a young, orphaned pup.
He's carried my saddle, and my worn-out old frame,
But now my old horse is at last goin' lame.

My horse loves the canyons and the clear mountain springs;
The verdant, pure meadows, the geese on the wing.

We've ridden dark trails where the lightning bugs glow
And hills billowed over with blankets of snow.
We've helped bunch the cattle all up in the fall;
Yeah, my horse and I have about seen it all.

He could fly like a rocket, down some desert dirt track,
Kicking dust up behind us, with his mane flowing back;
He'll share my warm fire, in some fold in the hills,
And I'll tell him my troubles—I don't need no one else.

He's my partner, my compadre, my very best friend;
But I fear our last trail is close to its end;
But I'll never forget how he's been by my side,
And I'll always think of him long after he's died.

My horse loves the canyons and the clear mountain springs;
The verdant, pure meadows, the geese on the wing.
We've ridden dark trails where the lightning bugs glow
And hills billowed over with blankets of snow.
We've helped bunch the cattle all up in the fall;
Yeah, my horse and I have about seen it all.

My horse loves the prairies, where the meadowlark sings,
The high mountain passes that green up in the spring;
He'll head for the barn if I ask him to go,
But he'd rather stay high up, with the towns down below;
Through blizzards and dust storms, he's been my best ride;
Now my old horse is headed for that last Great Divide.

They tell me that a cowboy is not s'posed to cry,
But I'll be spilling my heart out when this old buckskin dies.

They tell me that a cowboy is not s'posed to cry,
But I'll be spilling my heart out when this old buckskin dies.

My horse, he knows me; he knows what I love;
He takes me to places that I'm dreaming of;
My horse understands me, he knows what I dream;

My horse is half-human, or that's how it seems.

And I'll be spilling my heart out when my old partner dies.

Coal had to fight in a couple of places to keep tears out of his eyes, both because of thinking of Cody, and Prince, his father, and because of the beauty and feeling in Maura's voice. The song even reminded him a little of himself. Marines claim not to cry, and although it had been years since Coal's days as an enlisted Marine, he didn't always succeed, but he did his best to keep that standard. With Maura's heartfelt performance and wonderfully written words, it wasn't easy.

And perhaps it was harder because, deep down, Coal knew this was the end for him and Maura, the end until who knew when. She had disregarded his order not to come here, she had put herself in grave danger doing it, and she had caused them both to cross a line he had fought for a long time to hold. If he could manage to get them both safely away from her place this morning, he would not be coming back here until he could be sure his danger with the Mob was over—and there was a big question that he wasn't sure could even be answered: When one came into the Mob's spotlight, did that light ever extinguish while he was still alive?

CHAPTER SIXTEEN

When Maura suggested showering, she had a spark in her eye. Coal pretended not to notice and told her he needed to get to work and was already dressed anyway. Then he had to continue pretending he didn't notice the disappointment in her eyes and the ensuing change in her demeanor as she grew extra quiet and stopped stealing furtive glances at him and making eyes when he saw her.

While the woman was showering, Coal took a chance and made a quick phone call out to Jim Lockwood's house, then hung up before there could be any chance of a call being traced no matter how technologically advanced the Las Vegas Mob might be. When Maura came out of the bathroom quite a while later, her makeup was done, and she was fully dressed.

With his heart pounding, Coal began the conversation no man wants to start, at least not with a woman who has gotten into his heart.

"You know we can't do this again, right?"

Maura shrugged, and for a moment she remained quiet.

"Maura? Talk to me."

"Yes, I know."

"And you understand why?"

"I guess ... No, not really."

He drew in a breath. "I could be gone tomorrow. Even today. I could walk outside and take a bullet."

For the first time since the start of the conversation, she met his eyes directly. "And how is that different from any other time before this? Or after the Mob's gone?"

He stared back at her, his gears shifting. Of course she was right, if they wanted to stretch it. In fact, anyone, any time, could have his or her life snuffed out. He had to spin the wheels of his mind for a while before he could reply.

"You know that's different. I know what you mean, but look at it like this: Any normal day, we both live our lives like two people walking down the middle of a country road. Sure, a car could come along and hit us, but the odds are pretty low. Right now, I'm like a man running back and forth across a crowded interstate. My odds are high. Really high."

"And if we aren't together anymore, that's going to make it easier for me when you're gone?" She spoke like a woman who had been holding on to that question, knowing it would be like tossing a grenade into his argument.

He gave a tight smile, trying to be patient, and trying to be understanding. "Maura, you've got to understand. I'm standing in a mine field. I'm going to have to have every edge to get out of it. I can't be thinking of other things. I can't be watching out for other people. I've got to concentrate on myself. I'm trying to keep you safe the only way I know how. You're going to have to trust me."

Maura was silent, and he instantly knew he had struck a chord. Without speaking, and obviously trying to hold back her emotions, she walked to him stiffly and threw her arms around him. "Coal, I'm really scared."

"I know. So am I."

They drove away from the house with Maura toting Coal's new hat, still in its box, his guitar in its case, and carrying a suitcase full of clothing. As for Coal, he was carrying her promise that if he stayed at her house she would not come back to see him until he told her it was safe. What he didn't tell her was that he probably wouldn't stay there again anyway. He felt the need to be moving, staying at different locations around the valley, never giving the

Mob hitmen the sure knowledge of where they were going to find him next.

Keeping a careful eye on his rearview mirror, he drove out to Jim Lockwood's and went inside with Maura. While Betty served Maura coffee in the kitchen, Coal and Jim spoke alone in the back hallway. It was decided that Jim didn't need his Thunderbird today, and Coal could park his GMC around behind the back of the house and take the Bird into town. That way, he could take Maura back to Connie's without anyone knowing what vehicle to look for.

"I can't thank you enough, Jim."

"That's what brothers do," Jim replied. "Just try to keep my baby safe. And yourself too."

It was a little under three miles from Lockwoods' back to Connie's place, but when Coal left he turned the other direction. Maura threw a glance his way but said nothing.

He drove until he could dredge up some of that old Marine courage. "Hey." She looked at him. He suspected because "American Pie" was playing in Jim's tape deck, so good entertainment abounded inside the car, there was no reason to talk, and she didn't. But for him there was a lot of reason.

"I'm not sure what happened last night. I didn't mean to do that."

She still didn't speak. And she didn't reach over and take his hand as he had hoped she might.

"Maura, I guess we've changed some rules in our friendship. And now I'm not sure how to play."

"Well, it sounds pretty simple. You said I couldn't see you anymore." Her voice sounded flat. Not unfriendly, but more ... emotionless.

"Maura, before you I've never been with anyone but Laura." He might have already told her that during their trip. He couldn't remember, although he remembered thinking it.

"What do you think *I* am, Coal?" This time her reply was instant. "Some kind of slut? Other than my childhood, and that beast, no one ever touched me but the man who fathered my boys. So what are you trying to say? That we were wrong, and you wish you could go back and send me away last night? Is that it?"

Coal felt like he had stepped right on top of one of those hidden mines in the field he had been trying to make his way out of. He was standing on top of it now and had to figure out how to step off and keep from being exploded into a million pieces.

"I wouldn't go back," he replied quietly. And he meant it.

She sat silent for a long time, and he knew without looking over at her that it was because she was struggling against strong emotion. "Do you regret last night?" he asked her once he understood she was waiting for something more from him.

"Of course I don't. Not as long as you don't." Hearing this, he ached to reach out and take her hand, but he didn't. He was thinking about his childhood teachings, and principles that any Christian church would dole out in plenty. After what they had done last night, now the only decent thing to do was for them to get married—wasn't it? At least that was what a lot of folks would say. But what about all the kids? What about her boys, and the trouble with her ex-husband? A man and a woman in their position didn't simply walk into a church or a courthouse and get married on a whim, not if they wanted to have a good chance of their marriage being a successful one.

Coal thought about all the difficult implications of starting a life with Maura, and he imagined she must be thinking about it too, if she was smart. But suddenly he knew one thing: This wasn't the time to hash it out, as he had set out to do. If he survived the Mob, they would have all the time in the world to sort things through. His survival was the next big thing he had to concentrate on, and everything he had already told her was true. They had to fight to stay apart until he was safe to come for her.

With no argument, and no questions from Maura, Coal found a driveway to turn around in, and he headed the black Thunderbird back toward town. The ache in his heart would just have to stay there until he felt safe again, and knew he could keep Maura and his family from harm's way.

Even as he thought this, a dark blue Jaguar with two people inside drove past heading toward Leadore, and inside Coal swore.

He had to find out more about that car.

It hit Coal that in trading the GMC off for Jim's Thunderbird he had sacrificed his link to dispatch. In the pickup, he had a radio. In Jim's car he was just another civilian—no radio, no red light, no shotgun ... nothing he needed as a working sheriff. But then again, if whoever was in that Jaguar was after him, they would have no clue they had just driven right past him.

His first instinct was to find another turn-around and head southeast again. He slowed way down, looking for a wide spot. In the mirror he saw nothing but a semitruck bearing down on him. The truck soon veered around him, giving him a couple of short toots of his horn, which Coal took to be friendly. He glanced back, and the next vehicle in line was a red passenger car. Taking a breath to calm his nerves, he pressed down harder on the accelerator. The big 429 Thunderjet engine responded, taking them up to seventy-five miles an hour with no obvious effort, and the Ford floated up the road like a big boat on smooth waters. In no time, the red car faded behind, and no dark car ever passed it while Coal was watching.

At Jim's road, he made the corner way faster than was prudent, asking silently for Jim's forgiveness, and then stopped a ways up on the side of the road. This was a quiet road, and although he was partly out in his lane, he doubted anyone would come along soon.

He saw the red car pass. Next a blue one, but light blue. Then a blue-black Jaguar.

Maura had been silent this whole time, but she was alert and looking around. She seemed to be doing her best to seem unconcerned, but her curiosity was getting the best of her.

"Is something wrong?"

"I'm not sure. There's a car I've been seeing a lot of. It just passed us after we turned around and headed back toward town, and now it's headed that way too. I also saw it pass your house after I pulled in there."

Maura remained silent, and he didn't look at her. He didn't want to see her fear, but by now it must be there. She was too smart for it not to be.

Turning the wheel slightly left, Coal got back out on the road and gunned it. They neared another road, Old Lemhi Road, and Coal made the hard left turn. He spared no gas pedal here, going around curves way too fast, and before long he found himself coming up on Savage Lane from the back way. Here, he applied some serious brake around the corner, almost going into a fishtail as they neared the house.

He skidded to a halt on the loose gravel in front of the driveway. "I'm going to let you off here, okay? Just jump out and throw all your stuff out in the yard, then get up to the house as fast as you can." He met her eyes and hated the fear that this ride had written all over her face.

"Is everything going to be okay, Coal?"

"It will. I promise." He reached over and squeezed her hand, and she bunched her jaws and jumped her glance away from him, fighting emotion. "Go!"

When Maura had her suitcase, the guitar case and hat box out on the ground, and her door slammed, Coal hit the gas and sped down Savage Lane to Highway 28, where he sat to wait for several cars to pass. There was a lot of industry going on around the valley that year, and this time of morning traffic was brisk.

When the last car for a ways out went by, he spun out onto the highway again, heading back toward the little wide spot in the road known as Baker, where Jim and Betty Lockwood lived.

At Jim's, he pulled around to the back of the house again, then got out to stand at the corner of the house watching the road. A lot of traffic passed in the next frigid ten minutes, but none of them was a dark blue Jaguar. That didn't surprise him. Unless they had a bug on him, he had no idea how they could have followed him here. But there were a lot of other things about that car he couldn't explain.

* * *

Scabs Ravioli swore and slapped the dash. With a last study of his surroundings, he saw the house coming up where the sheriff had pulled in the day before. He felt the Jaguar slow, and commanded, "Drive on past!"

Menny Marcello stepped down on the gas again and drove a quarter mile. "Who do you think the dame was?"

Scabs shrugged.

"No idea?"

Scabs shrugged harder. "How should I know?" His voice was hard. And with his humor all gone he even forgot to use his partner's new nickname, which he was having a fun time wearing out on him. Well, he had to find a way to resurrect it.

They were coming up on another road sign a ways farther on the right, and he said, "Slow it down. What's that? Three Mile Road? Hey, take that one, would you? Twinkie?"

"Judas, Scabs. Enough with that already," Menny replied as he swerved off too fast onto Three Mile Road. "I swear I ain't never eatin' no Twinkie for the rest of my life. Least not if you're around."

Scabs chuckled. "Aw come on. You know it's cute."

Menny nodded, trying to be patient. "What now?"

"Just keep drivin'. Let's see where this takes us."

They went up a small distance and veered left to start following a small river, probably the same one they had been crossing numerous times out on Highway 28. If so, it was called the Lemhi River. They paralleled it for a while, then crossed it, and shortly came up to a Tee, where their Three Mile Road ended and a Lemhi Road went either way.

"Take a right," said Scabs, and Menny did, without comment.

They went along in silence until coming to Geertson Road, which Menny casually drove past.

"Hey! Geertson! Stop and back it up. Geertson, that's the other side of the sheriff's place."

Menny stopped, and after checking in his rearview mirror he threw it in reverse and sped backward for fifty feet, then spun the car expertly to put it in line for taking the corner.

Scabs grabbed his stomach and screwed his eyes shut for a moment as the car lurched forward. "Jeez, Twinkie, do you have to do that?"

"Do what?"

"Go backward so fast. I'm gonna lose my breakfast."

Menny let out a laugh. "I'll start driving backward fast everywhere if you keep callin' me Twinkie."

Scabs gave him a sour face, but he didn't reply. He wasn't going to trade away Menny's funny new nickname *that* easily.

When they got back to Highway 28, Scabs had Menny sit there for quite a while, watching cars pass. After twenty or more minutes, he told him to head on to the sheriff's house.

"So what about that dame?"

"Oh, give me a break, Twinkie! You back on that again?"

"Well, what about her? What if she goes back to the house before the sheriff does?"

"Is that what you're worried about?"

Menny gave him a blank stare, then looked away, frowning. "Yeah, I guess I am, sort of. I mean, I've never hit the wrong person."

"Well, she ain't, all right? She won't go back there before he does. You saw how she snuck in there like an alley cat in the middle of the night. What would make her go back there if he isn't even there?"

From across the road at the edge of the foothills they had been sitting in a stolen pickup the night before, a four-wheel-drive pickup they had hot-wired in one of the neighborhoods in town because they didn't want to get the Jaguar stuck out in the boondocks. They had returned the pickup in the wee hours of the morning, with its owner none the wiser, before walking a few blocks away to pick up the Jaguar and heading back to their hotel.

While sitting in the idling pickup, trying to stay awake as the too-effective heater lulled them into lethargy, they tried to keep an eye on Sheriff Savage's house through an infrared scope. Scabs had been shocked wide-awake when Menny shook him to tell him some woman had come walking up the road carrying a square package and what appeared to be a guitar case and gone behind the sheriff's house. Not much later, with Scabs watching the scope, the front door of the house flew open, and a man—obviously the sheriff—appeared. The woman came from the end of the house and went inside.

She had never come back out in the four more hours they dared remain watching.

Menny thought about his partner's question. What would make the woman go back to the house if the sheriff, obviously her lover, wasn't home? It was a good question, but ... He had seen stranger things. And the thought made him queasy. He was afraid of how killing the wrong person, especially some dame, would affect the rest of his life.

"Okay, Scabs, but what if she did? What then?"

“Judas priest. Well, we can’t account for everything—Twinkie. Come on. Lighten up. It’ll all work out. All right, man, pull in there,” he said as they approached the house.

“You sure?”

“Of course I’m sure! Pull in, dummy!”

Menny jerked the wheel and drove up to the front of the house. Both men scrambled out, and while Menny ran and opened the trunk with a spare key, snatching out a cardboard box, Scabs got behind the wheel of the car.

“I’ll be back in five or ten minutes. Be waiting around the back of the house, and when I honk, you come runnin’ an’ jump in. But don’t show yourself until I honk. We can’t afford havin’ anyone see us. If this works, we’ll be headed home real soon.”

He pulled away and swore with a grim smile as he remembered he had forgotten to say “Twinkie”.

CHAPTER SEVENTEEN

Coal was pretty sure he had accomplished his purpose by swapping Jim cars. He had gotten Maura back home safe and thrown off whoever was following him by driving an unfamiliar automobile long enough to do the job. Yet somehow the people in the blue Jag, and at this point both common sense and instinct told him they were the guys who were here to kill him, had caught the swap and gotten on his tail fairly quick.

One thing he knew he should have done, looking back. He should have lost the silver belly hat. Between the hat and his uncommon size, it wasn't altogether unlikely they had been stopped somewhere and spotted him inside the Thunderbird when he came by. He would be more careful from here on. But he was satisfied that thanks to all the other traffic on the road, at least this time he had pulled it off. Maura was safe. That is unless the name Savage Lane led them to go poking around there, where Connie's house and the Ledbetters' were the only two residences on the road.

He was on 28, racing back toward town, when he first got the idea to call in an APB on the dark blue Jag. He didn't have the plate, but he hadn't seen any other Jaguars in Salmon, dark blue or otherwise, so plate or no plate, spotting this one should be easy. No sooner had he called for dispatch to put out the bulletin to all agencies than he saw Maura's house ahead. He was thinking about stopping, although he wasn't exactly sure why, when the radio speaker began to crackle, and soon he heard Nadine's early morning voice: *Salmon dispatch calling Sheriff Savage. Salmon dispatch to the Sheriff.*

He snatched up the mic as he flew past Maura's with only a glance around her yard. It all looked pretty much as it had when he and Maura left, although at this speed that didn't mean much.

"This is the sheriff!" he almost yelled into the mic.

Good morning, Sheriff. Hey, when you get into town will you call me, ASAP?

"Sure. Can you give me a clue what it's about?"

I'm afraid so. It's in reference to Charlie and Bernice Cain.

"All right. It'll be maybe five minutes." He looked at his watch and stepped down deeper on the gas.

Coal was coming up Courthouse Drive when something hit him, and he swore. He had left the judge's paperwork on Richard Parker back at Maura's! He swore again and swerved into the parking lot, almost hitting a car on its way out. As he recognized young Vic Yancey's car, and Vic behind the wheel, he squealed to a stop. Vic had stopped too, and he waited until Coal backed up next to him.

"Hey, Vic. Sorry about the crappy driving. You all right?"

"Sure, Coal. Something wrong?"

"No, I just— Hey, hold on. I know you're off duty, but could you do me a big favor? Maybe a favor for both of us."

"Sure, anything."

"Pull back in, would you? I've got to make a quick phone call, and I may bring you out on a call if you're interested. You game?"

"Sure!" It wasn't often that Coal had a chance to see Vic so excited about anything. In fact, unless he was in the office pretty bright and early, he seldom had a chance to see him at all. Coal parked and almost ran down the stairs to put the phone call in to Nadine's house, where she kept the radio set she dispatched by on her shift, just as Flo did on hers. He saw Vic pull back into the lot and park as the phone started ringing.

Lemhi County Dispatch, Nadine speaking.

"Nadine! Coal."

Oh, hey, Coal. So we got a call especially for you from Charlie Cain. I don't know if you want to mess with this, but—

"What's it about?" he cut her off.

Well, I guess you know him, or he says you do anyway. He wants to see you, Coal, and he said it's really important. He said if he doesn't see you, and only you, he can't say what might happen.

Inside, Coal swore, but he didn't let on to Nadine. "Yeah, I know Charlie—unfortunately. Okay, I'll go out. Can you call him and let him know I'm on my way?"

Sure. And Coal, I could hear a woman crying in the background. I'm pretty sure it was Bernice.

"All right, Nadine, thanks. I'm on it." He was hanging up the phone as Vic walked in. He didn't even take the time to let him know he wouldn't be able to take him along after all. He had to try to catch Maura before she left for work.

The phone at Connie's rang and rang. After twelve or more rings, he finally gave up and slammed the handset down. Once more, he managed not to swear out loud.

Vic, in a nervous tone, said, "Everything all right, Coal?"

"Yeah. Well, no, not really. Hey, Vic, I have to apologize for getting you back in here. I was going to take you on a call with me, but it sounds like it's something I have to go out to alone, or it could lead to more trouble."

Of course Vic's curiosity was piqued, but he held his tongue.

Coal started for the door, then stopped. "You know what, though? There is one thing you could do. I forgot some really important paperwork out at Maura PlentyWounds's house, and I promised the judge I'd get it to him as soon as possible. I'm sure Maura's on her way into work at McPherson's right now. I couldn't get her on the phone. Will you do me a huge favor before you go home and stop down there at McPherson's? Tell Maura I'll ..."

He was going to say he would take her out to dinner as payment, but he realized under the circumstances that would sound like a tease.

"Just tell her this is hugely important and see if she can get off work and go back out to her house. I left the papers in a folder on the end table by the couch. If she can get them back in here and take them up to Judge Sinclair's office just tell her ... Tell her I'll owe her bigtime."

"I'd be happy to help, Coal. Good luck with whatever you're going on."

Feeling like a heel, Coal drove the GMC out Highway 93 toward Montana, where Charlie and Bernice Cain lived in a little log house Coal's grandfather had built around the turn of the century, and the Cains had inhabited ever since. Since it was at least a one-way drive of fifteen minutes or so, if the roads were clear, and that river road didn't leave a lot of room for driving errors, he settled back in his seat, pulled in a deep breath, and tried to think in advance of some magical words he could use on Charlie. He prayed the old guy hadn't been drinking. Especially at this time of morning, he only drank if he was thinking of killing himself—or someone else close to him ...

* * *

Scabs Ravioli skidded into the yard at Maura's house after going down the road a few minutes, then turning around and starting back. He was laying on the horn, and Menny Marcello came running from behind the house with a worried look on his face.

Throwing the door open and leaping in, he hadn't even gotten the door latched before Scabs was peeling out of the yard. "What the hell, brother! I thought we weren't supposed to be drawing attention to ourselves."

"Like hell!" As Scabs flew out onto the highway and gunned it toward town, he looked over at Menny. "I'm glad I just barely got the radio turned on." He pointed down to the radio set they'd been using to monitor local traffic.

"Why?"

"Because the sheriff just called in an APB on the Jag!"

Menny turned and looked up the road toward town. "Then why the hell you goin' this way? Straight into town!"

"We've gotta make a run for Challis, man, and fast. We try to head out on that long stretch to Idaho Falls, they'll nail us to the wall for sure."

"What about the Challis cops? And their county guys?"

Scabs thought about that for a moment, and then a sick look washed over his face, and he swore violently. "Well, I guess we're headin' for Montana." He and Menny had known all along this was going to be the most dangerous part of the job: The only escape was over one of three long, lonely roads, all of them long enough to get a chopper in gear and nail them before they could reach any place of perceived safety. And if it wasn't a chopper, it was going to be a road cop, and a running gun battle, at best.

Scabs growled cuss word after cuss word as he stared at the road ahead. He and Menny had scoured all the maps of the area, including the layout of Salmon. There was no easy way out. No matter which way they turned, it was going to be a miracle if they got out of this unscathed.

By the time they were coming into the edge of town, Scabs was pouring sweat. Menny, stiff as a surfboard beside him, had his pistol in his hand, and he seemed to be trying to squeeze it into molten steel.

Ahead of them, they both saw the flash of a red overhead light, a cop car on the side of the road. They were going to have to drive right past it!

Scabs swore again. "This is it, brother!"

"Turn!" yelled Menny. "Take a right!"

A road sign registered on Scabs as they were in danger of passing it, and without signaling he veered over and made the corner. The sign said Lemhi Road. It headed toward the mountains—away from Salmon.

* * *

Coal stopped out on Highway 93, looking between the rows of cottonwood trees that lined either side of the gravel drive into the Cain place. The property looked quiet right now. An aging, rusted out Dodge "truck of many colors" sat right in front of the front door like a great big banner announcing what kind of a place this was. Redneck all the way.

Sort of Coal's kind of place. But he didn't wear the redneck crown of kings that Charlie Cain did. No man could wear that crown with more honor than old Charlie, who would have been living off raccoon, opossum, and skunk soup if he had his way.

Steeling himself, Coal turned the pickup and drove on in. He didn't know whether his brand-new looking GMC should be proud, or embarrassed, to be parked next to Cain's, which didn't have an inch of shine left anywhere on it.

Before getting out, Coal obeyed old habit and once more pulled out his .44, checking the loads. Of course it was full of six. But too many nightmares with empty guns in them had trained him to keep on checking.

Coal knocked on the door, hoping Charlie wasn't drinking, and hoping he looked out the window first before blasting through the door with a shotgun.

The door cracked open, and a gray-whiskered face peered out, pale blue eyes bleary. "Hey! Coal Savage!" Now the door flew open wide, and there stood Charlie, wearing a red and black plaid shirt, the kind made famous in Charles Russell hunting art, with ragged Levi's held up by suspenders. He didn't appear to have shaved in days, and his face was thatched with silver.

There was no sign of his wife Bernice.

"I can't believe you akshully come, Coal. Bud, come on in. Come in! I made some coffee for just in case they found ya."

Coal grinned and shook Charlie's outstretched hand. "I hope you remembered how I like it, Charlie."

Charlie guffawed, tucking his chin. "Shoot! You like it just like I do—strong as a ox! How c'd I fergit? Come on, Coal. Come in outta that cold. Man, I ain't seen cold like this here in a tortoise's age."

Coal had to let out a laugh as he stepped in and Charlie shut the door behind him. "That's pretty original, Charlie. Everybody else calls it a coon's age."

"Well, I read a book where they said tortoises live longer," said Charlie, laughing with glee.

Coal kind of doubted that. He would have to have some kind of proof that Charlie could actually read.

"So what's going on this morning, Charlie?" Coal asked, hoping to put off a forthcoming invitation for him to sit down on one of Charlie's couches, where he was pretty sure Charlie was raising livestock when no one was around to see it. The smell of this place alone was enough to make Coal want to go take a bath in a snowdrift.

"Oh, nothin' much. Just wanted to see you."

"You— You're joking, right? See me about what? Dispatch told me— Surely you didn't go through all this trouble to—"

Coal heard the back door open, and Charlie turned toward it. It slammed shut, and Charlie yelled, "Hey, Ma, git in here. Coal come out t' see us."

Bernice came in, bringing with her whatever remained of hair that looked to be a mixture of dirty blond, silver, white, black, and gunmetal gray. Coal never could quite get a handle on what color her hair had been originally, but like now she always seemed bent on letting him get as close a look as possible.

"Oh, Coal, my sweetheart!" The old lady, who had looked seventy-five for as far back as Coal could recall, came rushing at him with arms outstretched, her pale eyes beaming at him far bigger than they should have been through lenses with heavy black frames. Coal cringed but met her embrace head-on, smelling dust, ammonia, and maybe rose water in her hair even though he had tried to hold his breath. He swore he wouldn't eat again for days.

"Hi, Bernice. Sure is good to see you." He couldn't help feeling a little dishonest, for although she really was like the smelly old hound that lay out back in the filthy dust of so many yards of the world and made it known far and wide that no one in the universe could be happier to see anyone, the smell and everything that came with visits to the Cains' just didn't make it all that enticing. Memorable, yes.

"You too," Bernice replied. And Coal had no doubt she meant it. "Say, I have somethin' for you." She pointed a finger at him. "You stay there, an' I'll be right back."

Coal was more than happy to stay standing where she had figuratively nailed him. He silently prayed again that Charlie wouldn't offer him a seat.

"Oh, boy, the old woman has somethin' yer gonna like, Coal. Boy, I'll say!"

He had no more than said this when Bernice walked back in. Coal almost jumped backward when he saw her holding a huge, heavy-looking double-barrel shotgun with barrels seriously browned with age. He sighed with relief when he realized the bores directed right at him had been only an accident.

"What do you have there, Bernice?"

"It's a shotgun, Coal."

Coal had to hold back a laugh. "Oh. You wanted to show it to me, huh?"

"No, I want to *give* it to ya, honey."

Coal stood silent, looking from the shotgun to Bernice. "I'm not sure I understand. That's a neat old weapon, Bernice. Why would you want me to have it?"

"Oh, shoot, hon. We ain't gonna live forever, you know. This belonged to my grandpa. It's a ten-gauge. Winchester. Made in 1878, or thereabouts."

Coal didn't know quite how to respond. He had come out here expecting to talk Charlie out of a suicide attempt, as Jim Lockwood had had to do so many times during his career, and as Coal had done a couple of times coming out with Jim.

"Well ..." Coal looked almost helplessly from Bernice to Charlie. "I'm not sure what to say but thanks a million. That's a beautiful old gun."

Charlie laughed gleefully. "Well, don't get all choked up about it. Old woman thinks I'm gonna shoot her with that thing someday. Ha!" He looked over at Bernice, who was scowling back at him. He ignored her and leaned in closer as if she wouldn't hear, speaking in a conspiratorial tone. "But I'd never shoot her. She makes too good o' biscuits!" He let out another laugh.

As Bernice thrust the shotgun out insistently at Coal, he took it with a smile and thanks. What else was he to do? And then, of course, they insisted he sit down on the couch and have coffee. It was far too long sitting in the urine and hair and other animal sign on the couch—at least he prayed it was all from animals—before the Cains decided Coal might have other chores to do as county sheriff and allowed him to go.

But he didn't go far. Just as he was reaching for the front doorknob, the phone rang, and Charlie said, "Hey, Coal, hold on jus' a minute, pard! Don't leave 'out sayin' g'bye."

Coal's fingers paused on the doorknob, and he wanted to curse but held it inside. He had been so close!

"Howdy—Cain home." Charlie stood with the phone to his ear, listening, then looked up at Coal. "Oh, sure. Sure he is. Standin' right here, jus' gittin' ready t' leave. You wanna speak at 'im? Okay, hon, jus' a second." Charlie looked at Coal and held out the phone to him. "Funny, son—it's for you."

Confused, then realizing Nadine knew he was out here, he picked up the phone. It smelled like cigarettes, beer, and the worst kind of morning breath.

"Hello."

Coal! Coal, you need to get back to town.

He should have let her finish, but he didn't. "What's going on, Nadine?"

I've been trying to call you on the radio for ten minutes, maybe more. We had another explosion. Blew up a house out toward your place.

Coal froze. He felt a chill run over his entire body, and his vision blurred. "A— Did you say an explosion?" Of course he had heard her very clearly. He was only hoping she would tell him it was some kind of sick joke.

Yes, and ... She was going to say something else, but she stopped herself. *Coal, you just need to hurry on back, okay?*

Heart pounding, breath coming hard, Coal almost dropped the shotgun. "Nadine, do you know any more about what house it was?"

Uh ... No, not really. And Coal knew on the instant that she was lying. *Just hurry back.*

The line went dead. When he tried to call back, he got only a busy signal. And out on the road, calling dispatch on the radio, he got nothing. Nothing but radio silence.

Nadine was ignoring his calls. She had a great big reason not to want to talk to him.

* * *

Grant Fairboune, with his hair sticking everywhere and his feet bare, dropped the phone back on the hook. His little darling Becky was staring at him as were the three older children.

"Honey, what is it?"

Although Grant had worked late, when the phone call came in, the dispatcher's voice sounded urgent, and Becky didn't think she could ignore it, so she woke Grant up regretfully. From there on, she had listened only to his side of the phone conversation, but she read the sick shock on his face, and it had transferred to her own.

"Another bomb, they think."

"No! Who was it?"

"They don't know yet, but it's out toward Coal's place. Hey, listen, hon, I gotta go." With his eyes still half-focused and swollen from too little sleep, he started looking around for his clothes.

Becky scrambled to get everything into one place for him as the children hung on her like bits of Velcro. Finally, Grant settled his black hat on his head and blinked his eyes, trying to clear them.

He looked down at his wife. "You sure look beautiful today, babe."

When he left the room, Becky was crying.

CHAPTER EIGHTEEN

At last, Coal heard traffic coming over the radio. Even in his state of near panic, it took him only a sentence to recognize his old friend Bob Wilson.

Salmon PD, number 2, calling Sheriff Savage. Sheriff, you still out there?

"I'm here! Talk to me, Bob."

There was a pause, long enough that Coal almost got back on. Then the line crackled again. *Hey, can you find a house and stop, Coal? Get by a phone? Then radio me. I'm going to run over to the house next door, and I'll call you to exchange phone numbers as soon as I can. Salmon PD out.*

Coal's eyes dodged left and right. He saw a little house, a newer-looking, prim white place with dark blue trim, a place he didn't recognize, built in a meadow where he used to watch winter elk roaming around looking for feed. He pulled in there too fast and slid to a halt on a sheet of ice, dangerously near their new concrete steps.

Jumping out, he ran up and knocked on the door. In half a minute there had been no answer, and he wasn't surprised, since there was no car anywhere on the property that he could see. But he tried the door, and it was unlocked.

Going back to the truck, he contacted Bob on the radio. *Yeah, I was just about to call you. Where are you?*

"Listen," Coal replied. "I'm not sure of the number. Just give me one where I can call you." He didn't feel it necessary to admit over the air that the county sheriff had illegally entered someone's residence.

Getting the number, Coal ran back in the house and made the call. The phone seemed to get torn off the hook before it could make a full ring, but when Bob's voice came on he didn't sound much less reluctant to be on the line than Nadine had earlier.

"Bob! What happened?"

Coal, I'm going to tell you, but you've got to promise to take it easy on the way back in, all right? Remember what they always say: No emergency is worth hurting yourself or someone else innocent. Okay?

"Damn it, Bob! Where are you?"

Another long pause. *All right, brother. I'm counting on you not to lose your head. The house ... So it's the place that belongs to your friend, Coal. Maura PlentyWounds.*

Coal froze. He felt goosebumps flood over his body, and his vision blurred. The world seemed to be turning upside down. "What happened?" he yelled back into the phone. "Where's Maura?" He was barely alert enough to hear a car pull up outside.

Coal, we don't know. Hey, the mayor gave the fire boys permission to come out of the town limits, and they're still on this, trying to knock the heat down. Whatever was left after the explosion caught fire, and ... Well, you know how fast trailer houses go. I have to warn you, bud, there just isn't much left here.

"Okay, Bob. Thanks." Coal knew his voice sounded numb, for that's how he felt. He couldn't help it, and he couldn't even bring himself to say goodbye. He just set the handset down quietly and turned to open the front door, where a middle-aged couple were standing outside his truck, looking in.

There wasn't much of an exchange between Coal and these two strangers. He didn't even introduce himself beyond telling them he was the sheriff and had needed to use their phone for an emergency. As they climbed their stairs and stood on the porch, trading him places after a brief but polite exchange, Coal got in his pickup and started once again for town. Bob needn't have worried about his speed. Coal could hardly get his foot to sink down on the accelerator. He seemed to creep all the way back to town, then turned on his red dome at the intersection onto Main Street, set it on the dash, and turned to head out on the last stretch toward the place he had been calling home. His guts felt like someone had emptied a gallon of gasoline into them and set it on fire.

The cloud of black smoke was visible a long ways out, in fact not much after leaving the town limits. Still, he drove slowly, not wanting to see what he was going out to see.

It was like a scene from a disaster movie. Not one, but two firetrucks, two city police cars, and Jordan Peterson's brown truck. He could see Jordan and Grant Fairbourne, standing together on the far side of the house, on the windward side. Bob Wilson was nowhere in sight, but Police Chief Dan George was sitting in his car watching the progress of the fire fight. Coal didn't blame him, as the wind was still blowing, and it couldn't be much over minus twenty degrees, even out of the wind.

Not long after Coal arrived, both fire engines shut down, and everyone stood around watching the flames consume whatever was left of the house. He thought of the paperwork on Richard Parker, which had seemed so important earlier that he would ask Maura to leave work and go all the way home to get it. And if Maura couldn't have done it, had his mother answered the phone when he called the house, he had planned on sending her, but she must have had to take the kids to school. He was kind of surprised they even held school today at all, as cold as it was. Crazy the things a man thought of at a moment like this ...

Coal sat as far to the right of his lane of traffic as he could, his light still on, and felt, more than saw, the surge of passing vehicles going both ways, to and from Salmon.

He had an urge to hit the gas and keep driving, but he didn't know where to go. South, of course. South, away from Salmon. Away from Lemhi Valley. He should have gone when he first got the call from Mikey Parravano. Then he wouldn't have been staying at Maura's house, and ...

Bile rose in his throat. With no warning, tears surged into his eyes, and he fought them back. He should have kissed Maura when he dropped her off. He should have gotten out and held her to his heart. Really, he should never have let her go at all. Why had he been so hard? Why had he let them part the way he had?

He saw Bob Wilson appear from behind one of the fire engines, where Captain Gary Hirschi was standing and watching the fire. Obviously, their tanks had run out of water, since there were no hydrants out here and no two fire apparatus running only on tank water could have extinguished a fire this hot. Bob saw him and started toward the highway, and Coal put his foot down on the gas. When he heard the engine rev, he realized he had taken it out of gear without realizing it. He looked down to re-engage it, but Bob was coming on. He couldn't just drive away.

With leaden feet, he started out of the truck, decided better of it, got in again and fired it back up, then drove into Maura's yard to park near the police chief's car.

Bob was stopping beside him as he got out. "Hey, brother. You all right?"

Coal looked past his friend. How did a man reply to that? Why would another man be fool enough to voice the question?

"Where's Maura's rig, Bob?" he asked numbly, scanning the yard. A little white over mint green sixties Datsun Bluebird with dull paint was the only vehicle close by that seemed out of place among the emergency vehicles, and he stared at it a while even as Bob searched the yard himself.

It suddenly dawned on Coal who the Datsun belonged to, and his eyes jumped about the yard again. "Where's Vic Yancey? That's his little car."

Bob followed Coal's eyes. "That Datsun?"

"Yeah. He was in it when he left the courthouse this morning. Where is he? I'm going to need to get him out of here."

"Hey, Coal, uh ... That car was parked in the yard when I got here."

"Huh?" Coal turned to stare at Bob.

"Yeah. There wasn't anybody around."

"But ... Where's Vic?"

"Coal. I have no idea, bud. All I know is when I got here that car was sitting there, and the other side of it is pretty black. It had to have been here when the bomb went off." Bob stopped and put a comforting hand on Coal's arm. "Hey. Coal. You all right? Maybe you'd better get back in your truck, man. I know how hard this has to be. Go on—get out of the cold for a bit."

Coal kept staring, trying to register what Bob was saying. He ignored everything about getting in his truck. "But Maura ... Bob, Maura drives a big Travelette. You know, an International."

Bob shrugged. "I know. I know that ugly truck. But I just don't know what to tell you, man. I was the first one on the scene, and that Datsun's the only car that was here. No International."

Coal was in a daze. Deep inside, his Marine training was trying to kick in. Suck it up. Get tough. Forge on. People die. Even close friends pass on. They go down all around you, all the time. Sometimes in tiny pieces, sometimes in a cloud of smoke, with the stench of burning pork.

All of a sudden, he blinked his eyes forcefully, and the cold almost made them freeze shut. He let out a growl, clenching his teeth.

Bob watched him closely. "Hey, man—you need to have the ambulance look at you."

"No. No, I'm okay."

As if the word ambulance had called them up, out of the corner of his eye Coal saw the meat wagon pull up in front of the house, hesitate, then slowly turn in, its tires crunching on the frozen mud.

Both doors flung open, and the driver and passenger stopped in their tracks, staring, two people turned instantly into statues of ice. The wind was whipping the long blond hair of the passenger around even as a third person, a man Coal recognized as his buddy Jay Castillo, climbed out of the back.

Coal's eyes returned to the passenger with the blond hair, trying to register on his mind what he was seeing. He heard Bob saying something to him as he walked away, but he didn't turn back to ask what his friend had said.

When he reached the blonde, he slowly put out a hand, gingerly touching her shoulder. She turned, and they stared at each other. Coal was unable to believe what he was seeing, and the woman didn't appear much more coherent. Her eyes were open wide with shock. Coal swore, this time without even realizing it, and Maura PlentyWounds fell into his arms, instantly wailing.

After a while, Coal heard snow crunching as someone approached, and he looked up to see Jay Castillo to his left, and Ronnie Davis, who had walked around the front of the ambulance and stood not far off beyond Maura, trying not to look at the pathetic scene of one of his partners publicly breaking down.

Sagely, Jay said nothing. And Ronnie Davis spoke, but only to swear. Coal could hardly blame him, and at the moment it seemed like maybe he and the often surly, arrogant medic were cussing comrades in arms.

After what seemed like an eternity, Coal forced Maura away from him, having to push her back to loosen the grip of her arms. "Maura ... How ... What happened? Did you see Vic Yancey, my jailer?"

Maura managed a nod, wiping at her eyes. The hardy trooper, she would try now to pull herself together, at least here in public. "I'm sorry, Coal. He came to the store and said you asked him to have me come out, but ..." Suddenly, she started shaking her head adamantly and rammed her eyes shut, reaching fumblingly out to get hold of the shoulders of his coat and hang on.

"Maura, what is it? What happened?"

She gathered herself together and looked toward the smoking remains of her house, where active flames continued to leap skyward from the rubble. Like a robot out of a bad sci-fi movie, she turned her face back to Coal, stopping only for a moment on the Datsun Bluebird.

"What?" Coal demanded.

"I was trying to figure out how to leave before any of the others had even got there. Florin had called to say his car wouldn't start, so it was just me, and I was trying to get some stuff off the floor before customers started coming, and ..." She stopped, probably realizing she was throwing out a lot of information that meant absolutely nothing important.

"Then what, Maura?"

"Then he—your deputy—he suggested he could drive out and get the papers. If I didn't mind." She turned and looked at the car, sitting there in the wind and cold. Coal recognized all the strength it took her this time not to fall to the ground, and he stepped closer and took her arms.

"So ... Vic came for the papers? And ..." His voice trailed off, and he looked over at the house again. He clenched his teeth so hard he couldn't speak. In reality, he couldn't speak anyway. Young Vic Yancey ... He had just started to get to know him.

It was only inches more to step forward and have Maura back in his arms, and Coal didn't care who saw it. He took her, and he held her, and he swore he was going to find a way never to let go of her again.

To Coal's surprise, while Jay remained his stoic self, a bastion of support for Coal and Maura, it was Ronnie Davis who walked over closer. Coal heard his heavy boots crunching on ice.

"Hey, man. That was one of your deputies, huh? Man, I'm sorry to hear that. That's a tough one."

Feeling confused, Coal looked up at Davis and blinked. Could it be that in their previous encounters Coal had missed something about Ronnie Davis? Did this man actually have a heart after all?

"Thanks" was all he could utter.

Coal heard a car door slam, and after a bit he heard the voice of Chief Dan George, who was now standing by Ronnie Davis. "I don't suppose you could hang around for a while, could you? I mean ... Well, the victim ... It's too late to help him, but with this cold we might need you to take care of one of our firefighters or cops. Okay?"

"Sure thing, Chief," agreed Davis. "We'll hang on."

Coal looked over at Jay, who immediately met his glance. "Hey, do you think you could do without Maura? I think I'd better take her back to Mom's."

"Oh, of course. Yeah!" He looked over at Maura and reached out to squeeze her shoulder, ever the strong, pragmatic, calm in the storm. "Hey, Maura, I'm sure sorry about your house."

The woman could only turn and give his hand a squeeze in return, nodding vigorously. She must not trust her voice yet.

Coal kept his arm around Maura and took her to the pickup, turning up the heat for her. "Stay here, okay? I'll be right back. I promise."

He started to turn away, but Maura's voice stopped him. "Yeah?"

"Coal, I ... I killed that boy. I thought all this kind of thing would end when we left South Dakota. Coal, why won't it stop?"

The look in her eyes was one of pleading, as if she thought somehow he could answer her, or that he could make everything all better. It was obvious Maura was in a state of emotional shock. But her question was one he kept asking himself, over and over until the words thudded like monotonous drumbeats in his head.

CHAPTER NINETEEN

Ex-Green Beret, ex-FBI agent, ex-everything but Nebraska State Cornhuskers fan and special ops man for an organization not to be named Samuel "Viking" Browning, and his pal, Alex "Q" Martinez, flew into Salmon, Idaho, not in a plane, but in a flake orange 1968 Mustang coupe, because Martinez hated to fly without four tires in contact with a road and because after learning what it was going to take to get plane tickets, fly into Idaho Falls, rent a car, and drive to Salmon, then not have his car with him, Martinez simply thought it sounded like the better option. That and he loved to drive, especially fast, sporty cars like his Mustang, which he liked to call Flash.

The inside of the pony car felt so toasty that if Browning and Martinez hadn't already had to step out into the air of the frigid north numerous times to re-fuel they would never have known they were going to freeze their lips off here in Salmon. That was another plus to driving—no surprises about what the temperature was going to be upon landing.

It was a drive of somewhere around seventeen hours from Lincoln, Nebraska, to Salmon, Idaho. Flash, the sparkling copper-orange Mustang, made it in nineteen. But that slight delay was only because after hanging up with Coal, Browning had to track down his old partner, make up a story to tell his wife and children about heading out to the West to sell farm equipment, and then he and Martinez had to pack their clothing, some food for the trip, then hit the highway on the fly. The drive itself only took fourteen hours.

Sam Browning leaned his big frame forward to look out the window at the mountains surrounding Salmon, at the slowly (at this point) roiling river, and at the stately buildings of the town. Martinez drove all the way southeast down Main, until it was obvious they were about to leave the city limits. Then he whipped it around and parked at the curb just west of Warpath Street—a fitting name considering why the two of them were here.

Martinez looked over at Browning. "Well? Now what?"

"I don't know. Go to the jail?"

"We can try that. It's the other way from where we turned, right? Up that hill?"

"Yeah, I think so. On the Bar."

"How did you learn so much about this place so fast?" asked Martinez.

Browning chuckled. "You must be gettin' old, dog. That's what we do, right? A couple phone calls, and wham! There it was. Now it's up here." He tapped his right temple.

"Uh-huh. I know. Like a steel trap. Only it's so tight nothing's ever comin' out again."

Browning had no answer for that but a laugh. He motioned forward with two fingers, and Martinez pulled into traffic and drove to where Main turned to Courthouse Drive, then went partway up the hill and turned in at the very obvious and very impressive Courthouse.

He drove slowly around the back, the 289 under the hood thumping along nicely. It hadn't minded the fast drive at all, it seemed. Even with the change of altitude, a few little carburetor adjustments and they were running like a top again.

Martinez drove along the back of the big building, and both of them saw "Sheriff's Office" over a set of stairs that led down to the basement. "I guess we start right there." He found a parking spot, and both of them got out to scan the lot. At this point, however, Browning was more concerned with stretching all the kinks out of his long body and heavy muscles. The Mustang was a nice car, but unlike his Monte Carlo it was never intended for a man of his size—not for any fourteen-hour hauls, anyway.

Seeing nothing of great interest, including nothing but white with green-lettered 2L Idaho license plates, which was the mark of Lemhi County, they trooped downstairs. Martinez peeked in the window before trying the door. The place appeared to be empty.

Walking in, they glanced around. Not only was the room empty, but it was a little cold as well.

"Not much help here," said Browning. "You think they've got coffee?"

Martinez gave his partner the look of "don't be stupid". "This is Coal Savage we're talking about. Of course he has coffee." He nodded toward the coffee maker. "Probably the best brand, too."

"Oh. So no MJB?"

Martinez didn't laugh or smile. Browning knew he was funny because of the look in his amigo's eyes, but that was all. Martinez had a thing about not laughing unless something really caught him off-guard.

"Want to go upstairs?" asked Browning.

"We can. Or you can. Maybe we'd draw less attention with just one of us. You go, and I'll wait here to see if anyone comes back."

Leaving Martinez in the office, Browning went back out in the cold, suspecting that his partner had simply not wanted to come out into the freezing air again so soon, then re-entered through the back door to the building's first story. He looked around until he found a likely looking office with the door standing open.

Inside, a heavy-set, plain-looking woman in a red dress looked up from behind a desk that bore the name of Cindy on a plaque.

"Hi, Cindy."

"Hi. Can I help you?"

"Maybe. I'm a friend of Coal Savage's. I told him I was coming into town, but he's not down in his office."

Cindy frowned, a sad expression. "I'm so sorry, sir."

"Sam."

"I'm sorry, Sam—are you *good* friends with Coal?"

Browning's heart leaped. Had the Mob moved so fast? "Uh ... Yeah, I am. Something wrong?"

Cindy laughed. "Oh, I'm silly. I'm sorry, that probably sounded bad. No, Coal's all right. We just had a ... Well, someone set off a bomb this morning—the second one in two days. This one set a whole house on fire, and I think Coal is either still out there or he might be with his family."

Browning looked appropriately concerned. He tried to react the way normal Joe-Schmo citizen would, although he wasn't sure he remembered how.

"That's scary! Two bombs? I thought this would be a really peaceful little town."

Cindy shook her head quickly. "Oh, please don't misunderstand! It really is peaceful, normally! It's just ... Well, it seems like since Coal came back—I mean Sheriff Savage—and became the sheriff, there has been a lot going on. It's almost like it all came back from the big city with him."

Browning pursed his lips, shaking his head. Oh, if Cindy only knew!

"Well, Cindy, do you think there's any way I can get hold of Coal, or will I have to wait in his office?"

She paused. "Umm ... You know what? It was Sam, right?"

"Yeah. Sam Browning."

"Sam, let me just make a phone call, okay? Hang on."

As Sam watched her, it was obvious she was using all her power to remember something, maybe trying to impress the stranger that she knew the sheriff so well. Seconds later, without having to use any reference at all, she had picked the handset off a fat, heavy-looking black phone, and squeezing it between her shoulder and cheek, she dialed five digits. Sam watched each of them closely, pretending not to.

"Hello. Connie? Yes, it's me, Cindy—calling from the courthouse? Yes! Fine, how are you? Say, I have a gentleman here from out of town wanting to see Coal. He said Coal is expecting him. Sam? Browning? Oh! Okay. I'll give him the phone."

Cindy held the phone out to Sam, and he took it, eyebrows raised. "She's calling Coal to the phone," Cindy told Sam.

* * *

Connie held her hand over the phone as she leaned down where Coal sat on the couch, his arm around Maura, squeezing her close. "It's some fellow who says he knows you. Sam Browning?"

"Oh!" Coal leaped up from the couch and grabbed the phone. "Hello! Sam?"

Yeah, hey, Coal! Before Coal could say anything else, Sam cut him off. *Hey, I've got Q sittin' down in your office, and I'm callin' you from Cindy's office.* He enunciated this last part carefully, knowing Coal would get the import of it. *If you can give me your number I'll go down and call you back from there so Q can say hi too.*

"Right," Coal replied. "Good thinking." Coal gave him the house number, and they disconnected.

The second the phone rang again, Coal jerked it off the hook. "Sam?"

Yeah. Me. Coal, what the hell happened? We got here as quick as we could.

"Don't worry, buddy—you got here in record time. Not fast enough, but I don't think if you had flown a rocket it would have been fast enough. They set off another bomb, at ..." Coal glanced over at the back of Maura's head, then looked at his mom and made an apologetic face. "Hey, Sam, I'm going to switch phones, all right?"

He turned and handed the handset to Connie. "Hang it up when I pick up the one in your room, okay?"

"Of course."

Coal ran down the hall into Connie's room, shut the door, and jerked the red handset off the receiver. "Sam?"

Yeah.

"So they blew up the place where I was staying when you called me back yesterday. We're still doing some investigating, but I think they killed my jailer in the process."

Wait. A jailer? Why him?

"Bad luck, I think. It's a long story I'll tell you later. Is there somewhere we can meet?"

I'm not sure. I'm trying to decide if anyone should see us together yet.

"Well, before you decide, see if this makes any difference: I put out an APB on the car I think the Mob boys are driving. No way to be positive, but a lot of coincidences. I think it's a dark blue Jaguar, a couple of years old at the most. Like I said, I don't know for a fact it's our boys, but it showed up a few days ago, and I've been seeing it way too often for comfort since then—and behaving strangely."

Okay, that's a start.

"Well, the reason I told you that," Coal clarified, "is no one has seen it since the APB. It's not parked at any of the hotels or grocery stores, nowhere around town, at least nowhere obvious. I think they must have a radio in their car and heard the bulletin go out, so they split."

Browning laughed. *Split? That doesn't sound like the old Coal Savage I know. You sure you're not a hippie imposter? So Coal, you telling me that APB went out over the air? Why'd you do that? Good way to tip somebody off.*

"Well, I was kind of in a panic. But if it got them to lay low and stop bombing people, then I'm all for it."

Okay. That might be a point. So hey, why don't you come on back up to your office? I think it'd be safe to talk here.

After Coal hung up, he sat down on the edge of the bed for a few minutes, his head in his hands. The feeling inside him was one of huge relief that Sam and Martinez were here. Those guys knew how the Mob played, especially Sam. He had made a hobby of studying them and their methods, and he could exchange punches with any mobster with the best of them. But it didn't change two facts: One, young Vic Yancey was almost certainly dead. And two, Coal had almost killed Maura, and he would have succeeded if she could have found a way to leave work. Every time he thought about it, it made him nauseous. Maura or his own mother. Either one and he might as well have died himself. Knowing he had been the cause of Vic Yancey's death was difficult enough.

He had just stood back up when the phone rang again, and he stared at it through two rings, deciding if answering it would be a waste of his time, or if it could possibly be Browning calling back for some reason.

Finally, he picked it up, knowing his mom was probably waiting for him to do so.

"Hello?"

Hello, came a weak-sounding voice from what seemed like a million miles away. *Is this Sheriff Savage?*

"It is. Who's this?"

Sheriff, this is Diana Yancey, out in Tendoy. I'm sorry to bother you at home, but I just called your dispatcher, and she said to call you here.

Coal cringed and swore, in his head when the name registered on him. Yancey! He swore again, then tried to pray. The two didn't seem to mix, so he stopped praying. Not swearing somehow didn't cross his mind.

"Yes, ma'am, Mrs. Yancey." He stopped. How did he go on? How *could* he go on?

Well, the reason I'm calling is my Vic, well he came out here this morning after he got off work, in a big hurry. He said he had to run a little errand back in town, and he wanted to take his little sisters with him for donuts and hot chocolate, since he hadn't seen them in a while. Little Nita's not feeling good, so she stayed home, but Vic took Tamara with him, and they aren't back yet. I'm sorry for bothering you, but I don't have any other ideas. Do you have any thought where they could be?

CHAPTER TWENTY

The drive out to the home of Victor Yancey's family, Clyde and Diana and their younger children, was one of the longest of Coal's life. He made the drive alone, mostly because he couldn't bear to put anyone else through something like this, but he was wishing he had taken Connie with him and just left her in the car, so he would have someone to talk to on the way back home.

After first calling back to the jail and telling Sam and Martinez to run and grab a bite to eat or something while he performed his deeply unpleasant job, a job he would have to ponder on a long time before finding someone he despised enough to wish it on, he said goodbye numbly to Maura and his family and drove away with orders for them to keep an eye outside and call for help the second anything seemed out of place.

Before making the drive east, because he knew his facts were not yet complete enough to talk to Diana Yancey, Coal went back to the remains of Maura's house and found the state bull, Lyle Gentry, conferring with the officers of the other agencies. Under the circumstances, with Vic being Coal's deputy and with the chances being unfortunately very good that Vic was the one who had set off the explosion, Gentry was going to take on the investigation of the explosion, possibly with some expert help from outside.

The bad part was that earlier when Coal was here, no one had had any information to go on other than the fact that there had been a devastating explosion and that Vic's car was parked out front. Now there was something new, something Coal wished he had never learned.

The other officers, to the man, saw something in Coal's face as he walked up to them. Whatever they had been discussing seemed to lose all importance, and the entire group went silent. They watched him, waiting.

Coal scanned the group, trying to decide if there was any important reason not to say what he had to say in front of all of them. The truth was any individual with a badge had a right to know.

"I just got off the phone with my jailer's mother," he said. Although a few of them glanced around at each other, no one spoke.

"She said Vic went to her house this morning and got one of his little sisters to take her out for a donut."

Coal was vaguely aware that out of all these men, Jordan Peterson and the police chief's faces turned palest. But that part seemed odd, because more than any of them Grant Fairbourne took the news on the shakiest knees. He seemed about to walk away rather than listen to any more.

"She was asking if I had any idea where they could be." Coal heard his own words as if someone else were speaking. It was strange. He had delivered several similar messages as a sergeant at the Long Binh Jail in Vietnam. Why did this kind of thing never get easier? And how, why, did he find himself so often the first one holding this kind of shocking information?

Officer Gentry swore, and now his face had gone every bit as pale as anyone else's. His eyes flitted over to the remains of the house. He swore again.

The men all looked around at each other. Ronnie Davis and Jay Castillo had wandered over as well, and Coal wondered how all these men were holding out against this kind of bitter cold.

"Do you think ..." Grant Fairbourne's voice faded away before he could finish his thought. He sniffed and wiped at his red nose.

Coal looked at him, knowing he had young children. He was much younger, less experienced with death than Coal. Coal wanted to send him back to town, but he didn't want to shame him that way.

Some of the other officers looked suddenly beyond Coal, and before he could turn he heard a man say, "I think it's pretty much down now if you want us to do a search for victims."

Turning, Coal saw big Gary Hirschi, the fire captain. Standing beside him once again was Brian Howell. And there to Howell's right was Ken Parks, acting in his part as fire engineer for the volunteer fire department. Coal's heart was pounding, and his breath never quite seemed to fill his lungs. He stared at all these men, silently begging for some kind of release. But he knew there was none.

One bad thing Coal knew more than anything else: As far as he knew the history of all the men gathered here, no one could have seen more violent, terrible death than he had. Also, he had had more time to prepare himself than any of the others, on his drive over here after talking to Diana Yancey.

"I'll go look." His voice sounded dull, almost lifeless. He ground his teeth together. "Maybe you ought to move everyone way back and warn them what I'm looking for, all right?" He said this last without looking at anyone. Whoever wanted to act could do with it what they deemed appropriate.

"You want my turnouts?" Gary Hirschi asked.

Coal looked at him, scanning him up and down. Gary was a big man. Not quite Coal's size, but probably big enough, in a stretch. Yet Coal had seen what the insides of firefighter clothing looked like after a few minutes' worth of hard labor. He didn't care to be soaked in anyone else's sweat. "No, thanks. I'll just get my coveralls. Don't let anyone go over there, all right?" This time he looked directly at Lyle Gentry, then went to the GMC.

Numb from more than just the sub-zero temperature and wind, Coal dug his striped gray mechanic's coveralls out from behind the truck seat and slipped them on. His fingers fumbled getting them zipped up, and he wished he could blame it only on the cold.

Tugging heavy leather gloves on, he turned and caught most of the group of firefighters, EMT's, and police officers watching him. The majority of them darted their eyes away the moment they knew they had been caught.

As Coal walked woodenly past them, Bob Wilson came and joined him, walking at his side all the way to the front of the house, where Coal stared at the remains of the deck and felt a tug at the corners of his lips, the tug of wry humor that only a frequent first responder to death and destruction can understand. Of all the bad things he could think about today, at least he hadn't wasted any time building Maura a new porch.

"You want help, bud?" Bob asked as Coal stopped, scanning left and right over the smoking remains of the house.

"No. No, Bob, I'd better do this by myself. If ... Well, I don't think it's going to be nice."

Bob nodded, and Coal felt more than saw or heard him walking away. Working slowly, not wanting to get too far into this job too soon, Coal tried to tear away the remains of the porch. Ironically, this part of the house that had seemed most precarious since he started coming here now appeared to be the most intact thing about the entire place.

Finally, he climbed up on it, testing its strength as he went. He knelt where the remains of the aluminum door were and managed to shove it aside. He pushed at a charred wall stud, breaking it in half and then flattening the lower half down to the floor plate. Then he tore at a section of plaster inner wall and the siding on the outside, moving it to one side. And he stopped. His search was over.

There just under the rubble were the unrecognizable remains of a human face. Man, woman, Coal couldn't immediately say which. Protruding from underneath the larger body and making the image of the legs of the Wicked Witch of the East jutting from under Dorothy's house pop oddly into his mind, Coal saw two smaller feet, the left shoe gone altogether and the right one melted onto the foot.

Reeling away from the door opening, he turned and leaped off the porch, nearly twisting his ankle when he landed on a frozen hump of soil in the yard. He walked like a robot, hiding his feelings, until he got to his truck, where he began stripping the coveralls off, intent on shedding them and getting back into his coat.

His main goal, however, was to get in the truck and turn it on, then try to figure out how to avoid talking to any of the more than half-dozen men who either were staring toward him or looking at the ground and wishing themselves somewhere away from this scene.

Bob Wilson finally walked over, as Coal was snapping his coat front but before he could climb in the pickup. Coal didn't look at his friend, but from the corner of his eye he recognized his gait. He forced himself to look up, seeing Chief George, Grant, and Lyle Gentry close on Bob's heels.

All three of them stared at Coal, the same question huge and looming in their eyes, but all of them speechless.

Clenching his jaw, Coal only nodded to affirm their unspoken question. He glanced once more toward the house, unable to erase from his mind that the bomb had been set here for him, and that he had tried to send Maura over here in his place. Maura, who then sent young Vic Yancey, who in his turn, wanting to spend some time with his sisters and do something nice for them, had brought little Tamara along. The only thing that had saved their sister Nita was the fact that she didn't feel well.

"You'll need to drive over to the Yanceys'," said Bob, his voice dull. He looked over at George. "Chief, I can go with him."

"No," Coal said, cutting them out of the decision. "It's way out of your jurisdiction. And it's not something I'd wish on anyone else. I'll go alone."

Gentry spoke up, his voice sounding half-hearted. "My jurisdiction too, Coal. I can go with you."

"No." It registered on Coal that his voice sounded almost angry. Didn't anyone understand English anymore? He had already told them no. How many ways did he have to say it? It didn't really register on him until the others walked away that he might be trying to protect himself, keeping the rest of them away from him in case he lost it on either the way to or from the Yanceys'.

Later, as Coal drove slowly back to town, not even aware that the speedometer said fifty miles an hour, he couldn't block the image of Diana Yancey from his mind, collapsed on her knees just inside the front room door, wailing out her grief as her little Nita crouched over by the couch, crying because of fear of the unknown, crying because she had probably never seen her mother this way. He had gotten on his knees as well, putting an arm around Diana Yancey because he didn't know what else to do. There was nothing to say beyond what he had already told her, and he was smart enough not to look for anything to fill the void.

Now he was on his way in to the service station where Clyde Yancey worked as a mechanic. He had stopped back at Maura's property only long enough to let them know he was taking care of that job as well. When they tried to stop him, calling on the question of jurisdiction, he shut them down flat. He had already been through hell, talking to Diana Yancey, and he was still walking through hell's furnaces. He might as well remain there long enough to talk to Vic's father too.

Earlier that day . . .

Vic Yancey was sleepy. But at the same time he walked with a jaunty step. He was finally getting something accomplished with his life, meeting some goals he had long intended to push toward. He had always been a little on the shy side, and he knew it. It was something he had always sworn when he got away from his home and moved out on his own he would work to overcome.

Renting a basement apartment in Salmon wasn't exactly his dream of living alone, but at least he was mature enough to be away from home, running his own life, and his family all thought he was doing great. Vic had become a man. Also, the old couple he lived below were good people, nice and quiet, and stayed mostly to themselves except for the times when they ended up making too much food (at least that's what the nice old lady claimed) and brought some down to him—generally enough to feed three or four people.

Vic had been wanting to talk to the new sheriff, Coal Savage, for quite a while, to see if maybe he could start taking on more responsibility, maybe go out on a few big calls, sort of see what the job of a real deputy entailed. He had approached him on the subject, which had gone well.

And now, just this morning, a windfall had dropped into his lap. The sheriff had sent him to McPherson's to talk to a woman Vic had always admired from afar, a woman rumor had it that Coal was sweet on, which seemed to be proving true, according to the stories around town that they had gone off on a long vacation together, from which they had only recently returned.

At first, Vic had had every intention of passing on the message and then heading home to sleep. He was happy just to have a reason to get close enough to Maura PlentyWounds to talk to her, even if only for a few minutes. But when the woman, who was even more beautiful up close than he had imagined, seemed to be worried about how she was going to get off work and return home, he came up with the big idea of saving the day for her and going out there himself. It was the perfect solution, and of course he would be a kind of hero to her—and to Coal as well.

In accepting his offer, which made the woman happy enough that a huge smile lit up her face, she told him she had made oatmeal chocolate chip cookies the night before, and she and Coal hadn't gotten around to eating any. She practically begged him to take them with him and share them with his family. Honestly, he doubted she even knew about his family, so that part she had just thrown in there. But as he headed out to Maura's place her offer got him to thinking that he hadn't seen his five-year-old twin sisters, Nita and Tamara, for several weeks, and since they lived too far out of town to attend kindergarten, he knew they would be home this time of day. It would be the perfect outing!

After picking up little Tam, Vic pushed aside his disappointment that Nita wasn't feeling good, and he and Tam headed off on their quest for cookies and monumentally important paperwork, eager to prove to the sheriff that he was ready to take on more responsibilities.

Tam was a chatterbox all the way to Maura's, talking about their new puppy, and a fish Dad had caught, and how Mom was making a new quilt with some other ladies, and Tam and Nita would lie beneath it while they sewed and look up through the bright colors at the lights on the ceiling. Eventually, however, her little mind returned to the cookies, and once again she wanted to know if they had chocolate chips in them, and not raisins. When he said he had been told chocolate chips, and pressed her as to why she was asking, she finally admitted that raisins weren't crunchy enough for her. They were even a little slimy. He laughed and tousled her dark hair.

Pulling up to the mailbox, Vic checked for the PlentyWounds name, and it was painted there, plain as day. "Come on, Tam. I'll go get the papers I need and we'll see how the cookies taste." He didn't know what he liked better—making the sheriff pleased in him, or imagining Tam's face when she bit into that first cookie.

They stepped up on the porch, and Tam's eyes got big. She must not have been much more impressed with the beat-up old plywood porch than he was.

Vic used Maura's personal key to open the door and pushed inside, reaching back to take Tam's little hand. He shut the door behind them and saw the paperwork on the coffee table by the couch, the cookies on the kitchen cupboard. He took one step, and Tam started around from behind him, for she had spied the plate of cookies too.

And then there were no more cookies, no more paperwork, no more little Tamara, and no more Vic Yancey, trying to work his way into being a full-time deputy.

And the entire front room was engulfed in flame.

CHAPTER TWENTY-ONE

When Scabs Ravioli took the Jaguar onto Lemhi Road, it was all he could do to keep himself from flooring it. But after taking a few deep breaths, he got himself under control again. It was the way of Mob hitmen to be cool under pressure, to adapt to whatever came their way, to make choices at a moment's notice that would make the difference between their own life and death. And everyone knew Scabs was one of the best.

Menny Marcello was the best explosives guy the Mob had. He had set the perfect bomb. Scabs knew this because Menny's bombs were always perfect. Now they needed only to wait, and Lemhi County sheriff Coal Savage, who seemed to think he was so smart and who without a doubt had been responsible for calling in the APB on them, was going to sneak back home after a hard day's work, making sure no one followed him home. He would hang around on the road before turning in, watch for strange vehicles—the things all smart operatives did when they thought someone was out to assassinate them. He might get out of his pickup in the yard, stand near it watching the highway some more, and then at last, when he decided he was safe, he would head for the house, wanting to settle down and relax for the evening.

"And that will be the end of Sheriff Coal Savage."

Menny looked over, startled at the sudden sound of Scabs's voice. "What's that?"

"Oh, sorry!" Scabs hadn't even realized he had voiced the thought out loud. "Nothin', man, just thinkin' we're almost done with this job. Talk about short and easy!"

"Uh-huh. Don't forget, everyone who has a radio will be looking for this car now."

Scabs grinned. "Yep. But we won't be drivin' this car."

Even as he spoke, they were passing a lonely little ranch house with no neighboring houses close by. Scabs drove on, letting Menny sit and stew in silence, trying to decipher his meaning. He had told Menny he would fix the problem of the ostentatious Jaguar, and he was about to do just that.

He pulled the car off the road a ways ahead, onto a little nothing of a farm road that if he had kept going on it would have been terrible on the Jaguar, although with everything frozen it probably wouldn't have gotten stuck.

It was pretty flat here, with no real way to do surveillance on the house they had passed, so Scabs made up his mind and decided to take a chance. He looked over at his partner.

"Make sure your piece is ready. And this time maybe you'd better put that silencer on it."

"It's back at the hotel," Menny admitted, looking sheepish.

"Well, son of a—" Scabs drew a deep breath and huffed it out. "Great."

"Is there any way to go back and get it? We gotta get all our clothes and stuff too."

"The hell we do. We can't ever go back there. Whatever's there is lost, brother."

Menny looked sick. He appeared to be going over in his mind whatever list he could recall of the things he had left at the Stagecoach Inn.

"You got the piece, though, right?" asked Scabs, suddenly worried.

"Yeah. Yeah, I got that, man."

"Good. Get it ready. Loaded up?"

Menny gave him a scalding look.

"Okay." That look was enough for Scabs, who knew the slim chance of a Mob hitman ever forgetting to check his loads.

He backed out onto Lemhi Road again and drove back down to the house they had passed, pulling in. There was a huge metal barn with a rounded roof across a dirt and gravel yard from the red brick house, and a beautiful blue Chevrolet Caprice two-door coupe parked beside the house. Scabs waved at it as he pulled up next to it and parked.

"Our new ride," he said by way of introduction.

Menny licked his lips and looked toward the house.

"Come on," said Scabs, and he drove around behind the barn, then parked the Jaguar out of sight.

They both got out and walked briskly toward the house, climbing the steps together. With a look around, Scabs knocked on the door. A kindly looking lady in a loose, flowery blue dress, possibly in her eighties, opened the door with a tentative smile on her face. "Hello there. Can I help you?"

"Ma'am, the ad in the newspaper said you have a pickup truck for sale," Scabs said casually. "Do you still have it?"

Looking confused, the woman started shaking her head. "I'm not sure what you're talking about. I'm sorry. We do have a pickup, but my husband just bought it last year, and he never told me anything about trying to sell it."

"Oh." Scabs tried to look properly disappointed. "Well, is he home?"

"Not at the moment."

"Drat," said Scabs, hoping it was a word people in the sticks used instead of cursing. "Any idea how long he might be?"

"Well, he's in Leadore right now, and I don't expect him back for several hours, but I really don't think he wants to sell his pickup. I think—"

The woman's mouth clamped shut when Scabs pulled out his pistol and shoved it into her ribs, his entire demeanor changing. "Lady, just get in the house, all right? It's damn cold out here."

A mouth that had been clamped shut fell open now, and the woman backpedaled into her living room, almost falling over backward. "Oh, please! Please! What do you want?" she began to wail. "We don't have much here at the house. Do you want money?"

"No, lady, we need your car. That's it. Just your car."

"Okay. Okay, you can have it. Let me just find the keys real quick." With her hands shaking, she went over to a board on the end of the kitchen wall, where it exited off the living room. Several sets of keys were hanging there, and she pulled down a couple that were obvious Chevrolet keys.

As she turned back with the keys, Scabs shot her twice in the chest.

When the old woman slumped to the floor, and blood began to soak the front of her dress, Menny looked at Scabs, a look of horror on his face. "What the hell'd you do that for? Couldn't we have tied her up and just taken the car?"

"Come on," Scabs said, afraid his voice sounded a little scornful. "You don't think she would have fingered us the second her husband came home and set her free? What've I taught you?"

Menny looked down at the old lady, then jumped his eyes away, looking sick. He had nothing to say, because he knew the reality of their situation. And he knew one other thing too. It just took his mind a minute to catch up.

"We gotta wait here for her husband now too, right?" He looked a little ill.

"You got it. And hope like crazy he's alone."

Scabs walked over to where an old Motorola radio sat on the kitchen counter and turned it on, monkeying with the antenna until the sound came in well. They were playing some country garbage on there, but at least it was noise. With the music—he thought the term loosely—in the background, he went and sank down on the couch, feeling weary and wishing they could be playing Dino Martin on the radio instead.

As he sat there, he fished around in a pocket for a couple of cartridges and reloaded his weapon, glancing over at Menny, who stood close to the woman, trying not to look at her, but his eyes being drawn back to her all the same.

"She reminds me of my grandmother," said Menny, his voice gone quiet.

"Shut up, will you? You see how old she was? Probably wouldn'ta lived another year anyhow." He too had had a kindly old grandmother—kindly except when she had too much wine in her and took the wooden spoon to Scabs—known to her, of course, as Saverio—and his brother Manuel. She didn't even care if it had sauce on it and she stained their trousers. But overall, she really had been a sweet old lady, and the truth was he missed her. But not so much that it would have changed his mind when he knew there was no choice about killing this woman, who was a complete stranger to them both anyway.

"Go find some bleach or alcohol or somethin', will you?" Scabs suggested to Menny. "We're gonna need to clean off anything we touch in here—like those radio knobs and that antenna. Never know when some smart aleck cop might actually know how to dust for fingerprints. I know it ain't likely, but ..."

"I know," said Menny. "You didn't live this long by being careless."

Menny wandered down the hall to the bathroom and came back with a quart of rubbing alcohol. By then Scabs was already asleep.

Menny went over and stared down at the old woman, whose eyes were still open. Sometimes he hated this job. That old lady shouldn't have had to die. He wanted to pull a couple of coins out of his pocket and put them on her eyelids, but then he'd just have to take them off later so his fingerprints wouldn't be on them. He swore. Maybe he should pull her into another room, at least.

In the end, he went back to a bedroom, tore a bedspread off the bed, and brought it back to lay over her body. At least he didn't have to see her anymore.

Going to the kitchen, he pulled out a handkerchief. He gave a moment's thought to the fact that he could have used it later to clean up two coins, but what the heck? The woman was covered now anyway. He used the handkerchief to open the refrigerator door and found what appeared to be half a casserole. Sniffing it, his hunger instantly revved high, and he set it out on the countertop and started looking for a plate and a fork.

Once he had a plate of the casserole, he used the plate itself as a heating surface, coupled with a gas burner on top of the stove. When the food was hot, he put it on a towel, sat and ate it, with a 7-Up out of the fridge.

Finally, wiping his mouth with his handkerchief, he used it and some alcohol to make sure any part of the plate and fork he might have touched, and the 7-Up can, were clean, and then he started for the living room to find himself a chair. Who knew how long they would be waiting here?

Before he could sit down in the big blue La-Z-Boy in the living room, he realized the song on the radio had ended, and a news announcer was speaking in grave tones. When he heard the words "Highway 28", he stopped and turned to listen more closely.

Then he swore. Loudly.

"Scabs! Hey! Get up!" He grabbed his partner's arm and shook it. He probably would have continued shaking, but Scabs came up in a flash, his eyes groggy, but his hand reaching for his pistol.

"What the— What's goin' on?"

Menny's whole body was covered with chills, and he knew it had to be showing on his face. He grabbed Scabs's upper arm, squeezing too hard before Scabs jerked away in pain.

"The house blew! The house blew!" Menny almost yelled in his partner's face, his body filled with shock.

"Huh? What are you talkin' about?"

"The house, man! The house! My bomb!"

Scabs dropped his hand away from his gun butt and stared. "It blew? How? When?"

"I don't know, man, it's on the radio! It wasn't the sheriff!"

Scabs stared back at Menny, trying to put a look of confident patience on his face. "Calm down, Menny. Take it easy. What do you mean it wasn't the sheriff? We already made sure—" As suddenly as he had begun, he stopped, and now the fear washed over his face too. "It wasn't that girl, was it?"

"No, man. No! It was some deputy of the sheriff's and his five-year-old sister! Scabs! Scabs! Oh man, I killed a little kid."

Scabs raised a hand and scrubbed it across his mouth, blinking his eyes exaggeratedly and shaking his head. "No. No, that can't be right. How? How would that even happen?"

"I got no idea, man! Scabs! Man, I killed a little girl!"

"Hey! Stop blubbering! Get a hold of yourself, brother. We've gotta figure this out. What'd they say exactly?"

The news segment was over, and some country bumpkin was massacring what otherwise might have been a perfectly good song.

"I don't know. I don't know! Somethin' about another explosion, this time in a house, and preliminary reports showing that it appeared to be a young guy who worked at the jail and his sister. It's gotta be that kid we talked to down at the jail! They said he was nineteen years old."

"All right." Scabs looked about, scanning the room. "Is everything clean? Did you touch anything?"

"I did, but I wiped it off with alcohol."

"Okay. Uh ... Okay, damn it. We've got to get out of here. You got anything left for another bomb, or is it all back in the hotel?"

"No, I ain't got nothin'." Menny looked like he was going to throw up.

"All right, all right. Okay, come on. We'd better head out."

Sweeping the house with one last glance, hardly even looking at the dead woman, Scabs went to the door, taking out a handkerchief to turn the doorknob. They went to the Caprice, and Scabs shoved the keys into his partner's hand.

"Drive this over to the barn. I'm gonna look for some gas."

In the barn, Scabs found two five-gallon cans, one of them pure gasoline, and the other diesel. Taking them both outside, he opened the passenger door of the Jaguar and put them on the floor. Then he motioned for Menny to follow him, and he went around and got in, started the engine up, and spun his tires out of the yard, heading farther along the road, to a place that looked semi-deserted.

Stopping the car and leaving the keys in the ignition, he got out and opened the trunk, pulling out anything that belonged to him and Menny, who took it as he brought it out and went to put it in the Caprice.

As Scabs began unscrewing the lid on the huge light blue can of diesel fuel, Menny said, "What are you doin'?"

Scabs gave his partner a blank stare. He looked from the fuel cans to the car, then back at Menny, giving him a moment to see if he could possibly catch up. Menny only kept looking at him, saying nothing.

"Are you serious? What's it look like I'm doin'? Burnin' up the car."

"How come?"

"How— Listen, you—" He stopped himself in half-angry mid-sentence. All of a sudden, he straightened fully up. "You know somethin', Menny, you got a good head on your shoulders after all, don't you?"

"It just seems like we could be a hundred or two miles away from here without anybody bein' suspicious if we just clean the fingerprints off here an' go. Right? A big black fire, somebody'll be up here in no time, snoopin' around."

"Yeah, yeah. I got it already, brother. No need t' get cocky. I got it. All right, get in and drive back to the house. There's a big empty hole in that barn. We'll clean it up and just stuff it back there. Good job, kid." Menny grinned. It was nice knowing Scabs could actually give out well-deserved praise.

After driving back to the farmhouse and secreting the Jaguar back in the barn where it wasn't likely to be found for a while, they went back in the house and got bleach and alcohol, using both of them to wipe down every surface of the Jaguar where they could have left prints. They had been careful not to leave prints on or in the house this time, so when they finished with the bleach and alcohol they left them sitting by the Jaguar and hurried back outside, checking before they went out to see if anyone had arrived. It was empty and bleak as a graveyard.

"You feel like you can drive?" Scabs asked Menny.

"Drive? Well sure. Yeah, man, I'm good." Menny might have been lying. He had seemed pretty upset over the old woman and the girl. But Scabs would have to take the chance. He didn't want to strip the man entirely of his pride.

"All right then let's scram. Drive the speed limit. Just take it easy going out of here. They won't be lookin' for this car—not yet."

"Hey, man," said Menny as Scabs got in and shut his door and they started to pull away, "I was thinkin' about the hotel. What about fingerprints we left there?"

Scabs sat silent for a moment, staring and completely still, like a vacant-eyed, perfectly life-like portrait of some tough Italian laborer done by a master portraitist. The entire artistic ambience, however, was shattered when Scabs quietly, with a squint to his deep-set eyes but very little other expression, began to unleash possibly the longest freight train of curse words Menny Marcello had ever heard assembled in one place, in perhaps the most artful arrangement in the history of mankind—or at least the history of the Mob.

CHAPTER TWENTY-TWO

When Coal drove away from the service station, leaving Clyde Yancey to his shock and grief, he headed up to the courthouse. He knew Maura probably needed him, and maybe the rest of his family as well, as the valley seemed to crumble and explode around them. But he had to get with Sam Browning and Alex Martinez. He had to forge some plan with these two men, a half-mad berserker and the only man who could keep him from trying to destroy every bad person in the universe—along with himself—before it was too late.

As he had hoped, when he raced down to the jail, pausing before going down the stairs because "fools rush in", and bending over to look through the window, he could see two men inside. It was obvious who they were.

Coal jerked open the door, and the three of them stared at each other. He had the urge to run across the room and embrace them, but neither of the others would be the embracing type, he suspected. And then again, unless it was the right person, perhaps he wasn't either. "Was the door locked? How'd you get in, anyway?"

Sam laughed, while Martinez allowed himself a small, cryptic smile. "That's seriously the best greeting you've got?" Sam said, his blue eyes narrowing with his grin. "You never excelled in tact school, did you?"

Coal couldn't return any laughs. These boys didn't know what his morning had consisted of. "*Tactical* school, yes. But no, not tact school. Thanks for coming, guys. I'm in a world of trouble."

He walked to them and shook their hands. Holding on extra-long, and firmly, was the biggest sign of how grateful he was to see them.

"We heard all the news down at the Inn," said Sam, while Martinez remained quiet and aloof, his *modus operandi.* "The dead guy, that was your jailer? And ... he had his sister with him?"

Coal nodded. Exhausted, he walked over to the coffee pot because he could smell fresh brew. Touching it, he found it warm, and he turned and looked at Browning. "This smells different from the coffee we've had in here. You bring this?"

"Yep. Best coffee this side o'—"

"I know, this side of whisky. I know." Now Coal managed to chuckle, as old memories of these guys came creeping back in. "Just like old times, huh? By the way, I don't want to swell your head, but I have to admit from the smell of it you still find the best coffee I've ever had."

"Thanks," said Sam Browning with a grin. "Wolverine piss is what gives it the punch."

Coal grunted and poured a cup. He sipped at it and closed his eyes. One moment of bliss and comfort, in the middle of a war zone—the devil's playground.

Walking to his desk chair, Coal sank down onto it, setting his cup on the desktop. "You guys pick the lock?" he asked.

Sam grinned. "There wasn't any welcoming committee. I'm just kiddin'. It wasn't locked."

With a tired nod, Coal said, "You wouldn't want to see the welcoming committee that's been greeting me lately. So where do we start sorting this out?"

"First, tell us everything," Martinez finally spoke. "What do you got?"

Feeling worn out enough to lay his head down on the desk and sleep, Coal went clear back to what had happened with Angel and Ray, then worked forward. He tried to put everything into chronological order so he would leave nothing out.

"Sorry about the deputy," said Sam as he took a little silver flask from a hip pocket, unscrewed the lid, and tipped it over to pour some yellow-ish liquid into his coffee. He raised the flask to Coal. "Medicine."

Coal nodded. He might have been concerned, but there were two things about Sam Browning he knew: One, he could hold more alcohol than almost any other man Coal had ever met; and two, when he was on a job like this, he wouldn't take more than a swallow or two. Anyway, he seemed almost to work better with it than without.

"I have to say, though," Sam said as he worked the flask back down into the tight pocket of his pants, "I don't like that it happened to your deputy and a little girl, but if it hadn't been him, it would have been you."

Coal didn't say anything about Maura or his mom. Right now he could barely stand to think about it. "Would it? I wonder. I thought about how I could have taken you two back to that house when I got off work, and if you had been in there instead of Vic, you might have spotted the bomb and been able to get rid of it before it went off."

Martinez looked quickly over at Sam. "Don't try to snow an old Bureau man, Vike. He knows the score as good as you an' me."

Sam nodded and looked back at Coal. "Yeah. Sorry. I wish we had been here sooner too."

Coal only nodded. "What do we do now?"

"You said you remember seeing that dark blue Jaguar at one of the hotels, right?" said Martinez. "Did you ever go check on it?"

"When I saw it, I didn't really have any reason to. It had Ada County plates, and those lowlanders are always coming up here to litter up the valley." He knew that wasn't really true. People in the Lemhi Valley could litter with the best of them. But it didn't make the rumor about the citizens of Ada, Bannock, Bingham, and Bonneville counties being responsible for ninety-five percent of the litter in this valley any less fun to spread.

"Well, it sounds like you have plenty of reason now. But you put out an APB, right?" Sam said. "How long ago?"

"This morning."

"Then I'll bet you won't find that Jag now. You don't think those guys would be drivin' around here trying to kill you without a police radio on hand, do you?"

Coal stared at Sam, then glanced over at Martinez. The Mexican was staring at the floor—saving Coal some pride.

"Huh." Coal swore, perhaps his favorite pastime. "I didn't think about it. I was hoping they'd get picked up right away, and it would be over."

"Wouldn't have been over anyway," replied Sam. "They would have killed whoever stopped them, and if they didn't, they probably would have blown themselves up. They're not about to get caught. That's their job."

Coal nodded. "Well, if they blew themselves up, that sounds pretty much like it would be over."

Sam shrugged. "Yeah, I guess. If you put it that way. And if it's only the two guys you've seen in the Jag."

The implications of that statement made Coal's heart begin to thump harder. "You think there are more?"

"Killer ants work together," said Sam.

"I think these guys are more like wasps."

"Yeah. Maybe. But I wouldn't hold my breath."

"So back to my question: Where do we start?"

"The hotel. Where is it?"

They went out in the parking lot, where Coal, embarrassed that he had missed it the first time, saw the red-on-white license plate from the “Cornhusker State” on the front end of a sparkling burnt orange sixties Mustang.

He looked at Sam. “A little small for you, isn’t it?”

Sam laughed with glee and turned his hand over when he pointed a finger almost accusingly at Martinez. “Blame him.”

“That’s a damn fine ride,” Martinez said. “Just because it doesn’t suit you jolly green giants doesn’t mean you have to knock it.”

Coal gave a smile, not even trying to backpedal. He didn’t have to. “Actually, I like it, Q. I don’t know if I’d fit in it, but I’d buy one like it any day.”

Martinez looked over at Sam, his eyes saying Coal had settled some kind of argument. But he kept his thoughts to himself, and they all crawled into Coal’s pickup and drove down to the Stagecoach Inn, parking in the loading zone.

Coal scanned the lot, and Martinez watched him. When Coal looked over, he said, “Not here, is it?”

Coal only shook his head, then turned to lead the way inside. Julie the manager was behind the desk, and she greeted him with her normal huge smile, but this time there was a nervous edge to it. “Hey, Coal. Are you doing okay? I’m sorry to hear about your deputy.”

“Thanks, Julie. Yeah, it’s been a rough couple of days. Hey, these are some friends of mine ...” He paused, realizing his friends, under the circumstances, probably would rather no one in town know who they really were. “John, and Terry.” He pointed at Sam and Martinez respectively.

“Good to meet you,” said Julie. “What can I help you with, Coal?”

“Well, there was a dark blue Jaguar in front of the hotel a couple days ago. Know anything about it?”

Julie frowned. “That’s a weird thing, now that you mention it. I saw that car when I came in to work one day and tried to check the card on it, out of curiosity. Honestly, I can't even say why. But there wasn't any card with a Jaguar listed."

Coal frowned. "Why would that be?"

With a shrug, she said, "Well, there isn't any law that says somebody has to put down their real information, right? You could be driving a silver Rolls Royce with Alabama plates and claim it's a green Chevy Nova from Oregon. Who's going to check? Unless there's a break-in or something, I honestly don't think I've ever checked up on what somebody wrote on their card in all the years I've worked in this business."

Coal nodded, disheartened. What she said made sense. He had never thought about it, he guessed because he had never had any reason to lie about what vehicle he was driving.

"Well, let me ask you this," Sam cut in from beside Coal. "Are your room patrons all checked out, or paid up for today?"

"Umm ..." She looked thoughtful. "Well, now that you mention it, I don't even know. Let me look." She flipped through a card file and pulled out four cards, scanning them quickly. "It looks like these four are still in the hotel. Two are staying over, and the other two haven't checked out yet."

"Any idea who any of them are?" asked Coal.

Julie fanned out the cards, looking them over with a studious frown. "It would probably be more helpful if Keri, my night clerk, was here. But ... Okay, this one I know. A younger man and his wife, and they have two little girls—cute as a button. I can't remember why they're here. It says they have a green Ford station wagon. Then this one ... Uh ... Two guests ... two guests ... Oh! I think I know who these guys are. They don't seem to be from around here, but they're nice enough. One good-looking guy and then his partner. Now that guy is tough! You know, the kind you don't want to get on the wrong side of." She punctuated that with a laugh. "It says they're in a gold 1968 Dodge Monaco with Idaho plates from Ada County. I don't remember that car, but that doesn't mean anything. I'm not that into cars. Those are the two who are staying over. The young man with the family reserved several days, but the other two guys just keep coming down every morning to pay for another day."

"What about your other two? When did they check in?" asked Coal.

"Umm ... It says here yesterday, for both of them. One drives a—"

"Did they say anything about how long they were staying?"

Acting puzzled at being cut off by Sam Browning, Julie blinked, then looked down at the cards again. "No. No, it just says they paid for one day."

A young couple appeared at the far end of the counter, and the man slid a key across the smooth surface. "Room 112, ma'am. Thanks. Oh! And the toilet has a weird problem. A leak in the tank or something. Keeps coming on throughout the night."

"Oh! All right, thank you," Julie replied, looking at the cards. "One-twelve ... There you are. Thank you, Mr. Vaughn."

With a surreptitious glance at Coal and Sam, both of whom dwarfed him, the man turned and took the woman by the elbow, and they left.

"So now there's just three?" asked Coal by way of confirmation.

"Yes, just three. Do you want to know about the third?" She flashed a glance toward Sam, perhaps wondering if he would interrupt her again.

"Um ... Yeah, why not."

"Okay, it says here it's two people they paid for, but they asked for a crib. Their car ..." She paused and looked at Sam, then back over at Coal. "Do you care what they drive?"

Coal shook his head, feeling a little distracted. "No, that's okay. Tell me more about those two men, the ones you said don't seem like they're from around here. Can you give me any better description of them?"

"Well, the younger one's a real looker. He could be a magazine model, or maybe an actor. Black hair, and he keeps it slicked back tight. Just really good-looking, and ... Well, I think he knows it. Then the other guy ... Well, wow. Don't get me wrong, he seems nice enough. Polite, anyway. But there's something about him. He looks like he might be a boxer. His face seems all swollen. And I noticed he has scars on his knuckles—a lot of them. I'm not sure what else."

"Why do you say they don't seem like they're from around here?"

"Umm ... Well, I don't know why I said that, actually. I'm not sure. They just have a foreign look. Dark olive skin, black hair ... They seemed out of place."

"Is there any way you could let us take a look at their room?" Sam asked.

Julie stared at him for a moment, obviously taken completely by surprise. She looked back at Coal, and her eyes dropped to the badge on his coat. She giggled, a nervous reaction. "Uhh ... Well, the rules are pretty strict about that, actually. I mean—well, Coal, isn't that the law: no searching a room without a warrant?"

Coal chuckled. "Yeah. Sam was kidding. Weren't you—" He stopped and cursed himself inside. It was John, not Sam! He grunted, hoping Julie wouldn't notice the slip. "Well, Julie, would you do me a huge favor? When those guys come back, will you call either my dispatcher or the city police and have them tell me on the radio? Or—" He paused and looked at Sam, then back at Julie. "On second thought, just have them call me on the radio and I'll find a phone and call them back. Tell them not to put anything about this over the air."

Julie paused, her face getting serious. In her eagerness to help in all the questioning, she must have gotten distracted and not given any thought to why Coal was asking about her customers. Now, from the look on her face, it all must have hit home, and she swore, then blushed.

"Sorry! Please excuse my French."

Coal laughed. "You'd better be. I hate that kind of talk."

"I'm sorry," she repeated. "Coal ... You're thinking the guys that set the bombs might be staying here, huh?"

Not wanting to scare her, he said, "Don't worry. We just have to check out everything in town. That's all. Anyway, just give dispatch a call when you see those guys, okay? But don't ogle them—not even that handsome one. Or at least not unless that's what he's used to you doing. Then keep ogling."

Julie laughed, this time keeping her cool. "Okay. I'll keep ogling." Saying this, as another clerk walked in, she reached for a coat hanging on a hook behind the counter. "I'm going to go out with you guys. I really need a cigarette."

Politely, the three of them waited for Julie to come around the counter, and they walked back out into the bitter cold, which was so overpowering it had crept several feet inside the front door.

As they stepped out, Coal looked over at a nice blue Chevrolet Caprice, parked five or six spaces down the way. Two men sat inside, not looking toward them.

Julie looked at the same time Coal did. "Oh, hey! Hey, Coal, I think that might be those two guys right there."

At that moment, the passenger looked toward Coal, and their eyes met. For some reason, a chill went over Coal, an almost instant gut reaction.

"Ohh ..." Julie's voice was quiet. "Yes, that's definitely them. And that's *not* the handsome one."

"I'd guess not," Coal agreed. "It's the one you wouldn't want to get on the wrong side of."

As Coal spoke, he started toward the Caprice, and Sam and Martinez followed. The driver put the car into reverse, starting to back out of his spot. Coal held up a polite hand and quickened his pace to cut him off.

CHAPTER TWENTY-THREE

Menny Marcello saw the badge on the big man's coat, and the white cowboy hat. Then he saw the two men standing with him, and he swore. Throwing the car into reverse, he started away from his parking spot.

They saw the big man raise a hand to stop them, and Scabs turned his head and barked at Menny, "Stop the car!"

"What are you talking about?" Menny kept backing.

"I said stop the car, moron, or I'm gonna bust your face in! Just stop! They don't got a clue who we are!"

The car was already moving three miles an hour or so, and when Menny slammed down on the brake pedal the tires ground gravel coming to a stop.

As calm as a summer morning, Scabs rolled down his window. "Hello, officer. Is there a problem?" He was watching the big man's face. He was a broad man, the hair just over his ears, and what anyone would call the perfect mustache on his lip—a true cowboy straight off the silver screen. But even while he saw all this, he saw something more important, and he kept his own hand away from his weapon: None of the three men had a weapon in sight—yet.

* * *

Coal scanned the Caprice's passenger. He could sure see why Julie hadn't put him in the best light. To say the man had a scary look about him was putting it mildly. The bridge of his nose, probably broad by genetics already, had been made even more so, doubtlessly, by fighting. His brows bulged with flesh the same way, and his cheeks and ears as well. This man was no pacifist. But at a glance both men had their hands in sight, and none held any weapon.

"No, there's no problem. I was just hoping to have a word with you."

"Oh. Well, my moron buddy over here left his hat downtown. Can you wait for us to go get it?"

"Where is it? We can call down and have them hold it for you. Besides, it's a small town—I'm sure nobody will take it."

The ugly fighter stared up at Coal through eyes as black as ... Well, as black as Coal's name. "Uh, to tell you the truth, we were talkin' about goin' to grab a bite to eat. What do you need? Can't it wait?"

"Well, I'd rather not," Coal replied, starting to feel cautious. "Why don't you step out of the car? It'll just take a minute." He tried to watch both their hands without being obvious, but that was a tall order.

"Listen, man, I'm sure you have your job to do, but I'm really not in the mood right now. I'm hungry, and I don't do so well when I'm hungry."

"He's diabetic, you know," said a voice from the other side of the vehicle.

Coal leaned down to look in at the driver, who was startlingly handsome just like Julie had said, the kind of handsome both a woman and a man would take note of. Coal looked back at the passenger. "Is that true? You're diabetic?"

"I don't much like everyone to know about it," said the man, pulling a sour face. "Can't keep that guy's mouth shut with a bag o' cement. Yeah. Diabetic."

"What type?" Coal asked.

"The crappy type," the man growled. "How the hell I know what type?"

Coal tensed. Trying to look casual, he undid the bottom snap of his coat to reveal his revolver. This man must be in his fifties, and he looked ugly, but he didn't look stupid. What fifty-year-old man didn't even know if he had adult onset diabetes? But he couldn't prove a man his age would know the designation of his diabetes, any more than this man could prove he wouldn't.

"Hang on a second." Coal stepped over and whispered to the others to get the plate number from the Caprice, and then he went back to the car, standing three feet away, his right hand always hovering close to his holstered magnum while trying to pretend he wasn't aware of it. "So why don't you guys show me some I.D.," he said, aware that Browning was walking behind the car to look at the plate. "I'll just talk to you when you get back."

He said that, but if these two gentlemen thought they were just going to drive away, they were wrong. He planned on being behind them wherever they went to get the driver's hat, and then wherever they went to eat. At least until he knew who they were.

"All right," said the passenger, "that's fair enough. But let's hurry this up, all right? I'm gettin' pretty weak."

"Yeah, you look weak," agreed Coal, smiling to pretend he was only an amiable small-town lawman.

With his heart pounding, not because he knew anything but just because of a bad feeling, Coal watched the two men pull out their wallets, then get their driver's licenses from them, which they handed over. One said Bryn Maurice Renault, and it had the passenger's face sprawled in all its ugliness on it. The other was Matthew Drew Hardigan. Both their addresses were listed as being in Boise.

"So what are you two gentlemen doing in this part of the state?" asked Coal.

"Hey, officer, I thought you were going to take our names and let us go eat," said Renault, sounding almost plaintive. "I can't do this all day without some food in me."

"Can I at least take some time to call your names in first?" Coal asked, knowing he was probably pushing his luck.

Renault grunted and looked angry. Finally, he slapped both hands down on his legs. "Hey, how about this? You just hold the driver's licenses hostage, and we'll come get 'em after we eat? Good enough? We'll even come up to the jail if you want."

Coal had felt his heart starting to beat faster and faster throughout his interaction with Renault and Hardigan. He couldn't pinpoint any reason, though, and that was perhaps the worst thing about it. The wheels of his mind were spinning. He had the driver's licenses, and Sam would have memorized the license plate. And in reality, these men hadn't done anything he knew of even to justify holding them here as long as he had. If he could just keep an eye on them and watch where they went, there shouldn't be a problem with letting them go.

"All right," Coal said. "Yeah, let me hang onto these and you come to the sheriff's office and pick them up. You know where it is?"

"Uh ... Well, I assume it's at the courthouse? We saw that while we were driving around."

"Okay. Yeah. Go behind the building, and the sheriff's office is in the basement."

"Thanks, Sheriff. We'll see you soon then," said Renault. "Man, I'm sorry for being so grumpy. I'm just ... Well, I'm really feeling under the weather. Nothin' a good omelet or somethin' won't cure, though."

Coal nodded and stepped away from the car. "I'll be waiting at my office."

As the car backed away and then pulled off, headed toward Main, Coal didn't even look at the plate, since he knew Sam would have it. Anyone trained at the Bureau could remember license plates the way a kid would remember his favorite cereal. He motioned to Sam and Martinez to follow him, said a quick goodbye to Julie, and jumped in the pickup. He had to gun the engine to get out in traffic before the Caprice could turn left on Main, and already he was three cars behind them, but that would be fine.

Without being asked, Sam leaned past Martinez, the unlucky one with the shortest legs who got to sit in the middle, and proudly repeated the memorized plate number. "Two L, five, seven, twenty-five."

"Thanks," said Coal, half listening. "Wait. What? You said two L?"

"Yeah, two L—"

"What the hell? That's our county."

"Crap, that's right! All right, we've got to catch up."

It didn't take long to do just that. After the Caprice pulled onto Main, Coal kept an eye on it until his turn came, then spun his tires getting in front of a station wagon coming down off the Bar, and probably earning a few well-placed curses in the process.

He saw the Caprice pull up in front of Wally's Café and stop, and he parked a few places back, the only place left. When the two men in the Caprice got out, Coal yelled them down. "Hold up a minute."

The two stood waiting until Coal caught them. "What's up with the local plates on your car if you guys are from Boise?"

With only a moment's hesitation, Renault said. "Oh! Yeah. Well, our truck is bein' a piece of garbage, and I saw this thing was for sale, so I asked if we could drive it around for a while to make sure it runs good. It's a long drive back to Boise in a car that don't run well."

"Yeah, of course. So where'd you pick this up?"

"Uhh ... Lemhi Road? Something like that. Some older lady."

"All right. Thanks for clearing that up. It was just a little weird."

"You bet, Sheriff. Any time."

With that, the two men continued on into Wally's.

Coal looked across the street, where the police station was, then turned to Sam and Martinez. "Let's go over there and check out their information. And then just for the fun of it maybe we'll see who that Caprice registers to and go pay them a quick visit."

Sam grinned. "Fine, but I hope you'll start lettin' me earn my keep sometime soon. So far, you seem to be doing just fine."

"Yeah, because no one's setting bombs off in my hat or anything. That's when I'll need you."

At the police station, they did a check on the two driver's licenses. There was nothing irregular about them. No arrest warrants, not even a speeding ticket on either of their records. The record actually showed their addresses as belonging to someone else, but the system was infamously slow being updated, so that meant little.

When the plate check on the Caprice came back to Bernard and Renee Schutmann, on Lemhi Road, Coal laughed. "Well, there are some folks I know. Let's go have a talk with them about their car, shall we?"

"You bet, man. What else do we have to do?" said Sam. "I don't suppose Renee's a good cookie maker, is she?"

* * *

Scabs Ravioli and Menny Marcello sauntered into Wally's. Scabs even stretched his arms, to add to the appearance of being tired and relaxed.

"Just have a seat, guys," said a woman with beautiful red hair kept up perfectly, and an apron that in spite of a job that didn't lend itself to being clean looked as if it had just come out of the dryer.

"Hey, ma'am," said Scabs, feeling the racing of his heart. "Before we eat, is there any way you could do me a favor?"

"Sure thing. What's that?"

"Well, our wives are across the street shopping, and they've been at it forever. We told them we were coming over here to save a table, but we're trying to have some fun with them, and when they come in we want it to look like we're not here."

"Okay," said the woman, getting a smile on her face. "So you're wanting a place to hide?"

"Actually, even better," said Scabs. "If you could show us out a back way, we're gonna sneak around the front and when we see them come in, we'll come walking in just when they're starting to think we ditched them."

"Oh, you boys are rotten," said the kind red-haired lady. "All right, just follow me. But I hope I get a nice tip for this!"

Scabs thought, *Sure, I'll give you a tip: Never trust a stranger.*

They followed the woman back through the kitchen, where a stout-looking man also wearing an apron gave them a surprised look. "Hi. Can I help you guys?"

"Don't worry about us, honey," said the woman. "I'm just showing these gentlemen out the back way. They'll be back."

The man laughed. "Okay, whatever you say, sweetie." He shook his head, still chuckling, as the woman who was evidently his wife led them through the back door.

"Well, there you guys go—freedom! But I hope you won't keep your wives waiting too long. I still say it's a rotten trick." She grinned, and her eyes opened wide with surprise when Scabs reached behind his back and drew out his wallet, then pulled a five-dollar bill out of it and handed it to her.

"There. That's for playin' along!"

"Well, thank you! Now I'm just going to make sure you have an extra helping of whatever you order. Or maybe even one of Wally's special cinnamon rolls."

"Sounds good. Thanks again!"

When the back door shut, Scabs turned to Menny. "Come on. We ain't got a lot o' time."

"Where we goin'?"

"Gettin' outta here, that's where. We gotta go before the lid blows off this place!"

They went down the alley until Scabs saw a newer model gold Plymouth Satellite, possibly a seventy-one. "Our new car," he said, and he lifted the door handle, which was unlocked as he imagined most doors in this little town would be.

"Get in," he told Menny.

"You haven't even started it yet!"

"I said get your butt in. When I start it we ain't gonna have time to sit around. We've gotta head for Montana, and now!"

Menny went around as he'd been told and got in the passenger side, looking about nervously. "So help me, man, if I gotta kill somebody out here in daylight over this, that's it. We're done for."

"Then don't," said Scabs in a strained-sounding voice as he leaned sideways and forward, messing around under the steering wheel. After a minute or so of fiddling, the car fired up, and Scabs turned and gave a smug smile to his partner, put the car in drive, and pulled out of the alley.

When they hit the next street, they turned right, drove down two blocks, made another right, and drove until they came to a tee. They made one last right, got to Main Street as Scabs had known they would, and the second they had a big opening he pulled sedately onto Main, heading west. They were crossing the river bridge moments later, and then they turned right onto Highway 93.

There might be some roaming state bull around that they didn't know about, but Scabs was pretty sure everyone else would still be in town, after the morning's excitement.

With that confidence, he sank the gas pedal to the floor, learning on the instant that the obvious big-block engine under the hood knew good and well what it had been intended for.

Grinning widely, Scabs reached into his left shirt pocket with his right hand and pulled out what appeared to be two cards, handing one to Menny. "There, *compagno*. If I'm not mistaken, that's the new you, Michael T. Mangione. And I'm ..." He paused and peered at his own driver's license, which he had to hold well away from his face to read. At that point he was going around a curve at eighty-four miles an hour. "I'm David B. Ragule. Sweet. Don't forget it, bud: old Bryn Renault and Matthew Hardigan just died back in Salmon and got reincarnated. Man, I already miss that Caprice," he added, "but damn, this baby can up and *move!*"

CHAPTER TWENTY-FOUR

Montana, same day

It was a miserable one hour and fifty-minute drive from Salmon up over Lost Trail Pass to the little town of Hamilton, Montana, and most of the drive was made in silence, other than the humming of the gold Plymouth's tires on the asphalt.

Menny took over the wheel and drove the entire way, fighting his instinct to put the pedal all the way to the floor and praying that in Salmon they had yet to discover this car had been stolen. He and Scabs had discussed it at length when trying to decide whether or not to ditch the car along the way and find a way to get another one, killing its owner so there would be no one to report the theft. They decided that with the car being parked where it had been, it likely belonged to someone who was at work in downtown Salmon, and with any luck they wouldn't discover the Plymouth's absence until the end of the workday. The danger of taking the time to find some other option for a vehicle, and then leaving another dead body, or even more of them, on the backtrail simply was not worth the trade-off. And so they drove on, and the death-like silence descended.

Menny felt sick. He would never speak to Scabs about it. In fact, he didn't know that he could ever speak to another living human being about it. But he couldn't get the old woman with the Caprice out of his mind, or the little girl he had killed with his bomb. Neither of those was supposed to happen. It might sound strange trying to explain to someone why he could be a paid hitman for the Mob and yet be so tortured by death, but the death of a sweet old lady and an innocent little girl were something completely different from taking out full-grown men. *Why?* Why did that deputy have to go get his sister and go to that trailer house? And that old lady. Why couldn't they simply have found a car and taken it, without ever even seeing its owner? It had worked fine with the Satellite.

There was more than one time, driving along that long, long stretch of road, when he felt like stopping to get out and throw up, telling Scabs he had eaten something bad. But he never had the luxury of throwing up and then feeling better. The sin of killing that little girl, and of even being in the room when Scabs callously shot that old woman, those two things were eating him up. In all his time as a hitman for the Mob, he had never been involved in anything like that. He started to dream about what other jobs the Mob might have to offer a man like him. He glanced over at Scabs, who was so calm and callous he appeared to be asleep, kicked back in his seat with his dark glasses over his eyes. How, he wondered, could a man be so hard?

Scabs Ravioli had his seat back, his glasses over his eyes. But he was not asleep. In reality, he was far from it. During all the excitement in town, with the adrenaline flooding through him like fire water, he had had no time to think about anything but sheer survival. He had been overcome with the deadly thrill of being so close to one of the men they had been sent to Idaho to kill, along with the two ex-FBI agents both he and Menny had studied so much prior to both of their disappearances: Samuel Browning and Alex Martinez. His active mind had been more than occupied with dreaming up reasons for why he had to leave the hotel, why he had to walk all the way through Wally's and out the back—the kinds of lies his mind could whip up as fast as another man could swat a mosquito.

But now? Even knowing how close he and Menny had been to three men whose reputations he and his partner had despised so much when the three of them worked for the FBI, other thoughts had come to cloud his mind, thoughts he had spent years trying to keep down deep inside him, because no other soul who worked for the Mob could ever know the real Saverio Ravioli.

The thing was he couldn't stop thinking about that little girl from the news. Before disappearing out of radio range, they had been forced to listen to the story again on Salmon's radio station, and he had had to sit there and pretend to be looking out his window, enjoying the scenery, when all he really wanted to do was reach over and turn the radio off. But if Menny, a hitman much younger and less experienced than he was, could sit there as cold as a block of ice and listen to the story of that little girl being blown to bits, then how could Scabs let on how it was affecting him? He couldn't. It was as simple as that. He could be every bit as strong and heartless as Menny.

And yet he couldn't stop thinking of his own little girl. Viola. Sure, she was older now. She was gone. Married to that damn doctor who had taken her so far away from her mother. And from him. But she was still his little girl. He could remember her face when she was the age of the girl on the radio. Her fifth birthday party. He remembered every minute detail. So many years ago, and he could still hear the sound of her voice. So sweet, so innocent. Even to this day she had no idea what her father really did for a living.

She thought he was a traveling salesman. And to this day, when she had three children of her own, she remained innocent. Saverio's little girl.

Why had that stupid jailer taken his sister with him to that house? Why could he not just go himself? And why were they even there at all? Stupid people. Why did stupid people always have to mess things up? Everything had been going so smoothly. Just another day, and he and Menny would have been well on their way back to Idaho Falls, still driving the nice Jaguar, still undetected, still guiltless.

Now they had killed a little girl. Scabs wouldn't drink alcohol on a job, but he would when he got back home. It was going to take a bathtub full, and more, to wash that little girl from his mind. He only prayed he would never see a picture of her face ...

It was with that thought that they pulled into the town of Hamilton, the first place of any size since leaving Salmon. The sign said there were 2400 and some people inside the city limits, and that was more than big enough for a car lot. This Plymouth was a beautiful car, and powerful under the hood. But it was a liability that had to disappear. It was time to get something legal and rid themselves of the worry of being picked up for grand theft auto.

* * *

With Martinez beside him, and Sam by the passenger door, Coal drove the GMC up Lemhi Road to the home of Bernard and Renee Schutmann, glad to be inside the cab, with its raging heater. Outside, the cold battered on. In fact, as the day crept on it seemed to grow even colder.

When they arrived at the house, there were no cars around. Before Coal could mention it, Martinez said, "I would have thought those two guys would have parked their car here when they took the Caprice."

Coal nodded. “Me too. Well, I can’t imagine Renee has another car, so she must be home—unless she’s with Bernard somewhere. Let’s go see.”

They went up on the porch, and Coal knocked on the door. He knocked again, with Martinez standing beside him. Sam wasn’t quite so patient and polite. While Coal was knocking, and Martinez was waiting, Sam walked along the porch and peeked through the window. Coal heard him swear, and he looked over. “What?”

Sam dragged off his sunglasses. “I don’t think you wanna know.”

Feeling dread start to erupt inside him, a dread he could never quite seem to escape anymore, Coal walked over to Sam, wordless, and peered through the curtains. He used the same word Sam had. There was a mounded bedspread on the floor, and from the end of it protruded the bottoms of two shoes—women’s shoes. Coal swore again.

After Sam picked the lock, the three of them went inside with gloves on, and Coal went straight to the bedspread, lifting it up gingerly. He hadn’t seen Renee Schuttman in years, and of course never with the pupils of her eyes fully dilated. But it didn’t take two seconds to know her face. With his heart jamming up into his throat, he slipped the cover back over her face and stood up, blinking rapidly. War. War ... This was only a war. It was not the civilian life of peace he thought he was returning to Lemhi County for. He had to get back into the mental mode of war, or he would soon go insane.

Walking to the phone, his hands still gloved, Coal called Nadine. He ignored the woman’s initial pleasantries, not because he wanted to be rude, but because he didn’t even realize she was asking him how he was doing. “Nadine, I’m up at 898 Lemhi Road—the Schuttman’s. Listen, I need you to send the state patrolman up here if he’s still in town. And the coroner.”

On the other end of the line he heard Nadine gasp. He almost felt as sorry for her as he did himself. He had never been a dispatcher, but it must be every bit as bad imagining the worst things as it was seeing them for real.

"Also, Nadine, can you go through our files and get the description of the kind of vehicle Bernard Schuttman drives? And then put an APB out for it. We need to try and find him as soon as possible. Please let the state cop and the coroner know I won't be here when they get here, but they can reach me on the radio. And do me another favor: Send as much backup down to the area of Wally's Café as you can find."

Not wasting any more time, even though he knew he was breaking a major rule by leaving the scene of a homicide, Coal and his cohorts bombed back down Lemhi Road. Inside Wally's, they found exactly what Coal had expected: No Renault, and no Hardigan. The blue Caprice was still out in front, but they were gone.

After speaking on the radio with the state bull to let him know the situation and what he was walking into at the Schuttmans', Coal, Sam, and Martinez returned to the Stagecoach Inn, and Coal made an emergency call to Judge Sinclair, seeking easily-obtained permission to search the suspects' hotel room. Julie, her face sober and pale, allowed them into the room.

It was as if Sam Browning, the explosives expert, had walked into a bomb maker's heaven. Besides all the suitcases and the clothing that someone fleeing an occupied hotel room in a hurry might leave scattered behind, there were a number of items that no run-of-the-mill tourist would ever have any need of traveling with: the equipment and materials of a bomb maker's trade.

Sam looked at Coal and raised his eyebrows way up. He gave a disbelieving shake of his head. "Well, if you never wondered before ..." Without saying anything, he reached into a hip pocket and extracted a pair of heavy-duty rubber gloves, which he slid over his big hands. Then, beginning at one end of the bureau in the middle of which the television sat, he began picking up items, some of them in boxes, and studying them, explaining each as he went. There were a number of pipe clamps in one box, sitting on top of a second box filled with industrial-strength magnets. The clamps would be used to connect the magnets to a pipe bomb, which a passing pedestrian could conveniently slap under a target's car in passing, perhaps pretending to tie his shoes or some similar task.

There was a can of potassium permanganate, a common disinfectant, and a bottle of glycerin, both available at any drugstore, but which when combined would create a hot enough flame to get a house fire going, and if done the right way could be delayed long enough for the arsonist to be long gone before any flames started up. "It's not much of an assassination tool," Sam admitted with a shrug, "but another tool in the toolbox, I guess—if you got some guy sleeping in a house and you want to quietly set his house on fire and be gone before it gets rolling."

Sifting through the hitmen's bag of tricks, Sam found two more similar items that would also cause a fire when mixed together: Iodine and aluminum powder. Nearby was a box of tin foil, and a coffee grinder. The foil would be ground up in the coffee grinder, then turned to a powder in a rock tumbler that was sitting unplugged on the floor.

"These guys had a little bit of everything but the professional military stuff," said Sam. "Interesting mix of things to start fires with, and a bunch of stuff most people would never think twice about other than to think it was odd to have in a hotel room."

Other tools the hitmen had on hand, all of which were mind-boggling to Coal, who never could understand why a professional hitman wouldn't just go out and buy a bomb at the Acme Bomb Store like Wile E. Coyote always did, were: a partial Hills Brothers coffee can partially full of what Sam identified simply as rust; two iron rods still hooked up to a car battery, which combined with a nearby bucket that had obviously contained salt water was how they had made the rust, or iron oxide; a coffee maker with dirty filters in the trash, used to collect the rust out of the salt water; a few broken light bulbs in the trash can; hydrogen peroxide; a can of Kool-Aid mix; and last of all some heater tabs, to be used for blasting caps.

Coal looked at Sam. "This is seriously something a professional hitman would be using? It doesn't look much more dangerous than a city dump in here to me."

Sam pointed a finger at Coal and clicked his tongue. "Exactly. To you and almost any other hick town sheriff in the country."

* * *

After parking the beautiful gold Satellite at the curb in Hamilton, Montana's only park, leaving the keys inside it and cleaning off any surface they might have touched, Scabs and Menny had walked to a local car lot and bought themselves a decent 1968 Oldsmobile Cutlass four-door sedan, three-speed manual with a 400 cubic inch engine under the hood and only 25,000 miles on the odometer. The car was sedate looking enough not to grab a lot of attention, but with all those horses under the hood plenty strong enough to jet them down the road in a time of need.

It had a soft black vinyl top, and the body was what Oldsmobile called "scarlet", but Scabs thought of as plain old red. It reminded Menny of blood.

Renting a nondescript room under Scabs's new name at a pointless-looking highway motel, they took their worn-out carcasses and their now-invisible, and in fact non-existent luggage in and threw both down on the bed. Scabs didn't even bother to turn on the television. Each man closed his eyes to sleep. And neither of them slept.

After a half-hour of lying on the bed pretending to rest because of course nothing affected Saverio Ravioli, he got up and went over to the phone. One of the specific rules in the Mob rule book was not to use the room phone in a hotel, but since today Scabs was David Ragule, he didn't really care. Thinking about rules today made him tired.

He dialed the front desk of the Flamingo Hotel in Vegas because he wasn't allowed to keep the bosses' numbers with him and didn't call Porc de Castiglione enough to have his number memorized. When he got to the right person, only then did he ask for the top-floor office of *Mister* de Castiglione—whom he had never wanted so badly to call Porc.

The voice, although almost a thousand miles away over a skinny little wire, still made Scabs's heart pound, and he hated Porc de Castiglione for that.

Hello? Castiglione here.

No "de" in front of the name? thought Scabs. Then be damned with that.

"Mister Castiglione. Saverio Ravioli."

Mister Scabs! You've certainly kept me waiting. You have some good news for me?

There was no point in dragging it out. "No, sir. Nothing good. Well, one thing: The prosecutor, Mike Fica, he's gone."

Good. Good. What else? I hope you ain't got bad news.

Inside, Scabs swore, and he wanted to call Porc a name—something less innocuous than Porc. But he could only imagine the hitmen Porc would set on him if he swore at him and hung up. "It ain't good, Mr. Castiglione."

Listen, Mister Scabs. De. *Hear me?* De *Castiglione. So what's your news?*

Scabs couldn't win against this man. "Well, we had some trouble. It looked like a sure thing. The sheriff is living by himself. We know where his family lives, but apparently he must be estranged from them or something. No idea, but he don't go where his kids are. Got some girl, though."

A girlfriend?

"As far as we can tell."

Okay, so? Is that the bad news? Come on, man. I got stuff t' do.

S.O.B. "Okay. Sure, boss. Sorry. Well, like I said, it looked like a sure thing—"

Just tell me already! Castiglione's growl was even harsher than normal. *You haven't had your valium today?* Scabs wished he could ask.

"So Menny sets a bomb at the sheriff's house. It goes off not much later after he went to town. But ..."

But it wasn't him, was it? Come on, you ass. You think I don't hear the news? You think Vegas is so far away we're out in the middle o' nowhere? I heard, ya bum. I heard about some dumb jailer and his little kid sister gettin' it. What the hell was that? What kind o' idiots would screw up an easy thing like that? Huh? Well? If you're lookin' for a great way t' get all the FBI in on this and who knows who else, you morons are goin' about it the right way.

"We screwed up, sir. I know. There never should have been any reason for that kid and his sister to go there, but they did. It was a total fluke."

Silence. There was doubtlessly a volcano building up on the other end of the line. Scabs of course wanted to shove something down it to keep it from erupting, but he couldn't think of one thing that would work. He just had to keep talking.

"We gotta come home, Mr. C— Mr. *de* Castiglione. Me an' Marcello, we gotta come home. That sheriff has seen us up close. That was a freak thing too. An' he's got some other guys with him now too, and—"

Who?

He hoped that detail would slip by. "Uh ... Well, some guys. Sir, he's got ..."

Spit it out, you imbecile. I'm runnin' out o' patience here.

"It's Agent Browning and Martinez."

Far, far away on the other end of the telephone line de Castiglione swore, but it seemed to tear in through Scabs's good ear and out the other one. *What the hell you talkin' about? They quit! They ain't with the Bureau no more, remember?*

"I know. But they're in Salmon. That's all I can tell you. An' they saw us both—up close."

De Castiglione swore again. Then silence fell, the same kind of silence that follows a major explosion, when everyone's eardrums are so badly shaken that no one can hear anyone else speak even if they could find the energy to try.

At last, there was a sigh. *All right. All right. I'm gonna try somethin' else.*

"So we come home?"

No, ya moron! You two stay put. Stay wherever you are, an' I hope it's a long ways off from that sheriff an' Browning an' Martinez. Let's get a number I can call you back on, and I'll get hold of you in a few days. Maybe a week. If this other thing works, then you can come home. But you can forget any Christmas bonus.

The line went dead, and Scabs sat there listening, then jerked the phone away and stared at it for a while. Did Porc actually hang up? He hadn't even gotten the number yet to call him back! With a sick feeling in his guts, feeling the eyes of Menny Marcello on the back of his head but not looking over at him, he started once again the long process of getting back through to the office of Paolo Oronzo Rustichelli de Castiglione—Porc. It took almost as long to get him back on the phone as it did to pronounce his cursed name.

CHAPTER TWENTY-FIVE

Saturday, February 10

Three days passed, and Salmon remained quiet. Coal, Sam, and Martinez stayed in various places around the valley, once with the Lockwoods, another time with Leo and Sharlene Erickson, the parents of his high school friend, rodeo tomboy Molly. The third night they stayed with the parents of another old rodeo buddy, Jeremy Snowball. His parents, Billy and Gertrude, were happy to have Coal and his friends, and everyone pointedly avoided talking about the devastating experiences Coal had gone through since his return to the valley. It was good simply to be among friends.

The big thing, the important thing, was that no one ever asked who Sam and Martinez were. That was one thing neither Coal nor his friends could share. Sam and Martinez had already put themselves in enough legal danger being involved in this matter with the Mob in the first place, and especially coming out in broad daylight like normal people, when neither of them had the kind of face that would soon be forgotten.

At Sam and Martinez's insistence, Coal had made an arrangement down at Quality Motors to park Martinez's Mustang, the Thunderbird, and the GMC in their shop at nights, and Coal drove a different used vehicle every day, paying the dealership a small fee out of the county funds. He had to make sure to be in a vehicle that could not be recognized as his. The bad thing was it left him without a radio in his vehicle. Luckily, the best backup he would ever need was always riding with him.

By far the biggest change for Coal was when Martinez and Sam convinced him to have Maura and his family pack up and leave town to stay in Missoula with friends. They took all the dogs with them, but the six horses were being fed and watered by Walt and Susan Ledbetter, their neighbors across Savage Lane.

It seemed to Coal now more than ever that Sam and Martinez were his family, for they were the closest to kin he had, and with him almost every waking hour.

After the rash of violent death in the last week, the town seemed overly quiet. Coal sensed a difference in the air, a difference wherever he went in public. People would be talking in seemingly normal tones, but when he appeared they would either end their conversations or settle into whispers. Perhaps it was his imagination. He imagined a lot of things lately that probably weren't real.

Coal, Sam, and Martinez sat in front of the television at the Snowballs' house after their three eerie days of quiet around Salmon watching *The Super Friends* and pretending to enjoy it. It had been half an hour since anyone spoke, and now Martinez cleared his throat.

"Hey, Coal. We should talk."

Coal drew in a big breath. He knew what was coming. He had been waiting for it, and he had dreaded it. "I know. We do."

They locked eyes, and Coal saw Sam's face turn his way as well. "Then I guess you've already thought about what I'm going to say."

"Try me."

"Well ... Nothing's happening anymore. Not that I want it to. But ... Well, you know we can't stay around here forever, just waiting. Eventually, we've got to head back home. We're brothers, Coal. As much as any three guys who aren't related by blood. And

I'd love to hang out here for the rest of my life and help you if we could. But you know it's not possible."

Coal blew out a long-held breath. "I know. So what now?"

"Let's give it another day or two, huh? Then we'll talk about it again. I hate to leave, but ... Well, you know."

"I know. You've done a lot already, guys, and I appreciate all of it."

"I don't think it's over, though," Sam cut in. "You know that, right?"

"I know. If they're laying low because they recognized you two," Coal said, "they'll be back. Maybe not those two, but someone."

Sam nodded. "They've got to button this up. Either you, or the Medinas. Somebody's got to get shut down."

When they drove into town later to check in with all the hotels and see what kind of new customers they had signed in, that conversation was all Coal could think of. Martinez had said another day or two. It didn't seem like anywhere near enough.

Coal didn't feel like dining out, so later, after checking all the hotels for anyone who might seem out of place, they went down to the Coffee Shop and got some hamburgers and fries, then took them back to the jail to eat. Coal, feeling reckless, even bought himself a six-pack of Hires root beer down at Saveway. If he was going to die, he might as well die with sugar in his veins—a happy man.

Sitting at his desk, Coal pulled three root beers from the cardboard container and passed two to Sam and Martinez. Neither of them was likely the soft drink type, but they thanked him anyway, and he pulled a bottle opener out of the drawer and popped his lid off, then tossed the opener to Sam.

"Hey, guys, as soon as we finish eating, I don't suppose you might want to go sit in the truck for a while, would you? I have a couple of personal phone calls to make."

Sam grinned, while Martinez leveled a serious gaze Coal's way. "Sure," Sam replied. "Q knows how that is—those personal phone calls."

When they were gone, Coal called out to Annie Price's and got a busy signal. Even in all the stress and strife of life here in the valley lately, the nurse had been on his mind a lot. He couldn't quite erase the events of that last strange night out at her house, and it seemed he was forever worrying now whether she was all right.

The next call was to Kathy MacAtee, whose words were normal but whose tone of voice let Coal know his instincts had been right: He was missed, but Kathy was trying to distance herself from him. It wasn't like he hadn't expected it, and he sure didn't blame her.

After that, the next call was long distance. An old friend, Don Hazekamp, answered the phone, sounding very far away, from his home in Missoula.

"Hey, Don. Coal."

Coal! Hey, brother. You doin' all right?

"I'm alive. And right now that's saying something."

No kidding! I'm sorry about all the crap you've been goin' through. That's some crazy garbage. Hey, I won't keep you. I guess you're wantin' to talk to your mom? Or is it Maura? He let out a little laugh, almost a giggle.

"Let's try my mom first. I don't want to seem desperate."

Laughing, Hazekamp went to get Connie.

It's funny how a man can grow up and be self-sufficient and well-respected by many, and yet a conversation with his mother can always make him feel like a little kid again. Connie had all the right words of comfort and love, and Coal's heart felt one hundred percent better after speaking with her. Each one of the kids took a turn after that, and they even got Sissy to come on the line. After some coaxing, she said, *Hi, Papa Coal.* And that was enough. It was also enough to make Coal glad he had sent Sam and Martinez out, so they wouldn't see the tears glisten in his eyes. That little Sissy had come so far since he first found her.

Last of all, Maura got her turn, and Coal could tell the rest of them had deserted the room—most likely herded away by Connie.

Hey. The voice sounded lost and forlorn. Lonely, but also broken. Perhaps worse than he had heard even during their ordeal in South Dakota.

"Hey. You doing okay?"

I ... Sure. I'm all right.

She wasn't. She wasn't even a good liar.

"I miss you, Maura." And he did. He was aware of the ache of missing her throughout much of every day, but he hadn't known how strong the feeling was until now, hearing her voice.

I miss you too. Coal ...

"Yeah?"

Nothing.

No, it was something. "Don't pull that one on me, woman," he said, trying to put a teasing lilt into his voice. "You know I'm the master at trying to hide things after letting out little hints. What are you thinking about?"

There was a long moment of silence, and he waited all the way through it. Finally, she took a deep breath. *I keep thinking about this all the time. I want to come home—but I don't have a home to come to anymore.* In the last few words, Coal heard her voice break.

Coal waited for a while, the pain and sorrow building up in him while no words of comfort that seemed to matter would come. He finally said, "I'm really sorry, Maura," because it was the only thing he could say.

She sat there for a while as he waited longer, and after five or ten seconds he heard her sniffle.

"Everything's gone. Everything. All the things I saved from when my boys were little. Their little baby shoes. All my photographs. My guns, my bullwhip. Everything. I don't have a thing left anymore."

After a couple of seconds he could tell she was breaking down again, and the thought of it broke his heart. He wanted to tell her she had him, but he had a feeling having him might be the very last thing she wanted right now.

Idaho Falls, Idaho
Saturday night

Jack Sheppard was one rough customer. Someone didn't even have to know him to recognize that. They only had to look at him. Jack wore his hair a little too long to look like a respectable citizen of the 1970's, and a white tee shirt stretched over the build of a guy who had too much time for the gym. He rolled a pack of cigarettes up in one sleeve—part of his James Dean complex, some of his colleagues called it. He had the rolled-up blue jeans as well, and black harness boots. And when it was cold, like tonight, he would don a black leather jacket, which he would remove the moment he was inside, because a man didn't want to lift all those weights only to hide the evidence.

But not all of Jack's appearance had to do with style choices. The real reason Jack Sheppard looked like a rough customer was his black eyes, his wide, flat, scarred mouth and broken nose. One corner of his lips appeared to have a permanent sneer, mostly from a years-old knife scar. Jack appeared tough, and he acted tougher. He looked around like maybe he was hoping someone would challenge him. Jack Sheppard wanted to hurt somebody.

Jack parked a black 1967 Ford pickup at the curb in front of a bar with a decorative vertical neon sign that said HUB, with an image beside the word of a cowgirl in hat and black boots, and a little red dress that appeared to have fringe at the bottom of it. That girl, even though only an image made out of lights, seemed to be having an altogether too wonderful time. Maybe Jack Sheppard would have to go inside and spoil it for her.

He walked into the Hub Bar almost as if he had never heard of the place and started looking around. It wasn't too long before his eyes found Bobby Jones sitting at the bar. Bobby had wandered into the bar tonight the same as Jack and struck up conversations with several people. In fact, he seemed to like making the rounds, speaking mostly to men. Of course, he would take the time to talk to a female now and then as well, but only if he could tell she was really alone or in the company of other females, and not with a man. One thing Bobby didn't want was trouble with anyone. Bobby wasn't looking for a fight. At least not with the wrong man ...

What Bobby *was* looking for, and waiting for, was for Jack Sheppard to find his way into the Hub. Now Bobby's real name was not Bobby. It was Leonardo Ossani, the Leonardo part generally shortened to Lenny. Most who knew him didn't call him Lenny, either, and they didn't call him Ossani. They called him Smiley. Because like all the patrons in the bar could swear to, all of Lenny Ossani's friends in Las Vegas would say the same: Lenny Ossani—Smiley—was smiling all the time. If he was happy, if he was sad, if he was in pain, or even if he was angry, Smiley had a smile on his face. On the inside, that might be a different story. But Smiley was careful: No one ever got on the inside.

Jack Sheppard, standing inside the barroom door and studying the crowd, saw Bobby. And Bobby saw Jack. Of course, Jack's real name wasn't Jack any more than Bobby's name was Bobby. Jack's name was Diego Gentile. His Mob colleagues called him "Gentle", but only to be funny. Gentile and Smiley knew each other. They had worked together before. In Seattle. In L.A. Even once in Oklahoma City—which was under extra special circumstances, because in the Mob, men generally made a habit of avoiding places that were the size of a city but put forth the mentality of a village of hicks, and it was rare to have one of their people detained in such a place as OK City. But Smiley Ossani and Diego Gentile would take their act on the road any time the Mob had what they called a "situation", where one of their men had become a liability, or someone else had wronged one of the Brotherhood, and said party happened to get himself into a place where nobody else could reach him. Sometimes, rarely, it was a woman. The Mob had special females who took care of those cases.

But the rest of the time, when the trouble was a man, Smiley and Gentile were there. And job satisfaction for Smiley and Gentile was monumental.

The fight seemed to start over nothing. A silly little incident involving a spilled beer, not much more imaginative than a scene in a Grade B movie. Any aspiring author in junior high might have written the script. But this was a bar crowd, and a fight was a fight. Half of them had consumed too much alcohol by eleven o'clock at night to recognize the difference between a real fight scene and a staged one anyway. Besides, when someone wants a fight, any little thing is an excuse to throw the first punch.

At least that was the case for Diego Gentile. That was why he had come.

This brawl wasn't that out of the ordinary: Bobby spills beer on Jack; Bobby tries to apologize; Jack hits Bobby—a *real* hit; it turns out Bobby is pretty good at warding off Jack, but mostly his defense is to keep smiling and trying to talk Jack out of trouble; he even offers Jack some money, to make up for the accident. Or a pack of smokes—which Jack of course conveniently turns down.

From that point, the fight went around and around, with Bobby keeping out of the reach of Jack, and the bartender trying to stop it on his own, then finally calling a bouncer from a back room. That was where it got tricky. Jack proved tough enough to put that bouncer down. But then he had to take the consequences of bouncer number two—without getting hurt so badly he might end up in a hospital, where it would be impossible for him to complete his special assignment.

Jack, after making sure he had been there plenty of time, managed to break a long-neck beer bottle on the edge of the bar and, using it as a threat, he backed out of the bar. Fortunately for him, by then someone had long since called the police. As belligerent as Jack had seemed, everyone was surprised to see the cops take him without a fight. He went down to the jail, with a rolled-up piece of plastic containing two very deadly pills stuffed up into a dark and smelly place where no cop was ever going to find it, and where within half a day or so Jack would have access to it, if all moved well.

The next day, Bobby, who was really Smiley, sat in a hotel across town watching TV, planning out his call to the local prosecutor to tell him he had decided not to press charges against Jack. Meanwhile, Jack, who was really Diego Gentile, got his first little recess at the jail, and that was where he first saw Angel Medina—and Angel saw Diego ...

CHAPTER TWENTY-SIX

Sunday, February 11

Diego Gentile, alias Jack Sheppard, had been lucky in the night. Lucky in that things "moved" to his satisfaction, and he now had two little plastic capsules in his pocket that contained sodium cyanide, the deadliest, fastest-acting poison known. So Jack, acting on behalf of Diego Gentile, made his move.

Diego gave a slight smile as he approached Angel Medina. Angel still wore his dark glasses. He always wore them. Diego walked casually to him and sat down near him, but neither man gave any indication of familiarity. After a moment of seeming to pass the time as two strangers, they shook hands.

Then Diego leaned closer. He told Angel the Mob had a big plan. They were going to get both him and his brother out, and they would both be shipped out indefinitely to the remote Seychelles Islands. The big thing, Diego said, was they couldn't reveal anything about the plan to Rey yet. Just let him hang cool. Don't say a word. Wait. The big spring was coming. And then, when he was walking away from this apparent casual encounter, Diego smiled.

"Big spring". Didn't that have a nice ring to it?

The next morning, Diego made sure he and Angel sat together to eat. There was tension in the air, a tension Diego completely understood. Angel must be on pins and needles waiting to see how the Mob was going to put their big plan into action.

Halfway through the meal, as Angel finished his water, Diego downed his own in a couple of gulps. He lunged out of his seat. "Hey, brother, I'm gonna go get some more water. If you'll watch my tray, I'll get yours too."

Angel nodded thanks and handed his glass to Diego. Diego sauntered to the water cooler, casually emptied the contents of both capsules into Angel's glass, then filled them both with water, taking care to drink his own glass down by a third so there wouldn't be any mix-ups at the last deadly second. That particular error was a kind that Diego Gentile never made.

Back at the table, Angel took his water and drank half of it down. The toast that morning seemed particularly dry. He continued eating. The grits weren't terrible, as far as grits go. After a minute or so, Diego saw Angel clutching his stomach, an inconspicuous movement at first. He took another bite of his grits and then another long drink of water, and Diego noticed sweat beginning to bead up at his temples.

"You all right, man?"

Angel turned to him, seeming to study him. Through the black glasses, nothing could be said for certain.

Finally, when Angel must have made some decision in his mind after looking at Diego for a while, he said, "My guts ... Hey, I gotta—"

Just as he started to stand up, he turned around, barely avoiding showering the man on his other side with vomit. He fell to his knees, clutching at the bench where he had been sitting. This time when he turned to look at Diego, Diego was certain. Even with the black glasses, the look was plain. The awful truth had finally slapped Angel in the face.

Angel fell over on his side and started to convulse. Diego yelled for a guard, and two men came running, but all they could do when they arrived was to tell everyone else to stand back and give Angel some air. Neither man lowered himself to get down near Angel, and with the vomit all over the floor, Diego didn't blame them.

Angel ended up on his back. In that position, if any normal sick man were to throw up, he might aspirate and choke. But that was the least of Angel Medina's issues.

Diego still couldn't see Angel's eyes, but he knew they would be huge. And full of shock. Angel, who had been so bad to so many other men, and most likely women, in his time, and would have been bad to so many more, if he had lived longer, lay spasming, and choking. In spite of the orders from the two guards, ten or twenty inmates had crowded around, staring down at him in shock and horror. Even Diego Gentile stared, in the exact same shock and horror, although the people who really knew Diego would know full well that almost zero percent of it was real—if Diego Gentile had even *zero* shock and horror to offer. But Angel Medina didn't care what anyone thought. Angel was already sliding away to be with the other angels.

Salmon

Later, there was a little crowd out at the Lockwood residence. Coal, Sam, and Martinez had come once more to invade Jim and Betty's privacy, and they all sat around the living room watching TV. When the phone rang, and Jim got up to answer it, he seemed surprised.

"Savage? Yeah, he's here. Sure, hang on."

Coal got up and reached for the phone as Jim put his hand over the mouthpiece.

"Nobody I recognize, but he says he's from the Bonneville County jail."

Coal answered the phone, and over the line he heard, *Sheriff Savage, this is Vern Brawver, with the Bonneville County Sheriff's Department. I'm not sure if you remember me.*

"Sure, Vern. Sure I do. What's up?"

Well, it's a little bizarre, Coal. I'll dump it all in your lap and let you sort it out. Sorry if it comes as a shock, but the older of the two Medina brothers you brought for us to keep is dead.

Coal was pretty sure he grunted out something in his surprise, but Brawver cut him off and kept going.

It was pretty odd how it happened, and we suspect foul play, but it was just this morning, right? So we really can't prove anything yet. But to be on the safe side, we're making arrangements to get his brother out to another jail. Some place we won't publicize. After Coal's extended silence, the voice came on again. *You still there?*

"Yeah. Yeah, Vern, I'm here. All right. Thanks for the call. Any idea where Ray will be moved?"

Right now we're thinking Salt Lake City. Their jail's big. And pretty safe. As safe as any, at least.

Coal thanked Lieutenant Brawver and hung up, turning to see Sam, Martinez, and Jim all standing there watching him. Betty was the only one with the couth to stay in her seat in front of the television.

"Angel Medina's dead," Coal said quietly. "Suspicious circumstances."

Sam and Martinez looked at each other, and Sam nodded. "I guess that explains the peacefulness around here the last few days."

"So you think it was the Mob?" asked Coal.

The look Sam and Martinez gave him pretty much told Coal he was stupid for asking. They didn't even have to speak.

"What about the brother?" asked Martinez. "He's still alive?"

"Yeah. They're moving him somewhere else—maybe to Salt Lake City."

Sam swore, and Coal looked a question at him.

"It would have been nice if they got them both. That would be your ticket to freedom. Two possible Mob squealers gone, no witnesses for a trial, no dirt on the Mob. So no reason to keep after you, or anyone else around here. But now they're moving the brother, that leaves you in the same boat you were. In fact, now if they can't find where that brother's gonna be put, they might double up on you. They're gonna get worried that the brother's gonna crack, with his brother being killed that way. The authorities will use that against him to *make* him crack, and the Mob knows it. Sorry if that isn't what you wanted to hear, but it's the hard truth."

Coal nodded quietly. "It wasn't what I wanted to hear, but it makes sense."

"So I guess we're stuck in Salmon for a while, huh?" Sam looked over at Martinez.

"I guess we are."

That evening, the phone rang again, and this time it was Connie. She had some surprise news, and it wasn't the welcome kind. In spite of all Martinez and Sam's best intentions, Connie was bringing Maura and the children home tonight. When Coal pressed for a reason, Connie turned to speaking in quieter tones, and the TV on her end went quieter, so Coal knew she had gone into another room.

It's Maura. She doesn't want to stay here anymore. She told me she would get a bus ticket home unless I wanted to go, so I don't really feel like I have any choice.

Coal bunched his jaw muscles and sighed. *Stubborn women,* he said to himself, and swore. "Do you think it would do any good if I talked to her?"

After a moment of silence, Connie said quietly, *Do you think you can stop the sun from rising?*

"All right, Mom. When will you be back?"

I guess sometime tomorrow afternoon.

When Coal walked back to his chair, he was looking purposefully at the television screen, avoiding looking at the others. But it didn't matter; this time he couldn't hide what was on his mind.

"Coming home, huh?" asked Martinez.

"Yep. Thanks to Maura."

"Sounds like you got a gutsy woman there."

"I've got a stubborn fool, Q. That's what I've got."

Monday, February 12

It was three degrees above zero when Coal, Sam, and Martinez headed into town the next morning, having climbed from the night's low of two.

Coal had let Sam take the wheel this time, since the car they were driving, courtesy of Quality Motors, made Sam feel like he was back in Nebraska. It was a brand-new Monte Carlo, this one in a color General Motors called midnight green, with perfect seats of tan-colored leather that made the interior smell like heaven. The car showed thirteen miles on the odometer.

Before they got to Annie's house, Coal told Sam he was going to have him pull over there. He went to knock on the door while Sam and Martinez sat in the idling car, but he knew it was futile because her blue Buick wasn't in front. Disappointed, he went around back, where he had found her door open once before, and went inside, where he left her a note.

I'm just checking on you, Annie. I wanted to make sure you're doing okay. Coal

It was all he would say. All he *could* say. For some time he had sensed Annie slipping away from him. And down deep inside he knew it was for the best. God seemed to be making it pretty plain, in spite of all the struggles and strife, who he needed to choose to complete his life. He only needed to find the strength to do it. Seeking out other women was only an emotional tactic he guessed he was using to avoid the inevitable.

He returned to the Monte Carlo, and they continued on to town. The same nagging thought that made him stop to try and see Annie made his mind turn to Kathy MacAtee before they reached town. Their recent phone conversation had left him feeling lost as to how to act around his old buddy's wife, but something drove him to want to see her in person, to read her feelings in her eyes. Then maybe all of this would be easier. Maybe then he could release her and Annie, and, finally, they could release him.

Coal had started to have feelings for Maura PlentyWounds that he didn't know how he could deny, and with Valentine's Day just around the corner ... Well, in the back of his mind he was formulating a plan that might change her life and his, forever ...

Hamilton, Montana

The phone rang in the middle of Scabs's television show, and he swore. After looking at it stubbornly for two rings, he went and drew it off the hook. "Hello. Mangione here."

This is Castiglione. We did our best, Mr. Ravioli. But we failed. Angel Medina is ... shall we say, disposed of. *But not his brother, and now word has it they're movin' him out t' somewhere they won't say.*

Scabs cringed and looked over at Menny. He had suddenly lost all interest in the TV. "So ... now what, sir? I don't think we should go back to that town now that they're onto us. Do we come back home?"

You got those little pills we gave you?

Scabs stared at the wall, his mind whirling. "Pills. You mean the suicide pills? The cyanide?"

No, the damn vitamin C pills.

Scabs gritted his teeth. It didn't take a rocket scientist to see what was coming. "Sure, Mr. Cas— I mean Mr. *de* Castiglione. We always have them."

Then I would suggest you get on with what you went up there for. This ain't no vacation, you know. You get in trouble, you know what to do. All you guys know what to do. Go out the honorable way. Or get the damn cop. Capiche?

"I get it." Scabs knew his voice sounded flat and sullen. The truth was, he didn't really care what he sounded like right then. He was finding he had feelings of hatred for this crime boss perhaps worse than he had ever felt toward any man he had been sent to kill. In fact, he *knew* they were worse, because the men he went to off were strangers. And Porc Castiglione was anything but.

Here's my suggestion, though, Castiglione went on. *Might save you some heat. No motels, no hotels. None of that. Go rent some place, maybe out of town. Buy you a car that don't draw much attention. Blend in. Become a good neighbor—but a quiet one. Hell, you both know your job. Do it. And listen, Scabs: That's a hick town. This ain't no big city job. I'll give you one more week up there to get this done, and then we're cuttin' all ties. And if that happens, you ain't gonna be able t' find a hole deep enough t' hide in. Capiche?*

Cut it with your corny Italian, Scabs wanted to say. "Yes, sir, I understand," was his actual reply.

And one more thing: Call me as soon as you get a place back there and get set to work. I'm sending three guys up there to make sure you don't screw up no more.

Scabs felt sick, and he almost didn't ask the question, but he had to. "Can I ask who you're sending, Mr. de Castiglione?"

Well, of course. We're sending Derasmo and Giampa. Oh, yes—and Baresi.

Scabs Ravioli heard the last name, and he cringed. Porc had saved it for the last on purpose. And he emphasized it very carefully. If Scabs hadn't hated him enough already, now he wished him dead.

CHAPTER TWENTY-SEVEN

His real name was Jacopo Baresi, but people in the Mob called him *La Pistola Rossa,* or "LPR"—in English: the Red Pistol. Baresi was a hitman. He was a trouble shooter. He was the Mob's last defense, the man people like Porc de Castiglione would call on when all other options were exhausted.

La Pistola Rossa was deadly, even blood-thirsty. He didn't kill only for money. Anyone who knew him would attest to the fact that he would kill for free if his services were no longer called for professionally. He killed for the money, because a man had to make a living somehow, but he also killed for the thrill of killing. The sheer joy he found in it. Old men, young men, crippled men. Women. Children. Babies. If La Pistola Rossa had any reason to kill, he killed, and he did it with a friendly smile on his lips which some called a leer.

La Pistola Rossa had come by his name honestly.

The man was so brutal he was hated and feared even among his own colleagues in the Mob. He couldn't kill clean. He couldn't be counted on to kill with any mercy. The more pain he could inflict, the happier it made him. No one, for Jacopo Baresi, was out of his reach—including anyone in the Mob. Step on the wrong toes, disappoint the wrong people: meet the wrath of LPR.

And now Castiglione was sending LPR to Salmon. Was it only to babysit? To make sure Scabs and Menny did their job right? Or was there a more sinister intention behind his appointment, to be accomplished once killing the sheriff was behind them?

The other two men, Olivina Derasmo and Americo Giampa, called simply Vinny and Rico by their cohorts, were inconsequential when compared to Baresi. They could do their jobs, and they would do them with competency, but they didn't do the job because they loved to kill people. And that was something everyone knew was Jacopo Baresi's driving motivation.

Scabs didn't have to think about it very long to come to an absolutely certain conclusion: The Mob had decided he was expendable, and probably because of their association that included his partner Menny Marcello as well. They were willing to let him continue with this job, and with any luck he would succeed. Or perhaps they would find it even more fortunate if he were killed while trying. But if he wasn't, then afterward he would face the Red Pistol. And no man ever walked away from him—not while the Red Pistol was still alive ...

Even with all these dire thoughts in mind, Scabs and Menny, in silence, prepared to make a trip to a couple of stores. The bombs they had brought with them from Vegas had been left in the hotel in Salmon. Thankfully, Menny Marcello had a head full of information with which to improvise, and everything they needed could be purchased in any drug store or department store in town.

Salmon

In the midnight green Monte Carlo, Sam, Martinez, and Coal patrolled the streets of Salmon, and the roads leading into and out of town. They were looking for strangers, strange vehicles—any clue that might lead them to recognize someone who was a danger.

In the early afternoon, feeling guilty for having already put over a hundred miles on the brand-new car, which Coal had fallen in love with, they returned it to the lot and traded it for the GMC. Besides having his radio again, in case a call needed to be dispatched, there was an even bigger benefit: Coal was back in control of the wheel. More than almost anything else, Coal hated being a passenger in an automobile being driven by someone else. He didn't feel like a control monster in very many things, but in driving, he was.

While cruising the streets, Coal had spotted Annie Price's Buick in the parking lot of Steele Memorial. He said nothing about it, because there was no reason to, but when Sam Browning mentioned feeling ravenous, Coal dropped him and Martinez off at the Coffee Shop with the promise to come back for them, because eating was the furthest thing from his mind, and he drove in a beeline for the hospital.

Inside the hospital, the air smelled fetid. Someone had obviously had a bowel or some other kind of gut issue, and Coal immediately knew that his lack of appetite was now a sure thing for some time yet to come.

Mandy, the dark-haired hospital receptionist, sat behind her desk, ready with a sour expression the moment Coal looked at her. When he matched her disgusted look and shook his head, Mandy laughed, making the skin around her deep brown eyes crinkle up.

"Pretty bad, huh?"

"Not pretty good, that's for sure."

"You want Annie, I bet."

Coal bunched his lips. "Well, I did—but not anymore if she's the one dealing with *that.*"

"Then I guess you're stuck with me," said Mandy with another little laugh. "You wanna go grab a Coke or something?"

Coal looked at her, trying to decide if she was serious. It was plain that she was. "Or maybe some Vicks to stuff up my nose."

Mandy giggled again, standing up. "Oh, come on. Follow me."

She took him down to the break room and shut the door behind them, pulling open the door on a fat mustard-yellow Frigidaire and reaching in to pull out a bottle of Coca Cola. "Coke?" She turned to look at Coal.

He shrugged. "Anything less toxic in there?"

"Like ... coffee?"

"Not out of the fridge, but if you have a hot cup, then yes."

Walking to the coffee maker, she put her hand on it. "It's still lukewarm. But I can heat it on the stove."

Coal looked at the gas stove, across a tan oak cupboard from the fridge. "Ah, don't worry about it. I've probably had my quota anyway." The truth was the coffee was probably no good, since most coffee in the world wouldn't meet with Coal's standards. "You know what? Maybe I'll take that Coke after all."

Even as he was taking the bottle from her and popping the top, he couldn't believe it. He didn't drink five bottles of pop in a year. He was much more likely to drink a whisky, and he almost never did that either.

Mandy sat down at a little round table with marbled blood-red Formica on top, which squatted in the center of the room. She waved Coal to a seat. "Jeez, Sheriff, I wish you'd sit down. I forgot you were so tall."

"It's Coal, remember?"

Another giggle from her. "Sure, but it's been so long since you came in I thought maybe you changed your mind and wanted me to be formal."

With a laugh and a sigh, Coal sank into the chair across from Mandy, raising a hand to rub at his eyes. He blinked and looked back up at her. She was sure an attractive young lady. He took a sip of the Coke and winced. It was so nauseatingly sweet he wasn't sure how he would finish it.

Mandy seemed to enjoy giggling, or maybe Coal just brought it out in her. "You look like you just swallowed a toad."

"Ha! I think I'd rather. How do you drink this stuff?"

She shrugged. "Umm ... Carefully, I guess? Hey, Coal—personal question."

"Shoot. I'll try to think of a personal answer."

"Are you doing okay?" Her face had taken on the expression of a caring girlfriend or wife.

"Of course. Why?"

"Oh, well, nothing. I'd feel stupid ..."

Again, Coal sighed. "I look like crap, right?"

Mandy allowed another giggle to escape her, this one obviously born of embarrassment. "Yeah, kinda. But in the best way."

"Sure. Well, I have to say you don't look like crap. Did you get a boyfriend yet?"

Laughing outright, Mandy pulled up a chain from inside her white blouse, and a pretty diamond ring dangled from it. "I hope not! My hubby would kill me."

Coal matched her laugh, hiding the fact that he hadn't known she was married. He had never had any reason to. "Well, then I'd have to throw him in jail."

Mandy's face went serious again, and she studied Coal. "It seems like it's been really hard here in the valley for you. Do you ever regret coming back?"

"I'm not sure if I can answer that. Well, wait. Okay, yeah. There is a part of me that has regretted it. But not enough to leave."

"I think you need a good woman to rub your shoulders after work and kiss everything better." She said that, and then she blushed, probably realizing how the last part sounded.

"Sure, I guess."

"What about Annie?" Mandy said boldly. Her eyes pinned his in place.

"Annie?"

After sitting there for a few seconds giving him the eye, Mandy raised her eyebrows. "Yeah, you remember—the lady you came in here looking for until you smelled the bowels of hell out there. *That* Annie?"

Coal couldn't help but laugh. "Okay, so what about her?"

"Well, she could use a good man to rub her shoulders too ... and other things." She seemed to have decided that blushing was a wonderful experience, because this made her do it again. When he didn't reply, just looked at her, she said, "I think you two would be great together. Don't you? Listen, I'm serious."

"I don't doubt you are," Coal replied. "And I'm not so sure you're wrong, but ... Well, you know what? My life is complicated. Having everyone want to kill me doesn't seem to be very attractive to women."

She laughed again. "Really? Try to tell James Bond that!"

"Uh-huh. Half the time the ones that want to kill him *are* the women!"

Mandy grunted and took several not-so-dainty swallows from her Coke. "I still think you should take Annie on a date."

Coal stared Mandy down. He was trying to decide if Annie was actually so secretive that she hadn't told her co-workers about her date to the movie with him. "You know we've gone out, right?"

"No! Really? Annie never said a single thing." She seemed vastly pleased with his revelation.

"Yep. And now I can't even remember what movie it was." He thought back with a guilty conscience on how hard and long Annie had begged him before he caved in. Why couldn't he remember the movie? Most likely because he could only think about and look at Annie, who without a doubt was one of the most attractive, alluring women he had ever spent time with.

After Mandy finished her drink, and they both finished the small talk, they went back in the hall, and the stench had grown no better. Coal had lost all interest in saying hi to Annie Price face-to-face. "Tell Annie I came by, would you? I've got to go meet a couple men across the street, so I'd better take off."

Mandy's face fell. "All right. I'm sure she'll be disappointed."

He gave her a sad frown. "I would have liked to stay. I'll try again—and hopefully it won't smell like this!"

Late that afternoon, Coal was driving with his protectors back from where they had been sitting by the roadside at Ellis, watching the Challis highway for strange vehicles coming in. He was really starting to feel bad that he had already tied up so much of Sam and Martinez's time, when Flo Hawkins's voice came over the radio. *Salmon dispatch to Sheriff Savage. Sheriff Savage, please respond.* Alarmed at the sound of the woman's voice, Coal picked up the mic and answered her. *Hey, Coal. Your mom called and asked me to pass on her message that everyone's back home.*

He frowned. "Okay, Flo. Thanks. Is that all?"

You bet.

"All right, thanks again." He slammed the mic back on its hook harder than he meant to. "Why do women always have to sound so dramatic about everything? I thought someone else got blown up."

Sam chuckled. "It did kind of sound like she was about to tell you the world fell apart again, didn't it?"

Alex glanced at Coal. "Women sure complicate things, don't they?"

"That woman at my house sure does. Or were you talking about my dispatcher still?"

"No, the woman at your house."

"You like her?" Sam cut in.

"Like her?" Coal glanced toward the big man, then hurriedly away. "Well, sure I do. I mean, she's okay."

"Well, don't listen to Q. Married life isn't so bad, if you find the right woman."

Sam wasn't so tactful. His comment was insulting to Coal because it intimated that he had found the *wrong* woman on his first attempt, and insulting to Martinez because it also intimated that he couldn't find one at all. And perhaps both were true. Martinez was trying and couldn't seem to line up with a halfway sane woman, and Coal had found one and then had his knees taken out somewhere around second base.

A stray thought raced through Coal's mind that had been plaguing him for too long. It was a thought about Maura, Annie, and Kathy MacAtee, and all of them seemed almost to blend in strangely together. Maura and Annie, both of them incredibly passionate and equally beautiful, but both with emotional and possibly mental problems Coal wasn't sure he could live with for long. Either or both of them might in the end turn out to be no more sane than Laura had become. Then there was Kathy, his best friend's widow. Kathy. Almost too good to be true. She owned her own ranch, she sat a horse like a twenty-year-old rodeo queen, she was gorgeous, with the deepest brown eyes in Coal's universe and a smile that could lure a beaver drunkenly away from a green aspen sapling. She was smart, funny, loving ... and lonely. The perfect woman for Coal, with three sweet and very well-behaved girls (because he certainly needed a lot more children around!). And to ice that cake, she even owned a LeMans blue Z/28!

She was everything Coal might dream of, but for some reason he wasn't drawn to her in all the ways one might have thought he would be, and he feared it was because of Larry. Even deceased, he was standing in Coal's way.

And then reality came crashing back down, and even all thought of the coming Valentine's Day passed out of Coal's sights. No matter who the right woman might be, no woman deserved a man like Coal in her life. His own impending death seemed assured unless something happened soon to stop it, and he simply could not be the man who put any of the three sweet women in his life through that, but especially not Kathy, not after what she had recently been through.

Yet he found the memory of her out at the ranch, sitting on that tall blue roan quarter horse, engraved startlingly in his mind.

Right at that moment, he hated himself. His mother was hoping he would find a wife. His children deserved a loving, nurturing mother figure. But as sheriff here in Lemhi County, Coal had rendered himself absolutely unmarketable as a husband, and no sane woman could ever think it was a good idea to settle down with a man someone somewhere was always wanting to kill.

If the woman came along who thought that was all right, it would be Coal who had to turn her away.

CHAPTER TWENTY-EIGHT

Hamilton, Montana

They say it never hurts to try, and if anyone knew anything about Saverio Ravioli, they knew he had plenty of try in him, to use a true Western saying. He had thought of something at the end of his conversation with Porc Castiglione that made sense, and he had mentioned it to the crime boss. To his surprised delight, Castiglione had agreed. When it came to going into a real estate office in Salmon, or even simply flipping through the classifieds and calling a private number trying to find some place to rent, it made more sense having someone do it who hadn't already been pinpointed by local lawmen as a paid assassin.

With that realization in mind, Castiglione had agreed to send Vinny Derasmo, Rico Giampa, and Jacopo Baresi up to Salmon to secure a place big enough for all of them to stay. Scabs and Menny, meanwhile, would wait in Hamilton for someone to contact them and let them know it was time to make the drive back and meet their destiny. Of course Castiglione hadn't voiced that last part, but Scabs had read the writing on the wall.

After hanging up, Scabs felt Menny's eyes on him as he scooted back on the bed and stuffed his pillow behind his head, zeroing his eyes in numbly on the television screen. Menny was curious as to the plan, as any man would be, but Scabs wasn't ready to talk.

The Mob was a cruel bunch to work for. Scabs had seen it many times, and so had Menny. They could treat a man like a brother, pay him handsomely, provide him with a wonderful life, and then, in the most fickle way, decide that his time was up, that he was a failure—and stamp out his life like an earwig. But were there so many hitmen now that a guy like Porc Castiglione could so easily write off two men who had been as faithful and hard-working as Scabs and Menny, who had loyally carried out every job ever given them without complaint?

Scabs wanted to believe he was wrong. He wanted to decide Castiglione was simply being cautious deciding to send LPR Baresi up to Salmon to work with them. But he didn't believe it. The truth was he had been noticing something in Castiglione's manner for some time now, and not only his manner but that of other members high up in the "family". Something in their manner, something in their eyes. For whatever reason, Scabs and Menny had become a liability, and Scabs didn't understand it. He had always done right by his bosses and his mentors. He had always done what was asked of him, and done it with the best attitude.

But now that he was getting close to retiring, and perhaps speaking of it too often, the act of quitting his avocation was all it took to be considered a liability. *If* that was indeed the reason for their dissatisfaction with him, which he could only assume.

So what about Menny? Was he going to be taken out simply for the unfortunate fact of being Scabs's partner? Or in the end, would it have something to do with the mistake of killing the jailer's little sister, back in Salmon? Anything Scabs came up with would be conjecture. He didn't even know for a fact they intended to kill him. It was only something spoken to him down deep in his guts.

Tired of feeling Menny watching him, Scabs spoke without looking over at him. "Hey, Twinkie, I'm gonna go find a phone booth, huh? I think I'll make a call home and check on Nicola."

"That's fine." Menny didn't even acknowledge the nickname. "Hey, Scabs, you all right? You didn't tell me nothin' about what Porc said."

Scabs looked over at his partner and forced a grin. "I'm great, man. I just hope they don't got this place bugged. Porc hears you call him Porc, you'll be the one gets barbecued."

Menny scoffed. "He's the one that came up with it."

"Yeah, uh-huh. You might admit to somebody you're a butthole, but if your kid calls you that you're still gonna show him the back o' your hand."

Menny let out a laugh. "Maybe true. Okay, be careful out there."

Scabs went into the hall and looked around. He felt naked without his pistol, but having it on him wasn't a liability he wanted right now. Besides, he was in Hamilton, Montana. What need would he have of a pistol? To shoot some redneck rock chuck?

He walked a ways downtown and went in the first corner phone booth, sitting down on the little bench. Letting out a big sigh, he reached up and dropped a few dimes in the change slot, then dialed his home number, setting a stack of more dimes on the edge of the window frame in case he needed them.

The phone rang five times, and each time his heart sank a little more. The Ravioli place was nice, but it was only an apartment, and not that large. They didn't need big now, not with all the kids gone. An immaculate nine-hundred square feet with a balcony, plush carpets, and gold faucets, now that was living.

Just as he thought he was going to have to disconnect the line, he heard it pick up, and his falling heart leaped. He heard Nicola's voice on the other end, and his heart began to pound.

"Hey, sweetheart. What, you stuck on the pot again?"

Ignoring his joke, Nicola exclaimed, *Hey! Cuore mio! How are you, amore? I have missed you!*

The terms of endearment were flowing at the Ravioli residence. Maybe Nicola had had to drag her intoxicated self to the phone, and that was what took her so long. "My heart", and "love", both in just two exclamations. Scabs was scoring tonight.

"I'm good, sweetheart. Real good. I've missed you too."

They spoke softly for a while, the way lovers talk to each other, and after over fifty years together that still amazed Scabs. He and Nicola had found the same true love as his Mama and Papa, and he wished Papa could see it. He had always said his own love with Saverio's mother could never be matched, but Saverio had proved his papa wrong.

Unfortunately, after talking a little bit about the children, Giorgio, Nicoló, and Viola, followed by a long moment of silence, Scabs had a reminder that his sweet wife of all these years had honed her instincts like a fine-edged sword when it came to the realities of life. *Mi amore. Talk to me. Something is wrong.*

"Why do you say that?" Scabs asked casually, chuckling. "You always worry for nothing."

It isn't for nothing. You are worried. I can hear it in your voice. Tell me, Tesoro. Tell me what is the matter. He had scored another one: *Tesoro* meant "treasure".

"Don't worry, sweetheart." His voice was soft. Soft in a way he would never speak to a soul if anyone else had been around to hear him. "I just missed you. I had to hear your voice. Hey—you all good with money and things? I mean, you got all you need?"

What're you asking, Saverio? What do you mean? What's wrong?

"Hey. Stop. I just want to know if you're doin' okay. Can't a husband be concerned about his wife?"

Not while the wife is busy being concerned about her husband. You know something? You truly are mia vita. I don't lie when I say this. You are my life. But you know I will shoot you myself if something ever happens to you, right? You're comin' home safe, aren't you, mi amore? You promise me?

"I'm comin' home safe. Of course! Stop bein' silly. Hey, sweetheart, my dimes are gonna run out, k? I love you. You always remember that, don't you?"

Saverio, stop! Stop. Don't talk like this.

"No, no. Seriously, you always remember I love you. Just tell me."

Scabs hated to hear his wife on the verge of tears, but right now he heard the first hint that he had driven her to that point.

Yes, Tesoro. Yes. I always remember that you love me. I will see you soon, okay? You call me before you get on the plane, and I'll cook you some good food, light some candles, and get out the old Dino Martin records. We'll have a good time, okay?

Scabs heard Nicola's voice break. "Sure we will, sweetheart. We'll have the best time ever. I'm sendin' you big kisses. See you soon."

He dropped the phone down in its cradle with a heavy clunk, smiling when after a second or so he heard the rattle of change, like the sound of a winning pull on a slot machine, and reached into the hole to find that the payphone had spit out every single dime he paid it.

He was still smiling as he walked back toward the hotel with all his dimes back in his pocket, but he was surprised to realize he actually felt a little guilty. Not guilty because he had cheated Ma Bell, but guilty because he had spoken with his beautiful wife, and he had had to pay nothing for the privilege, when he would have paid out a hundred dollars for that gift.

Very odd. Scabs Ravioli had felt guilty for almost nothing in his life.

* * *

At seven P.M., Coal Savage sat behind his desk at the jail and stared at the phone. Sam and Martinez were gone. For once, they had decided not to bother anyone in the valley looking for a place to lay low, and instead they had taken a nice room at the Stagecoach Inn. Coal was a little surprised they had let him out of their sight, but he guessed since Angel Medina's death had occurred only that morning they were still figuring whatever was coming would take at least a day to develop. So Coal was alone. For the first time in what seemed forever, he had no babysitters, no bodyguards.

He stared at the phone, wanting to call someone, wanting to hear a friendly voice. Trying to decide whose. Wondering where he should try to sleep that night.

There was a part of him, deep inside, that had decided whoever his first choice was to call might be his subconscious mind telling him whatever it was that his conscious thoughts could not come up with, or at least would not admit.

He sat there while the clock ticked on and on, a clock that was normally so quiet he would not have noticed it. Now it sounded like distant, perfectly spaced gunshots.

Maura ... Annie ... Kathy ... Who would he call? And why did he feel driven to call any of them? He had already decided he should leave them all alone, keep them as far from him as possible while he waited to take a bullet, or take on a bomb. He had thought Maura's name first. Did that mean she was the one?

He swore at himself. He was like a kid at the candy store, with only enough change in his sweaty hand to pay for one piece of candy. He had to choose carefully.

In the end, he called Connie. And then instantly knew why: because Maura would be out there. She had nowhere else to go.

Hello, Savages.

He expected Connie's voice, or Katie's. Maybe even Cynthia's. Virgil of course wouldn't take the responsibility of answering upon himself.

But Maura apparently would.

"Hey."

A long silence. Each tick of the second hand on the clock seemed to match with the beats of Coal's heart.

Hey.

"So you know I was trying to keep you safely away from this valley, right?" He had truly intended to scold the woman for insisting on coming back, but the harsh words he had practiced slipped away like greasy little pigs.

I know. But ... She ceased speaking, and it was almost as if she had fallen asleep, and the clock and Coal's heart ticked on.

"But what?"

But I missed the valley.

And maybe she missed him? He wondered, but he wasn't fool enough to put the question out there. "I still wish you weren't here."

Thanks. I miss you too.

Apparently it wasn't the thing she had wanted to hear. "Maura ... Do you think maybe we could talk sometime soon?"

She probably wanted to laugh. She normally would have. But she didn't. *I thought we were talking now.*

"You know what I mean."

Oh ... I do?

"Yeah, I mean face to face."

What happened to you not knowing me?

"I think we might have one safe day. I think the guys that were up to get me are away right now."

She didn't ask him how he had come to that conclusion. *I've really missed you, Coal.* He sat there wondering why he couldn't hear loud, fast hoofbeats. Where was the sound of the wild horses it had taken to drag that admission out of her?

He ran a hand back through his hair. There were a million things he could say. And a dozen he should say. And the one he was thinking he kept to himself, locked in his heart like a hideaway gun.

"I'm going to come home tonight, okay?"

I don't think you can.

He paused, confused. Then he realized she was teasing him. "Why's that?"

Because I'm sleeping in your bed.

The thought nearly made the beating of his heart stop, and for a few seconds his ears were even dead to the tick of the clock. *Save yourself, Coal. Think of something funny ...*

"I suppose you're sleeping with Dobie, huh? Look what happens the first time I'm out of your sight."

He had scored. He had coaxed out Maura's first giggle of the night. *Yes, and he is one hot guy, I'm telling you!*

"Not as hot as Shadow, though."

Shadow sheds like a November elm tree.

Coal laughed. "Wow, that was actually pretty funny, Maura."

I try.

But she hadn't been trying lately, he was sure. Not since losing her house. He had been pretty sure he would never see her smile again, not after listening to her on the phone the other night talking about all the things she had lost in her house fire.

"Hey. If I come home tonight, do you think I could see you smile?"

After a few seconds, she said, *I'm pretty sure if you came home I'd smile a lot.*

"Do you think I could hear you play your song again?"

She paused, this time much longer. *I'm not sure. I don't feel very much like singing anymore.*

Neither did Coal, but he couldn't tell her that. He didn't feel like singing; he felt like making love, for what he feared might be the last time. The false peace in the valley couldn't last, and the forces that had so far been sparing his life certainly could not hold so strong forever.

There was darkness looming in the Lemhi River Valley, and that darkness would consume Coal Savage's soul.

CHAPTER TWENTY-NINE

Coal drove home down 28 far more slowly than he had to. It was already seven forty-five, and he should have been racing, trying to get home to spend as much time there as he possibly could. The children would be going to bed soon, for they had school the next morning, way too early.

But thinking about Maura, not to mention the nagging thoughts of Kathy and Annie, made him nervous about being home just yet. Whatever he did, he couldn't make any mistakes tonight. He had to stop himself from saying the wrong things, from jumping too fast, from acting like he had made any life-changing decisions.

So many thoughts plagued him, so many thoughts of things that would alter his existence drastically. Some of them he should have brought up with Connie, but there never seemed to be a right time. And besides, he didn't want to give his mom any false hopes. It seemed like she was way too attached to Maura to give out any truly helpful advice about Coal's situation. After all, she hadn't seen the troubled side of Maura that Coal had. She had only seen all the wonderful, perfect things Maura could be.

Coal, on the other hand—sometimes it seemed like he could still feel a bit of the ache in his jaw from where Maura had struck him. He already had so much trouble in his life; was he ready to marry into a potentially troubled relationship, for mere love?

In the happiness of the evening's long-awaited reunion (or at least to Coal it seemed long), the little things that kept nagging him were in the main forgotten. They managed to creep back in only now and then, and a happy smile and a hug from Connie, Maura, or one of the kids would instantly drive them away like that last wisp of morning fog when the sun bursts over the mountain.

Supper was over, and the dishes had been all cleaned up, but that didn't stop Connie from breaking out the ingredients for chocolate and coconut no-bake cookies. His mother's skills were finely honed when it came to making sure that last little bit of fleece remained over Coal's muscles that would have kept him from ever competing on a bodybuilding stage—if he had ever had any such silly desire. Standing in front of hundreds of people on a stage in his underwear had never been one of the goals he aspired to.

For the first part of the evening—an evening on which Connie had decided the children could stay up late, because in her words it was a special occasion—Coal had a hard time talking to Connie or Maura about anything serious. Between Dobe and Shadow, both falling all over themselves like six-month-old puppies at his sudden appearance, and the children, who stayed gathered around him as if they had been thinking they would never see him again, it was impossible to talk "adult stuff".

The hopeful matchmaker side of Connie tonight didn't even bother asking Maura if she wanted to come to the kitchen to help with the cookies. She let Maura stay on the couch, pressed as close to Coal as she could be without being on his lap. That would have been hard anyway, since Sissy wasn't going to give up his lap for anything. That little girl, in vying for Coal's attention and nearness, would win top dog award over Dobe, Shadow, or any of the others. And to have her holding onto him for dear life as she did tonight, Coal had to admit was one of the most heart-warming experiences of his life. It was like one more unexpected chance at those lost years when Katie was a tiny girl, and he was so often away in some distant, violent place.

When the cookies were finally gone, and after them the children—all except Sissy, who couldn't be carried away by a herd of wild pterodactyls—Coal sat with Maura pulled as tightly to him as he could, Sissy on his lap, and Connie in her chair. Both dogs had finally collapsed from the sheer exhaustion of the after-effects of their happiness at having Coal home. The fire crackled bright behind its screen shield, filling the room with that deep, satisfying warmth that only wood or coal can give, and with the wonderful aroma that coal can't.

"Hey, Maura," Coal said to the top of her head.

She looked up.

"You think you can hang onto this little monkey for me while I go have a word with Mom?"

"I bet I can," she said with a smile.

Maura would have lost money if they had bet. There was no prying the little girl away from Coal. When she realized they were going to try, she wrapped her arms around his neck so fiercely he thought she was going to choke him out.

"All right, Sis," Coal said, laughing. "Okay, you win. You can go with me." He reached out and squeezed Maura's leg, then stood up with Sissy pretending to be a necklace and motioned for Connie to follow him down the hall.

Locked behind the barrier of his mother's door, standing by her bed, Coal created a seat for Sissy with his arms, feeling the overwhelming emotions only a little child can impart. Connie reached out and squeezed one of Coal's hands.

"You're pretty popular."

He laughed. "She just doesn't want to be cut out of the will."

After they both laughed together, something Coal hadn't been too sure they would ever do again, Connie said, "So what's up, Son? This secretive meeting sure has me on the edge of my seat."

"Well, Mom, this one is pretty huge."

Her eyes got big, and he was pretty sure he saw them grow moist. "Oh, Coal! You—" She stopped, containing herself although it was obviously the last thing she wanted to do. "Sorry. Keep going."

"Mom, it isn't what you're thinking, okay? Not yet." He tried not to feel bad about the disappointed look that came over her face. "But it's still big. I've been thinking a lot about this, and I want to see what you think. How would you feel about starting the ranch back up? Like when Dad was here."

"Wait—what? The ranch! Coal! What about your job?"

"We could do it. We could do both."

Her roving eyes and bunched lips proved that her mind was running wild, trying to figure out in a few seconds all the logistical things Coal had been mulling over off and on for a long time, actually long before Maura's house was destroyed.

"This is a lot to digest. Wow. How in the world did you come up with such a thing?"

"I don't know. Inspiration. Now here's the part I think you'll like. I was kind of hoping you'd agree to add on to the house. We could add on a whole section, with another bathroom, a kitchen—the whole works. It would be like another house, a small one, with its own living room, two or three bedrooms—and all joined up with the old house by a hallway, and a door that could lock, but would open up into our house. We'd have to figure out where."

"Son! What do you mean? What ... Okay, you've really lost me now. Why would we need that?"

He drew a deep breath. "Well, I'm thinking since I have my job, and it's pretty full-time ... What would you think about having Maura move over here? She could live in the attached house, and both of you and the kids could run the ranch when I'm working. I mean, her house is gone, and I don't know if she can afford to replace it. I haven't asked her any details. And she sure can't keep sleeping in your bed with you forever, especially if she gets her boys back, even part-time."

He stopped, then grinned. "I'm talking too much, huh?"

Connie laughed, the tears spilling into her eyes. "No! No, Son! I think it's a wonderful idea. I just ... Well, I've never thought of such a thing. You know, we could buy the land across the road, and there's still some of that Lemhi Road property open. And we still have the old hay fields above us, too. Did you know that? I've been leasing out that property, and— Well, it's not just you, is it? Talking about this is pretty contagious." She breathed deeply, letting it slowly back out. "So you haven't said anything to Maura yet, of course."

"No, I wanted to see what you thought first."

"Well, I don't want to be the meddling old lady, but ... Of course you know what it's going to sound like when you make the offer to Maura, right?"

He smiled. "Yeah. Do you think I'm ready, Mom?"

"You're the only one who can answer that."

"I know. It's killing me. I keep thinking about Kathy, and Annie Price. I'm almost forty-three years old. Mom, I can't afford to make another big mistake."

"Have you asked God about it?"

"I'm too scared to. I think God is pretty sure I've blocked him out."

"Then stop. Get on your knees. You're right, buddy. As much as I hate to admit it, you aren't exactly young anymore, and you can't afford to do something that will only make your life harder. Especially with those little boys."

"Now you're talking like you don't think Maura's the one anymore."

"I sure never said anything like that! But I really have been doing a lot of thinking about everything. You once said something, and I can't get it off my mind. That Kathy MacAtee, she really is such a sweet girl. And so beautiful. And those three girls of hers, they're real dolls. She has that ranch, and ... Well, I feel sort of silly even talking about all this, but I really do see the spot you're in, Coal. I think getting the ranch going again if you feel like you're up to it is a wonderful idea. It thrills me to think about. But you really owe it to yourself and everyone else around you to be sure about pulling Maura into it."

"But what about her house? It's my fault it's gone. They weren't after her. And she didn't have to let me stay there."

"You can't let that ruin the whole rest of your life, Son. We can try to help her financially. I know you'd do that anyway. Maybe we can borrow a little money from Cynthia, even."

"No! No, we're not going to ask Cynthia for that. She's going to need all that later. That isn't something I'm willing to do. I'll figure out something else."

"Okay. You're right. So we find Maura another trailer, if you decide not to have her here. It won't be that hard. I only want you to be sure."

"All right. But at least give me your gut feeling. What's your first reaction? And before you answer me, you know Valentine's Day is the day after tomorrow, right?"

Connie grinned. “I do. Believe me, it hasn’t been out of my mind for a month. I’m just surprised you would know.”

“Well, I may be a man, but I’m not completely oblivious. There are red hearts glued all over this town, and I do have this thing called a calendar on my wall.”

With a laugh, she said, “I need to start giving you more credit.”

“Yes you do. So what do you say? Gut reaction. First thought, without analyzing anything.”

“First thought. Straight from the heart?” Connie drew in another deep breath. “If you get an answer that it’s okay, I would love nothing more than to have Maura as my daughter-in-law.”

* * *

They came too soon. Too soon for Coal, Maura, and Connie. Too soon for Sam Browning and Alex Martinez. They came too soon because this was La Pistola Rossa, and La Pistola Rossa smelled the scent of death—the death that he would bring. He had been itching. Itching to kill.

As Vinny Derasmo turned the car off Highway 28 onto Savage Lane, he cut the lights. With Jacopo Baresi sitting in the passenger seat holding a Thompson machine gun, an antique he claimed had been owned by John Dillinger, and no one could prove otherwise, they stared up the midnight road, with Rico Giampa leaned forward from the back seat to peer between them.

The car was a 1970 Pontiac Bonneville, a deep dark color called Mariner turquoise that blended beautifully with the depth of the night. No onc could see them sitting there. No one spoke. Death waited. Patient. Cold.

But death would not have to wait for long.

When Baresi motioned forward, Derasmo started driving, the headlights still off. They pulled to a stop in front of the big log home at the end of Savage Lane. All the lights were off inside. The home was at peace. The thought made Jacopo Baresi grin.

There was a light green GMC pickup parked in front. That made him grin even bigger, and he licked his lips.

CHAPTER THIRTY

Still grinning, something like a rabid dog, Baresi looked over at Vinny Derasmo. “Well, I guess we ain’t gonna need Scabs an’ Menny, are we? The sheriff’s right here, an’ we ain’t even had t’ waste money rentin’ no house. Looks like this job’s in the bag.”

“What if he ain’t alone?” asked Rico Giampa from the back seat.

Baresi let out a little laugh. Then another, and another. They came in little bursts, much like the three-round bursts of his Tommy gun. Baresi didn’t laugh often, but he seemed to be enjoying the feel and the sound of his own laughter now. He seemed only to laugh when it had something to do with death.

“What if he ain’t?”

“Well, they weren’t happy about the little girl Marcello blew up.”

Baresi scoffed. “They weren’t happy the sheriff didn’t get blown up, dummy. They didn’t give a crap about that girl an’ you know it. What I’m thinkin’ here—we go in from both sides of the house, guns ready. You fire-bomb the back, I bomb the front, then we take cover behind their own vehicles, where they won’t want to shoot at us, and wait. Anybody makes it out of the house without burnin’ up, them’s the ones that take a bullet. Capiche?”

At the driver’s wheel, Vinny lifted one shoulder in what appeared to be a lackadaisical shrug. “I guess you’re callin’ the shots." He chuckled when he realized he had made a pun. "Castiglione just sent us along to back your hand."

"Remember that," Baresi said. "Any other questions?"

* * *

Shadow, the old German shepherd, hardly ever barked anymore. Even at her happiest at seeing Coal or Connie, she seemed always to have run short of energy, and barking took energy.

When the old dog stood up abruptly by Coal's bedroom door and let out a half-hearted bark, he rolled over, trying to see her in the dark. Reaching up above his head, he turned on a dim lamp he sometimes used to read—or at least he did back when he had time for such trivial pursuits.

Without warning, Dobe leaped right over Coal, hit the edge of the bed, then jumped down on the floor, trotting over next to Shadow and making a quick circle in place. Shadow was eying the door, and then she looked back at her master. Dobe, ears tightly erect, watched Shadow. It was obvious he had been disturbed by her commotion. Like Coal, he had no clue what was bothering the old shepherd.

Coal blinked his eyes tiredly, wanting nothing more than to lie back down. "You were already out, girl," he said. "Can't you hold it anymore?" He grinned to himself, but he started to get up anyway. He knew what it was like when you had to go.

When he opened the door, Shadow charged out and went down the hall. Coal heard her thumping down the stairs, quickly left behind by Dobe, who seemed to take them two or three at a time. He didn't know what Shadow was doing, but he certainly wasn't going to be left out of it.

Frowning, Coal reached under his pillow and dragged out his .44. Maybe it was just a nervous habit, but he liked having it with him. Other times like this there had ended up being something amiss, sometimes a stray animal out in the yard. Besides, just because it seemed like the Mob wouldn't be able to put people back into play immediately didn't mean it was written in stone.

Coal was in the habit lately of not getting undressed for bed, so all he had to do was get his boots and pull them on. He stuffed the .44 down the front of his pants, got up and left the room, going quietly down the stairs so as not to disturb anyone else in the house.

At the front wall, he pushed the drapes slightly aside to look out, his eyes barely focusing on the frozen yard.

On the road in front, a car was stopped. Its headlights were extinguished, and three men were slowly peeling out of three different doors.

Coal didn't have time to swear.

* * *

All three of them, Baresi, Vinny, and Rico, carried big weaponry. Baresi had his Model 1928 Thompson, with a box magazine of thirty rounds, Vinny carried a Beretta RS-200 pump-action "Combat shotgun" with six rounds in the magazine, and Rico had gone for the CAR-15 Commando, a Colt machine rifle which, like Baresi's, packed thirty rounds. Between the three of them, they had enough fire power to kill everyone in Coal's house eight or nine times over. But they didn't plan on firing a single shot. This slumbering family would be dead of smoke inhalation or burning to death long before they had a chance to escape the house.

With the dark Bonneville rumbling quietly on the road, facing back toward Highway 28 the way Baresi had directed, the three men had taken only five or ten steps toward the yard when Vinny hissed, "Hey, boss! There's a car comin'!"

Baresi whirled to see headlights coming up the road, still a long ways off. The car had just turned off the highway. Baresi swore viciously. "Get back in the car! Move!"

The three of them ran to the car and jumped in just as the on-coming headlights stopped. "Gun it!" growled Baresi. "Don't let 'em get a make on the car and the plates."

Vinny romped on the gas, making the rear-end go into a fishtail before the Bonneville straightened out and began to eat the frozen gravel road. "Watch it, damn it!" Baresi growled as they neared the other car. "Save some of them horses until we hit the pavement."

Grudgingly, Vinny slowed down. It was only at the last second that he reached down and turned on the headlights, already on bright. As the overly bright lights exploded over the road, they saw two men standing to the sides of the car in front of them, the one on the passenger side with his hand in the air, motioning for them to stop.

"I think he's got a shotgun," Vinny cautioned.

"Yeah, he's got a shotgun," Baresi said, and with that he started scrambling to roll down his window, letting in a blast of arctic air. "Don't slow it, Vinny. Go! *Go!*"

At the last possible second, Vinny swerved the Pontiac, nearly losing control as they hit the soft road edge. The driver of the stopped car threw himself sideways toward a fence line, while the other man, now on the wrong side of the Pontiac from Baresi, turned and fired two rounds from his shotgun at the fleeing car.

Feeling something warm sprinkle the back of his head, Vinny slammed his foot all the way back down on the gas pedal, and both he and Baresi ducked low as they heard another shotgun blast through the shattered back window of the passenger side. They didn't hear this one strike home as they had the first.

As they neared the main road, Vinny stomped down on the brake pedal, but he was nearly too late. The car skidded sideways, and as the tires caught on the main road it came up almost all the way onto its right tires. Through a barrage of swearing from Baresi, Vinny corrected it and laid the gas pedal once again to the floor.

The 455 cubic inch engine was driving over three hundred and seventy horses. It didn't take Vinny long jamming through the four gears before they were bombing down the winding road, now and then nearly raising up on two wheels again as they rounded curves at ninety miles an hour.

Baresi swore, his voice a roar. "That guy's behind us!" He swore again. "Shut off the lights!"

"What the hell! I ain't shuttin' off the lights on this road!" Vinny yelled back.

"Shut 'em off, or I swear I'll blow your head off!"

The car behind them, which they had both recognized while swerving past as a late sixties Mustang, struggled to keep up, but when Vinny cut the lights he also had to cut the speed. Soon, the Mustang was racing up on them, but whoever was back there must have realized this was a fool's game, for all of a sudden he backed way off.

Baresi started swearing again, and this time he scarcely bothered to find little windows to fit his normal words in-between. "Go, ya idiot!"

"I can't see! Jacopo, I'm stoppin'! You want the lights off, you drive!"

Strings of swear words, hot and red like chili peppers swinging in the wind off a Mexican balcony. "Pull over then! Ah hell! Just turn on the lights an' go. There ain't no Mustang in the universe can catch this car."

The second the lights came back on, Vinny's confidence surged back, and so did the 455. Baresi roared with the laughter of a lunatic. "Grind them gears, Vinny! Grind 'em!"

With one last surge, one last desperate hope of catching the Pontiac Bonneville, the driver of the Mustang came racing on, but his only hope in a race against this Pontiac was in the short run, and Highway 28 was a long road.

Then the two deer bounded across the highway, right in front of the Pontiac.

Vinny swore and swerved. Baresi just swore. He followed soon after with a laugh, this time the laugh of a man trying to cover the fact that he most likely had something inside his pants now besides his underwear and body parts.

* * *

With his gas pedal flattened, his eyes glued on the car ahead, Alex Martinez gasped when he saw their lights go out. For a second, the thought went across his mind that maybe the car had gone around a curve, or maybe even wrecked. But the lights wouldn't have gone out completely if it wrecked, and he surely would have seen it making a curve.

After too much reaction time, he slammed down on his own brakes, knowing nobody could drive this road in the dark, and the other car must be right in front of them.

"Go!" yelled Sam. "What're you doin'?"

"Don't be stupid!" Martinez snarled. "He's gonna be right there—waitin' for us."

Sam sank back in his seat. "Oh. Yeah. Maybe you better back it up then. If he disabled the brake lights and the back-up lights, they could be coming back at us right now."

Before Martinez could even react to that thought, the lights in front flashed back on, the suspect vehicle not much farther along than when they first shut off the lights.

Sam frantically started rolling down his window. "Go, Q! Get on it!" With a ferocious growl, then a heart-pounding roar, the little Mustang bombed into motion just as Sam was getting out his window, his rifle ready. He sat right on top of the door, hooking his foot underneath the dash, and yelled down in to Martinez. "Hold it steady!" They were in his sights. He was going to make those thugs wish they had never come to Salmon, Idaho!

Both Martinez and Sam saw blurred motion ahead of the other car. Martinez was quick to think deer, for this was a long, lonely road, with willows and foothills and the river all along it, and it had to be prime country for wildlife.

But the other car only touched its brakes, then kept going, so Martinez rammed back down on the gas. They were only a hundred yards or less behind the other car now, and it was a now or never shot for Sam Browning. Both of them had already seen what the other car had to offer in the way of highway speed.

"Take the shot!" Martinez yelled, hoping his partner could hear him over the roar of the road and the wind in his ears. "Take it, Vike!"

Out of nowhere, about where they had seen the blurred action moments before, another deer came, and Martinez swerved a little to miss it, with Sam only in the back of his mind. He missed the deer, thankfully.

But then there was another. No, two! Martinez thrust his foot down on the brakes as the right front portion of the car smashed into the second deer's front end, sending it spinning off to the right and knocking out that headlight. The car went into a swerve, with Martinez's teeth ground together, creating the only barrier to the dictionary of curse words that had bottle-necked up from the back of his throat to the tip of his tongue.

The car screeched to a stop, rocking up precariously to the right. When Martinez looked over, Sam Browning was gone.

CHAPTER THIRTY-ONE

"Where we goin'?" Vinny Derasmo asked Jacopo Baresi, who had sat on the passenger side silently for the last ten or fifteen minutes clutching his Tommy gun.

"Hell if I know," Baresi replied, his lip curling. "Well, we have to go back that way eventually. Or find another way back to town. Hey! Pull off right there!"

Where he was indicating, there was basically a wide spot in the road on their left, with a little white store on which were painted the words "Tendoy Store". Passing the far side of the store was a little northbound road marked by a sign that said "Tendoy Lane". Vinny slowed and took the road.

"Now keep on it," Baresi directed. "We'll go up a ways and pull off till we can figure out where we are an' if there's a way t' go back toward town without bein' on the main highway. Hey! Rico!" he said to the back seat. Silence was his answer, and he swore. "Flip the overhead on," he ordered Vinny, and Vinny did. When Baresi cranked around in his seat and peeked over, he saw what was left of Rico Giampa slumped over on the seat, and blood and other matter on his clothes, the seat, and the back of the front seat. A glance over at Vinny showed Baresi what he suspected, and he let out a gleeful-sounding laugh.

"Looks like you get to take a shower when we get a place. You already got showered once—but not with water."

Vinny cringed, both at the thought of what Rico must look like, and at the sound of Baresi's sick laughter. He wondered if that man cared about one person in the world. Vinny hadn't wanted to check on Rico because ever since the man with the shotgun fired at them and he felt the warm liquid spray the back of his neck he figured what condition his partner would be found in. He had hardly stopped thinking about it in all the miles since.

A ways up the road, they came to a Tee, and Baresi had him turn left, which pointed them back toward Salmon. Once they made it to a quiet area where no lights could be seen, a quarter-mile up the road, Vinny pulled off, trying to crowd thoughts of Rico out of his mind. Without even addressing the issue of what they were going to do with Rico, Baresi pulled out a map and shook it open, studying it closely in the dim light. He could have been a father trying to get his family to a motel in the next town for all the emotion he showed over their comrade in the back.

"All right, we're in luck. I think if we stick to this road long enough, through a bunch of twists and turns and crap, it's going to land us right back at the outskirts of the town. In fact, it'll take us right past the sheriff's house again, from the other side. Pretty ironic, right there."

"Yeah. Ironic. What we gonna do about Rico?" asked Vinny. "Is he ... ?"

"Is he what?" Baresi stared at Vinny as if he had a tongue sticking out his eyeball. "What do you think? Yeah. His head's a mess, and yeah, he ain't breathin', not even a little. We gotta lose him. And we gotta make it so ain't nobody ever gonna know who he is. Get out an' pull 'im outta there," Baresi ordered.

"I ain't touchin' him," Vinny countered. "You pull 'im out."

Baresi glared at the only partner he had left. His eyes were flat and deadly, but otherwise rather emotionless in the lights of the dash. "Fine, sit on your butt an' don't do nothin'."

Getting out, Baresi snatched Vinny's shotgun from where it had been leaning by his left leg, next to the Tommy gun. He threw open the back door, and after sounds of a brief struggle Vinny heard the body slide outside, and the door shut. Six blasts from Vinny's own shotgun followed, every one of them making him cringe. Finally, Baresi slipped back in and slammed the door, turning to glare at Vinny.

"Now drive the car. We gotta go find some way t' get this thing cleaned up before we can get anything else done. Then we'll look for a place t' stay." Baresi looked over at Vinny then, while Vinny pulled the car back out on the pavement and started driving down the road, staring straight ahead. "Hey. What's wrong with you? You look like you're gonna be sick."

* * *

Coal slammed on his brakes, skidding to a halt in the middle of Highway 28. Ahead of him, a confusing sight greeted his eyes.

In the middle of the highway, turned sideways, was the flake orange 'sixty-eight Mustang owned by Alex Martinez. Taking a deep breath, Coal let out the clutch and inched the pickup forward. In the dim light, he could see shapes moving beyond the car, but the movements weren't fast and frantic, as he would have expected if there was a fire fight going down up there. In fact, from what he could make out in the dim light of his headlights, all movement was a little sedate.

With the .44 on the seat beside him, ready to take up at a moment's notice, he pulled closer. Suddenly, two faces turned toward him. He couldn't be positive at this distance, but by the heights and general appearance he guessed it was Martinez and Sam.

He pulled up closer, and soon the full light from his headlights was illuminating the Mustang and the two men it was now obvious were his friends. He had his headlights on them, so he could see who they were, but with the glare in their eyes it was obvious they wouldn't know it was him, and as Martinez ran to the car and snatched out a rifle, motioning for Sam to get in the driver's seat, Coal decided it was high time he identified himself.

Throwing the truck in neutral and setting the brake, he stepped out on the road with his big flashlight in his hand, flashing it toward them. "Hey! It's me, Coal!"

Martinez started to move in a lot more relaxed manner, motioning for Sam to back the car out of the road, which he did. Coal started to get back in the pickup when a noise in the brush to the right startled him, and he jerked his eyes, along with the beam of the flashlight, over that way, falling into a crouch. There in the dim light he made out the form of a struggling deer. Stepping closer, he could see it was badly injured.

The *boom* from the Smith and Wesson seemed to shake the entire night, and the head of the wounded deer slowly sank down into the grass.

Now fearing the real reason Martinez's car was stopped in the roadway, Coal got back in the pickup, set his flashlight and pistol on the seat, and drove farther up.

Sam was out again and sitting on the trunk of the car, one hand down squeezing onto his right leg at the knee. Martinez was crouched at the front of his car, and he stood up as Coal parked the pickup and got out, walking toward them. Coal had a dozen questions in his head, the foremost, he was ashamed to admit, how Sam and Martinez had come to be here tonight. Only secondary were his questions about whether they were all right.

"What's going on?" Coal asked as he came up to Sam, a breeze that felt like it had ice chips in it making his ears ache and his eyes water. "You guys okay?" He looked down to see a huge tear in Sam's pants, and where his hand was squeezing his skin appeared to be bare.

Martinez came over. "I hit a deer."

"I took care of it. He was hurt pretty bad. How's the car?"

Martinez scoffed. "It's ugly. That right side is messed up, and the headlight's smashed. That's the second time in six months I've trashed this car. I'm starting to think I wasn't meant to have it."

Coal looked over at Sam, whose face was down. "Vike? I get why your leg would be hurt, especially since I know you enough to know you weren't belted in ... But why the ripped pants?"

Sam gave up a lopsided grin. "Oh, man. Long story. But this is the result when you try to sit on top of the door to shoot somebody and your driver can't stop smacking into deer and crap."

A glance at Martinez showed Coal an irritated face. Apparently, wrecking his beautiful car subtracted his sense of humor from all his other senses.

"That brings me to my next question: Why in the hell are you both out here?"

Sam jerked a thumb over at Martinez. "Him and his Mexican instincts."

A questioning look from Coal was answered by Martinez. "We figured out you weren't coming to the hotel, so I called your dispatcher on a whim. She said you called her and told her you were staying at your house tonight. We figured you were pretty safe for the night, so we went to bed."

"Come on," Sam prodded. "Tell him."

"So I had a dream. I dreamed some guys found you and were burning down your house. I woke up in a sweat and couldn't go back to sleep."

"So I told him we'd better go drive by your house," Sam finished the story.

Coal nodded, trying to digest everything they had said. "Well, your timing couldn't have been any better. My German shepherd woke me up, and when I went downstairs and looked out I saw three guys with guns coming toward the house. They had a car parked out on the road, maybe a Challenger or something with the same lines. I couldn't make it out, or them."

"Well, we know one thing," Martinez said. "It was definitely the Mob. Another lesson learned, too—they got back in action a lot faster than I anticipated."

"Yeah, I thought you guys were pros," said Coal, trying to lighten the mood.

Sam laughed. Martinez didn't.

Coal looked back at Sam. "You all right then?"

"Ha! Hell, I'm made of steel, buddy. Truth is, though, I'm glad I had on my coat and my long johns. I don't know how I'd be looking if I hadn't. You don't make your roads out here very soft, do you?"

"No, not generally. Well, let's take a look at your car." Coal went and got his flashlight, then returned to the front of the Mustang. He shook his head, with Martinez and Sam standing beside him. "Looks like it'll limp back to town, but you sure aren't going to want to drive it much until you get it fixed."

"Yeah. I'm about ready to drive it into the river."

Coal chuckled. "Tell me about the Mob car."

"Not much to tell, other than it's a dark color, and he's got a beast of an engine," replied Sam. "There was no catchin' that thing once it hit the highway. But I think I put a mark on 'em. I hit 'em with two twelve-gauge rounds as they came past us on your road."

"Taking a chance, weren't you? What if that would have been some dumb Boy Scouts out for a joy ride?"

"If they were dumb enough to try and smash into Q's car right in the middle of the road I figured they deserved to get shot."

"Good point. I'd shoot 'em too if they tried to smash up a great car like that ... used to be." Coal added that last off the tip of his tongue, momentarily thinking once again that it might lighten the mood and then instantly wondering why he cared about lightening the mood. He was in a life and death struggle. It was no time for light moods.

Before Martinez could respond to his inappropriate attempt at humor, Coal said, "Well, let's try to limp you back to my place. I know a good auto body guy we can take it to tomorrow."

"I was thinking about the same thing," Sam said. "Heading back to your place. Is there any other way back to Savage Lane?"

Coal's heart leaped. He thought suddenly of the old Lemhi Road. "Yeah, if it hasn't been closed off there is. Let's go."

No sooner had he got to the truck and threw the door open than he heard the radio crackling. *Last call for sheriff's department. Anyone out there?*

Cursing, Coal ripped the mic off its hook, fearing the worst. "Yes! I'm here!" The voice on the other end wasn't anyone he recognized. For one thing, it was male, and both of the county dispatchers were female. This must be the city police dispatcher.

I've been trying to reach you. We got a call from somebody out on the old Lemhi Road, just west of Tendoy Lane. He said he heard some shooting from what sounded like a high caliber weapon. He couldn't give me any other information.

Coal's first thought was that someone was out poaching. But this was February. What was to poach in February, at least that was worth poaching? And besides, they were too close to where Sam and Martinez had lost the Mob car. Telling the dispatcher he had copied, Coal slammed the door and marched toward the Mustang as it was getting turned around in the highway. He told them about the call.

"What do you wanna do?" asked Martinez. "We're not going to see anything in this light, right?"

"Yeah, my vote is to fly back to your house," Sam cut in. "Chasing phantom gun shots seems like a losing proposition to me—and a potentially dangerous one, for your family."

Coal nodded, taking a deep breath to calm himself. "Yeah, you're right." He thought about home again, and how vulnerable they could be now that there was no doubt the Mob knew right where he lived. He wasn't sure what anyone would have to gain by killing any of his family, but they might think if they kidnapped someone it would give them leverage to get Coal to go to them.

"All right, I'll turn around. You get in behind me and let's get to the house." Coal hurried back to the truck, feeling anxious, but not enough to run, like he wanted to.

Back at the house, the lights were on, but the drapes were drawn. Connie was smart enough not to let anyone see in, and probably smart enough to keep anyone who was up from walking in front of the window and making a silhouette as well.

He honked three times as he pulled into the yard, with the Mustang rolling in right behind him. When no one came immediately to the door, Coal nodded his satisfaction. Connie Savage was a pretty savvy lady.

Motioning for Sam and Martinez to follow him, Coal went up on the porch, hollering to his mother. The door flew open, and Connie's scared eyes flashed across Coal and found their way to the two men standing behind him.

"Coal! What happened?"

"I'll explain it all, Mom," he said as he pushed his way in. He invited Sam and Martinez in and introduced them. They had been by once before, fortunately, which was why they had known where to come looking for him, but he hadn't brought them in. "Can we find some blankets? These guys need to stay here tonight."

"We won't need blankets, ma'am," Sam cut in. "I doubt we'll be sleeping much."

Big Dobe, seeing that the two strangers were accepted by his master, was sniffing at Sam's leg now, and Sam was scratching him behind the ears. Shadow had warmed up as well, and Martinez was giving her the attention she loved so much.

Soon, Coal heard the toilet flush, and the bathroom door opened to allow a rush of yellow light into the hallway. Maura appeared, the light behind her throwing her into shadow. She rushed down the hallway faster than her normal pace by about double and threw her arms around Coal. After squeezing the life out of him for a while, she pulled back and looked at his eyes. "What happened?"

Coal lost against an urge to kiss the woman. Not caring one bit who saw, he bent and crushed his lips to hers, returning the favor of hugging her so tight she couldn't breathe. "I'm all right, Maura. It's okay. Let's uh ..." He ended his sentence simply by nodding toward the kitchen.

As Connie, Coal, Maura, and Martinez trooped for the lighted kitchen, Sam said, "I'll stay over here by the window." Nobody needed to ask why.

The other four sat down at the table while Coal and Martinez tried to explain all that had happened since just before Coal's sudden departure from the house to the collision with the deer, and even the dispatch about shots fired.

Maura and Connie failed in their attempt to hide the fear in their faces, but Maura was the worst. Tears filled her eyes, and the skin of her face was pale. When Coal looked directly at her, she dropped her eyes to her hands, twisted together on the tabletop.

Connie caught Coal's eyes and made a sideways jerk of her head toward the hallway. Coal managed to forget he was a dim-witted man long enough to catch her meaning.

Standing up, he reached down and took Maura's arm. "Hey. Come with me for a minute, okay?"

Without any smart comments, because judging by her face those were all used up—or at least bottled up—Maura stood, and she and Coal walked quietly down the hall. For Coal's part, he was really glad none of the kids were up. He hadn't asked about them, but knowing kids he assumed they had slept through everything.

Coal pushed Maura into his mother's bedroom, which was fast becoming their not-so-secret rendezvous point, and before saying anything he took her in his arms once more, and she responded willingly. "We'll never be safe again," she moaned into his shirt. "Will we?"

Even though his shirt muffled her words, he couldn't fail to make them out, especially since he had been expecting her to say something like that.

"No, Maura, it's going to be okay. I promise. Sam and Q are going to stay here and help."

"They almost— Coal, they almost had you." Her voice nearly broke.

"No they didn't. Not with Shadow around. Hey. Hey, you." He leaned back and lifted her chin up with his curled forefinger so he could see into her eyes. "I'm not going anywhere, all right? You're just going to have to live with me."

She searched his eyes, although he was unsure with the flood of tears in hers how much she was really seeing. "Live with you? Is that a proposal?"

Coal froze. He hadn't even thought out his words, but they sure sounded like that! It took him a stunned moment to understand that it was now Maura's turn to try and lighten things up a little.

"Ha! Well, I would probably be on one knee right now if I did that, and hopefully I'd have something more eloquent to say, too."

She laughed quietly and leaned back into him, and he breathed deep and thought this was the second time in one night he had dodged a dangerous bullet. That was some wry humor he would keep to himself, however.

"What are we going to do, Coal? We can't find any peace anymore. It's like this valley is cursed, at least for us."

Coal gave her a tighter squeeze, then patted her back. "It won't last. Things like this go in stages. It'll probably be years before we see something like this around here again."

She shook her head but didn't speak. The head shake said it all, though: She didn't believe him. And at that point he wasn't sure he did either.

CHAPTER THIRTY-TWO

Hamilton, Montana
Tuesday, February 13

Porc de Castiglione called at four o'clock in the morning. Why would he care if anyone else could still get a few hours' sleep if he couldn't? Scabs Ravioli jerked at the first ring of the phone and lay there blinking, wondering what had wakened him. The second ring came, and he rolled his head to the side and stared at the darkness where he knew the phone was. With the third ring, he finally knew it was real, and yet Menny Marcello hadn't even stirred. How did a man sleep through a sound as horrible as the ringing of a phone?

Thinking better of fumbling for the lamp switch, Scabs chose instead to fumble for the phone, and he came wider awake with a start when he almost fumbled it right back onto the base. Finally, he got the handset situated at his ear.

"Hello. Ravioli here."

That name don't even make me hungry no more, came the distant- and angry-sounding voice. *I used to like you two*—and Porc de Castiglione called Scabs and Menny a bad name. *But believe me, I don't no more. You wanna know somethin'? You remember Americo Giampa? We called him Rico? Yeah, you remember him?* By now Scabs didn't know why Porc kept wording things like questions, when he obviously wasn't going to give any time for answers. *Yeah, well, he's dead. Rico's dead. If you two bums had done the job you went there for, Rico wouldn't be dead.*

Scabs felt obligated to ask what happened with Rico.

What happened? I'll tell ya what happened, ya bum. That sheriff. That sheriff I sent you twos t' kill. He done Rico in. You hearin' me?

So the boys had made it to Salmon. That, apparently, was the good news. Porc went on to tell the rest, how Jacopo Baresi had decided he didn't need Scabs and Menny at all, and how on the way driving into Salmon he, Rico, and Vinny had decided to pull off on Savage Lane, where all official records showed the sheriff's family lived and where Baresi assumed they might find him, and lo and behold, there in the yard was the green GMC they had been told Sheriff Savage drove on the job.

The hit seemed like it should be a simple one, as far as Scabs could tell. Three grown men, all hired killers, deeply trusted by the Mob, against one worn-out small-town sheriff who shouldn't even have known they were coming. And yet, in spite of the ease of it, Rico was now dead. But did Porc make any mention of how maybe it was harder to kill Sheriff Savage than he had thought? No. Nothing. Scabs wanted to ask the surly old puke what he had against him, when they had always seemed to get along before half a year or so ago, but there were certain things you just didn't ask Porc de Castiglione.

Sounds like there was some other guys too, Porc finally admitted, as if this were a detail that pained him to admit. *Baresi and them run into some guys on the road, in a Mustang.*

"So now what, sir?" asked Scabs, and the "sir' was starting to hurt him to say. The fleeting thought crossed his mind wondering how hard it might be to go home, get Nicola, his beautiful, faithful wife, and get away from Vegas before anyone knew. But even if he managed to escape Vegas and start a new life in some other city, they would find him. And when he least expected it they would bring down their wrath. What had he done to make himself fall so hard from favor?

Now you start drivin' back to that little dung-hole town. I'm gonna give you a number, an' when you get close you call it. Got it? An' no screw-ups. You get up there, you're doin' what Baresi tells you. Anything *he tells you. Capiche?*

"I wish you'd quit sayin' that."

The sentence landed flat and sullen on the phone line between Hamilton, Montana, and Las Vegas, Nevada. Scabs, who had spoken the words, was stunned by them himself, and he waited for what seemed an interminable silence for the hammer to fall.

He finally heard de Castiglione's voice: *Did you say somethin'?*

"No, nothin'. Sir. What's the number I need to call?"

Salmon

Coal didn't even know anymore if his mother would care if he decided to take Maura and go to his own bed. But for his own conscience he wouldn't shame his mother in her own house that way, although he couldn't bring himself to walk away from Maura. The compromise was to sit holding her on the couch, with both Sam and Martinez nearby, along with good old Shadow and Dobe, his four-legged saviors.

No one spoke. The night quiet was too precious. One of them stayed awake at the window at all times, watching, waiting. No car ever disrupted the stillness of the frozen world outside. The whole scene reminded Coal in a terrible way of the recent events in Oglala, South Dakota.

When dawn began to break, Connie was already up, and Martinez sat in a chair he had pulled over by the window, watching through a crack in the drapes. At Connie's insistence, she had gone out to feed all the horses as usual, along with Chewy and Dart, Maura's heelers. Martinez kept an extra careful, nervous watch during this time, but it turned out to be wasted worry. The woman returned, throwing down her ear-flap hat and shrugging out of her gloves and great big coat.

"Did you see anything strange out there, ma'am?" Martinez asked.

"No, nothing. Listen, Mr. Martinez, I'm going to start breakfast. Since you're the only one awake, what would you like?"

"Whatever you want to make is fine," Martinez said.

From the couch, his arm wrapped around Maura, whose head had fallen on his chest, Coal said, "Don't let me fool you, Mom. The only thing asleep on me is my arm. I'd love some of that sausage you make with the potatoes in it. Is there any left?"

"Of course. I'll get some out."

When Connie went to the freezer to fetch some of her locally famous Norwegian-style sausage, a mixture of pork, beef, ground potatoes and spices encased in lengths of pig intestine, Coal turned toward Martinez, hearing Sam stir awake. "Well, what now? I was thinking we might want to go in and cruise the hotels again. I'll bet they made it back in by now. And we need to get your car into the shop, too. It could take a while to have it fixed."

Martinez grunted. "I'm not sure I even want it fixed. That thing's been a jinx for me."

Sam yawned and rubbed his eyes. "I was thinkin' earlier, Coal. I'm not too sure I like the idea of all of us goin' to town to take the car to the shop. Those guys came here once already. What if they come back and none of us are here?"

"Do you think they'd kidnap somebody?" asked Coal. "Doesn't seem like their style, does it?"

"Sam's right," Martinez cut in. "I think their style right now is desperation. You want to risk gambling on what a desperate man's gonna do? They've screwed up so much so far I'm sure the heat's on 'em from up top by now."

Coal shrugged one shoulder, looking down at the top of Maura's head as she began to come awake. "No, you're right. But

I don't know what else to do. I just spent some time over in Dakota mixed up in a bad situation and forted up in a couple of houses—three of them, actually. I'm not too fond of the idea of doing it again, and last night was already too close."

Martinez sighed heavily. "I don't blame you, but ... Well, I don't know. Vike can't use any of his explosives stuff. We don't know where these guys are stayin', and even if we did whatever we managed to blow up wouldn't belong to them. I sure don't think you'd want that in your bailiwick."

"No, of course not," Coal agreed. "We already know they've stooped to exploding a van and a house, but I'm guessing that tactic is used up. At this point, I'm thinking more along the lines of a sniper."

"Okay, but where? Is there any place they could hide that nobody would see them?"

As Sam spoke, Coal was thinking back on the day Hague Freeman narrowly missed taking his head off with a well-placed rifle shot. He had been saved only by stooping down to pet Shadow. And he had never figured out where that shot came from. So the answer to Sam's question was yes.

"I don't think any of these Mob guys are long-distance shooters anyway," Sam added. "Honestly. If they were, I think I'd have known it from all my research, but it's not their Modus operandi. They all work close up. Marcello is a bomb guy. The others use pistols."

"And nothing could have changed since your intel?" asked Coal.

Sam shrugged. "Never say never. I know. But anyway, if you're thinking sniper, then that's all the more reason for you to stay in. You could let me take the pickup or one of the other vehicles and follow Q into town. We drop off the 'Stang at your buddy's shop, then cruise the hotels and what-not. You stay here and keep the family safe. I think it's the best option."

Coal turned to look at Connie and Maura. He had to admit one big thing: He sure didn't want to leave them alone here, not now that he was sure the Mob knew where he lived and that he had family. It was something he should have known all along they would find out. Most likely, with a little work, there was nothing they couldn't learn about Coal Savage. Even about how badly he hated them, which was something they were about to learn if he had any say in the matter.

* * *

"I sure hope that old man didn't have anybody that cared about 'im," said Vinny Derasmo, looking dismally at a smear of blood on the white linoleum floor of the kitchen in the house in which they had forted up.

Jacopo Baresi flicked his thumb across a Zippo lighter and put it to the tip of the Saratoga sticking long and slender out of his lips. The cigarette and Baresi's mustache were about the same width. Baresi didn't even look at the blood spot that had drawn Vinny's morbid fascination. "Listen, you a killer or ain't you? Why'd you even sign up for this? Got nothin' better to do? That old man was an eyesore. Bet the whole place'll be glad to be rid of him. You got a cigarette?" He held his Zippo out toward Vinny.

Vinny's brow wrinkled as he stared at the man who by default had become his only partner. He realized after a few seconds that Baresi's question meant he was more than willing to let him borrow his lighter, but he wasn't about to waste a Saratoga on him.

"Uh ... Yeah." Vinny dug out a pack of Kools and shook one out of the pack, his hand trembling. Reaching out, he took the lighter and lit it, delicately planted the filtered end of the smoke between his lips, and sucked its tip into glowing life. Before handing back the Zippo, he looked at its engraved silver case. On its face was a little saying, and after studying it for a while a wry grin that couldn't be helped came to his face. The Zippo said, "Roses are red, violets are blue; I'm a schizophrenic ... and so am I."

As Baresi held out an expectant hand, a flat look on his face, Vinny put the lighter carefully on his up-turned palm. "You think that's funny?" asked Baresi.

Vinny stared at Baresi. Did he think it was funny, or didn't he? The question was plain in his eyes. He was afraid to answer Baresi the wrong way, so he didn't answer at all, other than with a loose shrug.

Once more, for the fifth time in the last half-hour, Vinny walked to the back door and stood staring out the glass. As luck would have it, the old man who had owned this little dump of a house they stumbled onto off Old Lemhi Road had owned a pen full of hogs. The hogs, unlike the old man appeared to be, judging by how skinny he was, were voracious eaters, it turned out, and with a sick look on his face, and a glaze over his eyes, Vinny watched the big animals, some of them pushing eight hundred pounds or better, rolling the dead man around in the icy mud and manure. Most of the old man's clothing was off by now, and parts of his body were off him as well. The hogs were a lot more destructive than Baresi. The only mark he had left on the old man was a tiny hole in his forehead the size of a .22 bullet.

Vinny jerked and swore at the sound of a phone ringing. He turned from the window in the back door to stare at his partner, then looked down at the telephone. Baresi looked over at the fat black phone, sitting on top of the kitchen counter, and drew deep on his Saratoga, squinting at a wisp of smoke in his eyes and at the heat of it going into his windpipe. The phone rang twice and went still. Vinny's eyes flickered up at Baresi.

Baresi held his smoke in for a few more seconds. Just as he was blowing it out his nostrils, looking distractedly at the phone, it rang again, then once more, and again went dead.

The third time, as it started to ring, Baresi eased the handset off the base and set it on his shoulder. "Yeah, this is me."

Saverio Ravioli. Scabs sounded far away. *I'm in a little place called North Fork, at a phone booth outside. Porc said to call you when we was close.*

Scabs's use of de Castiglione's self-given nickname that nobody else was allowed to use made Baresi chuckle. "Gettin' a little cocky, aren't you, old man?"

Go to hell, you fool. Where do we meet you?

Baresi's eyes flattened, but Scabs would have noticed no ill reaction to his directive to the killer, La Pistola Rossa, because of course he could only go by his voice—which many a man had been deceived by, even unto death.

"You two drive to town. Keep on drivin' through, headed back toward Idaho Falls. Got it? You'll get way out of town, past a place called Baker. Keep on drivin', and look for a little road on the left called Mule Shoe. Not long after that you'll cross over the Lemhi River, and then just a ways more you'll see a little white store on your left. Turn on that road. It's called Tendoy Lane. Come up to a tee, then turn left again. You'll be lookin' careful now, and after a while, maybe a mile or two, you're gonna see an ugly, hand-painted sign with red letters that says 'HOGS'. Pull in there and park around the back of the house by some pig pens. What you drivin'?"

A red Cutlass.

"All right. We'll be lookin' for you." Baresi clicked the phone back down on the base and turned to Vinny. "We're gonna get this mess fixed fast. I've already about had a gutful of Scabs Ravioli. It's just too bad about Marcello."

Vinny stared, almost choking on the smoke of his cigarette. He couldn't even form a reply.

They had only one more day until Valentine's Day. Maybe Vinny would be back in Vegas for a date with his sweetheart by that evening. Scabs and Menny were coming, and they all knew now where the sheriff lived. Four professional killers against somewhere between one and three mere ex-agents of the FBI. It wasn't even fair odds.

The four of them would take care of the sheriff, and whoever else stood in their way. And then ... Then they would take care of inside business.

CHAPTER THIRTY-THREE

Coal was standing at the window drinking coffee later when the phone rang. By now, he guessed he must have gotten used to the sound, because he didn't jump. He still hated it, and of course he still swore. He just didn't jump.

They had managed to get the kids on the bus that morning only by having them cover their heads with scarves on the way out, and relying on the bus itself to shelter them from the east. It was a risk Coal felt was pretty minor, and if he kept them out of school every time he was worried about their safety, Connie would be teaching them in an air raid shelter—which actually wasn't a bad idea as far as Coal was concerned. But Connie probably wouldn't agree.

Now it was only Coal, Connie, Maura, and the three younger children in the house. The twins were in the basement playing with their Johnny West action figures. Oh, to be a child again, thought Coal.

It had proved impossible to keep Sissy away from Coal, so she was standing by him at the window when the phone rang, and he felt bad that her little ears had to be assaulted—not by the phone, but by him. Connie had flour on her hands from a pie crust she was painstakingly constructing, and that left Maura with the phone.

Coal looked toward her on the third ring. She was watching him, her hand hovering over the phone. "It's okay. Get it."

Maura answered the phone in her most professional voice. "Why yes, in fact he is. Is this ... Judge Sinclair, right? No." Maura laughed at something Coal couldn't hear. "No, it's just that you have a very memorable voice. I'll get Coal for you. Hang on just a second. Yes. It's nice to talk to you again too, your honor." Once more she laughed. "Yes. Wiley. And yes, you can call me Maura. Okay, hang on."

Smiling, she held out the phone as Coal walked to her, limping noticeably for the cute two-legged lump that had grown to his leg. "Your friend Wiley," Maura said.

Coal studied her for a moment. Was she really feeling better, or was this only an act? Either way, he couldn't tell, and he liked seeing her smile again. As he took the phone out of her hand, he let his fingers brush the back of it, and it was warm. Valentine's Day—tomorrow—crossed his mind in a flash.

"Hello, this is Sheriff Savage."

Judge Sinclair here, Coal. How are you? Is everything all right?

For some reason the tone of the judge's voice, which matched the concern in his questions, touched Coal more than he would have thought, perhaps because the judge had seemed so stern at one time—even unfriendly.

"We're all right, Judge. It's been a rough stretch, but we'll make it."

Good. Good, I'm glad for that. You've been a boon to this county, Coal. Everyone speaks highly of you. By the way, we're not in court right now. I would like it if you call me Wiley.

"Sure. I'd like that." Coal tried to cover the surprise in his voice. "So what can I do for you?"

Coal, I don't want to bother you under the circumstances. I know you've had a lot of hard things going on. But I'm trying to button some things down, and Bryan Wheat came up this morning to chat with me. We were talking about Richard Parker. Remember him?

"Oh yeah. The pig guy. Right. What about him?"

Well, if you think it's appropriate, I wondered if you might try to get out and serve a warrant on him. I went ahead and had Bryan do that research I asked you for. I knew you'd been kind of snowed under. Anyway, the short of it is I have an arrest warrant for him now, so whenever you have a chance I'd like to have you run out there to his place and see if you can bring him in.

"Sure, I can do that." Coal hadn't wanted to leave, but the truth of the matter was that actually doing some real law enforcement work, rather than hiding here in a hole, would do him good. If nothing else, it would serve as a welcome distraction. "My mother's in the middle of making a pie, but when she's done I'll run her and the rest of my family over to Jim Lockwood's house for safe-keeping, then go see if I can find Mr. Parker. He's on the old Lemhi Road, right?"

Yes. The judge cleared his throat, then read off the address slowly, so Coal could write it down—which he didn't do. He had long since learned to memorize addresses, and he seldom needed notes for that kind of thing. *And by all means, let your mother finish that pie. That sounds like a top priority, in my book.*

"Thank you, Judge—Wiley."

When he hung up, he looked over to see that little Sissy had found a new home, in Maura's arms. The woman was watching him. "Imagine that, huh? It wasn't that long ago I remember you didn't like the judge all that much."

Coal shook his head and smiled. "Yeah. I think it was you that made the difference."

"Sure. Maura the lion tamer."

"You tamed me," Coal said quietly. "And I'm a Leo." He wanted to kiss her. So he didn't.

An hour and a half later, Coal dropped Connie, Maura, Sissy, and the twins off at Jim and Betty Lockwood's place, and then he started for Richard Parker's pig farm, on Old Lemhi Road.

He had no idea the sort of pigs he would find lurking there.

* * *

Scabs Ravioli and Menny Marcello had pulled off the old highway onto Richard Parker's property an hour earlier. At the hog pens, they had parked and glanced around, and when they got out the rank air twisted their nostrils.

"Man, I'm glad it ain't summer," Menny said.

"No kidding."

They started to walk toward the back door of the house when Menny looked too closely at the hog pens, where several large hogs were rooting around. Suddenly he swore, turning white-faced to Scabs.

Scabs stared at the place Menny had been looking at, where torn clothing and a few objects that looked like bloody bones were all that remained of some unfortunate human being. After a moment, Scabs said, "I wondered how they already had a place to stay."

Saying this, he took a deep breath, hardened his jaw, and turned toward the house.

"Wait." He stopped, looking at the house. "Stay here for a second," he ordered Menny. He went back to the car, threw open the driver's door, and honked the horn twice, then twice more. On a whim, he went to the trunk and pulled out a shotgun. He was carrying his pistol in a holster under his left arm, but suddenly he wondered if he might need something more.

As Scabs and Menny approached the back door, it swung open as if on its own. A voice Scabs hadn't heard in some time, other than that morning's brief conversation, and sometimes hoped he would never have to hear again said, "Come on in. And hurry, would you? This sure ain't Vegas around here—it's cold!"

Scabs steeled himself, and with Menny following him he stepped through the doorway which, even with the door standing wide, was very uninviting.

Dragging a measure of cold air and pig stench in from outside, Scabs eyed Jacopo Baresi carefully, looking for signs of aggression, before stepping aside to let Menny pass him and shut the door. It took a moment to realize there was a contest going on around this property: What smelled worse, the outside of the house, or the inside?

"Couldn't find any place that smelled better?" asked Scabs, looking at Baresi.

Baresi, a man with no wasted flesh on his body, even in the over-sized brown suit he wore looked slight in comparison to Scabs, although they were of an equal height. His lips were tight under his cigarette-sized mustache, and his eyes were tight under trimmed black eyebrows, as he glared at Scabs. It seemed to take a while for him to find his tongue, perhaps because he was working at calming himself down inside.

"It's actually perfect here. Yeah, it stinks, but I'm bettin' this clown lived alone here. He ain't gonna have no visitors. See?"

Scabs nodded, looking over to see Vinny Derasmo standing at the exit from the kitchen. "Hello, Vinny. Long time, no see."

Vinny nodded, swiping at his upper lip, which was moist with sweat. "Hey, Saverio. Good to see you. Menny."

Menny nodded. "Good to see you too, Vin. Real good."

"Let's do away with the small talk," Scabs cut in. "Porc tells me you're in charge now, Baresi, so what's the plan?" He was trying not to let on how bad he hated the idea of taking orders from the likes of La Pistola Rossa, but he doubted it was working. He deplored this man so much it had to be engraved all over his face.

Baresi drew deep on a Saratoga, then deliberately dropped it to the floor at his feet and ground it into the wood with the heel of a brown Oxford. "Now that Menny's here an' we got a bomb guy, we'll talk. What you got set for blowin' stuff up?"

"A bunch o' nothin'," replied Menny. "We left all the finished stuff—the good stuff—in our hotel room when we had to run. The stuff we have now is just crap from a drug store and what-not. More fire-bomb stuff than anything."

Baresi swore. "Wonderful. I was thinkin' of somethin' *big*. Real big."

Menny shrugged. "I know how to make somethin' big, if that's what you're after. Yeah, sure. It wouldn't be any finesse job, but we could still do it. Probably blow up that whole damn house if that's what you want to do. Just don't look for it to be some sneaky hideaway deal. The bomb I'm talking about would be the size of a van."

A tight smile came to Baresi's lips. "Well, Savage's whole family lives there. His mother, four kids. And since you blew her house up I'm bettin' his little whore lives there too."

"Yeah, that's true. Then I guess we'll think of another plan, huh?" said Menny.

Baresi drew his tongue across the inside of his lower lip, giving himself monkey lips to blow a long tube of smoke at the ceiling. He looked at Scabs, then back at Menny. "Another plan? What for? No, we're gonna blow 'em all up. That's what happens to families of guys who mess with *our* family."

* * *

Coal drove toward Richard Parker's hog farm. He was guessing he had less than a couple of miles yet to go. At last, he was going to get to meet the infamous, much-maligned Dick Parker. He couldn't think about it without his mind going back to Bern Hargis and his dairy. It sounded from what he had heard like Parker and Hargis would have gotten along fine.

Coal picked up the radio mic and called dispatch. Flo answered. "Hey, Flo, could you do me a favor? See what vehicles we have registered to Richard Parker, out on Old Lemhi Road, would you?" He was thinking it would be a good idea to know in advance when he got to Parker's place if he was actually there, and knowing his personal vehicles would be a good place to start. "Also, check and see if you can find any records of anyone else living out there with him. Oh—and Flo?"

Yes, dear?

"There might be a couple of friends of mine calling you sometime soon. If they call, just tell them I'm going out to serve an arrest warrant."

I will, Coal. You sure you don't want some backup?

Coal almost laughed. If he was going to cry for help in Lemhi County, he might as well hang up his gun and turn in his badge now. "No, ma'am. I'll be fine."

Coal was almost to the turn-off to Old Lemhi Road when the radio speaker crackled on again, and Flo was calling him, probably about Sam and Martinez.

Hey, Coal. I think I have a nasty one for you. What's your location?

Coal cringed. "I'm just turning onto the old highway."

Oh, really? That's great! I just got a call from Conrey Combs, who lives up a ways there on the old road. He says he found a body, and it's a mess.

Slowing almost to a stop, Coal said, "Wait— Did you say a *body?* A person?"

Yes, hon. Sorry. He says it's a man, but that's about all he can say. She gave him the location where he could find Combs.

Coal let out a long sigh. "All right. Then will you call Judge Sinclair and advise him I'm not going to make it to Richard Parker's place? At least for a while. And maybe if one of my other deputies will answer the phone at the jail or at their house you might want to start them this way as soon as possible."

Coal turned left at the dead end of Tendoy Lane, putting him on the old highway, and not much farther on he spotted a red and silver Ford pickup tilted at a crazy angle on the grassy road edge, its hazard lights flashing. He pulled up behind the pickup, seeing two cowboy hats moving around in the cab. When he got out, so did both of them, and he had his .44 in his hand—just in case.

Conrey Combs was a middle-aged rancher with reddish blond hair, at least what was left of it. A huge red-blond mustache hid his upper lip, and his light gray Stetson concealed the baldness of his head. He wore an insulated brown Carhartt coat and mittens. When Coal recognized him, he holstered his pistol. Combs had his hands in the air.

"Just me, Sheriff. Just me."

Coal nodded. "Sorry, Combs. So Flo tells me you found a body?"

"Yeah, man. A nasty one. I was comin' up the road, and a pack of coyotes took off running from the side of the road. Those hides are pretty nice right now, so I got out to see if I could knock one over, and then I saw this ... Well, come on. I'll show you."

Coal looked over at the other man, who was actually a boy of fifteen or sixteen. Coal didn't recognize him, but he looked so much like Conrey Combs he guessed it was a son. Right now, he looked about as white as the cowboy hat on his head.

The body lay in the weeds only six or seven feet off the road. Combs was almost parked on top of it. The shock of seeing it made Coal step back, and after the initial shock a wave of alarm went over him. This body had been mangled purposely. The face was obliterated, obviously by a shotgun, and both hands, especially the fingertips, had been treated the same. Someone was covering identifying marks.

Combs looked up from the dead man's head at Coal, appearing as if he were about to throw up. "That's pretty bad, huh? What the heck you make of it? No face, hardly any hands."

Coal swept the area with his eyes. The surroundings were mostly sage-covered hills, now speckled with shiny bits of ice that a frigid sun glared through, pretending to offer warmth but in reality providing none. A couple of farm buildings. Two lazy-browsing horses and a mixed clot of Herefords and Anguses, along with what appeared to be one red Limousin, thrown in for variety. When he realized his hand was on the butt of his Smith and Wesson, he eased it away, pretending to be casual when it was the last thing he felt.

"Let's get your address and a phone number, Combs," said Coal. "Then I'm going to have you move along, all right? We'll be treating this as a crime scene."

After Combs and his son had driven off, Coal sat at the road's edge, waiting on Kerry Updyke, the coroner, Lyle Gentry the state bull, and whoever else Flo might round up to send his way. There was one positive side to this morning: If Coal had known nothing about murder investigations when he arrived back in Lemhi Valley, he was sure getting a fast and furious education since.

It was a full two hours before Kerry Updyke's vehicle rolled away bearing the un-identifiable corpse, and Officer Gentry pulled out at the same time, both of them making their way back toward the main highway.

Coal was still sitting at the roadside, craving a cigarette for the first time in weeks, and thinking of the stash of them they would surely have at the Tendoy store. Behind him, in a Hemi orange 1970 Dodge Dart the boys down at Quality Motors had loaned them, sat Sam and Martinez, a cloud of steam rising away from their tailpipes as they sat in the idling car, waiting for Coal.

Coal descended from the pickup and walked back to them. They both got out when he was almost to their car. Sam was sipping at a Husker's mug. "You had any coffee yet?"

Coal stared at him. Coffee was the last thing he had expected to talk about. He shook his head, not even interested in answering. "Well, what do you think?" he asked.

Sam shrugged his massive shoulders, which looked even bigger in the light blue down-filled coat he had purchased at McPherson's. "He's obviously one of them. I'm sure I hit the back window. I guess he was in the back seat." For all his emotion, Sam might have successfully swatted a fly. "But don't ask me who he is. Even I can't do miracles."

Martinez nodded, shivering. "Yeah, from the looks of it they pulled him out first, then threw him down, and made sure he couldn't be identified. Good friends, I'm guessin'."

"With friends like that, who needs enemas?" Sam interjected, grinning. Coal and Martinez turned to stare at him for a moment. Coal almost smiled.

Looking back at Martinez, who apparently was the only one mature enough to converse with, Coal said, "Yeah. They'll do the same thing to us, too. Well, I have to go serve a warrant, since I'm all the way out here anyway, and the guy I'm after is just up the road. You guys learn anything else today? I'm assuming not."

Appearing crestfallen that his humor had been wasted on two men who had no sense of humor, Sam shrugged. "We hit all the hotels. Not just the parking lots, but the offices too. Nothin'. Nobody strange in town, or at least that's what all the clerks said. An' nobody weird going into the real estate offices. That was our last shot."

"Well, we know they're here somewhere," Coal said. "They aren't just sleeping in their car."

Again, Sam shrugged. "You got a big county, Coal. I don't know what else to tell you. Hey—since we're out here, you want us to go serve that warrant with you?"

"No, I doubt it'll be that exciting. He's just an old pig farmer—a *perverted* old pig farmer, if all the rumors are true."

"Don't trust all those rumors," said Sam. "They used to say that about me, too." A huge grin split his face in two, and he let out one of his giggles, making Martinez roll his eyes.

"See what I have to put up with? And you wonder why he needs a babysitter."

Coal laughed. "I never said I was wondering." Then he turned back to Sam. "They used to say you were a perverted pig farmer, huh? Weird. I never heard you were a pig farmer."

Sam giggled. Maybe someone else actually had a sense of humor after all.

Getting back in the pickup, Coal watched Sam jockey the orange Dodge back around in the highway and drive back toward Tendoy Lane. Then he let out a long sigh and headed for Richard Parker's pig farm.

It was nice that the judge trusted him to take care of this for him, but he sure wished it could have waited for some other day. Where was a pig farmer going to disappear anyway?

CHAPTER THIRTY-FOUR

Coal didn't really need Richard Parker's address, although having it memorized did get him in the general area. There was a huge, hand-painted sign before the driveway that said HOGS, in bright red letters, apparently in case some passing motorist wanted to stop in and get a new pet—or wayward lover, as the case might be. What more direction could a lawman need?

Coal pulled in and looked around the junk-strewn yard, reminded once more of the Bern Hargis dairy farm. There was rusted farm equipment, a broke-down trailer whose tires had rotted completely apart, and here and there some scrap of pig hide or bone. One thing that wasn't in sight was the 1958 Ford pickup that apparently was the only rig registered to Parker, according to county records. That didn't mean he couldn't have slipped over to one of the neighboring counties to have some other vehicle registered, however.

But the fact was there were no vehicles in the yard at all, at least not in the front. Stepping up on the porch, Coal could smell the reek of the house leaking out around the edges of the poorly-sealed door. He knocked, and was happy not to have any answer.

He thought about going around back. The judge would certainly be proud of him if he did so and ended up getting his man. But would Judge Sinclair have any clue whether Coal went that far or not? No. But Coal would.

Taking a deep breath, he stepped off the porch and started around back. The moment he saw the dark turquoise tail end of a car, he slowed down, putting his hand up on his gun butt. Coming around the house, he froze. The car parked there was a late model Pontiac Bonneville, possibly a seventy. And it's left rear window had been shattered.

With his heart pounding suddenly, wildly, Coal drew his revolver and fell into a crouch, scanning the yard. He also scanned the house once more, looking for any movement behind the windows. He was back in the Korean War, as it seemed he had been so many times since leaving Washington, D.C. Any second could be his last ...

He moved toward the vehicle slowly, picking the entire property apart with his eyes, but keeping most of his attention on the house, as it was so cold outside he had doubts anyone would be out here. Reaching the car, he paused to let his eyes carefully peruse the yard and the vacant-staring eyes of the windows in the house once more. Other than the sound of hogs rooting in a couple of nearby pens, there was no sound, no movement. Lowering his eyes to the shattered window, he chanced a look inside. There all over the back seat and on the backs of both front seats was the unmistakable staining of blood, and other matter he knew had to be brains. Whoever the dead man on the road was, he had been a passenger in this car.

Again, Coal looked over the yard. His pickup and its radio seemed endlessly far away right now. But it didn't matter. He wasn't going to get on the radio anyway, not under the circumstances. He could see a police scanner mounted under the dash of this car, and if there was a second car he couldn't take the chance that it didn't have one as well.

Looking around once more to make sure he had missed nothing, he moved to the house and used the bottom edge of his coat to open the door. The stench inside the house made him gag. Since it was warmer in here, the smells were magnified. Otherwise, they were pretty close to the odors outside.

He found the telephone and picked up a stale-smelling dish towel, which he used to pull the handset off the base. Then, using a knuckle, he dialed the number to dispatch and brought the phone to his ear.

When Flo answered, he stopped her immediately from asking her usual kind-hearted questions. "Flo! Send me Officer Gentry and any other units you can find. As fast as you can. Tell them to go to the Tendoy store, all right? I'll meet them there. Whatever you do, don't mention Parker's hog farm over the air."

Coal went back outside and peered into the Pontiac, looking for a key he hoped might have been left in the ignition. He would have liked to get into the trunk and see what there was to be seen, but there was no key.

He became aware that the hogs in the pen were overly rambunctious, even seeming to be pushing each other around. Curiosity drove him that way, and at the edge of the fence he looked in. He felt himself go pale at the sight before him.

Judge Wiley Sinclair's warrant would be no good here at Dick Parker's farm, he guessed. Judging by the scattered pieces of clothing and bones, if this had been Parker there wasn't enough left of him to fill a grocery bag, much less take up a bunk at the jail.

He stepped back in the house to call Flo back and have her send the coroner out again—although in this case it seemed almost pointless. It was going to be another long, long day.

*   *   *

Jacopo Baresi, whose fake driver's license read Jacob Rutledge, could be a very disarming conversationalist. As he and the other members of his team drove around Salmon in the red Cutlass Scabs had picked up in Hamilton, Menny sat in the back seat, directing him and Vinny where to go, and what to buy. Scabs and Menny, of course, could not afford to be seen, so they lay low in the Cutlass, both with their coat collars pulled up high.

Baresi's first order of business was to rent a U-Haul van, the smallest self-operating moving vehicle he could find. His alter-ego, Jacob Rutledge, was happy to sign all the forms and leave a copy of his professional-looking "Jacob Rutledge" driver's license at U-Haul.

Afterward, they went to the farm supply warehouse and bought an entire barrel of ammonium nitrate fertilizer, then ended up at one of the local filling stations, where they purchased the exact amount of diesel fuel to mix in with the ammonium nitrate so that the combination would be at its most explosive.

Last of all, they ended up at the hardware store and the gun shop, picking up a number of small items at the first, and a can of black powder at the latter. These items would form the detonator that would set off Menny's impromptu and ugly but very effective bomb, the bomb that would demolish the log house on the Connie Savage property and end every worthless, miserable life inside its walls.

Now, with Baresi at the wheel of the Cutlass and Vinny driving the U-Haul, and both Scabs and Menny hidden securely away in the freezing cold back of the U-Haul with the fertilizer and two cans of diesel fuel, they headed east out of town, back toward the farm where they had left a bunch of fat hogs dining happily.

Baresi started laughing to himself as he parted ways with the city limits sign. He liked a good joke as much as anyone, and this was going to be a great one: Coal Savage, his whore, his mother, and all of his children were about to be torn into a million pieces—on the eve of Valentine's Day.

"Yes, sir, Sheriff Coal Savage and family," he said aloud, grinning. "I'm gonna be *all* your valentine. The last valentine you'll ever need."

Valentine's Day was a day set aside for love, and for Jacopo Baresi it was no different.

Jacopo Baresi loved to kill.

Still grinning at the thought that on this very night, or maybe early the next morning, they were going to flatten Sheriff Savage's house and make a statement that could never be forgotten or ignored, Jacopo Baresi turned left off Tendoy Lane—into the jaws of the law.

His heart leaped as he saw vehicles in the road far ahead. It was too distant to know for sure, but they all seemed to be centered around the house he and his partners were using as their headquarters. How had they discovered that man's death so fast? He was no one! Just some scummy, filthy pig farmer. How did anyone care about him enough to check on him? What was he, some kind of socialite? The most popular man in town? Baresi gritted his teeth and kept driving, watching in his mirror as the red Cutlass pulled onto the road behind him.

A dozen yards farther on, he pulled over, got out and ran to the back of the U-Haul, throwing open the door. Scabs and Menny stared at him.

"Problems?" said Scabs.

"Yeah, there's a problem! It looks like the cops are at the house, and we're gonna have to drive by an' hope they don't stop us. Damn it! Hey." He grabbed a couple of heavy blankets that had come with the van, to be used for padding around furniture. "In case they want to check the back, throw those blankets on you and crouch down in the corner. Keep your guns close. An' you better pray they don't see you breathe. If they do, you know what to do."

"Why would they check the back?" Menny asked.

"I don't know, dummy! Why did the chicken cross the road? Just get under them blankets and hold still. I'll thump on the wall when it's safe."

Slamming the door again, he went back to where Vinny had stopped the Cutlass.

"What's up, boss?"

"Trouble up ahead. There's a bunch of cop cars in the road. So let me handle it if anybody tries to stop us. You got them Montana plates, and my driver's license says I live in Great Falls, so stick with that, all right? Passing through to see some friends. I saw a name on a mailbox a ways up. Luntgrens. All right? L-u-n-t-g-r-e-n-s. Luntgrens. The cops stop you, you're traveling with me on the way to Salt Lake City—to help me move from Great Falls. Got it?"

Vinny nodded quickly. "Sure. Got it."

Baresi went and climbed back up in the front seat of the U-Haul. He took a deep breath. And drove.

As he got close to the pig farm, he saw a man walking out to the road, a big man in a light-colored cowboy hat. A little closer, and he knew. He had seen this man's photo before leaving Las Vegas. This was none other than Sheriff Coal Savage. In person, he looked as big as a barn, and as muscular as a jaguar. But he wouldn't have a clue La Pistola Rossa was driving this van, and where Baresi was concerned, size never mattered anyway. Like they said, the bigger they are, the harder they fall.

The lawman raised a hand to wave him down, and Baresi swore and glanced around at all the other official-looking vehicles, then took a deep breath to settle his nerves. In spite of all the cars, there wasn't another person in sight.

He eased the van to a stop just before coming to the sheriff, and waited ...

* * *

Coal watched a U-Haul van coming down the road, a road not that well-traveled. Loosening his gun in the holster, he moved toward the road, walking between the pickup and Officer Gentry's patrol car.

When he waved the van down, it obligingly came to a stop. He watched the driver, wishing it wouldn't look so bad if he drew his gun; right now he trusted absolutely no one. Clenching his teeth, he walked over to the driver's door. A friendly-looking man with black hair and a well-trimmed slice of mustache, a gray golfer-style hat perched aslant on his head, looked out at him with a patient but concerned look.

"Hello there. Where you headed?"

"Up here a ways, to see some friends. Everything all right?"

"Sure. Just some local trouble. Who are you going to see?"

"The Luntgrens. Bob and Susan."

Coal didn't recognize the names, but that was no surprise, after all his years gone from the valley. "All right. You don't mind if I see your driver's license, do you?"

"No, sir, not at all. You sure everything's okay? Is it safe around here?"

The man looked earnest. If anything, maybe a little scared. "Oh yeah. Nothing to be concerned about." He took the man's license when he held it out. "Jacob Rutledge. From Helena, huh?"

A confused expression washed over the man's face, but after a moment's hesitation he said, "Yeah. Yeah, that's right. Helena. Moving down to Salt Lake, though. Got a job there with the Mormon church," he added like an afterthought.

"You don't say? Well, good luck with that."

"Thanks. Oh—and the Cutlass back there is with me, too. He came up to help me move."

"Good enough." Coal handed the man's license back to him. "I'll just stop him real quick. If you want, you can pull over here or just keep going."

"Yeah, sure."

A thought came to Coal, and he yelled at the driver before he could get his window all the way up. The man opened his door a few inches. "Yes, sir?"

"Hey, could I get you to put it in park and come open the back really quick?" Coal had no legal justification for this request, but past experience told him most regular citizens didn't know that, and if the man opened the door voluntarily there was no legal mis-step.

"Uh, sure. Is there a problem?"

"No. Just precautions, you know."

Still the man hesitated. He turned suddenly away from Coal, as if looking for something in his cab, and Coal's hand came instinctively up to his gun butt. He wanted more than anything to draw. He could justify it later. But somehow he convinced himself to stay his hand.

In a couple of seconds, the man turned back around, his hands empty, and got out of the van. Coal breathed more easily, and he waited as the man sauntered back toward him, now seeming to have a hard time meeting his eyes. Coal noticed that Rutledge was five-six, perhaps five-seven. He must feel like a dwarf next to Coal, but Coal was used to making other men feel inconsequential by his size.

Going to the back of the van, Rutledge fumbled with the latch. Something seemed strange to Coal, and then he realized it was the fact that there was no padlock on the door. He wasn't sure why, but it made him uneasy to see that, and he eased his .44 around in the holster, although he knew the man in the Cutlass behind him was probably watching him closely.

When that thought sank home, Coal turned a little more so his left side was toward the Cutlass. He motioned to its driver to pull past, and when he got up to Coal, he told him to drive up parallel with the van and wait for him there. Having a strange driver behind him simply didn't seem like a great idea, however innocuous these two looked.

By now, Jacob Rutledge was prying open the heavy van door, and he stepped to one side. Coal peered into the shadows, his eyes trying to adjust to the light. There was one fifty-gallon steel drum sitting there, and two fuel cans on the floor beside it. Coal knitted his brow, turning to Rutledge. "So ... I thought you said you were moving your stuff down to Salt Lake. You don't own much, do you?"

The man laughed, seeming nervous. "Oh! No, no. We haven't even gone to pick up the stuff yet."

"What's in the barrel?"

"Fertilizer, actually," replied Rutledge, his eyes slicing away from Coal's.

"Fertilizer? You plan on taking care of some forest on your trip?"

Again, the man laughed. "No, I told a friend of mine up there outside Helena I'd bring him a load when I came. I knew I'd have an empty van anyway."

Coal's mind raced, trying to figure out the convoluted details of Rutledge's story. He had a lot on his mind. Maybe on any other day it would all have made sense, but as it was none of it seemed to mesh.

"Can you step in there and pull the lid off that barrel for me?"

"Uh, sure. But why?"

"Curiosity's sake, that's all." Coal waited, keeping his eyes on the man's face but knowing all the while what his hands were doing—and hoping Rutledge didn't suddenly decide Coal had overstepped his legal boundaries. On the other hand, part of him wondered why he even cared what was in the barrel.

Rutledge moved up into the dark box slowly, much more slowly than his athletic, slender build made it seem like he could have moved. Coal followed him, keeping an eye on the open back door to see if the friend showed up. He knew he should have brought one of the other officers out here with him, but it was much too late to think about that now.

Once inside the van, Coal glanced around. Other than the barrel and the fuel cans, the only things in the van box were a couple of blankets, the kind moving companies rented out to pad things. "What's under there?"

* * *

Grant Fairbourne stood freezing near the hog pens as the coroner and Lyle Gentry milled around, taking measurements and photographs of the scene.

Grant wanted to be home. He wanted to be back with his family. He had seen enough death and destruction for a while and was starting to wonder if Lemhi County really had been the best choice for his family.

But then that nagging thought kept coming back to him. Was he here only to keep Coal Savage safe? It seemed stupid to think about. Coal was a veteran of two wars. Decorated. He had been an agent for the FBI. He knew what he was doing. Grant was certain any law-abiding citizen he ran into would tell him Coal was intelligent, cagey, and good at his job. Some *non*-law-abiding citizens would probably tell him the same thing.

Yet still he couldn't shake that thought. He started to look around as an uneasy feeling came over him. Where was Coal anyway? He had been right here it seemed only moments before. Maybe he had gone in the house to use the bathroom, or to talk to Martinez and Browning, both of whom Grant believed still to be inside, probably being smart enough to stay warm, even if the house smelled like a nighttime feedlot.

Grant scanned the entire yard. No Coal. Something began to eat at his guts. He couldn't explain it, but he had to find him. Fighting off a strange feeling of near-panic, he started toward the back door of the house. But something drew him to go around instead. Maybe Coal had gone after something in his pickup.

As Grant cleared the side of the house, he saw a big U-Haul van out on the street with the back door open wide but no one in sight. Strange. He hadn't even had time to move when a man appeared around the corner, coming from the direction of the road. The man's right hand was in his coat pocket—and it looked like a deep pocket.

A chill washed over the back of Grant's head, and he started forward, his hand on the butt of his gun. He tried to force himself not to run. Something was about to go down. Something huge, bloody, earth-shattering. Only fifteen feet away, he drew his gun halfway out of its holster as the stranger began to pull his hand from the deep pocket.

* * *

An unexpected and authoritative voice from outside startled Coal. "Hey! Stop right there. Is there something I can help you with?"

Coal had whirled around, his hand automatically on the butt of his .44. Standing outside the open door of the van was the driver of the red Cutlass. He wasn't looking at Coal but off to his right. "Stunned" was the best way Coal could have described the look on his face.

"No, sir. I was just looking."

"All right, why don't you go ahead and get back in your car, okay?" Grant Fairbourne came into sight from the direction of Richard Parker's house. The look on his face was not unfriendly, but it was full of caution. Coal noticed his hand firmly on the butt of his gun.

"Sure, man. Just curious, that's all." Without any further discussion, the man went back to his car, and in a moment Coal heard the door shut.

Coal looked at Grant, wondering why it felt so comfortable to have him suddenly standing close by. "Hey, Deputy. I'll be done here in just a minute." Turning back to Rutledge once more, he said, "I was asking about those blankets, right?"

Rutledge looked over at the blankets. He raised a hand to wipe at his mouth. "Oh. Yeah. It's just a bunch of burlap bags my friend wanted to put around some trees. It's been getting pretty cold up there. You want to see 'em?" As he spoke, he moved slightly more toward the open van door, making it so if Coal went to lift up the blankets the man would be directly behind him.

Coal peered closer into the shadows at the blankets. He took a step nearer, wishing his eyes would adjust, thinking they simply weren't as young and flexible as they used to be. Finally, he shrugged.

He took a breath and blew it out. "No, it's okay."

Rutledge nodded. "You still want to see inside the barrel, sir?"

"Sure, go ahead." The man went back to his struggle to pull the lid off the steel drum, and Coal looked into it when he had it off. More than just fertilizer, the contents smelled like some kind of oil. He looked down at the fuel can. "What fuel is that? Diesel?"

"Sure."

"What's that for? This van takes gasoline, right?"

"Oh, they put the diesel in the fertilizer to help it absorb better." The man was fast with his answer, and Coal studied his face looking for truth or lie.

"Huh. Never heard of that. Okay." His eyes were drawn to the loosely piled blankets again. "Well, it all looks okay. Let's get you out of here."

Outside, Coal watched Rutledge re-fasten the latch, acting almost as if he had never done it before. Then he followed him back toward the cab and watched him get in while Grant Fairbourne stood a ways behind him.

Rutledge pulled down the road fifty more feet, and that left the red Cutlass sitting alone in the wrong lane. Coal went to his open window. "Go ahead and pull into the other lane, would you? In case we get other traffic." The man obliged, stopping when Coal held up his hand. Then, like a well-trained citizen, he sat in the driver's seat with both hands in open sight on the steering wheel.

Coal gave him the same line of questioning he had given Jacob Rutledge, looking over his license. "Mr. Hanson. So you're with the U-Haul, he said."

"Yeah." Hanson seemed overly hesitant in his reply. "Yeah, just going up to Great Falls to help him pack up and move. I guess he probably told you—he's headed to Salt Lake."

Coal's guts tightened up. He was ninety-nine point ninety-nine percent positive Jacob Rutledge had told him he lived in Helena, and his driver's license had that listed as his hometown at the time of the license's issue as well. If this man was actually with him, why did he say Great Falls? It wasn't like the two places were that close to each other, especially not in name.

"Yeah, he said he's got a job as an artist down there or something, huh? In Salt Lake?" Of course it wasn't true, but he wanted to see if he could persuade the man into easy agreement with a complete lie.

The man in the Cutlass looked at him for a moment, seeming to study him. Finally, he shrugged. "Uh, well, I couldn't tell you that. I don't know that he ever said."

Coal nodded and handed back the man's license. "All right. I guess you're okay to go. Thanks for stopping. Oh—one more thing: Does Helena ring any bells with you?"

Hanson gave him a blank stare. Then Coal could almost see the wheels of his mind spinning behind his eyes. "No, not really."

"Huh. Okay. Your friend said he's from Helena, though."

The man gave a laugh that seemed almost forced. Coal was starting to wonder if he could even read people anymore. "Oh, jeez. Yeah, yeah. Well, Great Falls is the place I always think of when I think Montana. I used to have a girlfriend who was stationed at the Air Force base there. Yeah, right. I think it is Helena. Hey, I'm just sticking to the back of the van, all right?" Hanson smiled. "I was hoping I wouldn't have to remember anything and could just have a peaceful drive."

"Easy mistake," Coal replied. "Sorry about all the questions."

"You bet," the man said. "I used to be a cop myself. I know what it's like. Stay safe out there now, hear?"

With that, the Cutlass pulled away, and when the driver of the U-Haul saw him in the mirror, he too headed down the road. Coal stood and watched them go, his heart thudding dully. Helena ... Great Falls ... Maybe it wasn't that big of a deal. Anyway, he had nothing on them, and they seemed to know who they were going to see, so ... You're just being paranoid now, old man, he thought.

He turned to Grant Fairbourne, and before he could say anything Grant said, "That guy kind of gave me the creeps. Sorry. I didn't like him standing there behind your back like that."

"Honestly, I didn't even know he got out of his car. Thanks for having my back."

Grant gave him a grin. "Gotta earn my keep somehow, right? Hey, man, when I left Caldwell I sure didn't think I'd come back out to God's country and get so much action right away."

Coal had to chuckle, although for the most part it was a little hard to find real humor in this day. "Yeah, I would have agreed with you too. This is the craziest I've seen this valley. I think I'm a jinx."

Coal and Grant wandered back again to the stinky hog pens, where Kerry Updyke, the coroner, State officer Gentry, and Sam and Martinez were congregated. Coal had explained the presence of his two friends by telling everyone they had been with him in Vietnam and had come out from back East to visit for a few days, and the two men fit in so well that no one ever questioned anything more about them.

Coal went to lean up on the stout railroad tie fence with Grant, where the pen full of hogs were sitting on their haunches, their silk suits and black ties all soiled now, and wiping their snouts with slick burgundy-colored napkins. Only the best of living out here at the Dick Parker farm.

Like any old law enforcement officer worth his salt, Coal was falling back on black humor to survive the strain of this day. But he couldn't help wondering if the stories were all true about Dick

Parker, and if a bunch of fat, fickle hogs had just finished dining on unleavened, manure-seasoned lover-of-pork.

And then suddenly he thought about the Luntgrens ... Was it Bob and Susan? Maybe he needed to take a little drive up the road. Maybe he wanted to comfort himself by seeing that U-Haul van and the Cutlass parked outside some house up the way that belonged to someone named Bob and Susan Luntgren.

Hurrying inside the house, he dialed dispatch. When it picked up, he said, "Hey, Flo? Do me a favor and find an address for a Bob and Susan Luntgren, would you? Out on the old highway?"

Grant Fairbourne had followed him in, apparently to pick up something about how things worked in law enforcement out here in the sticks. Now Coal heard another set of footsteps, then another. He turned to see Sam and Martinez. They looked at Grant and smiled, but neither spoke. Still, Coal could feel their minds churning with questions.

"So we're going to visit the Luntgrens?" asked Grant. "Just to check on the guy with the U-Haul, huh?"

Coal nodded, but before he could speak, Sam cut in. "U-Haul? What U-Haul?"

While waiting for Flo to come back on the line, Coal told Sam about the van, the Cutlass, and the lonely barrel of fertilizer. "It seemed like there were some discrepancies with their stories, so—"

"Wait," Sam cut Coal off again. "What's that smell, Coal?"

"What, the pigs?"

"No, not pigs."

Coal laughed. "You can smell something past the pigs?"

Sam didn't even smile. "It smells like diesel."

His smile fading, Coal said, "Oh. Well, you've got quite a nose, buddy. Yeah, there were a couple cans of diesel in that van."

"You—" Sam stopped. "You said they had a barrel of fertilizer in there, right? Did he say why?"

"The driver said they mix the diesel in with the fertilizer to make it absorb in the plants better."

Sam's face went even more serious. "Diesel— Man, Coal, I don't want to make you feel dumb, but are you serious? Diesel? That stuff will tie up all the nitrogen in the soil and kill everything growing in it. Really? He told you that? No, I'll tell you what diesel mixed with the right kind of fertilizer *will* do—if it's ammonium phosphate. If there's enough of it, and a reliable detonator, it'll make a bomb powerful enough to make that big log house of yours look like a smoking game of Pick-up Sticks."

CHAPTER THIRTY-FIVE

Coal felt his face go white as he stared at Sam, digesting what he had said. He didn't hear the distant voice on the phone until Grant said, "Hey, boss. Somebody's yelling at you." Coal looked at him, and he indicated the phone, which now hung at Coal's side. He jerked it up to his ear.

"Yeah, Flo! Did you get it?"

Yes, Coal, I did, but— Hey, hon, I have another call coming in. Can you hold on?

"Only for a minute!" Coal barked, then regretted sounding sharp.

In less than a minute, Flo came back on the phone. *Coal, we have a bad wreck out on the highway toward Leadore. Sounds like two cars went head-on.*

Coal cringed and swore out loud.

Sorry! What should I do?

Grabbing at his forehead, Coal said, “Hey ... Damn it! Flo, can you dispatch the State? And send Grant Fairbourne. They’re right here with me. I have a situation I have to—” Suddenly, he felt sick, and a feeling of weariness mixed with it and washed over his body. “No, never mind, Flo. Where’s the wreck? It sounds bad. We’ll all go.”

When Coal hung up, he looked at Sam and Martinez. “I don’t know where that U-Haul’s going. Is there any way—”

“You don’t have to ask, boss!” Sam cut him off. “We’re on it!”

“Be careful!” Coal warned.

As Sam and Martinez headed out to their car to try and catch up to the U-Haul and the Cutlass, Coal and Grant ran to their own vehicles. Coal was hollering for Lyle Gentry before he reached his pickup. When he heard him answer, he yelled, “Bad wreck out on the highway toward Leadore!”

He made sure Gentry heard him and was on his way, and then he vaulted into the front seat and peeled out after Grant.

The wreck, only five miles out on 28 after pulling off Tendoy Lane, wasn’t anywhere near the disaster the caller had made it out to be. A pickup had been trying to pass a mining truck, and when he saw an oncoming sedan round a curve, he tried to back off. They had indeed struck each other, but it was more of a glancing blow, and the driver of the sedan was complaining of a sore neck, nothing more.

“Stay with them!” Coal ordered Grant, and then he got back in the pickup.

Because of traffic, and a narrow road, it took Coal a bit to get turned around, but once he did he floored it. He made it back to Tendoy Lane, screeched around the corner in time to see Kerry Updyke coming up to the highway stop sign, and gunned it once more.

Cursing over and over when a part of him knew he should be praying instead, Coal slammed his hands helplessly on the steering wheel. This was not the road to be driving seventy miles an hour on, and several times he nearly learned that the hard way. When he finally reached the address Flo had given him for the Luntgrens, whose names, she had mentioned, weren't Bob and Susan, but Doug and Wanda, there was no U-Haul around, no red Cutlass, and of course no Sam and Martinez.

Feeling sick because this road also connected to Savage Lane eventually, Coal ignored all the warnings in his head about driving too fast, and once again he gunned it. It didn't make sense that the Mob would go after his house when they knew he wasn't even there—and unbeknownst to them, neither was his family—but all the same he had to be sure.

The GMC had just flown over Kenney Creek when Coal thought he heard gunfire. Because his motor was revved and his window was up, the sound was faint, almost like the wind. He slowed way down, and at a glance up the next dirt road, which loosely paralleled Kenney Creek, he saw it: the top of the U-Haul van! It was coming up out of a barren field, climbing back toward the road of frozen mud. Then he heard another round of gun shots, and this time there was no questioning them.

Whipping the wheel, he turned up the farm road, driving as fast as he dared over the bad washboards that bordered an alfalfa field fallow with the winter. He didn't realize until he was almost on top of it that the U-Haul van had reached the road and was now bombing down it at breakneck speed—straight toward him!

* * *

Jacob Baresi pushed the gutless old U-Haul as hard as he could. Everything in his experience promised him the sheriff, along with who knew how many others, would be on his tail soon, and he had to try and find some place to hide before they reached him.

He was going so fast he almost missed the farm road that took off to the right, disappearing up into a fold between foothills. Slamming on the brakes, he skidded onto the road, and for a second he thought the van was going to tip over. He only had a second to wonder about the stability of the steel drum full of fertilizer and diesel before pushing down on the gas again and surging up the torn-up farm road.

A glance in the rearview mirror showed him that Vinny had also made the turn in the Cutlass, but he gritted his teeth looking at the road ahead. He wondered if the passenger car would make it. In fact, he wasn't sure about the van!

He was almost out of sight up the road, knowing the next best thing to a clean getaway was a secure hiding spot, and he had lost sight of the Cutlass because it was right behind him.

That was when he saw an orange Dodge Dart rocket past out on the highway. But it didn't go far. Suddenly, its driver slammed on the brakes, and the car slid to a halt.

Before Baresi could even get his throat clear of all the curse words he had memorized for special occasions like this, the Dart was spinning around and heading back for the farm road.

Baresi practiced a rhythm of swearing and slamming on the steering wheel, his foot trying to push through the floor of the van. Finally letting off the gas, he came to a stop and yanked the brake on. He leaped out and ran to the back, continuing his now very eloquent string of curses, somewhat like a song without a tune. Poetry! He fumbled until he got the door open. Scabs and Menny were waiting at the entrance.

"What the hell's goin' on?" Scabs yelled. "You know how close that barrel came to tipping over?"

"We're trapped, you moron! That's what's goin' on!" Baresi jabbed a thumb behind him toward the road.

Scabs looked toward the highway, and his face paled. "Okay. All right, we're gonna ambush 'em, got it?" In his state of panic, Baresi didn't even question the fact that Scabs was taking control.

"Sure! How?"

Scabs's eyes swept the terrain. It was frozen. Hard, empty fields of ice—or at least hard-*looking*. Ice all around, on the fields, the brush, the trees. They had to take a dangerous chance, because their tails were about to be caught in a crack. It could be the worst defeat the Mob had seen in years if they were captured here.

"We'll get the big guns out of the trunk, capiche?" He wantonly used the word he hated so bad. "You pull the truck out in that field, because that truck's the thing we gotta protect right now. Pull it out there in plain sight, then idle it until we get that orange car taken care of. Menny an' me will get up here in the trees with the rifles, and Vinny keeps drivin' up the road, as if all of us are in there with him."

"Okay, then what?" Baresi snapped, chancing a glance toward the orange Dart, which was starting up the road.

"When that car gets up here, me an' Menny open up on 'em. Blow that piece of junk to pieces. And that's when you take off and get back on the pavement. Turn right and find the first tight spot you can get into an' hide. We're just gonna have to find you later. Second thought—lay low long as you have to, then make your way back to Leadore. When we get outta here, we'll meet you back there."

"That damn Dart's gonna be on top of us!" Baresi yelled. Scabs smiled to think Baresi might be losing his famous cool.

"Fine. Last part of the plan: When they're good and scared, and they think they're pinned down, me an' Menny run down the hill toward the highway. That's when Vinny hits the field, too, just like you. Pedal to the metal, Vin!" Scabs looked at the younger man. "No kidding. Don't spare the horses. You gotta get across that field, and the second you can get back up on this road, you do it. We'll meet you partway down. Go!"

Even as Scabs was laying out the plan, Menny had had the presence of mind to run to the car and grab the key, then go to the trunk and throw it open. He got all the guns out, tossed a rifle and a shotgun in the back seat, then ran back to Scabs holding Baresi's Tommy gun and the dead Rico Giampa's Colt rifle. He threw the Tommy gun to Scabs, both of them looking spitefully over at Baresi to see his reaction.

To Scabs's delight, the supposedly tough-as-nails killer was too panicked even to notice, and already he was moving toward the van.

Scabs grabbed Menny by the shoulder. "Vinny, we'll get in with you until you get over that rise where they can't see you drop us off! Come on!"

They scrambled back to the Cutlass and climbed in, and just as Scabs had said, when they passed over the high spot in the road, Vinny dropped them off, and they crept up into a grove of aspens, their branches now barren with the winter.

* * *

The U-Haul van was bearing down on Coal, and there was hardly a place to go to avoid going head-on with them. And that van wasn't budging! At the last second, Coal whipped the wheel to the left, taking him over a bad spot at the edge of the farm field and nearly tipping the pickup over. It ended up stopped at a very bad angle, with the driver's door staring down at the ice of the field and the passenger side staring up toward the mountain horizon.

As the U-Haul bounced down the road toward the highway, Coal threw open his door and nearly fell out onto the field, clawing at his Smith and Wesson. He had gotten it free and turned to level a shot after the van when the *rat-a-tat-tat* sound of a machine gun lifted up from the hill across the road behind him, and he heard bullets striking the side of the pickup. Coal dove down onto the field, scrambling to get behind a tire.

The shooting up the hill went on. Then, out the corner of his eye, he saw the red Cutlass driven by the man who had passed himself off as "Mr. Hanson" bounding down the field on a route that closely matched the one the van had taken. Only in the car's case it didn't seem to have plans of getting back on the farm road. Instead, it was on a beeline across the empty field, bound for the highway.

Again, Coal turned to take a shot as the red car jangled and clanged past him on the rutted field some eighty yards away, and another burst of machine gun fire made him drop again. This time he heard the distinct sound of a tire going flat and smelled the stale air that accompanies a flat. He practiced some phrases he kept only for the best of moments such as this.

More gunfire from above. A couple of shots from another direction—Coal had to assume those were from Sam and Martinez.

Then silence fell down on the icy field and the foothills.

Coal looked down the field toward the red Cutlass, so abused by its driver, but so tough and resilient. It had almost made it clear to the road, and it would indeed make it all the way.

Even as Coal thought that, he saw two men come racing recklessly off the hillside to his left. They couldn't have been closer than a hundred and twenty yards away—a distance Coal and his friends used to shoot their pistols to see who got the lucky shot, and whom his friends had to treat to a free dinner downtown.

And Coal still had six shots in his revolver.

Crawling over to his rear tire and sitting up, Coal leaned his back against the tire and raised his knees, his feet planted flat on the frozen field and his elbows locked between his upraised knees. He followed the racing gunmen, who were only twenty yards or less from the Cutlass, which had now stopped at the edge of the highway.

Coal didn't tell himself this was a stupid shot. That was how his father had told him a marksman talked himself into missing.

Instead, he took the shot as if scoring was a given.

One hundred twenty yards. Two men who intended to kill him and his family. Men who had surely killed before. Targets. Running coyotes. Lead ... He's moving fast. Lead a little more ...

The crack of the magnum rang against the metal of the truck near Coal's head, setting his ears to ringing as well. He didn't wait to see where it hit but reared back the hammer once more, focused in on the front sight, and squeezed off another round a few feet in front of the slowest target, the one farthest from the car.

Even though he was pretty sure the second shot went low, that slowest target never made it to the Cutlass.

With the slower man now down on one knee, Coal leveled his pistol again. Before he could take the next shot, the Cutlass flew into motion. As he was about to squeeze off, the car lurched up right between the downed man and Coal's sights.

That didn't stop him. He let a little breath seep out his mouth and tripped the trigger anyway. The tinny echo of a hit drifted back up to him, as he was squeezing off another round.

Shooting at a running man one hundred twenty yards distant was one thing—chancy at best. Aiming a Smith and Wesson .44 magnum revolver with a six-inch barrel at a car the size of a Cutlass that was sitting still? To Coal, that was a sure thing.

He aimed at the car window, just above the driver's head, and sent another two rounds that way in fairly quick succession. He couldn't be positive at that distance, but he was pretty sure he saw the spray of glass on the first shot, and he thought he saw the man jerk a little after the second one.

And then the man stomped down on the gas and spun the car back the other way, bearing down on the highway. When he hit the pavement, the car lurched sideways, but the man quickly had control of it. Before Coal could empty the .44 of casings and thumb even two more cartridges in, the Cutlass was well out of range.

It disappeared when the toe of a foothill blocked it from his view. Coal sat silent and pushed the rest of the cartridges into the wheel, then slapped it shut again.

He almost didn't dare go up the hill looking for his comrades-in-arms.

CHAPTER THIRTY-SIX

It seemed more than a little miraculous to Coal when he found Sam and Martinez that neither of them was hurt—at least not more than their pride. For three men as supposedly well-trained as they were, they certainly had fallen into a trap, and the worst of it was it didn't even appear that it could have been a well thought out trap. It had been a trap of desperation, but it had worked anyway, and the hit-men couldn't have had more than a minute or two to come up with it. But then sometimes desperation is the father of the best plans, some wiseman once proclaimed—or words to that effect.

The orange Dodge Dart, as pretty a car as it had been when Quality Motors loaned it out to Sam and Martinez, was no longer a show piece. A show piece, perhaps, but only to show what a machine gun can do to sheet metal and fine-looking automobiles at close range.

Coal got on his radio once he knew his boys were all right and called in to dispatch to send a wrecker out. Then they sat in the Dart and waited, because at least while it was idling and the heater was running warm they were on flat ground, not tilted drastically over to one side as they would have been in the GMC.

It was Ken Parks, much to Coal's chagrin, who answered the call, but the mechanic didn't make a single wisecrack. Apparently, looking at the side of the Dart and the pickup sobered him a good deal. "Man, that's too bad, Coal," said Ken, looking at the ten or so bullet holes in the side of the pickup as he shook his head. "That was a nice-looking truck."

"Yeah, well thank heavens I've got a good friend who can fix stuff like that. It's the Dart that makes me sick. Ben Goodall over at Quality Motors loaned that to us, and I guess this is the thanks he gets."

Ken cringed. "Yeah, that stinks. Well, I'll get the truck righted, and then we can change that tire out. Looks like it's the only one they hit." Which wasn't the case with the Dart, both of whose tires on the passenger side were flat on the ground, besides having twenty bullet holes down its side and three shattered windows.

"It might look bad," Sam cut in, "but I bet neither one of these cars feels as bad as that guy Coal plugged."

Ken jerked his eyes over to Coal. "You hit one? With that?" He pointed at the pistol on Coal's hip.

"Yeah. He wasn't that far."

Martinez scoffed. "Yeah, only a hundred and thirty yards or so."

"One-twenty," Coal corrected quietly.

Ken laughed. "Dang! Remind me to bring a rifle if you ever challenge me to a gunfight."

Sam was limping around, and it took Coal a while to think about why.

"You've been hiding that pretty good, Sam. Still hurting from your tumble down the road?"

Sam shrugged it off. "It'll heal."

Coal was pretty amazed. Sam had certainly come by his tough reputation honestly.

Once the GMC was back on somewhat level ground and the spare on, Ken loaded the Dart onto his trailer, and then the three shame-faced crusaders got into Coal's truck and sedately followed Ken's tow truck back to town, by way of the old highway and then Savage Lane. Coal had made that special request of Ken to be sure there wasn't a big U-Haul truck sitting in his yard.

All the way back to town, Coal was quietly wondering just how smart the Mob really was. Could he know without any doubt that there was no way of their finding his family at Jim Lockwood's? After everything he had seen, he was beginning to wonder.

* * *

As they had planned, the four mobsters met in Leadore, where Jacopo Baresi, for all his tough shell, had been sitting for half an hour in a vacant lot biting his fingernails off before the red Cutlass rolled in next to him with a quiet crunching of gravel. By now, it was being driven by Menny Marcello, the only one of the three who had come away from Coal's .44 magnum unscathed.

Scabs Ravioli was seriously hurt. The .44 magnum sent its bullet out of the barrel at over thirteen hundred feet per second, and by the time the sheriff's copper-headed bullet had reached out the one hundred twenty yards to its target it had lost very little of its steam, and not a lot of elevation either. He had taken the bullet in the outside inch of meat on his left thigh, making it difficult even to walk. Even so, he was counting himself lucky for the low shot. If he had taken one ten or more inches higher it would have meant a hip ... or worse.

Luckily for Scabs, however, his good fortune had at least prevented it from hitting bone, so if he could get some decent medical care soon, he would recover probably with no ill effect other than a nasty scar. And although he was in no shape to be moving around and needed to be patched up, in his bare-knuckle boxing days he had suffered a lot of bad treatment, and his body had learned to recover from the effects of shock much quicker than men of a weaker caliber. So had his mind.

For Vinny Derasmo, on the other hand, the effects of his wound were far more mental than physical, although the physical part was bad enough. The bullet that had made Vinny jerk had sliced through the skin of his scalp across the top of his head, removing a furrow of hair a good two inches long and a quarter-inch wide.

He had managed mostly because of his galloping adrenaline to race away from the scene. But the shock had set in quickly, and when, due to the near disabling effects from the shockwave of the bullet and the blood that was running profusely down his forehead and into his eyes, he had nearly run the Cutlass off the road, Menny had forced him to pull over so he could take the wheel.

Vinny couldn't stop babbling about how close he had come to death, but by now the major aftereffect for him was a pounding headache that wouldn't likely go away soon.

Even hurt as badly as he was, it was now Scabs's sharp mind that proved to be running the show, in spite of any of Porc de Castiglione's wishes that Baresi be in charge.

Because the four of them still had their traveling bomb (which Scabs and Menny had miraculously managed to keep upright on the rough and tumble road), and they now knew where the sheriff lived—and maybe more importantly because they all knew what lay ahead at the hands of Porc de Castiglione if they failed in their mission—they had to remain in Idaho until the job was done. But to remain, they had to have a place to stay.

It was Scabs's clear-thinking, in the end, that convinced Baresi and the others that the safest place to stay was where they had already been staying: the pig farm. Who would ever believe they would go back there? It wasn't appealing, it had the stench now of more than one kind of "pig" all over it, and it was distant from town.

In short, it was the perfect hiding place for a bunch of thugs who hoped no one came out to check on their welfare.

The U-Haul fit nicely behind the property's biggest barn when they got back to Richard Parker's place, but it wouldn't remain there long. There was already a plan in place that called for its departure, a plan which, with Jacopo Baresi proclaiming himself once more in charge, he had dreamed up with the greatest of pride. While he would remain behind at the pig farm to nurse Scabs, as he put it, Vinny and Marcello would take the U-Haul, along with Parker's beat-up old pickup, for transportation back when the job was done, drive by the sheriff's house to park the van in the yard directly in front, then take the long-distance detonation device Marcello had invented and hide out on a not-so-distant hill to wait.

It didn't matter whether the sheriff's pickup was in the yard or not. If it was, and if there was a sign of life inside, the job would be easy, and fast. If it wasn't, on the other hand, then Menny and Vinny might have to wait in the old pig farmer's pickup for longer than they wanted. But eventually it was going to come to the sheriff's attention that the moving van he was looking for had been right in his yard the entire time, and he was going to go exploring it. When he did, Menny would use his hand-held device to touch off the detonator, and then they would drive sedately back up Lemhi Road and be back at the pig farm within fifteen minutes.

The problem was the Mob knew nothing about Coal Savage's dark green Thunderbird. And the T-Bird was his ace-in-the-hole.

Scabs sat on the couch with his wounded leg propped up. Good old Menny had turned out to be a fine partner. He was completely solicitous of Scabs's every need, bringing him water, soda pop, snacks—whatever he asked for. He even kept bringing fresh strips of a sheet he had dug out of a drawer—apparently the only clean sheet on the property—and cut up to use for bandages, because Scabs was still bleeding, although it had slowed considerably.

When Baresi went to use the bathroom, the other three men left in the living room looked around at each other. Scabs guessed by Vinny and Menny's faces they were thinking the same thing he was, and Menny proved it when he spoke.

"I don't think I'm all that keen on this plan, guys. Scabs, do you think we should do this?"

"What choice we got? Porc says Baresi's in charge, so if I try t' argue, you know how I get treated when we get back."

Menny's eyes met Scabs's, and Scabs stared back. Finally, he dragged his glance away. He knew what Menny was thinking. He was thinking it too: Was he really going to get back at all? They both knew the uses Jacopo Baresi had been put to before. Had Castiglione really sent his pet psychotic killer all the way to Salmon, Idaho, merely to kill a local sheriff when he already had two proven hitmen on the job? So Menny had made a little mistake. And it wasn't even his fault. There was no way anyone could ever have guessed that jailer and his little sister would go to that house. No way. No, it was something else. Porc simply wanted Scabs out of the picture. He couldn't prove it. He had no concrete evidence. But it was something he felt with every part of his being.

Scabs thought of his beautiful wife, sitting home alone. He wanted to call her. He wanted to tell her he would be home tomorrow night, in time for a nice little Valentine's Day candlelight dinner, like she had talked about. But there was only one phone, and he couldn't talk to her like he wanted to with the others around, especially Baresi. So he sat on the couch, and he waited.

And slowly, darkness closed in.

When Baresi said the word, it was well past midnight. He stood up and paced the floor a couple of times, both times looking out the front window by using a finger to drift the drapes to one side.

Finally, he turned. "All right, boys. Time to go."

"You sure this is the best idea?" Menny asked. He knew Vinny felt the same, but Vinny would never have said it. Anyone else sure would have said something. One close call with a bullet was plenty for one trip.

Baresi stared Menny down. "You questioning me, Marcello? I'll blow your guts out you don't get out there an' drive down the road. An' when I see you two's again that sheriff better be gone."

Vinny swallowed hard. Menny nodded. He took a deep breath and walked over to Scabs. "Hey, *amico.* You take care, huh? Soon as I get back I'll get you to a doctor somewhere. Promise."

Scabs nodded at his partner. His good, faithful Menny. “Sure thing, Twinkie,” he replied, dredging up the almost-forgotten nickname. Menny grinned and shook Scabs’s outstretched hand. He held on longer than two grown men should, and Scabs didn’t even mind.

After the two men had departed, Baresi went over and sat on the couch down from Scabs. For a while, he stared at the black TV screen, which he had already tried to watch earlier but found only snow. “Damn little Podunk villages,” he said. “No TV at night. No radio. Don’t know how people even live out here.”

Scabs didn’t reply. He was trying to block out Baresi’s grating voice, and the disturbing look of his ugly, murderous face. He was thinking about Menny, and Vinny, waiting out there in the dark all night, maybe longer. He tried thinking about his Nicola, sitting home alone, except for their dumb schnauzer, Pieta, and the goldfish, Baldini and Bud. He thought about his three wonderful children, Giorgio, Nicoló, and Viola. And he thought about Skoal tobacco, which he had run out of yesterday, and Ritz crackers with pickled garlic and mozzarella.

It was sure going to be nice to get back home to civilization. And to his beautiful bride of thirty-six years.

CHAPTER THIRTY-SEVEN

Sam and Martinez didn't seem to think it was a good idea for Coal to stop at Jim Lockwood's house and see his family and Maura. There was no point in drawing attention to where his family was staying. They told him he was going to be fine, that they would stay well back from the hitmen, and they would never even see them coming. They told him it was almost over.

Coal believed Sam and Martinez were probably right, that it was probably almost over. But whether or not he would be around to see the ending, that was another story, and one he had a hard time making himself believe.

As good as Sam and Martinez were, the Mob as a family had been at this killing thing a lot longer than they had, and Coal and his friends were outnumbered—at least as far as he knew.

When it was obvious that Coal's mind would not be changed, Sam and Martinez insisted on some precautions. To make sure the Mob had no way to track them, they borrowed from Ken Parks a vehicle no one would associate with Coal, a rusty, once-green old junker of a 1959 Chevrolet Biscayne. They wanted to get something with some power, but Ken didn't have anything like that on hand, and after what had happened with the Dodge Dart they certainly weren't going to crawl back into Quality Motors asking for another of their pristine vehicles. So they had to settle for the V-6 235 under the hood of the Chevy and pray if they had to chase another vehicle it wouldn't be faster than the U-Haul van.

When Coal pulled the Biscayne up in front of the Lockwoods', Sam kicked back in the passenger seat. "Leave the engine runnin', would you? Me an' Q will stay out here an' keep an' eye out. You're not gonna take forever, are you?"

Coal scoffed. "I'm not even sure what forever means anymore."

On Jim's porch, Coal turned and scanned his surroundings. The road out front was quiet. It was late evening, and an eerie orange glow tainted the western sky. In keeping with that eeriness, there was an overarching quiet about the yard, the air, and it seemed the entire country. Coal couldn't help but feel like it was the calm before the big storm.

He knocked quietly on the door, and in a moment the drapes parted an inch or so. Two seconds later, the door flew open, and Coal was under attack from every direction—black and tan missiles from hip level, upright little bombs that came to above his waist, and others that hit him around the chin. Dogs, children, moms—and Maura—could sure make a man feel loved.

When the initial greetings were over, Coal noticed that although Maura had hugged him right along with everyone else, she seemed to hang back now, as if purposely distancing herself. Coal gave individual attention to each of his children, which included the kind of advice a man might give his family before an extended trip away. Connie didn't miss this, and of course Maura wouldn't have either. But as Connie was drawing closer to him, Maura got farther away.

Acutely aware of his partners waiting in the car, Coal kept trying to force himself to cut the visit short. And yet he lingered. And lingered. Deep inside, something kept telling him to make it last. A man was never promised another week, another day ... even another hour.

As the children pooled around him, with Katie clinging to his side like a strip of Velcro to the side of a sheep and Sissy holding desperately onto his leg on the other side, Coal's heart kept on a constant downward trudge, because every time his eyes sought out Maura, wanting to talk to her alone, she seemed more distant. And it wasn't all physical. There was a closed-off look in her eyes, a distance he couldn't recall seeing in her before. His heart pounded in a dull, ponderous way, and he started to feel a strange difficulty getting his breath. Something was happening here with him and Maura. Some kind of dynamic he had no way to understand.

And on the eve of Valentine's Day.

Coal had once had a dream, not a week after his father died. His father, big, tough old Prince Colt Savage, had returned home, as if from a trip away. While Coal was detained by school friends who wanted to visit, he kept his eyes on his father. He had been certain his father was gone forever. Certain he was dead. Yet here he was, big as life, standing at a little distance away, waiting for Coal's friends to finish with him. There was a look in his father's eyes that let Coal know he had something important to say, and Coal felt anxious and impatient that his friends wouldn't leave him alone during this most important time between a father and his son.

Then he began to notice that as his friends drew closer and closer around him, almost forming a fence of human flesh, Prince began to fade back farther and farther away, not only in distance but in the solid-ness of his being. He was slipping away, graying out. Coal started to realize he was able to see right through him, as if his father were becoming transparent.

Desperately, he tried to fight through his crowd of friends, but more and more insistently they clung to him, grabbing his arms, his legs, holding him back. His father gave him a mysterious smile, seemed to shift his gaze off somewhere at a great distance, and then, like a wisp of cloud, he was gone.

Coal wasn't dreaming now. He was wide awake. And yet the look in Maura's face took him back to that dream, and in desperation he saw her fading away.

"Kids, can you guys give me just a minute with Maura? I'll be right back. I promise."

Even with his plea, it took Connie practically prying Sissy away with a crowbar to get her to let go of Coal's leg. Feeling almost frantic, because he couldn't shake the bad dream, Coal went to Maura, who stayed standing in her place, not taking even one step forward to meet him. Metaphorically, she seemed to be vanishing from right before him, just like the cloud the image of his father had been.

He was right in front of her, still surrounded by his family and the Lockwoods, and yet it felt like the two of them were alone.

"Can we talk?" He didn't know why, but it felt like they had had an argument and he was trying to get her to make up.

She shrugged one shoulder, both of her hands deep in her pants pockets. "Sure. Where?"

Coal turned to Jim, who was watching him. Before he could ask, Jim jerked his head toward the hallway that led to his and Betty's bedroom. "Use the loading room. You'll like how it smells in there."

Coal tried to smile back at his friend, and he took Maura's elbow as she turned and started down the hall following Jim's direction. There was no obvious warmth to the woman. He might as well have been leading a prisoner to her cell.

When they got to the loading room, Coal shut the door, immediately surrounded by the odor of Hoppe's Number 9 solvent, at any normal time a therapeutic aroma to anyone who loved guns.

Maura didn't turn fully toward him but kept her right shoulder away, and her left toward him as if she might need it to block any advance from him. The undeniable barrier kept him at bay.

"Are you okay?"

Maura found a little smile. "Sure. I'm fine. You?"

He smiled but didn't feel like it. "As good as can be. Hey. You know tomorrow's Valentine's Day, right?"

She tried to give him another smile, but he had seen smiles like this before and they never amounted to anything good. "Of course."

"Well, I was going to wait to ask you something, but ... Okay, so I can't wait."

He stood there watching to see if she would give him some kind of reaction, at least ask him what he wanted to say. She just looked at him, her eyes seeming, more than anything else, a little dull.

"I've been thinking about doing something big, and I wanted to see how this would strike you," he forged on. "And so you know, I was thinking about this before the fire." At the word "fire" another layer of film came over her eyes.

"I'd like to start the ranch back up again. At Mom's. We could try to raise some more Herefords, or even something more exotic. I even thought about Texas Longhorns."

"Wow. That sounds big." There was no change to her expression, or even her voice, that would make her words sound sincere, or as if the idea intrigued her whatsoever.

"I'd keep my sheriff job, though, and I was thinking Mom would need somebody to help run things when I wasn't there. What would you think about coming in on it? We'd put an addition on the house, a little self-contained log house attached right to our place, with a door on it you could lock or just leave it open, however you wanted, and come through to be at our house any time you wanted. It could be maybe eight hundred or a thousand square feet, with its own bathroom, and kitchen, and ..." He stopped here, searching her eyes, eyes that seemed unable to look right into his. This was so far from the reaction he had imagined.

"Maura, are you sure you're okay?"

A smile came to her lips at the same time that tears filled her eyes, which she tried to blink away. She nodded vigorously. "Yeah, I promise. Wow, Coal, that sounds neat. A real ranch. That seems so much like something you'd enjoy—especially the Longhorns. But ... I'm not sure about my part."

His heart was beating so hard it almost hurt. Maura ... fading away from him. "Why? Did I do something wrong?" He sounded like he was begging! He was a Marine! Marines weren't beggars. What was he doing?

"No, of course not!" Her eyes made her words into lies. "No. I just ... Well, it just seems so big. Such a huge change."

"Sure. Sure it would be—huge." He tried to bring to his voice all the excitement he had been so sure he would feel while he was asking her to come live at the up-and-coming Savage Ranch. But Maura's cool and distant demeanor had taken all that away. He was used to the passionate Maura, the Maura with the biting but fun-loving humor. He had even grown accustomed to the angry Maura, which a deep-down morbid part of him had almost even come to enjoy—as long as she wasn't punching him in the face. But this distant Maura, this was a woman he had never seen and was not equipped to understand or talk to.

Maura suddenly turned squarely to him, and his heart jumped a little when she even took a tiny step closer, reaching out a hand to lay it softly on his arm. "You've been thinking a lot about all this, haven't you?"

"I have. A lot." He couldn't even tell her how much, and how often. He didn't want to embarrass himself any more than he already was.

"Well, like you said, tomorrow is Valentine's Day, right? Maybe if ... If things are different tomorrow, maybe we can talk about it some more. Is that okay? It's sure a lot to digest."

There was still very little emotion in her voice.

"Yeah!" He tried to sound casual. "I sure wouldn't want you to jump at it." (Although in reality he had thought she would, and her reaction had done something akin to hitting him in the guts with a battering ram.) "So yeah, I'll come over tomorrow night, and we'll talk about it. And ... I'd kind of like to hear you sing that horse song again too."

A little smile came to her lips, but not her eyes. "Okay, that sounds nice."

Coal walked from the room with Maura once more in front of him, following her as if she were some stranger in the grocery store. In the front room, he hugged Connie and the kids, letting Sissy cling to him once more way too long. But when he looked for Maura, she was standing eight feet away, one shoulder again turned into him.

He looked at Connie. She was already watching him. He tried to give her a wink and a smile, and then he turned to bolt, nearly running into the door in his rush to get out into the freezing night air.

CHAPTER THIRTY-EIGHT

Wednesday, February 14

They had to pick Valentine's Day. So many cold, dreary, monotonous days in the frigid month of February, but they had to do this on a day that was supposed to be dedicated to love.

But then Valentine's Day had mostly become a day of big profits for the candy companies, the greeting card companies, and florists, a great big commercial venture like so many other things in the world. Coal hadn't celebrated a Valentine's Day in years. Did it even mean anything anymore?

This year he had intended for it to.

Before first light they came, first a single driver in a pickup that in the dimness matched perfectly to the vehicle that was supposed to be registered to the late great pig farmer-husbandman Dick Parker. From the hayloft, down on his belly in his heavy coat and gloves, Coal watched the slow passage of the pickup, which came from upper Lemhi Road, turned onto Savage Lane, and passed out to Highway 28. Beside him lay his battered old Winchester Model 70 .30-06, the weapon that had won him so many fun competitions in his youth—only competitions, of course, in which the master shooter, Hague Freeman, did not take part. The rifle was as accurate as any other he had ever owned, and he was better in its use than the next ninety to a hundred men. Today he prayed that would be enough.

Out in the field, in a much less comfortable position, lay Sam Browning, dressed warmly and covered in grass and weeds, camouflaged even too well for a careful search through Coal's binoculars to locate him. Martinez, meanwhile, was across the road in the willows.

It had been a long night, and with the bitter cold there had been no possibility that any of the three would fall asleep. Now they could only pray that their gamble had worked, that the men who had come to assassinate Coal would not dare wait now that their plan with the U-Haul had been discovered.

With the slow passage of the beat-up old pickup, it seemed the prayers had worked.

The Savage homestead was quiet. Quiet and dark. There were no longer even horses on the property, for in the night Coal and his partners had hauled them up to some beat-up old corrals behind the home of their neighbors, Wilber and Margie Rawson, to keep them out of harm's way. They had also left Maura's dogs, Chewy and Dart, up there in the Rawsons' garage. Now nothing stirred out there, not even a winter bird.

Another half hour had passed, and Coal's heart had returned to beating soddenly. Had the earlier passing pickup meant nothing? They had assumed the mobsters were the reason Dick Parker's pickup was never found on his property, that they had taken it somewhere and that maybe it would appear again being used by them. Now Coal was not so sure. He was pretty sure nothing on the place would have looked amiss to the killers. Why had the pickup, if it was driven by one of them, passed by and never returned?

Uneasily, he shifted his weight on the hard boards beneath him, protected only by a thin layer of lumpy hay which part of the time seemed to be more a curse than a blessing.

And then he heard the crackle of tires on frozen gravel again. Soon, another vehicle appeared, and inside Coal jumped. It was the

U-Haul! Once more, he carefully scanned the field. No Sam Browning. And in the willows Martinez made himself as invisible as a politician in a whorehouse.

It hadn't yet gotten light enough to be sure, but Coal only made out one person in the van. It slowed at the opening of the driveway. Then it stopped. On the frozen road, it sat idling, a cloud of white steam huffing away from the tailpipe. Coal's heart was pounding. This was the time of truth. The big test. They had to time everything just right, because if what Sam had said was true there were enough explosives in that van to take down the house, the garage, and the barn. And Coal was not ready to see the home of his childhood gone.

Yet he had to let whoever was in the van get out, and then if possible let their getaway car come in sight as well. They had one chance. They could never afford to let any of the killers get away, not when this was so close to being finished.

Another vehicle sounded on the road, and when it came into sight it was the pickup. It must have taken another road off the main highway to the east, gone up to Lemhi Road, and come back down. It came up behind the moving van and stopped, and then the van pulled on into the yard.

Coal rolled onto one shoulder to get into a better position to see the pickup. Again, it looked like the only person inside was the driver. But there should be others! Unless ... Had his shooting at the mobsters when they were fleeing from the area of Kenney Creek taken out two of them? He couldn't even hope for that kind of luck.

He licked his lips, regretting it almost immediately when the cold air contacted his saliva. His heart was racing. He wished he had radio contact with Sam and Martinez. What could the two of them see? Were they also seeing only two men? Were they able to see anything beyond the vehicles themselves?

Would this come down to Coal and the killers? Right now, where the two vehicles were stopped, he was pretty sure he was the only one who could get a clear shot.

Coal realized he was praying. He asked for patience, for calmness, and he asked to be allowed to stay here and raise his family. Then, finally, he set the binoculars aside and slid his Winchester closer. From now on, he would be looking through a single glass, with crosshairs in it.

The driver of the U-Haul got out, and now he was gone from sight. There was no sound of a slamming door, which was no surprise. Why give themselves away now?

The pickup was still idling in the road. There were only perhaps four feet of viewing area between the back of the van and the front bumper of the pickup. Coal's racing heart jammed his throat. He had decisions of a lifetime to make, either at this very moment, or when the driver of the van came into view. Who did he shoot first? The van driver? Did he already have the detonation device on him, or was it in the pickup? Did he shoot the driver of the pickup? Then what about the man in the van? Could Martinez get a shot at him before he made it back to the van?

Coal waited, frozen. To his surprise, he suddenly saw the van driver appear at the back door of the van, and he looked toward the pickup. Then, now hurriedly, he unlatched the back doors and latched them open. Before Coal could decide if now was the time to shoot, the van driver went back around the left side of the van, when Coal had thought he would get in the pickup, and to Coal's surprise he saw him reappear in the cab.

The van started moving up the road! Coal almost came up on his knees, then stopped himself from making that telltale movement. He thought of Sam and Martinez, but he didn't risk looking for them again.

After only ten feet or so, the van crunched to a halt with its rear right corner even with the driveway, then backed quickly into the driveway and rocked to a stop, the barrel in the back in plain sight, although sitting in dim shadow. Again the door flew open, and now the driver jumped out and strode toward the pickup.

Where was the detonator? Which of them had it? Coal's mind forced all thoughts of the house, the barn, the garage away from his mind. He pushed away his nostalgic memories of his father and mother feeding the cattle on a frosty winter morning, with steam rising off the animals' sides and from their nostrils into the frosty air, into the brilliant blue sky. He tried not to think—

And then the world went silent and white. Before Coal Savage there was nothing but a U-Haul van, a beat-up pickup, and two men who intended to see him dead.

He raised the rifle, lying on his side, and centered the crosshairs on the head of the pickup driver. He was praying again, and he didn't even know it.

The crack of the .30-06 was shocking in the early morning. It rang out across the frozen wasteland, hollow and eerie but a little underwhelming.

He saw the spray, that familiar, dreadful spray he had been forced to see so many times in Korea, at the Chosin Reservoir and other terrible places, sometimes a spray from the body or head of the enemy, or sometimes from his own comrades-in-arms.

A shattering sound of glass rocked back to him a second later, and then a yelp from the man who had been driving the van.

Coal heard his own voice, shocking to his ears: "Sam! Go! Go! He's running! Q!"

It was Coal's subconscious that had registered the sight of the second man running. The first one had slumped up against his steering wheel, the pickup had lurched forward half a foot, and steam no longer rose from its tailpipe. He must have killed it when Coal killed him.

Get him before he hits that detonator. Shoot him. Kill him.

Coal never wanted to kill another man, but this was war, and he was a soldier. That's what soldiers do.

Suddenly, the man pitched forward, on the far side of the pickup, and the delayed sound of a gun shot rang out from across the road. As he hit the ground, the man instantly rolled to the left, now out of Coal's sight.

"Get him before he gets to the detonator!" Coal heard his own voice almost screaming. "Go! *Q!*"

He had set up a pile of loose hay down below the loft door before going up there in the night, and now, with the rifle in one hand, he leaped out of the loft, landing in the soft hay and rolling.

He came up, instinctively scanning the yard and the rest of his surroundings, making sure the other two men weren't around.

"I can't see him!" Coal heard Martinez yell, and then he could hear Sam running in out of the field.

They had a grizzly bear wounded on the other side of the pickup. Only a fool ran in on a wounded bear.

Coal suddenly saw the man raise up behind the rear tire, and the door of the pickup flew open. "He's at the truck, Q! *GO!"* Coal started forward, motioning for Sam to go around the back of the pickup.

Coal heard Martinez swear. "Coal, he's grabbing something out! Shoot! *SHOOT!"*

A gun shot exploded from where Martinez was, and then another from Sam, who was only shooting at the side of the truck, because he couldn't see the killer any more than Coal could.

Martinez yelled out again, his voice frantic, just before he fired another round. *"SHOOT HIM, NOW!"*

* * *

Scabs Ravioli was sitting on the couch, his leg throbbing. It had been a long time since anything had hurt so bad. Across the room, the television was droning quietly. *Captain Kangaroo*, today, was in fine form.

In the kitchen, a little radio in a brown vinyl cabinet was on slightly louder than the TV. Today, by some miracle, they had a connection to both! Marty Robbins was crooning "El Paso." Fine song. Not Dino Martin fine, singing "My Rifle, My Pony, and Me" on the John Wayne flick *Rio Bravo,* by any means, but still a pretty good tune, and not a bad voice—even if he wasn't a fellow man of Italian roots like Dino or Frank Sinatra.

When the song ended, the deejay came on claiming to have a special breaking news bulletin. Jacopo Baresi, whom Scabs had believed to be asleep, perked up on his end of the couch.

The voice on the radio, which had otherwise sounded professional, funny, and entertaining throughout the morning, now had a quality of deep shock to it. After his introduction, the man continued, *We deeply regret to report that there has been a massive explosion reported perhaps half an hour ago, east of town out on Savage Lane. Apparently at least two homes and several outbuildings have been leveled in the blast. After initial investigations, it is believed that Lemhi County Sheriff Coal Savage and at least four other unidentified citizens were killed in the explosion. We will update the report as soon as we have more information, but in the meantime the city police and the sheriff's department are asking that no one call in with questions about the incident.*

Again, we regret to inform our listeners that it appears an early morning explosion from an unknown cause has taken the life of Lemhi County Sheriff Coal Savage and other unidentified persons.

Jacopo Baresi had a little smile on his lips, bending the ends of his mustache up ever so slightly. He let out a long, contented sigh and slapped the flats of his hands down on his thighs.

"So, I guess that's that. Mister de Castiglione is sure gonna be happy. Too bad about Menny and Vinny, though. I guess that leaves more fun for me."

Scabs sat there staring at Captain Kangaroo and Mr. Green Jeans on the TV. They were having some interaction, probably of the all-encompassing, earth-shattering variety. But Scabs couldn't hear a thing. All he could hear was the last words of his companion, Menneghetti Marcello, and the soft, almost musical sound of his voice. *Menny ... Menny ...* The words came into his mind, words he could never have said out loud to another man: *I love you, brother. Andare con Dio. Go with God ...* Twinkie was gone, and the world would never be the same. He couldn't imagine how he was going to bring the news to his partner's sweetheart.

"You want a snack?"

The words registered on Scabs, or actually more the sound of the voice. He turned and stared blankly at Jacopo Baresi, the man who had only ever cared about one person: himself.

"Huh?"

"I said I'm hungry, man. You want a snack?" This time as Baresi spoke he got up. He put his arms up in the air in a leisurely stretch, yawning. Was that a real yawn? Sometimes when Nicola's dog was embarrassed he was positive he caught it faking a yawn. Baresi scratched his belly with the fingernails of both hands, pulling the front of his shirt partway up. He yawned once more. And strolled toward the kitchen.

Want a snack? The words, so unlike selfish Jacopo Baresi, La Pistola Rossa, rang in Scabs's head as the other man disappeared into the kitchen, now hidden by the doorframe. A chill came over Scabs Ravioli. He felt the tiny hairs on the back of his neck rise up. In his head, he swore.

It was over.

Ten seconds later Baresi stepped back into sight. He had no sandwich, no crackers, no cookies, no jar of peanut butter or bag of nuts.

What Baresi had in his hand was a pistol—not the red one of his infamous nickname, but a very black one.

He swung it up to bear on Scabs Ravioli.

CHAPTER THIRTY-NINE

Scabs Ravioli squeezed his own trigger. Once. Twice. Then a third time. In the doorway, Jacopo Baresi cringed and bent sideways at the waist. Scabs raised his pistol out straight to shoot again—just as Baresi's gun went off.

Scabs started to shoot again as Baresi dropped to his knees, and his gun tumbled away across the living room floor. Scabs managed to struggle upright, his bad leg splayed out to the side. Baresi was looking up at him, clutching his chest, wheezing.

"Why'd you shoot me?"

Scabs stared at him. The words would hardly register in his mind. Did Jacopo Baresi dare ask why he shot him?

"Why'd I shoot you? You were gonna shoot me. How much they pay you?"

Baresi started to laugh. "Screw you."

Leaning down, ignoring the searing pain in his leg, Scabs shoved Baresi over backward and reached down to tear open his shirt. Like most of the Mob hitmen, Scabs preferred his quiet twenty-two to other calibers. The three holes it had left, all too far to Baresi's right side, were small, but they had certainly disabled him. Would he die? Most likely, but possibly not. Good medical care might save the man's worthless life.

"Get up," Scabs growled.

Baresi sneered up at him. "You shot me."

"No kidding. Get up."

Baresi made it up, wheezing heavily. "I can't breathe. You shot my lungs."

"No, just one of 'em. Shoulda shot your brain. Go out the back, Mr. *Red Pistol*. Head for the car. We're gettin' outta this valley while we still can."

Walking bent over at the waist, holding his chest and wheezing, Baresi obeyed. Scabs grabbed the car keys off the top of the TV and followed him out.

At the car, Baresi started around to the passenger side. Scabs's voice stopped him. "Hey. Pistola. Remember I said *we're* gettin' outta this valley? Yeah. I meant me—and the car—and my gun."

He leveled his pistol at Baresi again. "You were gonna leave me for the hogs, weren't you? Doin' Porc's bidding. Good old Porc. What beef did he have with me?"

Baresi, still clutching his side, grinned through his pain. "It was never against you, you idiot. Can't believe you two saps never knew nothin'." He almost laughed, but it appeared to cause him too much pain. "Porc was sleepin' with Menny's girl. Right under his stupid nose. That boy was a fool. Porc wanted him gone. That's all. He didn't want no mess. He only wants you dead because he couldn't trust you no more after he done away with Menny."

Scabs stared at the wounded man, his mind churning. Porc had never cared about him one way or another! It had all been his imagination. But he wanted *Menny?* A clear thought finally surfaced through the clouds of his brain. "So Menny's dead now, and you an' Porc didn't even do it! Nobody would ever have known you ever planned to. Why did you still try to kill me?"

This time Baresi couldn't hold back his laughter, though it caused him obvious pain. "'Cause I never liked you, Scabs. I just wanted to see you die."

Baresi was out of breath. He bent over at the waist, sucking hard. He started to laugh, then sucked harder for air. Scabs had once watched a man shot in a lung with a .22 drown on his own blood as it drained into his chest cavity. Baresi would not long be in this world, he surmised.

Scabs raised his .22 and pointed it at Baresi's head. The man's eyes grew big and he raised his hands to the sides.

"Back up, Baresi.. Back up."

Baresi started backing, wheezing. "Don't shoot me, Scabs! You don't have to do this!"

Several more steps, and he came up hard against the solid boards of the hog pen.

"Menny was a good partner, even if he never could see that girl wasn't any good," said Scabs calmly, and lowering his pistol he shot Baresi in a knee cap.

Baresi grabbed onto the top rail of the hog pen to hold himself up. His face twisted in pain.

Almost dragging his leg, Scabs hobbled to him. Then, with all his strength, he grabbed skinny Jacopo Baresi at the crotch and heaved him up and over the rail to land on his side in the enclosure with the hogs. Startled, the animals scrambled squealing across the pen to the other side. Baresi lay there writhing in the frozen mud and pig manure. A few of the braver hogs advanced toward him, sniffing the air, their wet, heavy snouts twitching back and forth, their lips still a little red from their last meal.

Leaning over the fence, Scabs took careful aim and shot Baresi in his other kneecap, then leaned both arms on the rail. For a moment, he watched the hogs milling on the other side, some of them trying to get brave but not knowing how much they trusted the man who was still upright.

Scabs lowered his eyes to Baresi, who was holding his legs and whimpering softly, his voice wheezing.

"Well, Baresi. Have a good life. I'd like to stay around to see which one of you is the biggest pig, but I gotta go see a man."

With that, Scabs Ravioli turned around and lurched his way to the Cutlass, climbing in. It was going to be a long, long drive to get home, but he would make it by the fall of night.

He could hardly wait to see the lights of Vegas as he crested over the hill. There was nothing in the world prettier than Las Vegas at night. Nothing except maybe his wife.

But as for Vegas, it was only pretty at a distance. Nothing in the world was uglier to Scabs Ravioli than the heart of Las Vegas.

He sure wished he could have said goodbye to his children.

* * *

When Coal had heard Martinez yelling that the man at the truck was down, and Martinez came running with his gun out, covering the downed man, Coal followed suit, coming around the front of the truck as Sam came from the rear. One of the two men Coal and his partners had seen outside the Stagecoach Inn, the strikingly handsome young one, lay on the ground, looking up at them with blood running freely out the side of his mouth.

"It's cold," the man said feebly. "And I gotta call my girl for Valentine's Day. Could you—" Slowly, his head sank down onto his outstretched arm. He tried to draw another breath, and then he was still. Several seconds later, his mouth snapped open as the sound of wind entering came to Coal and the others. The man's eyes flickered, and then the air seeped back out.

"Menneghetti Marcello," said Sam Browning. "I woulda had him two good, solid times if it wasn't for our pathetic legal system. Menny was his nickname. Menny Marcello."

Coal nodded, looking at a little device that lay beside the dead man's hand. Sam saw him looking at it, stooped and picked it up. When he stood, it lay like a dead bug on the flat of his hand. "Just what you think it is," he said casually. "I guess we better go get everything disabled before somebody accidentally touches this off."

Once Sam had rendered the barrel full of fertilizer and diesel fuel back to just those two ingredients, being worthless without a detonator, he stepped down out of the truck.

"You think the other two are dead?" asked Martinez.

Coal shook his head. He had studied these two dead men, the one whose head had met with Coal's .30-06 bullet, a man Sam wasn't familiar with, and Menny Marcello, dead by the gun of Alex Martinez. Neither of them was the man who had been driving the U-Haul the day before, and Coal had never even fired a shot at that man. "The guy I hit in the leg, who knows? A .44 could easily kill a man with a shot to the thigh. But the guy who was driving the U-Haul is still out there. I'll stake my life on it."

"I guess you will," said Sam.

The plan was a desperate one, and Coal only agreed to it as a last resort. After calling Connie out at Jim Lockwood's to let her know not to pay attention to the story on the radio, he called the owner of the radio station and asked him to write a news release and turn it over to his deejay without letting him in on the secret. Then he called McPherson's, because his mother had said Maura was on her way there.

But Florin Beller told Coal Maura wasn't scheduled to work that day.

After that, everything was a whirl. Coal's fevered mind couldn't stop thinking about Maura, wondering where she was and if she would be listening to KSRA. But even if she was, that matter was not life or death, and the matter with the Mob still was. He couldn't worry about finding Maura until he had done everything in his power to find the other men who had come to kill him.

It was Martinez who first suggested the Richard Parker pig farm.

"Can you think of any safer place? Anywhere those guys would think they could hide out without worrying anyone might look there? This isn't the big city. It's not like you guys are gonna have a team of investigators out there, and if you do it isn't gonna be right away. It's the perfect hideout."

Coal and Sam agreed with Martinez because they had no other idea where to look. Before leaving the house, Coal called Flo on the phone and asked her to put out a state-wide APB for the red Cutlass, and an APB into Montana as well, just in case the other two mobsters escaped the area. He tried McPherson's one more time, hoping Maura might have stopped in there, and then with a heavy heart he trooped outside.

The coroner's station wagon and the state bull were just pulling up, one in front of the other. When Coal got to them, Lyle Gentry shook his head, looking at the carnage on the road. "This is getting to be an ugly habit, Sheriff."

In Coal's pickup, the trio of hunters bombed east on 28. They turned left on Mule Shoe Road, then right when they hit the old highway, and they came in easy when they neared the sign that said HOGS.

Rolling slow, Coal came into the yard, scanning all around. Six eyes in total, and no one saw a movement or any vehicle but the Pontiac with the broken window.

Martinez swore quietly, and when Coal looked at him he simply shrugged. "Well, we're here, so let's look around anyway."

Coal set the brake and turned the pickup off, taking the key. He had had vehicles stolen out from under him in less bizarre circumstances than this.

With rifles in hand, the three of them surrounded the house, working slowly. There was no car in back, just the usual junk that was always there. While Coal and Martinez swarmed the inside of the house, covering each other, Sam crept around the back.

Half a minute later, Coal thought he heard a distant call, but he wasn't certain. Just as he held his hand up to stop Martinez from making noise walking, a gunshot sounded from out back.

CHAPTER FORTY

Ready to defend Sam, Coal bolted out the back door with his .44 at the high ready position. Sam was the first person he saw, standing out by the hog pens and looking calm. Without stopping there, Coal's eyes swept the yard. Nothing. He lowered his arms a few inches and looked back at Sam.

Sam was staring at him with his gun down at his side.

Coal stared back. "What the hell?"

"I wanted you to see something," said Sam with a little giggle.

Coal straightened up, his gun dropping down by his leg as if it weighed a hundred pounds. "Nice, Sam. Nice."

Sam grinned. He looked like he was embarrassed now, and well he should be. Jerking his head to the side as if trying to crack his neck, he said, "Well, you might think this is nice, or you might not."

With a feeling of morbid anticipation, because of the tone of Sam's voice, Coal walked in the direction Sam had indicated, toward the hog pen, and he could hear Martinez following him.

When they were close to Sam, he turned and strode alongside them. The three of them stopped. There in the hog pen was a ghastly sight. Most of the pigs had scrambled off at the sudden appearance of the three men over the top of them, but the two biggest ones, loath to leave their free meal, held their ground, staring up at the intruders with beady little eyes and snouts covered in gore.

"I guess we'd better pull him out of there," said Coal after a few seconds to recover from the jolt of seeing the mangled body.

"Yep. Guess you better," agreed Sam.

And he wasn't kidding. Neither he nor Martinez agreed to do anything but stand watch outside the pen with their guns in case the pigs decided to defend their meal. Coal opened the gate, went in and grabbed hold of a foot, then dragged the body outside.

The two biggest hogs were stamping around, shuffling back and forth between their front feet. They acted as if they were trying to decide whether it was worth rushing the opening until Martinez slammed it shut and latched it.

Within half a minute, all the pigs were wandering around the pen snuffling about on the hard ground, looking baffled as to how their latest meal had so suddenly vanished.

Disgusted by everything about this property and the wreck and stench of the house, Coal went in and called dispatch again, telling them to update the APB. They would now be looking for only one man in the red Cutlass.

When he hung up the phone, Martinez and Sam were standing there looking at him. Sam's brawny arms were folded across his chest. He nodded toward the compact radio still playing on the countertop, with an ironic song by Connie Smith called "The Hurtin's All Over."

"I guess the hurtin's all over for your friend outside," Sam quipped.

Coal only grunted.

"You know there's pretty much nothing left for us to do here, right?" Martinez added.

Coal stared him down. The question, actually more of a statement, gave Coal questions of his own, but he waited, assuming the two men had intentions of expounding on their cryptic wisdom. Finally, he couldn't take their silence anymore, so he caved.

"I planned on waiting to greet the coroner."

"So you can see his loving smile when he sees you again?"

Coal gave another grunt. "Yeah, something like that."

"He knows where to come, bud," Sam said. "And whoever's left, which I assume is Saverio Ravioli, the ugly guy you met the other day, he had to be listening to that radio announcement earlier. You can bet he's headed south as fast as he can go to get his paycheck. He sure won't be back here again. You got more important things to tend to than hanging around here."

"In fact, if you want someone to stay, we can do it," Martinez said.

"Why?"

"Why do we have to spell everything out, buddy?" Sam said. "You got a girl runnin' around this county somewhere that may or may not have been listening to the radio this morning. If she was ..."

Maura. She had hardly left Coal's mind since the announcement went over the air. He was only surprised to know Sam and Martinez had been thinking about her too.

"You sure you're all right to stay here?"

"We're all right," Martinez replied. "We'll hitch a ride back to town in the hearse. Might be kind of fun. We'll pretend it's Halloween."

"Thanks, guys. I owe you."

Sam grinned. To Coal, it almost looked like his white teeth sparkled. "Isn't that the understatement of the century."

With his heart pounding, Coal called the Lockwood residence. He spoke only briefly with his mother. She had heard nothing from Maura. He then phoned McPherson's one more time. Florin Beller sounded like he could almost cry when asked if he had seen Maura.

"You'd better find that girl, son. If she heard the radio there's no telling what she might do."

Coal hit the highway almost on two wheels, making up for pulling out in front of the car behind him by attaining seventy-five miles an hour within just over eleven seconds and not slacking the horses at all after that, even when he had to fly past a string of five cars at once to keep it there. He was pretty sure at least one of the drivers gave him a one-finger salute out the window, but Coal didn't mind. He was a man on a mission. It was Valentine's Day, and he had a valentine out there somewhere who might think he had been blown to a million pieces.

He had only made it a mile or so past Baker, and there was a big green semi coming at him. The second it passed, a sight exploded into view that he was not expecting: a big, ugly, white International Travelette!

Instinctively, as the Travelette flew by, going way too fast for the speed limit, like Coal was, he slammed on the brakes. In his rearview mirror he saw the Travelette do the same. Then he realized the traffic behind was bearing down on him too fast, so he gunned it again, praying for a nearby turn-off.

By the time he found it, a rutted farm road coming off the highway, passing through an opening in a barbed wire fence into a fallow field, and he went to spin around and get back out on the highway, he saw he didn't have to.

The Travelette was rocketing back at him.

Setting the brake, Coal jumped out as the Travelette careened off the highway, into the empty, frosted field, and bounced to a stop not far away from him.

The pickup door flew open and stayed open, its driver almost falling out, then stepping around it, holding onto its edge as if she needed the support. Maura PlentyWounds stared at Coal as if he were a ghost. He marched toward her, trying not to twist an ankle on clumps of frozen dirt but going as fast as he could.

Maura's face broke as her hand fell away from the door. With both hands up to her mouth, she came running toward him, slipped on an icy spot and almost fell. Coal was there to catch her.

Tears streamed down the woman's face as she got her balance and threw her arms around him, crushing him. She pulled away and stared through her tears at him, searching his eyes. He couldn't begin to describe the jumbled emotions all over her face.

She nearly screamed at him. "How? Coal! *How?* They said—" She broke again, this time in her face, her middle, her knees.

Before he could catch her this time, she sank to the ground, and he went down with her. She was sobbing loudly, almost crying out, releasing a kind of grief he hadn't seen displayed for him ... *ever,* he realized suddenly.

No other person he loved had ever believed him to be dead.

"I tried to reach you," he said, holding her, both of them kneeling on the frozen ground. "I called Mom. I called McPherson's three times. Maura, I'm so sorry."

"Everybody thinks you're dead. *Everybody!* Coal, why? What happened? Is your house—" Her voice broke up again, and he squeezed her to him. He was afraid he was holding her too tight, but she was returning the favor. Maybe under the circumstances there was no such thing as "too tight".

"Maura, no. No, everything's fine. Those guys are all gone, all right? We just had to put out that story to get them out of hiding. We ..."

Her grip on him relaxed enough to tell him she was trying to digest what he was saying. She finally pulled away from him, struggling to get up. He came up with her.

She stared at him, her face starting to fill with something that looked like anger. "You ... You *made that up?* You *told* them to say that on the radio? Coal! You can't do things like that! You can't—"

She struck him in the chest with the side of her fist, then again. “You can’t do that! You just can’t—” She lost her voice and burst into tears again, falling against him. This time he almost had to hold her up.

Coal tried to convince Maura to leave her truck in the field and ride back with him to the Lockwoods’. When she made it plain that she would drive her own vehicle and didn’t feel like seeing anyone else right then, he told her to go ahead and go back to his mom’s, and then he drove to the Lockwoods’.

Connie had her own car at the Lockwoods’, so after a tear-filled reunion between her and her son, and huge hugs from Wyatt, Morgan, and Sissy, they caravanned back to the Savage residence. The first thing Coal noticed was that Maura’s truck wasn’t there.

Before he could decide whether or not to go looking for her, Connie stopped him. “Son, we need to talk.”

He turned and saw the serious look in her eyes, which matched her voice. He didn’t speak.

She came over and put her hand on his arm. “That girl broke down yesterday. She kept talking about her house, and all the things that were in it. Mostly her boys’ photographs from when they were growing up. She has nothing left, Son. Nothing but horse tack and the clothes she had here when the fire happened. All her memories burned up in that fire.”

Coal nodded. “I know. I wish I could bring it all back. But I told her about the ranch. I told her she’d have a free place to stay.”

Connie shrugged. “She’s a broken young lady, Coal. She seems like she’s on the edge.”

“Of what?”

Another shrug. “I’m not sure. Breaking down? A real break-down.”

“How could she survive South Dakota and then break down here?”

"Son, try to understand. It's building up on her shoulders. First South Dakota, and then ... I think she came back here expecting to find some kind of peace at last, and then this happened. And they were so close together. After last night ... I wonder if she'll ever be whole again."

Coal's heart was aching. "I have to go try to find her, Mom."

"This is a big valley. Where are you going to go?"

"Back to her place, first."

"Why?"

"I don't know. Maybe because in a lot of ways she's like me, and when I feel like hell I can find peace in a barn, with the smell of hay and molasses feed, and ... I just think I need to try there."

Connie nodded. "Okay, Son. Do what you need to. I'm going to start a stew and then make some bread. Make sure Maura knows we want her back soon."

"I will," he said, and he hugged her.

He was driving slowly by the time he got to Maura's property, and a car flew past him, honking, as he slowed to fifteen miles an hour where the driveway left Highway 28. There on the far side of the barn he could see the protruding nose of the Travelette.

He parked the truck and sat there for a minute. Finally, he got out and trudged to the open gate of the corral, going in and walking to the barn. The big doors were closed, so he went in through the walk-in door and stood for a moment letting his eyes adjust to the darkness.

The loft. She would go to the loft.

Taking a deep breath, he walked to the ladder and climbed up. She was sitting almost buried in the hay, as if in a fluffier-than-normal beanbag chair. Her face was bathed in soft light from the open window, and she didn't look over at him, although the subtle change in her eyes let him know she knew he was there, and looking at her.

He walked over to her. "Is it okay if I sit with you?"

She nodded, staring out the window.

He sank down beside her. "It's Valentine's Day."

"Yep."

"I'm sorry about your house. I wish I could change things."

Her nod this time was small, and her eyes remained dry. "Me too."

He sighed. Maybe he shouldn't have come. Sometimes a person simply needed to be alone. He had felt that many times, and often having someone come to "comfort him" was no comfort.

"Mom wants you to be at the house for stew and fresh bread. I'd be willing to bet she's going to make cookies too. That woman should weigh eight hundred pounds by now."

A little smile came to Maura's lips, and now her eyes moistened. As she was swallowing a lump in her throat, she only nodded. Slowly, she reached out a hand and squeezed his knee.

"You want to be alone for a while?"

She only nodded, squeezing his knee harder.

Without another word, although there were a million of them trying to decide if they should get blurted out, he turned and went back to the ladder, climbing out of the loft.

Instead of going back home, he drove to Richard Parker's pig farm.

Kerry Updyke had just finished loading the ragged and bloody corpse of the gangster into the back of his station wagon. He frowned when he saw Coal.

"You're going to get rich off the county," Coal said.

"I'm afraid so. Are you all right? You've had a heck of a time lately."

"I'm all right. It's over."

Sam and Martinez were standing there over Updyke's shoulder, and after he pulled away and only the State police car was left, with Officer Gentry around back performing whatever he could of an investigation, they leveled a long, serious gaze at Coal.

"I made a phone call to some friends," Sam said. "Gave them a bit of description of that guy. You wanna know who that was?"

Coal shrugged. "I guess so, sure."

"That was Jacopo Baresi. La Pistola Rossa, they call him in Italian: The Red Pistol. LPR. He's the guy they send to take care of other assassins they don't like anymore."

Coal raised his eyebrows, nodding. "Wow. Sounds important."

"I guess he was. He's one guy I never got close to nailing. I didn't even know what he looked like." Sam drew in a big breath, then sighed. "Word will get out, you know."

"What's that?" Coal thought Sam was still talking about Baresi.

"It's going to get around that you didn't die."

"Oh. Okay."

"Okay, so ... You know the Mob's still in danger, right? They can't stop until you're gone. Or until all the witnesses who can testify against them are gone."

Coal shrugged and shook his head. He had no idea what Sam was trying to say, or what he was trying to do, beyond making him a nervous wreck.

"If that's the case ... I guess I'm dead. Someday if they keep trying they'll succeed."

Martinez nodded. "I guess so, unless ..."

"Unless what?"

"There is one other thing," said Browning.

"I'm all ears."

"Unless somebody could get to your Ray Christian guy."

"Get to— What are you saying?"

Sam shrugged. "He's the last one that could testify against the Mob in court, right?"

"I guess so."

"Then you know what we're saying."

At last, he took in a deep breath. Sam and Martinez were talking about somehow infiltrating the jail system and finding Ray Christian, the same way the Mob had gone in and found his brother. They were talking about silencing Ray forever to save Coal.

Slowly, Coal nodded. He thought of Ray Christian, the man he had gotten so attached to so fast, like a long-lost brother—even closer than his own brothers. He thought of the way Ray had tried so hard to keep innocent Moby Hargis out of trouble when he easily could have let him go to the wolves. He had really liked Ray Christian. But more importantly than that, it wasn't Coal's place to trade another man's life for his own, no matter how easy that might make things for him.

"I've sure appreciated your help, guys. But I guess this is the end of the trail."

Martinez nodded. "That's what we figured you'd say. I hope it all works out for you, buddy."

"Me too."

"So we're going to fly out this time," Martinez said. "I'm a little paranoid about driving."

Coal chuckled. "I don't blame you."

"You have any interest in a cool sixty-eight Mustang?"

Coal laughed harder. "Right."

"I'm not joking. You said you liked it. You want it?"

That question didn't take Coal long to answer. "If you're selling, I'd be buying."

"It cost me twenty-one hundred bucks when it had five thousand miles on it. If you want to give me a thousand and pay for the repairs, it's yours."

"It's not a Camaro, of course," said Coal.

"Exactly. I wouldn't dare ask that much if it was."

Coal laughed. "Sure, I'll take your Mustang. Something to remember you boys by."

"You're forgetting something else," said Sam, stepping forward.

"What's that?"

"My Russel Stover's chocolates. That was my price for all this hell you put us through, remember?"

CHAPTER FORTY-ONE

Las Vegas, Nevada, Late that night . . .

The lights of Las Vegas, as Scabs Ravioli crested over the rise in the highway, were as beautiful as he remembered them. He stopped his latest stolen car there and got out. It was raining lightly, and not quite forty degrees, but compared to where he had just come from, this was heaven. Limping, and holding on to his aching guts, he walked to the front bumper, pretending everything was fine, and leaned up against the front of the hood. For a while, the world seemed fine and good. Wholesome. Pure. He thought of how he used to take the kids up high like this when they were small, and they would sit on the hood, eating pizza and watching the lights. Life was good then. Life was real.

He lifted his hand and looked down at the big blood stain on the side of his shirt. That damn Baresi. La Pistola Rossa. Damn him! One shot! He had only gotten off one shot when Scabs was nailing him to the barn door, beating him at his own game.

But that one shot had taken Scabs. Right in the guts. It hurt worse than anything he had ever felt, and it made him feel sick to his stomach. That lucky shot, and the .44-sized hole through his leg, had made his drive home the longest of his life. The longest by far.

Finally getting back in the car, he cringed and almost cried out as the pain in his guts hit him full force. The hole in his leg hardly hurt at all anymore, not compared to the fierce and sometimes almost mind-numbing pain of that bullet Jacopo Baresi had put into his guts before going down.

He drove on out of the mountains into the city, and at the Flamingo he let someone else take the car to park it. They could put it wherever they wanted. It wasn't like he would need it again.

Pretending not to hurt, Scabs walked into the lobby, passed through and stopped at an office in the back. Everyone knew him there. They wouldn't dare question why the well-known Scabs Ravioli was here so late at night.

"Hey, Louie. Just goin' up t' see the boss."

A middle-aged, soft-looking man Scabs had always despised for that softness turned and eyed him. "Oh. Hey, Scabs. Keepin' late hours, huh? Sounds good. See you when you come back down."

"Yeah." Scabs turned and walked to the elevator, trying to hold himself together, mentally, emotionally, and physically. Financially didn't even matter anymore—and socially plain never had.

Up the elevator he went, all the way to the very top of the building. While he was traveling, Louie was making a phone call.

Porc de Castiglione not only worked way up high in the Flamingo, but he lived there too, in the most posh apartment in the building. Scabs had only been allowed into it four or five times in all the years he had worked underneath de Castiglione. But it was easy to remember the way.

He knocked. He heard a voice. He knocked again. "Who is it?" the voice yelled.

"It's Scabs Ravioli, sir. Reporting back."

He heard the man mumble something. A minute passed, and the door opened. There was no shock on Porc de Castiglione's face. He had been expecting Scabs. Porc raised a snub-barreled .38 special and shot Scabs in the chest without blinking. Scabs, surprised, raised his own pistol and put three bullets in his boss's fat gut with the sound almost of only one shot. Grimacing, Porc shot Scabs again. The fat man's face was now filled with shock and pain. He had thought he was invincible.

Scabs gritted his teeth. He hurt deep in his chest, but it was minor compared to the pain he had endured in his guts for twelve hours of driving.

He raised his gun higher and fired. Porc must not have liked having a bullet through his throat; he made a choking sound and folded straight to the floor, shot through the spine.

Scabs, using all the strength he had left, stepped forward and kicked Porc's gun out of his hand, then turned to leave.

His legs crumpled, and he landed hard against the wall, feeling the breath leave his lungs in a *whoosh.* His throat was gurgling. Liquid in his throat. He tried to clear it. Didn't have the strength.

When the three black-suited bodyguards rushed out of the stairwell, Scabs's eyes were fading. He thought of his wife, wondering if she had lit the candles yet for their special dinner.

Nicola ...

* * *

Salmon, an hour before dusk

Coal Savage, the sheriff of Lemhi County, had responsibilities he couldn't shirk, no matter how bad he wanted to be back with his family. No matter how bad he wanted to be with Maura for Valentine's Day. He first made a most important call out to Washington,

D. C., to his friend and one-time partner Tony Nwanzée, to whom he had made a promise to report the good news that he was safe. After a pleasant conversation with Tony, he went about his duties, he lined out his deputies for the night, and then, at last, he headed home. Beside him on the seat lay two dozen red roses.

He couldn't stop thinking about Maura, about how their life together would be. His heart pounded mercilessly, and at times he felt like he almost couldn't breathe. He was a kid again, heading out on his first date. But this date was going to be for the rest of his life.

He could make up to Maura for everything that had happened. He couldn't bring back her precious photographs of her sons, but he could build her a wonderful life, maybe not perfect, but more perfect than anything either of them had known in married life.

He raced home after driving past Maura's slowly to make sure her pickup wasn't still there. Maura was waiting at the house! He knew she would be. He loved this fast beating of his heart, the adrenalin-rush that rendered his breathing so labored. He was almost home, and Maura was almost in his arms again.

When he pulled into his mother's yard, he scanned it carefully. A little shock ran throughout his body.

There was no white pickup.

Grabbing the roses and jumping out of his truck, Coal slammed the door, listening to the familiar metallic ring of it across the yard. He almost ran to the front door, throwing it open to the greeting barks of the dogs. But no one else moved as he scanned the room hopefully.

Across the room, Virgil stood with his back to the corner of the wall going to the hallway. His hands were pocket-deep in his corduroys, and his head was down. Katie and Cynthia sat on the old couch with their backs to Coal. The TV wasn't on and yet neither of them looked his way. Were they afraid to?

Wyatt and Morgan sat on stools in the kitchen, and when they saw their father they turned their innocent eyes up to their grandmother, one of only two people gazing at Coal. Only Sissy dared approach him, and she did it like a rocket, physically pushing Shadow aside to get to him.

She was already sobbing before he could even pick her up. In confusion, with fear creeping in to replace it, Coal held the two dozen roses in his left hand, squeezed Sissy with his other arm, and looked his now severe concern across the empty space at Connie. His eyes scanned everyone in the room again, catching Virgil watching him. His boy averted his eyes.

Back to Connie. "Where's Maura?"

"She's gone, honey."

There was a sound of finality in his mother's voice he wanted to pretend away.

"What do you mean gone?"

"Gone. She ... Coal, do you want to go talk in my room for a minute?"

"No!" He was afraid his reply sounded angry. "Tell me where she went."

Connie's eyes took in the children at a sweeping glance, where they sat or stood like wax statues. Maybe she was looking for moral support, but she had to know young people enough to know there would be none, not in a situation like this. She returned her gaze to Coal as he walked near, carrying Sissy. Up close, he could see Connie had been crying, and so had the twins.

"Where is she, Mom?"

"She left."

"When's she coming back?"

"She isn't."

"I don't understand. Where did she go?"

"She ..." Another pointless, almost pleading glance toward the children. "She packed up her clothes and the dogs, told me to keep the horses or sell them, and then she drove off. She was so broken up she could hardly even say goodbye, but she told me she needed to be gone before you got back. She's moving to the Falls to be near her boys."

Coal stared, trying to make the words register. They couldn't be real. But finally, they sank into his fevered brain. "I've got to go get her!" he exclaimed, clutching the stems of the roses too tightly. He tried to pry Sissy loose so he could set her down, but she wouldn't let go.

"Honey, don't do this," Connie said. "You can't bring her back. She was ready. It was time."

Again, Coal tried to peel Sissy off him. When it was obvious he would almost have to hurt her to free himself, he changed his mind. "I'll be back," he said over his shoulder.

Then he stopped and turned, walking back briskly to his mother. With the help of the hand that held Sissy to him, he separated the roses he was carrying into two bundles, holding one of them out to his mother. "I got those for you, Mom. From Dad."

He whirled back around even as he saw the tears rush into Connie's eyes.

Still carrying the girl and the rest of the roses, he ran back out to the truck and got in, firing it up. He was finally able to beg Sissy to sit next to him on the seat, probably because his driving scared her so bad.

Out on the highway, he put the pedal to the floor. The curves along the river seemed deadly. If he had ever hit any ice they probably would have been in the river. And even with that knowledge, he still would have driven faster if he could, except for the life of little Sissy.

Every time the road straightened out, he poured the coals to it, a couple of times, around ninety, feeling the pickup start to shake.

He hadn't even realized it, but for miles he had been praying, hoping. Maura couldn't be gone. Not gone for real. She would never have left without telling him goodbye.

He was almost to Leadore before he saw the familiar tailgate ahead. At that point he couldn't push down on the gas any harder, so he prayed under his breath and held the pedal down, willing the pickup to hold together.

On the far side of Leadore he caught up. He started honking his horn and flashing his lights at her, but she sped up. Finally, he veered into the other lane and got alongside her. He motioned for her to pull over, but she shook her head and kept driving, staring straight ahead. By the red puffiness of her eyes, he could see what kind of a state she was in. How could she leave home when she was obviously still so full of emotion?

Coal had to stomp on the brakes and get back behind the Travelette when an oncoming semi threatened to hit him head-on. But the moment it was past he got beside her again, pointing adamantly to the roadside and yelling out loud. Beside him, Sissy was crying, now up on her knees, and she too was looking out the window toward Maura.

Finally a wide spot on the roadside appeared ahead, and Maura slammed on the brakes and peeled over into the gravel. Coal skidded to a halt a little late and had to back up, getting off the road just as a car flew past with its horn jammed to the bottom of the steering wheel.

Coal jumped out with the roses in hand, leaving his door open, and Maura threw her own door wide, revealing both her dogs inside, staring out at them. "Maura! What are you doing?"

"Coal! Go back. I told your mom ... Coal, you've got to just go home. Go to your family and try to keep them alive."

He grabbed at her arm, but she jerked away and took two steps back. "Stop! Coal, it's over."

"I don't know why you're doing this. I'm going to build you a place to stay. Maura, don't do this. I want you to marry me."

She stared at him for ten seconds that seemed like half an hour. A streak came past Coal suddenly and plunged itself against Maura, and she reached down to catch little Sissy. She and the girl were both crying. Coal's throat was too stopped up to cry.

Maura got down on her knees in the crusted snow and threw her arms around Sissy, squeezing her close. Coal stood and waited.

When he got the courage to step closer and put a hand on her shoulder, she didn't jerk away. She only squeezed her eyes shut and held Sissy closer.

At last, Coal sank down beside the two of them. "Maura, I'm begging you. Don't go. Please."

"Marines aren't supposed to beg."

"Who told you that?"

"You."

Coal tried to smile. His throat was so tight. "I don't remember saying that. Come on. Come home with us. We can talk about all this."

Maura closed her eyes again, holding Sissy until she stopped crying. Coal's knees were starting to hurt. But he didn't care. He would stay here until the pigs came home. For some reason, pigs, not cows, were the first thing on his mind lately.

After several minutes, Maura and the girl were quiet. Even the residual sobs were gone. She started to struggle to her feet, and Coal jumped up to help her, realizing his legs had both gone to sleep.

"Please take this little treasure," Maura said, looking down at Sissy and not raising her eyes to Coal.

"You take her with you. She wants to be with you."

"I'm not going that way."

"Wait. Maura, come on. Did I do something? What's happened?"

Her lip quivered when she tried to answer him. She bit down on it and waited, gathering strength. Finally, she met his eyes, briefly.

"Today I thought you were dead. I heard it on the news. It had to be true. And I wasn't even surprised. The way things are here, I expected it. It's never going to change. Ever. I'm always going to wonder when I'll hear that on the radio and it will be true. I can't go through that again."

"Come on, Maura. Please! I had to do that. I had to get those guys to think they won."

"I know. I know why you did it. But it doesn't matter. Someday it will be real. I can't be there when it comes true."

In Coal's aching heart he all of a sudden knew. His mother had been right, as she always was. There was no bringing Maura back. She had made up her mind, and she was leaving. There wasn't a single thing he could say to keep her.

The dusk was closing over them now. The last light had disappeared from the tops of the mountains, and they stood shivering in the half-light, as much from their high emotions as from the cold.

Coal had run out of words. He had run out of magic, if he had ever had any. The only thing he had left was a little bit of pride.

Reaching out, he took Sissy around the body. "Come on, Sis. Come with me, okay?" It was a job, but he finally pried her little arms away from Maura and squeezed her to his body with one arm.

He held the roses out. "At least take these, okay?"

Looking at the roses, Coal could tell the woman was fighting back tears. She reached out and took them, clutching them to her chest.

Coal thought maybe the roses would make Maura at least look at him. He even thought maybe they would convince her to give him a parting hug. She didn't do either one. With her lip quivering and her jaw clenched, she simply turned and got back in her cab, very sedately, pulled out onto 28 and drove on to the east, toward a new life.

The evening was cold, although Coal hardly felt it. The sun was long gone, and blues and purples painted the broken hills, maybe the same blues that painted Coal's insides. Silence had engulfed the universe, the kind of silence always deepened by snow on the landscape, and by the hush of another dying day.

As Sissy sat shivering in Coal's arms, unable to find any more tears, Coal watched the dimly beaming red eyes on the back of the Travelette fade away and blink into oblivion in the twilight.

THE END

Look next for ***BOOK 7: DARK BADGER***

Note to the reader

Maura. Ah, Maura. I am probably the biggest sap alive, worse than any of my readers. Maura's leaving broke my heart. Please don't be mad at me. Life has its way of making things work out. Someday, somewhere, Coal might run into Maura PlentyWounds again.

As Scarlet Butler said, "Tomorrow is another day."

This author's note might as well serve at the same time as my acknowledgments page, and here I want to thank all the good sports in these pages who are real people, especially my friend and boss at work, Sam Browning, who appears as himself on the cover and who gave me so much help in the arena of bomb making, where I admit to have been absolutely clueless.

Other folks I owe bigtime: Alex Martinez, former fellow security guard, also on the cover. Gary Hirschi, the best fire captain I ever had. Andy Holmes, one of my best friends, the best listener I know, and also a crackerjack of a fire captain and human being. Ken Parks, my mechanic and my friend.

Ashley Bullock, who portrays Maura PlentyWounds on my covers and who has brought that pain-filled girl fully to life.

And Brian Howell, who is no longer with us but whom I miss to this day. May his fire-fighting spirit live on forever. Also, for the first time in this series, I want to acknowledge Brian's mom, Connie, who was a large part of my inspiration in creating the character of Coal's mother and who seems so much like a mother to me as well.

And a cryptic thank you to those who don't even know they were used as character models in this series. You may never know who you are, but your contribution has been great. So thank you, Kerry Updyke and Ronnie Davies, whose real names may always remain a mystery to my readers.

I'm adding this last acknowledgment as a final edit to this

book, along with a comical story as to why. My son Clay is the main proofreader of my books as far as catching writing mistakes and giving his thoughts on many of the characters and scenes as they unfold in my books. I included my author's note when I sent him the manuscript to be proofed and edited, and in his usual comical way he added a paragraph about himself to the end of this author's note.

He meant it to be funny, of course, but it didn't take me long into reading it to realize that he, of all people, really does deserve a big mention here, because so many pieces of this book have been perfected because of him, and also because of Debbie, his mother and my sweetheart of thirty-three years.

So here I will say, "Thanks, Debbie!" and then I will add this edited version of the big nod Clay wrote himself but which should have been here all along.

And last but not least, thank you to my second son, Clay, for his tireless efforts to edit this book as my outstanding proofreader. (He is also an author, so check out his book series called *The Descendants of Light*!) I cannot thank him enough ... (And the rest of these words are mine, not his.) ... for all the hours of hard work he has put into reading this book and making some very helpful and some very hilarious comments that made reading his notes almost as entertaining as writing the book itself.

Partnering up with Debbie, and now with our son Clay, were the best choices I ever made, and none of my books would ever be the same without Debbie's dedicated heart and Clay's relentless search for every little mistake, coupled with the highly comical and often emotional critique I look forward to like a little kid to Christmas.

About the Author

Kirby Frank Jonas was born in 1965 in Bozeman, Montana. His earliest memories are of living seven miles outside of town in a wide crack in the mountains known as Bear Canyon. At that time it was a remote and lonely place, but a place where a boy with an imagination could grow and nurture his mind, body and soul.

From Montana, the Jonas family moved almost as far across the country as they could go, to Broad Run, Virginia, to a place that, although not as deep in the timbered mountains as Bear Canyon was every bit as remote—Roland Farm. Once again, young Jonas spent his time mostly alone, or with his older brother, if he was not in school. Jonas learned to hike with his mother, fish with his father, and to dodge an unruly horse.

Jonas moved to Shelley, Idaho, in 1971, and from that time forth, with the exception of a few sojourns elsewhere, he became an Idahoan. Jonas attended all twelve years of school in Shelley, graduating in 1983. In the sixth grade, he penned his first novel, *The Tumbleweed,* and in high school he wrote his second, *The Vigilante.* It was also during this time that he first became acquainted with Salmon, Idaho, staying toward the end of the road at the Golden Boulder Orchard and taking his first steps to manhood.

Jonas has lived in six cities in France, in Mesa, Arizona, and explored the United States extensively. He has fought fires for the Bureau of Land Management in five western states and carried a gun on his hip in three different jobs.

In 1987, Jonas met his wife-to-be, Debbie Chatterton, and in 1989 took her to the altar. Over some rough and rocky roads they have traveled, and across some raging rivers that have at times threatened to draw them under, but they survived, and with four beautiful children to show for it: Cheyenne, Jacob, Clay and Matthew.

Jonas has been employed as a Wells Fargo armored guard, a wildland firefighter, a security guard for California Plant Protection and Inter-Con, and police officer. He is now retired after almost twenty-four years of proud employment as a municipal firefighter for the city of Pocatello, Idaho, and works full-time as a private security officer guarding the federal courthouse under contract with Paragon Systems.

One of Jonas's greatest joys in life is watching his second son, Clay, become a recognized writer of much talent in his own chosen field, that of fantasy and science fiction, with his current series *The Descendants of Light*. There is no greater compliment a son could give to his father than to follow in his footsteps.

Books by Kirby Jonas

Season of the Vigilante, Book One: The Bloody Season
Season of the Vigilante, Book Two: Season's End
The Dansing Star
Legend of the Tumbleweed
Lady Winchester
The Devil's Blood
The Secret of Two Hawks
Knight of the Ribbons
Drygulch to Destiny
Samuel's Angel
The Night of My Hanging (And Other Short Stories)
Russet
A Final Song for Grace
Windfall
Tenn Rhoades to Hell
Jinx: A Novel of the Great Depression

***Savage Law* series**

1. *Law of the Lemhi, part 1*
   Law of the Lemhi, part 2
2. *River of Death*
3. *Lockdown for Lockwood*
4. *Like a Man Without a Country*
5. *Thunderbird*
6. *Savage Alliance*
7. *Dark Badger*
8. *Morgan Rose*

***The Badlands* series**

1. *Yaqui Gold* (co-author Clint Walker)
2. *Canyon of the Haunted Shadows*

***Legends West* series**

1. *Disciples of the Wind* (co-author Jamie Jonas)
2. *Reapers of the Wind* (co-author Jamie Jonas)

***Lehi's Dream* series**

1. *Nephi Was My Friend*
2. *The Faith of a Man*
3. *A Land Called Bountiful*

Gray Eagle series (e-book format only—forthcoming in print)

1. *The Fledgling*
2. *Flight of the Fledgling*
3. *Wings on the Wind*

Death of an Eagle (e-book and large format softbound)

Books on audio

The Dansing Star, narrated by James Drury, *"The Virginian"*
Death of an Eagle, narrated by James Drury
Legend of the Tumbleweed, narrated by James Drury
Lady Winchester, narrated by James Drury
Yaqui Gold, narrated by Gene Engene
The Secret of Two Hawks, narrated by Kevin Foley
Knight of the Ribbons, narrated by Rusty Nelson
Drygulch to Destiny, narrated by Kirby Jonas

Available through the author at www.kirbyjonas.com

Email the author at: kirby@kirbyjonas.com or write to:

Howling Wolf Publishing
1611 City Creek Road
Pocatello ID 83204

Made in the USA
Monee, IL
02 November 2023